Praise for *An Invitation to Seashell Bay*

'A lovely, sunshiney story, bursting with wit and joy.'
Milly Johnson

'*An Invitation to Seashell Bay* has the Bella Osborne hallmark combination of wit, wonderful characters and meaningful conflicts that never fails to provide a fantastic read.'
Sue Moorcroft

'Sparkling and laugh out loud – Bella's books are like a glass of the finest bubbly.'
Phillipa Ashley

'Bella's done it again, another gorgeous page turner of a story. From the opening chapter I was completely hooked by this fresh, funny tale full of Bella's trademark wit and warmth.'
Jules Wake

'*An Invitation to Seashell Bay* is the summer invite you need to accept. It's a funny, warm and gloriously uplifting romance with loveable characters and, like all Bella's books, is the perfect blend of hilarious and heart-warming.'
Cressida McLaughlin

'Pure, joyous escapism bu
absolute del
Christi

An Invitation to Seashell Bay

Bella has been jotting down stories as far back as she can remember but decided that 2013 would be the year that she finished a full-length novel. Since then, she's written nine bestselling romantic comedies, two bestselling book club reads and won the RNA Romantic Comedy Novel of the Year Award.

Bella's stories are about friendship, love and coping with what life throws at you. She lives in Warwickshire, UK with her husband, daughter and a cat who thinks she's a dog. When not writing Bella is usually eating custard creams and planning holidays.

For more about Bella, visit her website at www.bellaosborne.com. You can follow Bella on Twitter @Osborne_Bella, Instagram @BellaOsborne Author, TikTok @BellaOsborneAuthor, or on Facebook – BellaOsborneAuthor.

Also by Bella Osborne

BELLA OSBORNE

An Invitation to Seashell Bay

avon.

Published by AVON
A division of HarperCollins*Publishers* Ltd
1 London Bridge Street
London SE1 9GF

www.harpercollins.co.uk

HarperCollins*Publishers*
Macken House
39/40 Mayor Street Upper
Dublin 1
D01 C9W8

A Paperback Original 2023
1
First published in Great Britain by HarperCollins*Publishers* 2023

A catalogue copy of this book is available from the British Library.

ISBN: 978-0-00-858797-0

Typeset in Minion Pro by Palimpsest Book Production Limited, Falkirk, Stirlingshire
Printed and Bound in the UK using 100% Renewable Electricity
at CPI Group (UK) Ltd

MIX
Paper | Supporting
responsible forestry
FSC™ C007454

This book is produced from independently certified FSC™ paper to ensure
responsible forest management.

For more information visit: www.harpercollins.co.uk/green

For Trevor and Brenda Nutt – thank you for everything.

Chapter One

'Mind the gap,' said the voice over the underground tannoy as more people squeezed into the already full carriage and Nancy felt like sausage meat being squeezed into a skin. Today was a blooming big day for Nancy. Big didn't really cover it. It was more of a make-or-break kind of day. One of those pivotal points in life. What Nancy didn't know was whether it would be wall-to-wall celebrations or the day her life turned to absolute poo. It all hinged on whether her little fledgling business properly took off or nosedived into a puddle, but she wasn't going to let that stress her out. Whatever happened she wanted to look back on today and at least know she'd done everything she could to seal the deal.

The offices of All Things Crafty were in Paddington, London, which was a tube ride away from her own business premises in Dagenham. Her lodger, Alice, had helped her choose her outfit for the big day. Alice was a fun character and Nancy enjoyed having her around more than she'd anticipated. After an hour of Nancy trying on everything in her wardrobe, they'd gone for Lady Boss with a hint of art student. Nancy wore a beret, bright top and her best suit. She'd redone her mass of curly hair in a number of styles before settling on a bun. Her mother always said her hair had a mind of its own which was the kind way of saying it frequently resembled a dropped pan of spaghetti.

She had her plain black laptop bag slung across her body one way and another large bag containing sample products going in the opposite direction, which meant there was no hope of taking off her jacket. It was May and although warm outside, the many people rammed into the early commuter train made the carriage hotter than a sumo wrestler's armpit. She was regretting the beret; she pulled it off and shoved it in her bag. It was okay because she was so early she would have time to pop to the toilets and put on some fresh deodorant. Nancy had literally thought of everything. She always did.

She emerged into the sunshine at Lancaster Gate tube station as serious-looking people swarmed around her, making her glad she no longer had to commute into the city every day. After five years in various office jobs, she had started selling crafting goods online. That little company, Having A Ball, had blossomed enough for her to quit her office job and run her own business full time. It hadn't been plain sailing but if she could land a contract with the crafting giant, All Things Crafty, she would be well on her way to securing her company's future. Having A Ball was an online yarn and wool shop that specialised in ethically sourced products and she was very proud of it, especially the name – Nancy loved a pun. She knew all the statistics: on average 1000 companies went bust every month in the UK and almost one in five new businesses failed each year. But she was sure her business would be different. For a start, none of the others had her running them. Nancy was more determined than a seagull near a chip shop: opportunist, fiercely competitive and tenacious to the point of a restraining order.

2

She checked her watch. She was far too early. Plenty of time for a coffee and a trip to the loo. She chose a café close to the All Things Crafty offices, popped to their loo to sort out her armpits before joining the queue of sullen-looking suited people. But the smacked-bum faces couldn't bring Nancy down. She was already on a high. This was a huge opportunity and while she was a bit nervous, she was also very excited. She placed her coffee order and moved to join the less ordered group of anxious people waiting for their first caffeine hit of the day. A few large men moved in front of her making her shuffle back and then have to apologise to a tutting person for reversing her bags into them.

'Grande skinny mocha,' said the barista, putting the cup on the counter.

'Excuse me,' said Nancy, inching forward. Her hand reached for the cup at the same time as one of the men.

'I think that's mine,' said the man with a frown and a hairy hand on her drink.

Nancy kept hold of the cup. She had been in front of him in the queue so even if it was the same order as his, then it made sense that it was hers. 'Sorry, I think you'll find it's mine.'

'It's not. Let go.' He tugged on the cup but Nancy wasn't going to give it up that easily.

'Remove your hand and see what name's on the cup,' she suggested.

'You're being ridiculous.'

The barista reappeared and took in the altercation but in true London style he chose not to get involved and plonked down more cups. 'Tall cappuccino. Venti coconut latte with an extra shot, grande skinny mocha.'

Nancy's head swivelled in the barista's direction. 'Who is the mocha for?' she asked.

With a sharp blink the barista conveyed his annoyance

at the question. He turned around the cup to reveal the name in marker pen – Richard.

Nancy had never felt so smug in all her life, with the possible exception of the day the school bully walked into the side of a bus shelter. 'Are you Richard?' she asked the man whose hand appeared glued to her cup.

He let it go as if it had morphed into the business end of a toilet brush and picked up the correct cup – the whole time shaking his head like it was Nancy's mistake – and turned to leave without even offering her a cursory apology. Nancy was riled, she hated rudeness. 'You're very welcome, Richard,' she called after him.

Sitting down at a table she unloaded her bags. It was a welcome relief to her shoulders. Nancy pulled out her notes and put her laptop bag on the chair next to her. She was pleased with the presentation her small team had pulled together at short notice – they'd worked into the night on it. The slides were slick and professional, her pitch was punchy and compelling – all she had to do was deliver it.

'Excuse me,' said a young man in a baseball cap who appeared at her shoulder, making her turn slightly. 'I am very sorry to disturb you, but you look like you might be kind enough to direct me.' He gave her a tentative smile.

She'd lived and worked in London for years and like most locals prided herself on her knowledge. 'Of course, where do you need to get to?'

He pulled out a map. 'I'm looking for Talbot Square.' He pointed at the map, drawing Nancy's eyes to a red felt tip splodge.

'That's easy, you're really close. If you go out of here, take the first right and then Talbot Square is about halfway down.'

'You are so kind. Thank you,' he said, folding up his map and giving little bows as he reversed away from her.

'You're very welcome.' Nancy turned back to her notes. As she picked up her coffee, she realised her laptop bag had gone.

'Shit!' said Nancy, jumping to her feet and promptly knocking her coffee into the bag of samples. 'Double shit!' She spun around. A few people were glancing in her direction, but most were trying to avoid making eye contact. 'Thief!' she said, pointing to the door, but the young man had gone and so had his accomplice with her laptop. She needed her computer. It had the presentation on it. Nancy grabbed her things and, ignoring the coffee dripping out of the bottom of the bag, she raced from the café.

Outside she scanned the street in both directions. There was no sign of the young man or anyone carrying her laptop bag. But then it wasn't exactly distinctive. She had two options: to go left or right. He wouldn't have gone right because that was the way she'd directed him. She turned to go left. Or was it a double bluff? Nancy froze for a second. This was wasting time. She decided to go right and dashed off down the street at a half jog. When she reached the corner of Sussex Gardens she knew she was wasting her time. She felt the drips of cold coffee trickle down her tights. Nancy had been outwitted and she was furious. She'd lost her laptop and her notes. No, she hadn't, the notes had been on the table. At least she could salvage those. Nancy turned around and stomped back to the café.

The table she'd been sitting at was freshly wiped down and there was no sign of her notes. She hovered around the counter trying to catch the barista's eye. 'Excuse me.' He looked up, which was a result. 'I left some important notes on that table over there, do you have them?'

'You left a mess over there,' he said.

'Yeah, sorry about that. I'd just had my laptop stolen

so I had other things on my mind. Anyway, if you've got the notes that would really help.'

He reached under the counter and passed her a bin bag. 'They're in there.'

Nancy took the bag and peeped inside. A strong waft of coffee hit her. She jiggled the bag and watched bits of cake, a banana skin and brown sludge tumble about. Underneath it all she saw the corner of her notes, she reached in and pulled them out. They were covered in coffee grounds and dripping – the words were barely visible. She gave the paper a little shake.

'Thanks,' she said to the barista as she handed back the bag.

'Have a nice day!' he chorused, making her want to tip the bag over his head.

Nancy wasn't sure what was worse – turning up to the most important meeting of her life without any presentation or looking like the piece of coffee-soaked paper was her best effort at one. But her notes were a sort of comfort blanket even if they did now look like she'd wiped her bum with them.

Twenty minutes later Nancy gave herself a mental shake as she walked into the impressive offices of All Things Crafty. She gave her details to the receptionist, took a seat and waited to be collected. Eventually, a friendly woman slightly older than Nancy arrived to take her to the meeting. She introduced herself as Madeleine the Head Buyer and Nancy had to suppress her inner child and the images of heads on a shelf. Madeleine asked if Nancy had travelled far which was Nancy's opportunity to regale her with the nightmare she'd had.

'That's awful. Did you want to rearrange?' asked Madeleine.

Nancy looked at the coffee dripping from the samples bag. Like her dad said, sometimes you had to know when to quit and Nancy figured the point where someone had nicked her presentation, her soggy samples were ruined and her notes barely readable – this was probably the time. 'That might be a good idea.'

'The diary is pretty rammed because we're focussing on a big project from next week so it might be a few months before we can fit you in. Let me see.'

'But we only had a few days' notice of this meeting from Lord Boyle's secretary,' said Nancy.

'You're a cancellation. Once a month, Lord Boyle or Sir Richard, as he prefers to be called, allocates a small amount of diary time for new supplier meetings. This slot came free because the company who was pitching went into liquidation.' Madeleine beamed a smile. 'What's your diary like for September?'

Nancy scrunched her eyes closed for a second while she processed the situation. It was a gamble either way. If she waited the four months, would her own company have gone bankrupt? But if she presented today was she and her soggy samples enough to win them over? The thought of her company's lopsided balance sheet was the nudge she needed. 'Actually, I think I'll pitch today if that's okay? I'm sure if I explain the situation with my laptop . . .'

'Hmm. Okay.' Madeleine didn't look convinced.

Nancy had time to have a bit of a sort-out in the toilets. She redid her deodorant, brushed the worst of the bin contents off her notes and salvaged the best of the samples from the bag. She gave herself a sweep of lipstick, tucked in a couple of stray wisps of hair that had escaped from her bun and straightened her shoulders at her reflection in the mirror. She was Nancy Barraclough. She didn't let anything get in her way and today was no different. She put on her best winning smile and prepared to win herself the contract of her career.

Nancy walked into the meeting room full of determination and unease. Madeleine was chatting to a slightly older dark-haired man and they both got up when she walked in.

'Hi, I'm Peter Dixon, Digital Trading Manager. Madeleine has just told me about you being mugged.'

'I wasn't exactly mugged they just stole my laptop.'

'And chucked coffee over you?'

'Well . . .' She was about to admit to doing that herself but thought better of it. 'Anyway, let's not dwell on the bad start I've had to my day. Let's focus on the partnership we could build if you like the ground-breaking products I'm about to show you.' Nancy loved that she immediately had their full attention. Who needed a swanky presentation? 'Everything I'm going to share has been sustainably sourced and we pride ourselves on our neutral carbon footprint. It has been scientifically proven that the rhythm of crafting techniques like crochet and knitting helps with serotonin release. This is the chemical transmitter that helps regulate anxiety, happiness and mood so it's great for mental health as well as the social aspect of making friends and crafting together. There are four key products I want to share with you today and I'm offering these on an exclusive basis to All Things Crafty and—'

The door opened. 'I'm sorry I'm late, bloody nightmare, Jocelyn is off, so I had to get my own coffee and there was this bloody wom . . .' He stopped talking at the sight of Nancy. The man who had tried to steal her coffee had just plonked himself down in a seat next to the others.

'We've only just started,' began Madeleine. 'This is Nancy Barraclough.'

'Hi, Lord Richard, we've already met,' said Nancy, deciding to brazen it out. She reached across the table with an outstretched hand.

His mouth dropped open for a second before he recovered and shook her hand with an overly forceful grip. 'It's *Sir* Richard.'

Nancy felt her cheeks heat up. Bugger. That wasn't quite the confident introduction she was going for. 'Of course. My apologies.' This guy was everything she hated about the upper classes – the sort of jumped-up oik who had been told at private school how special and elite he was while being taught how to keep the riff-raff in their place. She despised the British class system and everything it stood for. But for now, she needed a deal so she would put all her prejudice aside and fix a smile on her face.

'Is that the product?' He reached across and grabbed the crocheted koala. His tight squeeze made coffee dribble out of its bottom and across the table as if the koala had a bad case of diarrhoea. He stared at the brown puddle. 'Is it meant to do that?'

'No. I was just explaining to Madeleine and Peter that I had my laptop sto—'

'Crocheted animals aren't very original.' He dropped the koala, pulled a hanky from his pocket and dried his hands. 'Anything else?'

His bluntness was off-putting but Nancy refused to be derailed, especially not by the bloke who tried to nick her coffee. 'Yes, we have what we call the three-in-one set. Which starts off as a beginner's crochet square and can then either progress into a blanket or a poncho and it comes with the patterns for each of the projects and a choice of yarn combinations to make it unique.' Nancy held up their best colours: Wild Ocean Waves and Hawaii

Palm Fronds – now both with a hint of mud thanks to the coffee.

'Choosing blue or green doesn't make it unique. Anything else?' Richard was looking bored.

'We have blankets which have been exclusively designed by online TikTok sensation Junip—'

'No, blankets have been done to death. That it?'

Nancy had one last product, but it wasn't ideal because it didn't get her merchandise on the shelves of All Things Crafty. 'Our craft box subscriptions are already doing very well. I can email you the stats on those. We send out four boxes a year and each box contains a new project and everything they need to undertake it. There are also online tutorials and the option to change the box contents to an alternative before it's posted. It would be an online product and we would do all of the fulfilment.'

Sir Richard at last looked interested and leaned forward. 'Exclusive to All Things Crafty?'

'Sorry no, I can't offer that.' It was Nancy's bread and butter and the regular income that the subscribers were giving her was much needed so she couldn't hand that all over to All Things Crafty who may or may not promote it on their website.

'Shame. What else?'

Nancy clenched her jaw. That was everything she'd planned on pitching. She searched her mind for the things they had discounted. 'We have some exclusive cushion patterns in our own colour range so they're not available anywhere else.' Sir Richard was already shaking his head. 'Teen-focused sets using banana fibre yarn to make bags and pouches for tablets and laptops.'

'Exclusive?' he asked.

She'd not planned on offering this one exclusively, but

she was fast running out of options. 'Yes,' said Nancy determined to come away with something.

'Send over the costs by the end of the day and we'll let you know.' He pulled out his phone and swivelled his chair away from Nancy. He really was so rude.

'Thanks for coming in today,' said Peter, standing up to shake Nancy's hand.

Madeleine handed her back the soggy koala, its diarrhoea now down to a trickle. 'I hope you have a better journey home.'

'Me too. Thanks for your time. I look forward to hearing from you,' said Nancy. When there was no response from Richard she added. 'Goodbye, Sir Richard, lovely to meet you.'

He didn't turn around but responded by holding up a hand dismissively. *What an arse*, she thought, as she picked up her samples along with what remained of her pride and left the meeting room. She went to retrieve the stuff she'd left in the ladies' loo. She bundled everything together and gave herself a mental talking-to. She had done the best she could in the circumstances. Her earlier encounter with Sir Richard obviously hadn't helped. Nancy thought of the rest of her team waiting back at the Having A Ball office and she felt terrible. They were all invested and had worked incredibly hard on this. It felt like everything had been building up to this moment. And now it had turned to poo. She squeezed out the rest of the coffee from the koala's bum into the sink. Perhaps she'd handled it all wrong. Maybe if she'd apologised to Sir Richard at the start things would have gone better.

As Nancy came out of the toilets someone was striding past and she very nearly bumped right into them. 'Sir Richard, I'm so sorry.' He was about to sidestep her when she decided to seize the moment. 'I'm really pleased I've seen you again. I just wanted to say I am very sorry about earlier in the coffee shop.'

'Fine.' He stepped to the side. But Nancy wasn't done. She moved with him. He frowned, but she countered with a smile.

'I was mugged this morning and I lost my laptop so my presentation wasn't as good as it could have been. Our products are exceptional. Our tutorials are fun and engaging. We are an excellent fit with your company. Shall I send you details of all of the items I went through today?'

'No. Just the teen stuff will be fine. Could you let me pass now?'

'Look. I'm sorry and I'm a bit desperate here. I need this deal. I know you hate me, but the products are excellent. My team has worked so hard and we—'

'I need to be somewhere important.' He pointed past Nancy.

She bit her tongue. 'Of course. Thanks for your time.' She stepped to the side and he walked away shaking his head. Nancy sighed heavily. She'd tried but she had a nasty feeling she'd just lost any potential deal and the lifeline her company so badly needed.

Chapter Two

Alice hadn't had the best day at work: Bonnie had tipped her water over three times, William had stabbed her hand with a pencil, Hamsi had screamed because she decided rain was the sky melting and Kayden had pooed himself sending everyone else rampaging across the room. Although in Kayden's defence he was trying to turn himself into The Hulk at the time. It wasn't an unusual day for a teaching assistant, but Alice was ever hopeful that things would be less eventful tomorrow. She'd been desperate to live and work in London, but the reality was vastly different to her dream. While she loved the work, the pay was dire and London was noisy and expensive. Annoyingly her parents had been right.

Thankfully a friend of Alice's aunt had a daughter, Nancy, who lived on the outskirts where she was able to rent a room cheaply. Luckily, they did get on despite Nancy being older and both of them being very different people. Alice was aware that she wasn't paying the going rate for the area so on days like today, when Nancy had messaged to say she was working late, Alice liked to show her appreciation by cooking them both a meal.

That evening, Alice stood in the kitchen, and stared at the beige mass she'd been diligently stirring. It didn't look like the picture on the internet. In fact, it didn't resemble anything edible. Although she did remember her mum going through a phase of cooking meals for the dog and this didn't look dissimilar. If she remembered correctly, the dog had wolfed the stuff down, but then she did literally eat anything, including part of the sofa and Christmas decorations.

Nancy's ragdoll cat, Carrie, trotted into the room and halted abruptly a few feet away. She dramatically sniffed the air in a style reminiscent of the child catcher from *Chitty Chitty Bang Bang* before violently retching. 'Helpful,' said Alice. Carrie gave her a pitying look, turned tail and stalked away. Alice took the hint and lit one of Nancy's fancy candles.

Nancy arrived home, kicked off her shoes and came into the kitchen. 'Ooh something smells . . . like someone's been cooking.' Carrie yowled a warning from the safety of the hallway as Nancy peered over Alice's shoulder.

'Lentil, artichoke and mushroom casserole,' said Alice as an ominous bubble belched out of the substance.

'Great,' said Nancy with forced enthusiasm. 'I'm so hungry I could eat a scabby horse.'

'It'd probably taste better than this.'

'Nonsense. I'm sure it tastes great.'

A few minutes later Alice was nudging the beige sludge into the composting pot and Nancy was preparing beans on toast. 'I'm sorry.'

'Stop it,' said Nancy. 'It's the thought that counts.'

'As long as you realise the thought wasn't, "Can I make my own pig swill?"'

'Stop worrying about it. I bloody love beans on toast.'

'I'll grate some cheese to make it a bit special.'

'Perfect,' said Nancy. She really was too kind.

They chatted over their non-gourmet meal and updated

each other on their disastrous days. 'Anything important on your laptop?' asked Alice.

'Apparently there were only a couple of things because most of it's on the cloud. Claudia changed all the passwords as soon as I told her it'd been stolen so she said not to worry. She reckons they will have dismantled it for the chip within minutes.' Nancy gave a shrug. 'At least it's insured, but it's always an arse ache to claim for stuff.'

'I can't believe that someone who is a lord didn't cut you some slack after the morning you'd had. Some people.'

'I know, right? Turns out anyone can be a tosser. Anyway, let's talk about happier things. How are things with Bonnie and Jaxon?'

Despite the children only being five or six years old some of them attempted to make attachments to others very early on and Bonnie and Jaxon's ongoing love story was one Nancy was addicted to.

'There've been big developments,' said Alice solemnly. Nancy leaned in, enthralled. 'I wasn't on playground duty, so I don't know exactly what happened. But Jaxon came back into class after break holding hands with . . . Delilah.'

Nancy gasped. 'The player!'

'Exactly. Bonnie spilled paint pot water over Jaxon's picture. He moved tables to sit near Delilah and Bonnie cried until going home time.'

'My word,' said Nancy. 'There's more drama than an episode of *EastEnders*.'

'Certainly more action than my love life,' said Alice with a sigh.

'Mine too,' said Nancy. 'It's been over a year since Chris and I split up. At least you've got Whizzer.'

'Let's be honest,' said Alice. 'Whizzer's like a delinquent chimpanzee. The only difference is he doesn't throw poo.'

'Yet,' added Nancy and they both laughed.

They cleared the dinner things away, Alice made them both a coffee and they went through to the small living room. The house was a Victorian two up, two down with the addition of the bathroom at the back of the kitchen.

Alice was annoyed on Nancy's behalf at the way she'd been treated by Sir Richard. She saw how passionate she was about the company she was building and the many hours she put in. 'Are you sure you're okay about this All Things Crafty business?'

'I don't have much choice,' said Nancy. 'There's nothing else I can do. I could kick myself that I cornered him in the corridor, I should have let it go.'

'Best not to dwell on it. Can you come up with something else and pitch to them again?'

'Easier said than done,' said Nancy. 'We've been working on these products for months, testing the market, pricing up materials and packaging, working out margins and volumes. There's hours and hours of effort gone into this.'

They sighed in unison. Carrie waltzed in and jumped up into the tiny gap on the sofa between Alice and Nancy, making them both move a fraction to give her a bit more room. She paced around in circles a number of times before carefully arranging herself in a neat ball. 'It must be nice to not have anything to worry about,' said Alice.

Nancy turned swiftly, scanning Alice over. 'Are you okay? What's wrong?'

'Nothing new. My parents rang earlier and asked when I'm planning on coming home.' It was a fairly regular thing. Alice's mum and dad frequently bombarded her with pleas for her to stop her silliness and leave London.

16

She knew it was because they worried about her, but it was *her* life and the only way she was going to be able to live it was to be somewhere they weren't. She hated to sound mean or ungrateful because her parents had always cared for her but that was the problem, she was their project – the thing they focused on and tried to protect 24/7. That basically translated into them trying to control her life.

'What did you say?'

'I said they can visit whenever they like but that they need to accept that I have a home, life and a permanent job here.'

Nancy tilted her head. 'Does that mean you've passed your probation?'

Alice couldn't hide her grin. 'It does.'

'You complete blooming star!' Nancy wrapped her in a hug. 'I'm made up for you. This calls for a celebration.' She put down her mug and went to the kitchen, returning with two beers. She popped the caps and handed one to Alice. 'Congratulations!'

Alice clinked her bottle against Nancy's. For the first time she was in charge of her own life and it felt great. Even if she would always have that little dark cloud that followed her wherever she went.

* * *

The next day at Having A Ball, Claudia and the team were being extra nice, which wasn't helping at all. It just made Nancy feel even more guilty for messing up the pitch. Nancy went to the coffee van across the road and brought back drinks for the whole team. It wasn't a big round – there were only four of them including herself. She delivered Filip's drink first as he was in the warehouse downstairs and then went up to the offices above. It was a small out-of-town industrial site with a window supplier on one side and on the other a laminate flooring company called Wood 4 U which always made Nancy smile. It wasn't the poshest location, but it worked for them. Nancy was also proud of the London address – she had London offices. She'd really thought she was going places when she'd moved in ten months ago. Although now she wondered if the move had been a bit premature, but they'd outgrown their old place and if they wanted to expand the business, they needed a bigger building. London premises weren't cheap, so they had to keep growing if they wanted to survive.

Claudia joined Nancy at the big table. There was a vast open space at the bottom of a metal staircase which Nancy liked to call 'the ideas station' but the large table she'd found in a skip was used for many things, including coffee breaks and meetings.

'Thanks. Are you okay?' Claudia reached for the coffee and Nancy held the cardboard tray tight so she could pull it free. Claudia had been born with thumb hypoplasia which meant she was missing a thumb on her left hand.

'Absolutely fine,' lied Nancy.

'Right, because last week you said you weren't buying any more drinks from the "fry pan van" because you thought he was topping up the coffee with a grow bag.'

'Oh yeah. I forgot,' said Nancy, sipping her coffee and remembering. She grimaced. 'We need to get a cheap coffee maker.'

'I'll add it to my list.' Claudia twisted her lips.

Nancy felt something tug at her subconscious. Something she'd forgotten. 'Shit, I've not done anything about the admin assistant role. I was kind of waiting until we'd secured the contract with All Things Crafty.'

'It's okay.'

'No, it's not. You're rushed off your feet, so am I, we

need to find someone and fast. Do you think we'd get more interest if we titled the job personal assistant?' Nancy took another sip of coffee and instantly regretted it.

'We might do. I guess admin sounds a bit dull. But do we want to employ someone new if . . .' She didn't need to finish the sentence.

'Good point.' Nancy put the coffee cup to her lips and then thought better of it. They sat in silence for a moment. Nancy's phone vibrated and the preview told her it was an email from Madeleine at All Things Crafty. 'I'd best get on.'

'Me too,' said Claudia and they both returned to their little glass offices.

Nancy took a deep breath and opened the email. She hated looking at emails on the tiny screen – she'd be glad when her new laptop arrived. A scan of the information made her stomach plummet, that or it could have been the effects of the grow-bag-doctored coffee. Madeleine said it was lovely to meet you, blah, blah, blah really sorry but Sir Richard has decided not to procure your products at the current time. Thank you blah, blah, bugger it. Nancy slumped back in her seat. It was what she'd been expecting but it didn't make it any the less depressing. She hit reply all and started to compose a response but then thought better of it and backspaced to delete the obscenities she'd typed.

She took a few moments to feel sorry for herself and then pulled herself together. She was Nancy Barraclough and she wasn't that easily beaten. There were other crafting stores. They weren't as big, but there were definitely other options. She didn't need Sir Richard. She'd got this far without him. Nancy took a deep breath and checked her lengthy to-do list. Admin assistant. Should she recruit someone new? She was bogged down in stuff she shouldn't be doing, and so was Claudia; they definitely needed someone to do the grind. She fiddled on her phone until she found the local recruitment site. She tapped the screen a number of times trying to get their email up. She swiped and lost it. 'Bloody hell.' Doing emails on her mini mobile made her feel like a sausage-fingered idiot.

She managed to access the job description and change the title to personal assistant. She added in a line about managing her diary and saved it. She jotted a covering email, attached the document and pressed send. She ticked it off her list with a flourish. Then she realised that sending an email wasn't actually recruiting, so she added interview and hire personal assistant to the bottom of her growing to-do list.

She was busy at the weekly team meeting when an email from Madeleine came in, so didn't have a chance to read it until an hour later.

Hi, Nancy, Sorry I don't think this was for me. FYI it went reply all. All best, Madeleine.

What was she on about? Nancy scrolled down. There was the email she'd sent to the local recruiters about her PA role only she hadn't sent it to them she'd managed to send it to Madeleine and other people at All Things Crafty, including Sir Richard. Now he would think she was a complete plank. 'Oh come on!' said Nancy loudly, before flopping forward and banging her head repeatedly on the desk.

'Your day got better then?' asked Claudia from the doorway.

'Bloody fantastic,' said Nancy through her mass of hair.

'I'll hurry up that coffee machine,' said Claudia.

'Thank you,' mumbled Nancy.

Nancy was on an escalator heading into the bowels of the London underground when a call interrupted the music in her earbuds. She pulled out her phone to see who it was. It was outside working hours and she was about to lose signal any second. When she saw who was calling, she immediately turned around and tried to go back up the down escalator in her desperation to get a stronger signal. There was lots of tutting and she turned back and raced down the escalator hitting accept as she went.

'Madeleine, hello. Lovely to hear from you,' she said, her heart pounding. Had they had a change of heart? Was this the big break her little company had been after? The place on the shelves of the biggest crafting chain in the country?

'Nancy, it's Sir Richard.'

Nancy froze which was never good on the left-hand side of an escalator in rush hour. 'Sir Richard, goodness—'

'You're meant to stand on the right,' came a gruff voice behind her, followed by another stream of tutting.

'I'm sorry,' she said, trying to slot into the right but there was a person on every step. 'Excuse me. Can I just . . . Sorry.'

'I think we can dispense with the apologies now,' said Sir Richard.

Shit, mouthed Nancy. 'Thank you,' she said out loud and then covered the microphone with her thumb in case she had any more interruptions.

'Nancy, I wanted to put a proposition to you . . . if you could help . . . beneficial to both of us . . . much trouble but—'

'I'm sorry you're breaking up,' she said, clutching the phone and pushing one earbud dangerously tight into her ear in her desperation to hear what he was saying as she went further and further down and away from any whisper of phone reception.

'Can you hear me now?' he asked clear as day.

Relief washed through her. 'Yes. Yes, I can.'

'So I was saying . . . proposition . . . slot into place . . . important in securing . . . obviously make it worth your while.'

Bugger it! Nancy pushed through the melee at the bottom of the escalator and began climbing up the one going in the opposite direction. 'Excellent,' said Nancy, liking the sound of the bits she could hear.

'I understand it's a big ask but . . . candidate . . . responsibility and experience . . . undertake the PA job . . .'

'Sorry, are you also recommending someone for my PA job?' This call just got better and better.

'Yes, it's slightly . . . of a friend . . . skill and capability . . . estate . . . in exchange . . . agree a price . . . if you're in agreement.'

'I'm certain we can agree a price that works for everyone, Sir Richard.' She was prepared for this to initially be on a small margin if it got her brand out there and she was also confident she'd make a good profit thanks to the predicted volumes through his vast store network.

'So you would be happy with that arrangement?' he asked.

She couldn't confess that she'd missed half the conversation. 'We'd need to iron out some details but in principle, yes.'

As she rose up the escalator the signal improved. 'That's jolly good of you, Nancy.'

'My pleasure,' she said. 'Would next steps be contracts?' She was keen to seal the deal.

'Sure,' he said. 'Authenticity will be key. Obviously, this is just between us. I can count on your discretion, can't I?'

Nancy wasn't sure why it would be all secret squirrel

unless they wanted to do some big announcement of the exclusive deal. Her heart fluttered at the thought of the PR. 'Of course, Sir Richard.'

'I'll get Freddy to call you and you two can finalise the details.'

'That would be wonderful. Thank you so much, Sir Richard. And what about the PA candidate?' But the line had gone dead. Nancy closed her eyes, hugged her phone to her chest, not noticing she'd reached the top where she spectacularly flew off the end of the escalator.

Chapter Three

Alice reached out an arm to touch her boyfriend but the sheets beside her were cold. She opened her eyes and checked the room, both he and his clothes had gone. She flopped back onto her pillow. Boyfriend – the same word whether you were four or thirty-four and it struck her that it was sadly apt. She was twenty-one and she was still dating boys. Boys who showed her a bit of attention and then cleared off back to their lives of drinking with their mates, playing video games and bumming around in low-paid jobs. Not that she minded the latter, she was in the same boat where pay was concerned, but was there a point when boys actually grew up?

'Alice, your bloke has pissed on the bathroom floor again,' called Nancy from downstairs.

Alice sighed. 'Sorry. I'll clear it up.' Alice got out of bed and joined Nancy where they both surveyed the toilet, lightly sprayed with urine. 'He has a thing about not switching the light on because the one at home lights up his parents' room and his mum's a light sleeper.' She realised she was trotting out the excuse he always gave. 'Dirty little Whizzer.'

'He certainly lives up to his name,' said Nancy.

'You'd think he'd be potty trained by now.'

'Maybe have that as a minimum base requirement when you're picking men,' suggested Nancy.

'Good advice. Thanks.'

Nancy gave her shoulder a squeeze as she passed. 'I'll put the kettle on and get out the rubber gloves.'

Alice started her working day by having to calm down a distressed parent who was extremely worried about the eagle his child had been attacked by at playtime the previous day. The school office had been entertained by the many messages the dad had left on the school answerphone. He'd even called London Zoo to report the escaped bird. Alice explained that a *seagull* had swooped down to steal the sandwich his son had sneaked out at break time. The father told her he'd been totally convinced because on the walk home from school his son's eagle story had been backed up by two other children. Alice pointed out that neither of those students were there at the time of the sandwich theft and the dad had finally seemed mollified.

She'd made it to break with no further events but there had been a playground incident when some of the younger children had ventured out of their designated zone and accidentally into the middle of a football match which had been a huge catastrophe for all involved. Apparently, a Year Six had missed a penalty and Bonnie had taken a tennis ball to the back of the head, Alice had been alerted by Hamsi's screams. Hamsi was like an early warning system for any potential drama.

Alice had an interesting conversation about hacks for cleaning paintbrushes with another teaching assistant at lunchtime. She only ever had conversations with other TAs, the teachers didn't mingle with them. There was a very definite divide and on day one it had been made clear which side she was to stay on. The comparison with the kids in the playground was not lost on Alice. There were strict but unspoken rules about which cupboard you put your mug in depending on which group you belonged to and while the teachers took the comfy sofas the TAs were relegated to the hard seats in the dark corner at the back of the staff room.

Although Alice counted herself lucky that the teacher whose class she worked in, Mrs Robinson, did interact with her occasionally. Some of the other TAs had horror stories to tell. Mrs Robinson's interaction did sometimes constitute her checking Alice's spelling and asking if she was okay to do some cutting out unaided, but she also included her in lesson plans and discussions about students.

Alice had led that morning's session on phonics, which had gone very well, despite William yelling 'bum' every time the letter b was mentioned. Jaxon had a love rival in William. He was trying to impress Delilah and, interestingly, it appeared to be working. The little girl had mastered the fake laugh and employed it each time he shouted out. Alice hoped Delilah would learn to set her sights higher as she grew up – she feared William was another Whizzer in the making. Things were frosty between Jaxon and Bonnie and they'd had a scrap over coloured paper.

The last lesson, where they were gluing and sticking, had gone a lot better than Alice had feared it might. She was still having flashbacks to a previous session which had ended with her having to have an inch cut off her hair. But today there had been no squirting of glue and everyone had been calm and focused as they created their summery pictures. Smiley sunshine faces and blobs of coloured flowers brightened every sheet of paper.

Unfortunately, there had been a small incident at the end of the day – Alice had been out of the classroom and the teacher distracted for a moment which was all it had taken for a hand to be pushed under the tap and half the pupils at the back to be subjected to a cold shower. The tables and floor had also taken a dousing, so Alice had cleared up while Mrs Robinson matched children to parents – a task deemed far too important for a TA.

'Miss.' The tiny voice pulled Alice away from mopping the floor – it was Bonnie.

Alice glanced at the clock. 'Why are you still here?' she asked.

Bonnie's lip started to wobble. 'I went for a wee wee and I had trouble with my tights. They're 'diculous.' She lifted her skirt to show Alice her predicament – her pants were in a roll around her thighs with her tights pulled up over the top.

'I hate it when that happens,' said Alice. 'Shall we sort you out?'

Bonnie nodded. 'I think I missed Daddy. Because he's not outside.' There was the lip wobble again.

'I don't think so. Let's sort out your tights and then we'll find your daddy,' said Alice. As they walked past the school office Alice popped her head around the door and whispered. 'Please can you call Mr Fisher, he's late again.'

With some direction and coaching Bonnie was soon more comfortable in the pants department and they went to stand near the gates to wait for her dad to arrive. Alice had noticed a couple of things, like Bonnie's hair not always being brushed or her not having a coat on a rainy day but she feared she was adding two and two and making five. Then again, it was her job to be vigilant; they took safe-guarding very seriously, and Bonnie's care had to be her number one priority.

'Bonnie . . .' began Alice, sorting the words carefully in her mind.

'Yes, miss.'

'Is everything all—'

'Miss Pelling!' Mrs Robinson called to her. 'You've left the classroom in an awful mess,' she added, marching over.

'I've not finished tidying up. I was waiting with Bonnie because her dad's been delayed.'

'I see. Then I will wait with Bonnie because Mr Fisher needs to know we have a three strikes policy on lateness and this will be his second.'

'Is Daddy going to get into trouble?' said Bonnie with wide fearful eyes.

'No, don't worry,' said Alice, ignoring the hard stare from Mrs Robinson.

'You need to get back to sorting out that mess, Miss Pelling.' Mrs Robinson pulled her chin in and waved Alice away like a bad smell.

'Take care, Bonnie. I'll see you tomorrow,' said Alice. Mrs Robinson wasn't an ogre, but sometimes she was a bit of a cow.

* * *

It made Nancy feel old that as she was getting into her PJs after a long soak in the bath at the same time as Alice was getting ready to go out. She liked that Alice was singing along to the latest tunes. Nancy hadn't realised, but until Alice moved in, she'd been quite lonely. While she had Carrie, who was a house cat, she was still independent and the conversation had been very one-sided. Having Alice dancing around definitely cheered the place, and Nancy, up. Not that long ago that had been Nancy but there wasn't much time for enjoying herself these days. She was either working or was exhausted from it. She couldn't remember the last time she'd taken any real time off. Maybe she needed a break. An image of a rainy walking holiday with her ex, Chris, and his mum brought her to her senses. What was she thinking? Now was not the time to be slacking off. She'd come so close to securing Having A Ball's future, she needed to ramp up her efforts not go on holiday. She banished the thought from her head although worryingly the sight of Chris's mother in extremely tight shorts still lingered.

'Don't wait up,' said Alice, popping her happy face around the door. She was squeezing every ounce of fun out of her London experience and Nancy admired her for it.

'As if,' said Nancy. 'I'm not your mother.' They both smiled. 'But be careful and come back safe.'

'Will do. See ya.' And with a flick of her glossy black hair, she was gone.

Nancy found herself alone and contemplating going to bed when her phone rang. It was a mobile number she didn't recognise. 'Hello Nancy Barraclough.'

'Hi, I'm Freddy.'

She didn't recognise the very posh voice, but the name did ring a bell. 'Oh, hi Freddy. Sir Richard said you'd be calling.' She hadn't expected that call to be at almost eleven o'clock at night but if it meant they sealed a deal she would have taken the call at two in the morning. She straightened her pyjama top and sat up tall.

'Fabulous,' said Freddy. 'I'm so glad we're on the same page. He said we should sign a contract as soon as poss. I'm assuming a non-disclosure agreement. That sort of thing. Just so everyone is clear on this arrangement.'

Nancy checked her diary. She had back-to-back meetings but she could move her first one to another day. 'I'm free at nine o'clock tomorrow morning if you want to come into my office. Or should I come to . . .'

'No, your place would be better. But nine?' She heard him puff out a breath. 'Anything later in the day?'

'I'm sorry, I am literally in meetings all day. Maybe we could do another date.' Not that she wanted to delay sealing the deal. She quickly checked her schedule for the week. 'Thursday morning I'm free at nine-thirty.'

'That's not really any better timewise. Whereabouts are your offices?'

'Dagenham.'

'Crikey, that's out of the way.'

Nancy bristled at this. She was very proud of securing a London address but she needed to give a better first impression to Freddy than she had to Sir Richard, so she quelled the desire to defend Dagenham. 'It's also our warehouse so I can give you the tour, show you how the whole operation works. I'll text you the details, now I've got your number. So, Monday or Thursday? Which is best for you?'

'That's like choosing your favourite poison.' A throaty laugh rattled down the phone. 'Let's do Monday, get it out of the way.'

Nancy wasn't sure how to take his comment. Maybe Freddy just wanted the formalities sorted so that they could get her product selling which was exactly what she wanted too. 'I agree. I'll look forward to meeting you at nine a.m. on Monday.'

'A.m. not p.m. Got it!'

Was he joking? Nancy forced a laugh that sounded more like her neighbour's old Capri firing up. 'Great. I'm really looking forward to . . .' Three little beeps told her Freddy had hung up. Oh well he was clearly very busy. If he'd been working so late in the evening, he was likely even more of a workaholic than she was.

Chapter Four

Alice absolutely loved London. She'd grown up in a tiny village on the Essex coast full of bungalows and walking frames, where nothing sensational ever happened. The local paper headlines were testament to the level of excitement in the area, declaring such things as – 'Bus Timetable Change Throws Town Into Chaos', 'Pensioner Rescued From Roundabout and Nuisance Neighbour Fined For Listening To Cliff Richard'. Now she was in London. She'd always dreamed of moving to the city, she'd missed a lot of schooling which had had a knock-on effect on her grades, so her plans of a London-based university were quickly scuppered.

Thankfully her aunt had come to the rescue much to the annoyance of her parents. Alice's Auntie Julie was the best. When Alice had been little Auntie Julie had let her stay up late, always had sweets and had taken her to places her parents feared were too dangerous, like ice skating and climbing – all the fun stuff she felt she was denied. When Alice had been feeling low it was Auntie Julie who dragged her out of her doldrums. Her parents had consoled her, of course they had, but she knew secretly they were pleased that she wouldn't be leaving home to study. They had offered suggestions of safe little local jobs.

'The newsagent is hiring,' her mother had said. 'You could walk to work.' There had followed two years of jobs she loathed: care home worker at one of the many seafront nursing homes and then receptionist at the local caravan site. She was working hard while her peers were living it up at university – she'd felt well and truly left behind.

Auntie Julie sat her down in front of her laptop and encouraged her to find out what she was qualified to do with the mix of average GCSEs and a merit in Health and Social Care. After a few false starts the job of teaching assistant had popped up. Alice hadn't been too sure to start with. It felt like she'd basically be going back to school which was one of the things she was trying to escape from. But her aunt showed her it could be the first step to a career in teaching. There was on-the-job training and the opportunity to further her own education. When she'd searched for TA jobs there were literally hundreds all over the country but there was only one place Alice wanted to be – London.

She'd thought her wonderful plan was dead before it had even begun when she saw the TA salary and the cost of renting in London but after a few phone calls Auntie Julie had sorted that too. Her friend's daughter Nancy had a spare room and was keen to help.

Since moving to London, Alice had made some like-minded friends who were also on limited budgets and were gifted at sourcing cheap nights out. A quick stop at her friend's flat to preload on some bargain cider and then she'd be on water most of the night while they danced their cares away in fringe clubs on discounted entry. Alice was living the dream.

In one of the smarter clubs they frequented her friends had managed to dive into a booth which was timely as Alice had been dancing non-stop for an hour and now her feet were stinging. She squeezed in next to her friends and they shared the bottle of tap water they'd sneaked in. On the opposite side of the booth three men were drinking beers. Two very student-looking types and one with equally wayward hair but dressed in a fitted shirt. One of the student-types in a blue top leaned forward. 'It's my mate's birthday.'

'Happy birthday,' the girls chorused. Alice noted fitted shirt had sad eyes and didn't look like he was having a good birthday at all.

Blue top pointed at Alice and continued. 'How about you give him a birthday blow job?' He slapped the fitted shirt guy heartily.

Fitted shirt guy leaned forward and shouted to be heard over the music. 'I'm so sorry, he's an arsehole, but as compensation can I get you a drink? What would you like?'

'Fruit cider, please.'

He nodded and shoved the others out of the way so he could exit. Alice slipped out of the booth to join him. 'Sorry about my mate. He thinks he's funny.' He looked genuinely embarrassed.

'It's okay.' She gave him a thumbs up. 'I'm Alice,' she said.

'What?' He cupped his hand to his ear.

'My name is Alice.'

'Sorry. I'm Dom.'

'I've not seen you here before?' she shouted in his ear. She definitely would have remembered him.

He winced. 'I've not been out for years.'

She laughed at his joke. They stood side by side at the bar and waited. This was awkward. Alice tried to think of things to talk about, but it was really difficult to hold a conversation when the music was loud. Dom eventually got served. He handed her a bottle of cider, paid and turned to go.

'Thanks.'

He turned his head as he hadn't heard her. She launched herself at his ear to repeat it but as he came back to face her, she found she was heading for his lips. In that split second and with a few drinks inside her spontaneity took over and she kissed him. He was startled at first, but he responded and kissed her back. But it wasn't the usual passion-fuelled snogging she was used to. It was gentle and tender and surprisingly erotic. The noise of the club melted away and for a moment she was lost.

Dom pulled back and studied her briefly. He pulled his phone from his pocket. 'I'm sorry. I have to go.' Before she could even ask for his number he was lost to the crowds, but that kiss was something she would remember for a very long time.

* * *

Nancy had changed outfits a couple of times before settling on the dark grey suit. It didn't help that Alice had shrugged at her over her Rice Krispies, declaring that all Nancy's clothes looked the same. Alice wasn't being unkind and she did have a point. Nancy had made a mental note to update her wardrobe as all she'd bought over the last couple of years was dull business suits and white shirts. Alice had lent her a bright beaded necklace to add a splash of colour. Nancy now felt ready to face Freddy the executive from All Things Crafty. After the disastrous pitch with Sir Richard she was determined everything was going to go smoothly this time as she had a second chance to make a good first impression.

In the office Nancy briefed the team on key things coming up in the week ahead and then delivered the good news that there had been a change of heart from Sir

Richard and they had secured a contract with the big crafting giant after all.

'All the products?' asked Claudia, balancing a notebook on her knee as she jotted things down.

'It was a very brief call so I don't know exactly which products. I think we should assume it's just the student range but we can clarify that when Freddy arrives. Even if it's just one product it's a start and if this goes well it could open doors for us.'

'Freddy who?' asked Shona, their marketing manager.

'Ah, he didn't say and if I'm completely honest the call was late on Thursday evening when I wasn't firing on all cylinders so I forgot to ask. But I like first name terms, I think that's a good sign.'

'Will Freddy want a tour?' asked Filip.

'I'm not sure how long he has with us but I only have an hour so my plan is to talk him through the products, check through the contract terms and then if he's got time, I think a tour would be great.' Filip gave her a thumbs up.

'We're a great little company, he can't fail to be impressed with what we've achieved. And that's down to all of you. Thank you,' said Nancy.

'Stop it, you'll make me blush,' said Filip, spinning his wheelchair away and whizzing back to the picking and packing area.

'You okay?' asked Claudia.

'Yeah. I am. I'm actually really excited about this,' said Nancy and she was more than excited; she was hopeful.

Nancy didn't feel quite as excited as nine o'clock came and went and there was no sign of Freddy. Nancy had checked and double-checked the information she'd sent to Freddy and tried to call to see if there was a problem, but it just went to voicemail. Had there been a change of plan? A little dark cloud of gloom was making her feel that all was not well, that Sir Richard had changed his mind and that the contract wasn't going ahead. She tried to think positively, there was probably a more rational explanation. It was more likely a transport issue or a last-minute emergency he'd had to deal with, although in both those situations surely Freddy or his PA would have thought to let her know.

A reminder popped up for her next meeting. It took a lot of moving parts to keep the business running smoothly and she couldn't afford to take her eye off the ball. Claudia was primed to update her on any news. Nancy pulled up the document she needed and dialled the number for her next call and tried very hard to push thoughts of the contract with All Things Crafty to the back of her mind, for now.

Nancy was just finishing up her eleven o'clock conference call with a potential new supplier when Claudia popped her head around the door and grinned at her. Nancy held up a finger. 'Thanks again for your time. If you can come back to me on those key points that would be brilliant. Thanks. Bye.' She ended the call.

Claudia was still grinning. 'Your nine o'clock has turned up and he's as hot as f—'

'Thank you, Claudia. That's irrelevant. At least he's here.' She'd been seriously worried that Sir Richard had changed his mind. And thanks to this meeting finishing much earlier than planned she had twenty minutes spare. She gathered up her papers and dashed from the office.

A broad-shouldered man with sun-streaked hair was leaning on the railings watching Filip make up orders in the warehouse below. Nancy tried to contain her excitement.

'Hi, I'm Nancy Barraclough, you must be Freddy. I'm so pleased to meet you.' She held out a hand to shake.

Freddy stood up straight and shook her proffered hand. He was rather tall and filled his suit well. 'Old school. I like that. How do you do?' he said, shaking her hand confidently and appraising her. She pulled her shoulders back but then remembered that made her boobs stick out, so she moved her shoulders forward and now probably looked like she was braced for impact.

'I'm great, thanks. Would you like to come into my office?' Thrusting her boobs at some senior executive was not really the first impression she'd wanted to give.

She noted he didn't have a briefcase with him but then these days most contracts were electronic. She ushered him into the glass office and ignored Claudia who was grinning at her. Nancy sat down and took a deep breath, she needed to be completely professional. But then she'd always been true to herself, what the heck, she'd already thrust her boobs at him. 'I was so pleased that Sir Richard called me. I think this is a great opportunity for all of us.'

'I'm glad you see it like that. So do I need to sign something?' He glanced at his watch. 'Because I've a luncheon appointment.'

Nancy was slightly wrongfooted. 'I assumed All Things Crafty would be drawing up the contract.'

He pouted his full lips. 'Uncle Dickie said you were sorting that.'

'Uncle Di . . . oh Sir Richard.' Nothing like a bit of nepotism. Most likely that was how Freddy had got up the ladder at All Things Crafty. She tried to keep her working-class chip firmly balanced on her shoulder. Whatever she thought about jobs for the boys mustn't influence how she interacted with Freddy. She was so close to landing this deal. The last thing she needed was her prejudice to derail it. She took a calming breath. 'That's quite unusual when we are supplying goods to a big chain they like to set out the terms and conditions.'

Freddy narrowed his impossibly blue eyes and leaned forward. 'Supplying goods?'

'Yes. I spoke to Sir Richard, your Uncle Dickie, last week about us exclusively supplying a variety of different crochet kits, I can show you some samples if—'

'That won't be necessary.' Freddy pouted again. 'Is this part of the deal?'

Nancy emitted a tinkly laugh. 'It's all of the deal.'

'Hmm.' Freddy bent forward over the desk and beckoned for her to lean closer, which she did and caught a whiff of aftershave which she could only describe as heady and expensive. 'I'm here about the job.' Up close he really was flawless which was quite distracting.

Puzzle pieces swirled in her head along with the parts of the conversation with Sir Richard that she'd been able to hear. 'You're who Sir Richard was recommending for the role of my PA?' She blinked more times than was necessary.

'Yes!' Freddy made a tick in the air with his finger.

She looked at Freddy afresh. She hated to make assumptions, but he really was the last person she would have pegged as a personal assistant. 'Then you're part of the deal?' she asked tentatively. Her dad had always said if it looked too good to be true then there was definitely a catch. The last-minute change of mind on the All Things Crafty deal had seemed like that and now she understood why – Freddy was the catch. She bristled at what she was being asked to do. Hire Freddy as a favour to his Uncle Dickie in exchange for a contract.

'Right, well I was planning to hold interviews next week but . . .' Who was she kidding? All the CVs she'd received had been beyond awful and if she wanted the contract with All Things Crafty then clearly taking on Freddy was part of the deal and the key bit of information she'd missed during the ill-fated call on the underground. She needed this contract. Throwing it away over principles wasn't smart and surely Sir Richard also had a reputation to uphold, he wouldn't have recommended Freddy if he wasn't up to the job.

'Interview?' Freddy was pulling a face.

'Yes. An interview is standard process.' She didn't want anything to jeopardise the deal, but she also had some scruples. 'As we're both here now, why don't you just tell me a bit about yourself?'

Freddy relaxed back into the seat. 'My pleasure. I'm Frederick Leopold Astley-Davenport. Freddy to everyone except my mother. I'm in line to be 13th Earl of Langham. I achieved a 2:1 from University College London in History of Art . . .' Clearly this was his favourite subject. 'I drive a Maserati, like horses and dogs and enjoy polo, skiing and rugby. I spread my time between London, Devon and St Kitts.' He leaned forward, twitched an eyebrow. 'Now tell me about yourself, Nancy.'

'I've got one A level in Geography, drive a six-year-old van and I spread my time between here, a two-bed terrace and Aldi.' Nancy scrunched her eyes up. What the hell was going on? 'Freddy, I think we are operating at cross-purposes. I was under the impression you wanted the job as my personal assistant. Is that right or am I way off course here?'

'Correct.' He pointed a finger at her. 'Although it isn't that straightforward. Didn't Uncle Dickie explain?'

'I was on the underground, so my phone kept cutting out. Why don't you explain it to me?'

'Happy to. I'm currently having a contretemps with my parents whereby they are demanding I provide proof I am responsible enough to take on the family estate.'

'I don't want to sound insensitive, but doesn't your dad have to die for you to inherit?'

'Normally that's the process but dear Pa is of delicate health mainly due to the demands of the estate. He wants to retire early to St Kitts and pass the millstone to me. To that end they have devised this preposterous scheme that I work in an ordinary job for six months before they will sign everything over. This is where you come in, Nancy. All you need to do is provide a few favourable updates, a reference at the end of the six months and once the estate has been transferred to my name, I will pay your fee. Did you and Uncle Dickie talk numbers?' She was about to answer but he clicked his fingers as if having a lightbulb moment. 'He's offered you the contract instead. Is that right?'

Freddy had hit the nail on the head. This was why Sir Richard had appeared to change his mind. After she'd inadvertently emailed the personal assistant job details, he must have cooked up the plan. Nancy had to unclench her jaw before she could speak. 'It looks that way.'

'Excellent.' Freddy clapped his hands together and kept them there as if in prayer. He smiled at Nancy. 'Are we done?'

'Not so fast.' Freddy's smile slid away. Nancy wasn't entirely sure what she was doing but there was something at her very core that meant she couldn't just roll over and let this Hooray Henry get everything handed to him on a plate. 'I believe in honesty and integrity. Do you get me? I'm building my business. And if I'm to provide verification of you working for me. You will need to well . . . work for me.'

Freddy's phone started to ring. 'Absolutely. I'm really sorry but I need to take this call.'

Nancy held up her palm. 'I need your email address and national insurance number.'

'Just a sec,' said Freddy into his mobile. 'Of course. Here's my card. Message me, and I'll reply with whatever you need.' Nancy took the thick bevel-edged business card. 'And thank you.' He gave her an earnest nod. 'I really appreciate this. But I'm terribly sorry, I must dash.' He pointed at his mobile and put it back to his ear. 'Ludlow, you prize wanker. I hear you're back in Blighty.' The door closed behind Freddy and thankfully Nancy managed to control the urge she had to hurl something after him – never a good idea in a glass office. Freddy Posh Git hyphen Davenport was her worst nightmare. The rich kid who sailed through life, probably quite literally as those sort of people owned yachts, and while bobbing around the Mediterranean they did deals and pulled in favours which made climbing the ladder so much easier than it was for people like her. But the truth was she'd somehow managed to get herself into this mess and all she could do now was grit her teeth and make the best of it. From the tightness of her jaw it would appear that she had already perfected the first requirement.

Chapter Five

Alice stopped laughing long enough to ask a question. 'Let me get this straight. In exchange for selling a few crochet kits you have to employ some toff because he's spent his life sponging off mummy and daddy?'

'That about sums it up,' said Nancy with a huff. She took a long swig from her beer bottle.

'Can he even do the job?'

'I've no idea but if he wants my sign-off then he has to do the work. And the point is I do actually need someone and he's well turned out, articulate and I'm guessing with a very expensive education behind him he will be able to pick things up. I'm choosing to look on the bright side.'

'Which is, you have a contract with All Things Crafty.' Alice clinked her bottle against Nancy's.

'Exactly. Although I'll be in more of a mood to celebrate when we've signed something.'

They sipped their drinks. 'Thanks for the beer,' said Alice. She was aware that Nancy put most of the food and drink in the fridge and she was grateful. Nancy was like the big sister she never had but without the sibling rivalry and the unfair judgements. She also knew that Nancy was there for her if anything should happen and that was reassuring too.

'It's okay. I know you're only staying in with me because it's the end of the month and you're skint.'

'Noooo,' protested Alice. Nancy gave her a look. 'Kinda. But I like having a girls' night in sometimes.'

'Me too. Although all I seem to do these days is have nights in.' Nancy had never been a party animal but once upon a time she did know how to enjoy herself.

Alice sat bolt upright. 'You and I should go out clubbing together! We'd have a great time.'

'I'm not so sure. I think I'm past the clubbing stage.'

'You're not that old. You're like what thirty?'

'Twenty-nine,' squeaked out Nancy.

'See that's not old at all. And if you don't mind me saying, you spend all your time working so it would do you good.'

'It's true that I have no life outside of work. My bins go out more than I do.'

'There you are then. Maybe you'll even hook up with someone. You've never had a bloke back as long as I've lived here.'

Nancy tilted her head. 'Ah yes, I remember sex. Although it's been so long I think I might have forgotten how to do it.' Things had ended with Chris over a year ago and there'd been no time for anyone since. It had all been a bit awkward. They had ended things when she discovered he'd emailed her suggesting that they take a break because she didn't have time for him. As she hadn't bothered to read his email or reply for almost two weeks she could hardly argue.

'It's like riding a bike,' said Alice. 'Not that I'm calling you a bike.'

'No, Alice, I didn't think you were. I'm not looking for a boyfriend or a hook-up right now. I need all my energy for the business so it's not fair to date anyone. But don't let that stop you hooking up.'

'I'm not looking for anyone either.' Although that was a lie. She had been on a hunt for Dom, the guy she'd kissed in the nightclub, but he'd vanished into thin air like a hot, sexy ghost and now he was all she could think about.

'Because you've got Whizzer?' asked Nancy.

Alice laughed. 'Blimey, no. Whizzer's not my boyfriend. We're more friends with benefits. Although he's not really my friend.' She was also struggling to identify any benefits off the top of her head. She didn't want to think too much about exactly what sort of relationship she and Whizzer had.

'That's good because you can do way better than him. I always think being in a relationship is like being a semi-detached house. However much effort you make you'll always be judged by the state of your other half.'

'Wise words,' said Alice, thinking that she definitely didn't want to be stuck attached to Whizzer for any great amount of time. She really did need to call a halt to whatever their arrangement was.

'Thank you. Strong women don't need men, only if we want them or something like that.' It appeared Nancy had run out of wise words.

'So you'll come out then?' Alice crossed her fingers.

'We'll need to go clothes shopping first because I genuinely have nothing suitable to wear for a night out.'

'Is that a yes?'

'Yeah. Go on, then,' said Nancy. Alice launched herself at Nancy and gave her a hug.

'We'll have the best time. We'll pull an all-nighter, drink shots and dance till we've got blisters. You'll not regret it.'

Nancy's expression told Alice she wasn't convinced.

* * *

Nancy knew Claudia had sent numerous emails to Freddy because she'd been copied in on every single one. They'd had one reply from Freddy which had returned the signed employment contract and shared some details including an address in Belgravia – where else? – his national insurance number and date of birth. When the other emails had triggered no response, Nancy had rung and left a message explaining that she needed an update. She'd received a texted reply of – *It's all good*. After bristling, muttering to herself about the upper classes and a strong coffee, her response had been – *Then I will see you 9 a.m. on Monday*. His reply was simply – *K*. Was it pure laziness to abbreviate OK to just K or was she that out of touch? Nancy knew she sounded like her mum when she moaned about young people, so she didn't. And anyway, Freddy was the same age as she was. He was evidently more down with the kids.

After their first meeting Nancy was already expecting Freddy to rock up two hours late and had had the conversation with him in her head a number of times so she was ready to rebuff any public-school cleverness. She was almost disappointed when he strode in at 8.59 precisely.

He wasn't wearing a suit but he was smartly dressed in an expensive logo'd white shirt, navy tie and dark trousers. He bounded up the metal stairs, making the sound reverberate around the building.

'Freddy Astley-Davenport reporting for duty, ma'am.' He saluted Nancy.

'Good morning. We're pretty informal here so you can dispense with the ma'am. You've got a busy day ahead, Claudia and I have mapped out an induction and there's quite a lot to cover. But first coffee and meet the team.'

Claudia shot from behind her desk uber-fast with her arm already outstretched like Supergirl. 'Hi, I'm Claudia.' She had a dreamy look in her eyes as she enthusiastically

45

shook his hand. 'I'm the operations manager which basically means I'm a glorified dogsbody.' She laughed.

'You don't really feel like a dogsbody. Do you?' Nancy was concerned. She knew Claudia was swamped but she thought she loved being busy like Nancy did.

She widened her eyes at Nancy. 'I was joking. She's a great boss. You're going to love it here. We're meeting later because I need to take you through health and safety.' At last Claudia let go of Freddy's hand, but to give him his due, he was smiling broadly.

'It's my pleasure to meet you, Claudia. I can't wait to properly get to know you and learn all about health and safety.'

Nancy thought Claudia was actually going to swoon. 'Anyway, Claudia, did you want to show Freddy, how the new coffee machine works.'

'Love to. The stuff from the van is vile and it's too far to walk to a decent coffee shop.' Claudia led the way downstairs to the small kitchen area.

'You are out in the sticks here,' said Freddy, following Claudia.

Nancy bristled. 'I wouldn't call it the sticks, it's East London.'

Freddy pulled a face. 'Historically it was Essex.'

She couldn't let it go so pursued him downstairs. 'Yes, it was, but it's not anymore. It has two tube stations.' She would always defend Dagenham and its London borough status.

'Both at the extreme edge of zone three.'

Claudia stood at the bottom of the stairs and held up a mug to get their attention. 'We have pods for americano, caramel macchiato, latte, hazelnut praline latte, chai latte, cappuccino and hot chocolate.'

'Claudia may have gone overboard with the pod ordering,' said Nancy.

'What would you like?' asked Claudia, standing proudly by the new machine.

'Black americano would be lovely. Thank you,' said Freddy.

'Right. You lift this bit up and the pod goes in here. The mug under there, press the button and hey presto,' explained Claudia although Nancy wasn't sure Freddy was paying much attention.

'It means we can offer any visitors a decent drink now,' explained Nancy. 'We also have some suppliers who come in and as you know we're building our client list.' She was proud of her segue. 'On that subject have you heard anything about the All Things Crafty contract?' She was keeping her side of the bargain and she expected Sir Richard to keep his.

'No. Did you want me to speak to Uncle Dickie?'

'Please, that would be a weight off my mind.' Relief washed through Nancy and the tension eased in her shoulders. She'd had another bill land; rent was due on the premises and it was all starting to feel like things were closing in.

'My pleasure, Nancy. Whatever I can do to help, you only have to say.' He fixed her with sincere eyes. This was a far better start than she had anticipated. Maybe she had been far too quick to judge Freddy Astley-Davenport.

Chapter Six

Over coffee in the tiny break room next to the kitchen area Nancy gave Freddy an overview of the business and her vision of the future and he nodded in all the right places. She was proud of what she'd achieved and explaining it to the new recruit reminded her how far she'd come. 'You've joined at an exciting time. This is a key stage for the business's development.'

'I feel like I should be taking notes,' said Freddy.

She liked that he was taking it seriously. 'There's no need, most of it is documented which I can share with you.' Nancy put her empty mug down on the edge of the coffee table so she could email the files straight to Freddy.

'Funny story,' he began as he uncrossed his legs. His knee caught Nancy's mug, sending it flying, saloon bartender style, across the table. They both tried to save it and dived the same way, banging heads. Nancy recoiled and watched her favourite Harry Potter mug hit the floor and smash.

'Whoops,' said Freddy. 'Are you all right?' he asked as he picked up the broken pieces.

'Fine,' said Nancy, rubbing her head.

Nancy took a deep breath. She couldn't blame Freddy entirely for that. 'Let me introduce you to Filip and the working heart of the company.' She led him out into the warehouse where Filip wheeled in their direction with a basket on his lap.

'Filip, this is Freddy. Please can you give him an end-to-end process run through and a demo?'

'Of course. Welcome aboard, Freddy.' The two men shook hands. 'I'm thrilled to have you here.'

'Are you?'

'Too right. The only bloke with three women, I'm a proper minority and that's before you factor in the wheelchair.' He laughed.

Freddy peered at a label on the wall of multicoloured yarn. 'A Sprinkle of Cinnamon. Is that a fancy name for brown?'

'Spot on,' said Filip. 'The fancier the name, the better it sells. Hint of Misty Morning is our bestseller.' Filip pulled a ball out from further down.

'Grey,' said Freddy.

'Exactly. Let's get you to work, it's the easiest way to show you how picking and packing is done.'

Freddy looked a little apprehensive. 'When the orders spike we have an all hands on deck approach where everyone mucks in to make sure the orders go out on time,' explained Nancy.

'It's dead easy,' said Filip. 'Orders are printed off here on double slips, you collect the yarn or whatever from the bay or drum on the slip, pop it in a basket, then we wrap and pack it, put it in the big cage and hand it over to the postie at the end of the day. Here you go.' Filip handed him an order.

'I'll leave you in Filip's capable hands. Then at twelve, Claudia is going to take over.'

'And will I see you for lunch?' he asked.

'I don't really do lunch. Claudia usually grabs me something from the sandwich van.'

49

'Okay. Maybe another time we could do lunch. I know a fabulous little place in Wimbledon.'

Wimbledon was miles away. Nancy wasn't sure if he was joking or not. Maybe he was used to long lunches, in which case Freddy was in for a shock. 'I'll think about it.'

Nancy left them to it and went in search of paracetamol as her bumped head was throbbing.

She had a busy morning but every so often she could hear Freddy's laugh and it was always accompanied by one of her team. He was already fitting in well. There was a tap on her door and she waved for Freddy to come in. 'Claudia and I got you lunch. It was quite the experience queuing at the sandwich van. We got you a brie and cranberry baguette which Claudia assures me is quite the delicacy around here so I've gone for the same.' He handed it over.

'Thank you. How's your morning been?'

He pulled up a chair which hadn't been what she'd meant but a quick glance at the clock on her new laptop told her she had time. 'It has been an actual revelation.'

'Really?'

'Completely. Your staff are all amazing people and they are absolutely devoted to you. Did you realise that?'

Nancy felt her cheeks flush and a lump form in her throat. 'We're a great team.'

'And you must be a great leader.'

'Thank you.'

'I've got a question,' said Freddy.

This was promising. Questions showed interest and engagement. 'Fire away.'

Freddy scrunched up his pretty features. 'I'm afraid I'm going to make a blunder by asking it.'

'There are no stupid questions.'

'But there might be ableist ones.'

'Ah,' said Nancy, cottoning on to where Freddy was heading. Having met the team he had obviously worked out what they all had in common. 'I'm a disability positive employer.'

'They've all got them,' said Freddy, sounding astonished. 'I thought Shona didn't but then Claudia explained that she has invisible disabilities that include chronic pain and epilepsy. I think it's brilliant that they all work here but I'm guessing it's pretty unusual.'

'You're right. The first time I tried to recruit someone I had very little interest via the usual job agencies. I couldn't offer top money and nobody had the right skills or experience that I needed. I put an advert in a local online disability forum and I was inundated with enthusiastic people. I interviewed three people and offered the job to Claudia. The others were all so capable that as my business has grown I've employed them too. Filip had been out of work for years. He runs picking and packing like a well-oiled machine, literally nobody is quicker.' Freddy looked doubtful. 'Seriously, we've had races. Filip wins every time.'

'I think it's inspired. Anyway, I'd best leave you to your baguette.' He said the word like it was something alien.

'Thank you.'

'My pleasure. I am learning heaps and I can't wait to drop things into conversation with Ma and Pa. Thank you so much.' He reversed out of the door. The encounter had left her feeling happy that her staff felt the same way about her as she did about them and that maybe Freddy was an excellent addition to their tight-knit team.

Shortly afterwards Nancy had something for shredding, she realised she no longer had to do tasks like that herself so she called Freddy in.

'Confidential waste gets shredded. The shredder is downstairs, Filip will show you.' Nancy handed him the documents.

'Right away, Boss.' Freddy took the papers and bounded off.

This was great. Nancy was scanning her list for other things she could pass to Freddy when there was a commotion downstairs.

'Help! Help!' called Freddy.

Nancy left her office and hot-footed it down the stairs closely followed by Claudia. Filip was already at the shredder which was making a very strange noise and starting to smoke.

'What the hell?' said Nancy.

Filip spun out of the way to reveal Freddy bent over with his tie in the shredder which was slowly mincing it.

'Would someone mind awfully, switching the thing off?' asked Freddy, his face getting closer to the machine's teeth.

Claudia stepped forward and pulled the plug from the wall.

'Are you okay?' asked Nancy. Freddy was looking a little flustered as he loosened his tie, pulled his head free and straightened up.

'Bit of a close call.'

'How on earth did that happen?' asked Nancy.

'Hands up,' said Freddy. 'I thought it might be a wheeze to put my tie in there. Didn't expect it to chew it up quite so quickly.'

'Freddy, I have no words,' said Nancy. 'But I think Claudia might need to go through health and safety with you again.'

Freddy grinned at the assembled staff. Claudia and Filip shook their heads.

'Oh come on. It was just a bit of fun.'

'You've killed my sodding shredder.' Nancy pointed at the machine as a final wisp of smoke escaped. 'That cost two hundred quid.'

'I love your accent. Is it authentic East End or is it merely more pronounced when you're agitated?' asked Freddy.

'Seriously?'

'My apologies. I'll um . . . fix it.'

'You've done enough. Back to work please.'

'Absolutely . . . I just need to um . . .' Nancy left Freddy trying to tug what remained of his tie out of the machine.

For Nancy the next couple of hours were peppered with phone calls and her ever growing pile of emails. When there was laughter she looked out of her office to see Freddy was at the big table on his mobile. Nancy got her head down and ticked a few things off her list. When she next looked Freddy was still chatting and now had his feet up on the table. She had a sneaking suspicion that it wasn't work related. Instead of emailing Claudia she came out of her office.

'Claudia, I need a meeting set up with the post office about our contract as that's up soon and given predictions I'd like to think we'd need to increase our daily package numbers. Should I speak to you or Freddy?'

Claudia looked in Freddy's direction but gone was the dreamy look and in its place contempt. 'I've tried to show him how to log on and add a meeting to your diary, but he wanted to tell me a story about the time Digby stole a penguin. Thankfully it was interrupted by a call from someone called Piggers and he's been on the phone to them ever since.'

'Right. Leave it with me.' Nancy walked down to Freddy and waved a hand in front of his face to get his attention.

'Two secs, Piggers,' said Freddy into the phone before putting his hand over the microphone. 'Nancy, what can I do for you?'

'I'd like you to log in to your laptop and set up a meeting for me please. Here are the details.' She handed him a sticky note.

'No worries. I'll get straight on it once I've finished this call.' He went to turn his chair away, but Nancy held onto the arm. Confusion shot across Freddy's features. 'Problem?'

'We're all really busy so . . .' She pointed at his mobile.

His expression changed. 'Got it. I'm naffing people off.' It was a fair summary.

'You are.'

'Message received.' He pointed at his phone. 'Piggers, let's catch up face to face. Where are you this week? Uh huh. Either Barcelona Wednesday night or Valencia on Thursday would work best for me.' Nancy intensified her glare. 'Okay, Piggers. Let's do Barcelona. See you Wednesday. I'll have the cava chilling.' He laughed loudly and finally ended the call. He put down his phone and put his hands together in prayer. 'Apologies.'

'I can't imagine Sir Richard stood for personal phone calls in work time,' she said.

Freddy appeared confused for a moment. 'Oh I've never worked for Uncle Dickie.'

Her suspicions were aroused. 'Have you had a job before, Freddy?' she asked.

His eyes went to the metal framework of the roof above them. 'Did a bit of farm work after my A levels. Ended badly. Old tractor, delinquent cow and flimsy barn.' He grimaced. 'I liked a girl at uni so got a job in the gym she went to doing inductions. Overdid some weights when I thought she was watching. Hernia wasn't pretty. Rugby tryouts—'

'So the short answer would be no.'

'A little unfair but that doesn't mean I *can't* do a job. It simply means I don't have experience of one.'

'And without experience you can't get one. That was Shona's problem.' Nancy wondered if perhaps it didn't matter what walk of life you came from some issues were the same. She didn't want to be too hasty with Freddy. 'If you can keep the personal calls to breaks and lunch. Okay?'

'Absolutely. There won't be any more.'

'And you'll sort out my meeting?' They both looked around for the sticky note and spotted it on the floor at the same time.

Freddy swooped down a hand to claim it and held it aloft. Nancy veered away, keen not to bang heads again. 'On it, Boss.' He jumped to his feet. Nancy went back to her office happy that she'd got her point across without being an ogre.

When she'd finished a few emails she looked up, but there was no sign of Freddy. Claudia had her head down but seemed to sense Nancy because her eyes popped up above her laptop. She pointed down into the warehouse. Nancy assumed this meant Freddy was picking and packing so she gave Claudia a thumbs up. Claudia shook her head and went back to her laptop. Nancy was puzzled. She pulled up her next email but was distracted by a cheer from the packing area. She needed to investigate. She left her office and as soon as she reached the stairs, she could see what had caused the whoops of delight. Filip was diligently picking orders while Freddy tried to drop kick balls of yarn into the basket on Filip's lap.

'Hey, what's going on?' Nancy came downstairs so fast

the noise was like a stampede. Filip held his hands up as if surrendering and when Freddy turned around, he pointed rapidly in his direction and mouthed 'nothing to do with me'.

'Target practice,' said Freddy. 'I'm bloody good. Watch this.' He drop-kicked a large ball of Ash of Vesuvius yarn into Filip's basket from a good ten yards. Freddy celebrated.

'My office, now,' said Nancy, turning on her heel and stomping back up the stairs.

She sat and fumed in her seat for a few moments before Freddy appeared and popped his head around the door. 'Problem?' he asked.

'Yes, big style! I don't know who you think you are but—'

'You've not googled me, have you?'

Nancy's rant was momentarily stalled. She shook her head. 'Why on earth would I?'

He shrugged one shoulder. 'It's just what women usually do.'

'Women? I'm your boss, Freddy.'

'Irrelevant.'

'Nah uh. Completely relevant. You work for me. Although I use the term loosely because I am yet to see you do anything that remotely resembles work.'

'I'm "working" for you,' he said, making finger quotes. 'Maybe we should clarify what that entails?'

'Easy.' Nancy bashed a few keys on her laptop and spun it around to show Freddy. 'Job description for the role of personal assistant already emailed to you which you'd know if you'd bothered to log in.'

Freddy scanned the screen and narrowed his eyes. 'I thought I explained that I don't have to actually undertake the role, you just have to say I have in a letter.'

'And I explained that I can't do that.'

'Why ever not?'

'Because if I have to produce something that says you worked for me then I need to have a record of that employment, which means I need to register you for tax against a salary I need to be paying you. I can't risk getting into any trouble with HMRC. We either do this properly or not at all.'

'You're saying you want to pay me for "working for you".' He did the quotes thing again and she wanted to grab his fingers and stick them up his nostrils.

'Yes. I want to pay you.'

'That's terribly kind of you.'

Nancy threw up her hands in exasperation. 'It's what employers usually do in exchange for their employee working.'

'But it's not for long.' He checked his watch. 'What time do you shut up shop?'

Nancy scrunched up her eyes in thought. Was he really asking what she thought he was? 'Your contracted hours are Monday to Friday nine to five, i.e. five days a week.'

It was his turn to look confused. 'I wasn't planning on coming in after today.'

'Un-bloody-believable!' Was he for real? Her patience was stretched thinner than school loo roll. 'I'm afraid, Freddy, that's how a job works.'

He gave her a long-suffering look. 'I understand that but as we've already discussed I don't actually need the job I just need you to tell—'

'And I've explained I'm not doing that unless you actually work for me. You also signed and returned the digital contract Claudia sent you, so technically you'd need to give me two weeks' notice of your resignation. I think that's what you call a stalemate.' She put her hands on her hips and stared him down.

Freddy drew in a long breath. 'I'm not sure you've thought this through. I mean I admire your moral standing, I genuinely do. Most commendable. But I'm not really cut out to be an employee.'

'But, Freddy. You are employed. You're on our systems and those of HMRC. And I had a deal with Sir Richard.'

'And how does that work if I don't come to work after today?' asked Freddy.

'Then I would fire you.'

'Then maybe we short-circuit that loop.' He drew a circle in the air.

'You want me to fire you?'

'Probably for the best. Let's face it, I make a terrible employee.' Freddy sighed deeply. 'Truth is I'm not very good at anything much. Apart from polo, and there was a time on the rugby pitch . . .' Nancy glared at him. 'I digress. I'll just say this. I have had a surprisingly good time. You are excellent at what you do, and it's been enlightening. Any chance of a letter saying I've worked for—' Nancy crossed her arms and intensified her glare.

'Obviously not. Anyway, it's been an absolute pleasure to be sacked by you.' He held out a hand and her manners got the better of her and she shook it. 'Goodbye, Nancy,' he said and walked out of her office.

Chapter Seven

Mrs Robinson was meant to be on playground duty with Alice but announced when the bell went that she was 'Just going to grab a coffee.' That had been fifteen minutes ago and break only lasted twenty minutes.

Bonnie had, yet again, taken a ball to the head but this time she was on her side of the playground and it was the tennis ball that was straying so that was confiscated. Bonnie was now running around having been fixed by the obligatory wet paper towel. They were the answer to every school calamity.

Delilah ran to Alice in floods of tears. When she'd finally calmed down to the level of sniffing in between words she said, 'Jaxon called me a baby.' Which triggered more tears.

'Come on let's find him,' said Alice and Delilah led the way.

'Jaxon,' said Alice. 'We don't call people names, do we? It's not nice. I'd like you to apologise to Delilah.'

'I didn't call her a name,' said Jaxon, with a pout.

'You called me a baby,' said Delilah, her pouting even more pronounced than his with the effort of not crying.

'No I didn't. I said *Hey, baby*.' Jaxon looked sheepish. 'My dad says it when Auntie Natalie comes over and gives her a big kiss and—'

'Ah okay. Got the picture,' said Alice hastily, keen not to hear any more about his dad and Auntie Natalie. 'I think there's been a misunderstanding. But Delilah has been upset by what you said to her so please apologise to her.'

'Sorry, baby,' said Jaxon with a big grin on his face. Delilah giggled, which was not helpful.

'No. Try again,' said Alice.

'Sorry, De-li-lah,' said Jaxon in a bored sing-song voice.

'Thank you. Now play nicely,' said Alice and she returned to her post as Mrs Robinson finally made an appearance with her coffee mug. 'Did you get me one?' asked Alice.

'Sorry, did you want one?' *Really, some people!* thought Alice.

Alice's afternoon was mainly spent marking some books that Mrs Robinson was meant to have done already. It clearly wasn't in Alice's remit as she'd had strict instructions from Mrs Robinson to alter her handwriting and make sure the head didn't catch her doing it – like it was *her* who was fiddling the system. After that she had the thankless task of cutting out frames for the latest display. It meant she had to cut a million strips of multicoloured zigzag card. Maybe not a million, it just felt like it when you had a rubbish pair of scissors to do it with.

When Alice went through to the hall (which also doubled as the assembly room, sports hall and canteen) another TA had already put up the display for her class. The theme this term was Romans and Alice was pretty sure some of the pictures displayed had not been done by the other Year One class. If they had, then there was more than one budding Van Gogh in there. Whoever had made the suspiciously good mosaic wasn't as much of an issue as the fact they were now significantly overlapping with Alice's section. As she'd measured out her cardboard and stapled them together to make frames, she didn't want to have to trim everything down. She was pondering her dilemma when another TA stuck her head into the hall. 'You've been Hardinged,' she said.

'Sorry?'

'Mrs Harding tries it on with all the newbies. Just go over the top of hers. She paints most of them herself anyway,' said the TA with a giggle before going very stern. 'But say I said that and we're both dead.' And with that she disappeared. While Alice was learning a lot about teaching, she was also having to get her head around a lot of classroom politics and that was a lot harder to comprehend than any of the lessons.

Mrs Robinson had an appointment she had to go to which seemed to happen quite regularly with very little explanation. It left Alice to finish off for the day so she gave the class a little quiet book time, sang their letters songs with them and then it was time to put on coats and get ready to go home. Alice was still getting to know all the parents, so she double-checked with each child who was there to collect them before letting them leave the classroom. As the numbers inside the class dwindled, she noticed Bonnie start to hang back.

'Is one of your parents here yet, Bonnie?' she asked over her shoulder. Bonnie shook her head and looked glum. *Oh come on, dad*, thought Alice. She let out the last five to waiting parents and then returned her attention to Bonnie. 'Come on, let's get the office to give your daddy a call.'

'But Mrs Robinson will be cross with him.'

'It's okay. I won't tell her.' Alice had a quiet word with the friendliest of the ladies in the school office and Alice made the call to Bonnie's dad.

He was already talking as he answered the phone. 'I know, I know. I am incredibly sorry. I know I promised you last time that this wouldn't happen again, Mrs Robinson, but you see—'

'It's Miss Pelling, Mr Fisher.'

'Oh right. You're the nice one.'

'Sorry?'

'Well, that was embarrassing. It's what Bonnie says. She always says you're the nicest person at school.'

Alice was touched and glanced over her shoulder at the forlorn sight of Bonnie sitting on a chair outside the office, her head bent and legs swinging. 'That's lovely but the thing is, I've got a dejected little girl here. I know you're on your last warning, so I'll not be raising it with Mrs Robinson. But I will say this: it's not so much about the school insisting that you're here for a certain time, it's the repercussions for Bonnie when you're not. She's the last child in the school right now. That has an impact, especially when it's a regular occurrence. So please bear that in mind when you're making choices about what time you leave to get here.'

'Bloody hell. That's the nicest bollocking I've ever had. Sorry, I shouldn't have said boll . . . anyway. Thanks for not ratting me out, Miss Pelling. And your name always makes me smile. Miss spelling.' He chuckled.

'I'd like to say I've not heard that before but . . .'

'Got it. Sorry. I'm five minutes away.'

'Okay. Don't rush. My mum always says better five minutes late than *dead* on time.'

'Right. I'll be there shortly.' The line went silent.

Alice joined Bonnie on the chairs outside the office. 'He's a few minutes away. He'd not forgotten you, I think it's probably the traffic. Shall we wait outside?' She offered Bonnie her hand to hold and she took it.

'Okay.' Bonnie rolled her lips together. 'Daddy's boss doesn't like him having to leave to pick me up. He gets into trouble with him but if he's late he gets into trouble with Mrs Robinson. He says it's a shit sandwich. What's a sh—'

'Must be tricky,' said Alice.

'Can I tell you a secret?' asked Bonnie.

'I love secrets,' said Alice.

Bonnie stopped walking and Alice bent down so she could whisper. 'Daddy says Mrs Robinson is a bit of a cow.'

Alice suppressed her giggle. 'Hmm. It's not nice to call people names so you probably shouldn't tell anyone else that. Or about the um . . . sandwich.'

'I won't.' Bonnie seemed to ponder something. 'Miss, which bit of a cow do you think Mrs Robinson is?'

Alice thought it wise not to share her thoughts on this with a five-year-old. But she was interested to find out if everything else was all right at home. She hoped the late pick-up was the only issue Bonnie had but it could be indicative of other problems. They waited by the school gates. 'Bonnie, at home is everyth—'

'Here's Daddy!' she exclaimed as a car pulled up at speed and braked heavily. A flustered Mr Fisher got out. He looked clean but dishevelled, a lot like his daughter. Hair a bit too long, fitted shirt partially untucked. 'I am so sorry. I was in a meeting and—'

Realisation dawned on them both at the same time. 'Alice?'

'Dom?' He was the guy from the nightclub out for his birthday with his rowdy mates. She thought she'd never see him again. Her lips pressed together involuntarily as if remembering their kiss and Alice felt a flush of chemicals race through her system. That definitely wasn't something she was meant to do with a parent.

'I didn't know it was you, Alice.'

Bonnie giggled and they both looked at her as if they'd forgotten she was there. 'Her name's Miss Pelling,' said Bonnie, putting her hands to her mouth as more giggles escaped.

'I better get this one home,' said Dom but his eyes were fixed on Alice. 'And again, I'm really sorry.'

'It's okay, but the office do keep a note of late pick-ups. Three strikes and you'll need to see the head.' Bonnie gasped. 'Not you. Dom will. I mean Daddy. Mr Fisher.' Alice's embarrassment escalated with each error.

'It won't happen again. I promise,' he said, scooping up his daughter and hugging her tightly. Alice couldn't stop staring at him. He was the epic kisser who had disappeared without a trace and here he was in the flesh looking hot as hell. She realised she was staring and tried to look at something else but then that looked even weirder. Dom smiled at Alice's awkwardness. 'Nice to meet you again and thanks for waiting with Bonnie.'

'It's my job and my pleasure. It's what anyone would do. Anyone from the school because it's our job.' She was rambling now. 'There's a slip in Bonnie's bag because she took another tennis ball to the head at playtime.'

'Oh no.' Dom stuck out his bottom lip and Bonnie copied him – it was the cutest thing. 'Was the tennis ball okay?' he asked earnestly.

Bonnie giggled. 'They're both fine,' said Alice. 'A wet paper towel solved the problem for all involved.'

'Ahh, I remember those. They're like magic. But you're okay, sweetheart?' Alice was about to answer when she realised he was talking to Bonnie. Of course he was talking to Bonnie.

'Can we have chips for tea?' asked Bonnie. The adoring look she gave her dad melted Alice's heart.

'Sure, we can.' He turned back to Alice. 'Lovely to see you again, Miss Pelling.'

'Ditto, Mr Fisher.'

Chapter Eight

For a Monday evening both Alice and Nancy had a lot to say as they recounted their day's events.

'So, Bonnie's dad is the mystery kisser. That's brilliant news,' said Nancy, having heard a detailed account of the event. Alice had seemed astonished and moved by the encounter at the time and bereft that she would never see him again. If Nancy was being honest, she'd felt the story had been a little romanticised as she'd been to the club in question many moons ago and her memory of it was sticky carpets, tacky tunes and even tackier men and she doubted it had changed. Therefore, it was more likely Alice's view of things had been coloured rose by too much cheap cider and she'd simply had a snog with some chancer who had done a runner. But it appeared Nancy had been proved wrong. Alice's old movie version of events seemed to be a possibility.

'I don't want to pop your balloon but is he single?' asked Nancy.

Alice chewed her lip. 'I don't know.'

'Surely it's easy to find out. "Bonnie, do mummy and daddy live in the same house?"'

'I can't ask her that. Goodness. Although . . . I was thinking maybe I could look at her school record.'

'Are you allowed to do that to find out if a dad is worth hitting on or not?' asked Nancy with a grin, quite enjoying the conversation as it was taking her mind off her disastrous day.

'Of course, I'm not. But before I knew who he was I had honestly planned to have a look at her file to see if Bonnie's mum was around because her dad, Dom, seems to be struggling a little.'

'Ooh I think we're blurring the lines of our remit there, Miss Pelling.'

'Stop it,' said Alice, taking a playful swipe at Nancy and missing. 'Anyway, let's over-analyse your day and what you're going to do about Freddy wotsit-doodahs. He sounds yummy.' Alice settled herself on the sofa and got out her phone.

Nancy's cheek twitched. 'He's okay if you like your men posh and useless. It's impossible for me to see past that.'

'You know you have an unnatural dislike for the upper classes.'

'Yeah well, I have good reason.'

'I know, but one person doesn't represent them all.' Alice turned back to her phone. 'Let's have a look at Freddy.'

'Let's not,' said Nancy, sipping her Coke and wishing it had a vodka in it. 'Don't do it, please,' she begged. She knew Alice was going to google Freddy and she couldn't see how that was going to help the situation.

'Too late.' Alice's eyes pinged wide as she scrolled through the search results. 'OMG. He's rich and famous.'

'So is sticky toffee pudding and too much of that will kill you.'

'Yeah, but what a way to go.' Nancy wasn't sure Alice was talking about pudding. 'He is a hotty. Listen to this . . .'

Nancy groaned and let her head flop back on the sofa, there was no stopping Alice. '"Freddy Astley-Davenport Pretended To Interview Celebs With A Banana."' Alice giggled. 'Here's another one: "Fortnum's Freddy Blew Up My Ferret!" Do you think that's a euphemism?'

'Please stop,' said Nancy.

'It's okay. It's a story about him giving a pet ferret mouth to mouth. Ahh that's cute. Ooh . . . "Funtime Freddy Rules the Waves – Freddy Astley-Davenport was cautioned after stealing a yacht from Benalmadena Harbour while shouting I'm Jack Sparrow!"'

'Do you see why it's best that I sacked him?'

'Not really. He sounds like fun.' Nancy glared at her. 'Okay, probably not the perfect PA but isn't this contract with his Uncle Dickie kinda crucial.'

Nancy picked up a cushion and hugged it. 'I need that bloody contract or we face bankruptcy.'

What she wanted to know was what firing Freddy meant for her contract with All Things Crafty but seeing as nobody had been in touch, she couldn't see them wanting to keep up their end of the bargain even if she had done her very best to keep hers. There was a lesson to be learned in all of this. In future the first thing she needed to do was get a contract signed and sealed. Although a bigger lesson was probably not to get involved in anything like this ever again.

'Then you know what you need to do,' said Alice.

Nancy pretended to cry into the cushion. 'I need to reinstate Funtime Freddy.'

'There you go,' said Alice, patting Nancy on the shoulder as she rocked gently.

Nancy took a deep breath and tried his phone, which went straight to voicemail. 'Hi, Freddy, it's Nancy Barraclough. Please can you give me a call ASAP. You've got my number. Thanks.' She'd tried. Alice pouted as Nancy ended the call. 'What?'

'You can't just wait for him to call back.'

'Why not?' Nancy curled her feet up under herself on the sofa.

'Because you need to get to him before he tells Uncle Dickie otherwise the deal will definitely be off. In this article – "Playboy Freddy's Favourite Places" it says he's a regular at this club I go to in Seven Dials.' Alice handed Nancy her phone. 'We should track him down. You could accidentally bump into him and offer him a last chance. Come on!' Alice dashed from the room but when Nancy didn't follow she eventually came back.

'I don't know.' Nancy had never chased after anyone in her life but then she'd never had a company's future hang in the balance either. 'I have nothing to wear.'

'You can wear something of mine. It'll be fun.' Nancy very much doubted that would be the case.

'Stop pulling your skirt down,' said Alice, as she led the way out of the tube station.

'But it's so blooming short I had to wear leggings underneath it.' Nancy gave it another tug.

'So it doesn't need pulling down, then.'

'Still.' Nancy didn't feel comfortable. 'If we're just finding Freddy I could have worn a suit.'

'Then he'd know you hadn't accidentally bumped into him,' said Alice. Nancy wrinkled her nose. 'Here we are!' Alice pointed to a dark doorway.

Nancy pulled her head back. 'Are you sure it's safe?'

Alice just laughed. As she stepped inside a large bouncer appeared. 'Hey, Kwame, how's things?'

'Hi, Alice, it's quiet tonight.' He stepped aside.

'Actually, I'm looking for someone. I don't really want

to pay if they're not here.' Kwame nodded his under-standing. Alice went on tiptoe and whispered in his ear.

'Nope. Sorry. He's not been by tonight.' He checked his watch. 'It's early.'

Nancy checked hers it was way past her bedtime.

'Cool. We'll come back later,' said Alice.

'You might try The Ivy. He's a member there,' said Kwame with a smile.

'You're a star, thanks,' said Alice and she led Nancy in the direction of Leicester Square.

'They won't let us in The Ivy. I should have worn my suit.' Nancy pulled the top up to cover her cleavage which exposed her tummy and Alice pulled it down again.

'It's worth a try.' Alice bounced along full of energy and Nancy wobbled behind on borrowed heels.

'Slow down, Alice. Remember—'

'I know, I know.'

As Nancy had suspected they were only welcome at The Ivy if they were members or had a reservation. But Alice wasn't giving up that easily.

'Actually,' said Alice. 'We're friends of Freddy Astley-Davenport so if he's here he'll sign us in.'

The maître d gave them both a pitying look. 'I'm sorry, lots of people try that one. He would need to have put your name down prior to your arrival and . . .' He checked his tablet. 'Mr Astley-Davenport has no guests planned for this evening.'

'Thanks,' said Nancy, pulling Alice away until they were outside the diamond-paned doors. 'That was embarrassing,' she added.

Alice laughed. 'No, it wasn't. Where shall we try now?'

Nancy yawned. 'It's gone half eleven. I'm knackered. I'm thinking chips and home.'

Alice's shoulders dropped. 'Aww I thought we were going to make a night of it.'

'On a Monday?' Nancy was shocked. 'I'd rather set fire to my pubic hair.'

'Okay. I'll see if any of my friends are out.'

Nancy was pleased to have a get-out clause that made her feel less of a let-down. Alice began speed-messaging people. Nancy saw her cue to leave. 'Right, well I'm going to head that way and—'

'Nancy?' The posh voice behind her made her spin around. It was Freddy. 'I didn't know you frequented this old place.'

'Hi, I'm Alice,' said Alice, doing a half curtsey.

'He's not Prince William,' said Nancy in hushed tones. Alice giggled.

'Hello, Alice, very pleased to meet you. Are you Nancy's friend, life partner?'

'Friend,' said Nancy quickly. 'This is a coincidence, bumping into you like this.'

'I would assume so because otherwise it would mean I have a stalker.' Freddy laughed hard.

Nancy joined in briefly. 'It's a shame things didn't work out. Perhaps we should have tried harder to make it work.'

'Nancy, it's fine. As they say, it wasn't you, it was me.'

'Oh definitely,' said Nancy with gusto which made Freddy snort a laugh. 'But here's the thing. You need an "ordinary" job.' Nancy did the finger quotes she so loathed. 'So why not come back?'

'I can think of many reasons. Why would you want me back?'

'I like to make things hard.' Freddy's eyebrows twitched. Nancy cringed. 'I mean I like a challenge.' Freddy didn't look convinced. 'How about we wipe the slate clean and

I'll see you at work tomorrow?' Freddy narrowed his eyes but said nothing. 'What do you think?'

'I think it's a lovely offer. So thank you. But I'm really not cut out for anything that involves responsibility.'

'But that's where this is perfect because it's baby steps. You start off with things you can cope with and by the end of six months you'll be ready to run the estate just like you and your parents planned.'

'I'm afraid that's a no from me. Sorry, Nancy. I need to be somewhere.'

Nancy could feel it all slipping away and she panicked. 'Then I could tell the press about this. About the deal. Expose everything.'

Freddy turned slowly to eyeball her, there was a coldness about his stare, but she pulled back her shoulders and held his gaze, ignoring the fact her tummy was now on show.

'Blackmail? Really? Nancy, you wouldn't blab to the papers. You're a better person than that.'

Nancy swallowed. 'You're right about me not going to the press.' For a moment Freddy looked relieved. 'But that's because I'm thinking of cutting out the middleman and going straight to your mum to tell her the whole scheme and how I inadvertently said yes to it and have offered you a proper job, but you've turned it down.'

They eyed each other for what felt like ages. Stalemate. Nancy held her nerve, she wasn't going to be the one to crack first. And anyway, he was lovely to look at. Freddy puffed out a breath. 'After today why on earth would you want me working for you?'

'Because I need the contract with All Things Crafty. And I don't see why I should miss out on a deal that me and the team have worked super hard on.' Freddy slowly blinked. 'But I also despise people who have everything handed to them on a plate and swan through life getting off scot-free.'

She felt the familiar bubble of anger at the injustice of the British class system and the impact it had had on her family.

Freddy pulled his head in. 'You think I'm someone who's had everything handed to them?'

'Freddy, I know you are.' A cab came trundling down the road and Nancy decided she needed to draw their discussions to a close so she held her arm out to stop it. 'Look that's the proposition. Take it or leave it.'

'And if I don't, you're going to squeal to my mother?'

Nancy pressed her lips together. 'You'll only find that out if you don't show up for work tomorrow.'

'Fine. But you don't know what you've let yourself in for.' Freddy shrugged.

'I fear I do!' Nancy opened the cab door and Alice got inside. She turned back. 'One more thing, Freddy. If you don't take this seriously, I will be straight on the phone to Mummy Astley-Davenport. You have been warned.' She got in the taxi and shut the door feeling like the queen of bloody everything.

'Hang on a sec,' called Freddy, interrupting her dramatic exit.

'Stop the cab,' said Nancy as Freddy appeared at the window. After a few attempts she managed to lower it. 'What?'

'I absolutely can't make tomorrow. Important prior commitment.'

'Fine, I'll see you Wednesday.'

'Any chance I could also have Wednesday off because I'm seeing a friend—'

'Not a chance.' And this time she got to have the last word.

Tuesday was a nice calm day, but Wednesday morning was exactly as Nancy had imagined it would be. Everyone at Having A Ball was busy as usual but there was no sign of Freddy. No message, no text, no nothing. Quite rude really. But what was she going to do about it? Was she really going to rat him out to his parents? For a start she had no idea how you got hold of people like that.

Nancy and Shona were in Nancy's office going through the marketing plans and tweaking the budget for various different crafting magazines and online paid adverts when they were interrupted by the sound of someone coming up the stairs. People generally didn't just come up as all deliveries were usually intercepted by Filip. Nancy looked up to see Freddy bounding up the last few steps. Designer sunglasses in place, jumper loosely tied around his shoulders over a polo shirt and dark trousers – he looked like he'd stepped off the set of *Made in Chelsea*. Nancy was slightly wrong-footed by his return and that probably showed on her face.

She stood up quickly and banged her leg on the desk. 'Sod it. Freddy.'

'What a lovely welcome,' said Freddy stony-faced.

'The sod it was for the desk not you. Although it might be, depending on whether or not you have a good excuse for being late.'

'Can we talk, please?' he asked.

She turned to Shona. 'Do you mind?'

'We're pretty much done here anyway,' said Shona, smiling at Freddy as she left. Why was everyone smitten with him? He was basically an out of work layabout in fancy clothes. It irked Nancy. If he had greasy hair and tracky bottoms they wouldn't look twice at him.

'Okay,' said Nancy, beckoning Freddy into her office. He sat down, slowly removed his sunglasses and put them on his head.

'So you drive a van.'

'Yes. It's practical, it has our logo on it so it's free publicity and it has double doors at the back so it can easily take large objects.' *Like your carpet-wrapped corpse*, she added in her head. 'Freddy, you said you wanted to talk.'

'Absolutely. How have you been, Nancy?' He studied her intensely.

'Since Monday evening? I've been looking forward to day two of having a new personal assistant. Given the very high standards you set on day one.'

'Splendid.' Nancy was fairly certain he'd not been listening to her reply. 'I've been thinking over our dilemma and I have a proposition for you.'

'Does it involve you working here Monday to Friday, nine to five?' she asked.

'No.'

'Then no dice.' She folded her arms and stared him down. The contract mattered to her but, when faced with it, her scruples mattered more.

'Hear me out. Please?' said Freddy, giving her puppy-dog eyes.

'Fine. But hurry up, I'm busy.'

'I know you think that I have to physically work for you but nobody from the tax office is going to check something like that. Who in their right mind would pay someone for not actually working? I want to offer you some money on top of the contract with Uncle Dickie. How much would it take?' he asked.

'To buy me?' Nancy was narked.

Freddy winced. 'I wouldn't put it like that. It's merely an additional gift to show my appreciation for what you're doing. And in exchange you provide the letter confirming my employment and obviously you don't go to the press or Mother.'

'I don't want your money, Freddy. But I do want you to take this job seriously.'

'Okay. Can't blame a chap for trying. Coffee?'

Nancy was surprised he was giving in this easily. 'Umm skinny mocha, please.'

'Coming right up.' Freddy flashed her a smile as he left her office. 'Claudia! Would you be a star and show me how the coffee machine works again?' he called and Nancy was almost certain she heard Claudia's eyes roll.

Nancy caught up with Freddy an hour later. 'How are you getting on?' she asked.

'I'm logged into the computer and ready when you are,' he said, looking quite pleased with himself.

'What do you mean ready when I am?'

'For you to tell me what to do.'

'When you were here on Monday, I asked you to catch up with Claudia who would explain the role.' Out of the corner of her eye she saw Claudia slink behind her laptop screen.

Freddy leaned forward and whispered. 'She said a lot of stuff on Monday and because I thought I was only here for the day I basically switched off.'

'Then I suggest you ask her again and this time take a pen and a notepad with you.' She said it as calmly as she could manage.

'Good idea,' said Freddy, picking up a biro and wheeling his chair over to Claudia at speed.

Claudia made a series of faces at Nancy so in response she blew her a kiss. Claudia stuck her tongue out.

Nancy was quite pleased with herself for getting Freddy to commit and it was pretty timely because another of the irons she'd had in the fire was starting to warm up.

When they all gathered together for the team meeting

in the packing area, Claudia took her to one side. 'He's an idiot,' said Claudia.

'Come on now, Claudia. Tell me what you really think,' said Nancy with a smile.

'Funny. I mean it. He is an *actual* idiot.'

'He can't be that bad.'

'He's worse.' Claudia checked over her shoulder. Freddy was chatting to Shona who appeared enthralled. 'He has the attention span of a toddler. Everything I start to show him triggers a funny story which he feels compelled to tell me. I explain how to do something, he nods along and then asks if I can show him. I did it the first time until I cottoned on that's basically me doing it while he watches.'

'My diary isn't too bad tomorrow so I'll have him shadow me which will give you a break and I can get him to focus on Friday. Okay?'

Claudia looked momentarily relieved. 'Thank you. Hang on. By Friday do you mean—'

'Hello,' said Freddy, waving a hand in front of them both. 'Please excuse me interrupting but I really do need to pop to . . .' He pointed over his shoulder in the general direction of the toilets.

'Of course. You don't need to ask, Freddy,' said Nancy.

'Splendid. Thank you.' He gave them another wave and disappeared.

'You're letting him loose on the new project?' asked Claudia, looking doubtful.

'He'll be supervised and there's quite a lot to do. He can learn on the job. Anyway, let's crack on with the team meeting.' Nancy and Claudia joined Shona at the bench seats.

Filip wheeled his chair into place on the end. 'Is Freddy on flexi-time?' he asked.

'He was late in this morning, but things have been

resolved so I'm sure he will keep to office hours going forward,' explained Nancy. The last thing she wanted was to upset her current employees.

'Right. Because he's just left for the day,' said Filip, sounding disgruntled.

'No, he's just gone to the loo,' said Nancy, scanning the area.

'He's meeting a friend in Barcelona tonight,' chipped in Shona. 'Isn't that exciting?'

'I saw him walk out.' Filip pointed a finger at the door.

When Freddy had said he needed to pop somewhere Nancy had assumed he meant the loo not bloody Barcelona. He was impossible.

Chapter Nine

Before school, Alice and Mrs Robinson were going over Alice's to-do list, which appeared to be a lot longer than Mrs Robinson's. She knew that teaching was a very important job, but she did feel like Mrs Robinson's personal assistant sometimes. While Alice didn't want to add to her own lengthy to-do list, she did want to see if she could find out some information about Dom and get some brownie points with Mrs Robinson at the same time.

'I was wondering about some lessons we could do with the children and I have some ideas I'd like to discuss with you.' She had one idea so hopefully that would be enough.

'Go on,' said Mrs Robinson.

'I thought it might be both fun and educational if we talked about the different jobs there are and maybe incorporate some dress up, picture work and link it back to home with what occupations their parents do.' Alice was very pleased with her well-thought-through pitch, she'd gone over it countless times in her head on the way in to work.

Mrs Robinson smiled, which was a good start. 'They tend to cover that area in Key Stage One but we avoid asking what their parents do as many don't know and we don't want to inadvertently shame any students who have unemployed parents. But it's good that you're thinking about this, Alice. What were your other ideas?'

'Err. Erm.' For goodness' sake this wasn't how it was meant to go. Alice raced over her conversations with Nancy about Freddy Astley-Davenport – was there anything there she could salvage an idea from? 'I thought we could look at family names and what they mean and why some are double-barrelled but most aren't.' She ran out of steam and looked hopefully at Mrs Robinson.

'I like that idea. You could look up all the children's surnames so they would know where they originated and what they meant, like Smith being a derivative of Blacksmith. They could paint their own coat of arms. That would make an excellent display. One to rival Mrs Harding no doubt.' Mrs Robinson seemed to have drifted off for a moment. 'As well as looking up each last name you'll need to make and cut out thirty-four shield templates. I'll leave you to sort that all out. Next week okay?'

Alice had no words. She'd totally stuffed herself up. She was no closer to finding out anything about Dom's marital status and she'd added a truckful of stuff to her already busy workload.

Her brilliant plan had been foiled so she planned a different approach during lunch break. She lost some time helping a member of kitchen staff clear up after one of the boys had brought in a banned substance (a can of fizzy drink) which had showered him and everyone on his lunch table like a winning Formula One driver, only everyone was left a lot stickier. Alice went to the school office still marvelling at how tacky her fingers were. She walked in, putting her sticky thumbs and fingers together like a crab. The nice lady wasn't there. A face popped up from behind two giant monitors. It was the thin woman with glasses that curved up at the edges making her seem quite villainous. 'Yes?'

Alice stopped doing her sticky crab impression. 'Hi. I'm Alice, from Year One, Class Two. Is it okay if I have a quick look at one of the student's records?'

'Which student?'

Excellent, thought Alice. That was easy. 'Bonnie Fisher.'

'Why do you want to see her records?'

Maybe not as easy as she'd thought. 'Because I need to check if there is any information about her home situation so I can be mindful of that in class.'

The woman narrowed her eyes at Alice. 'What's made you suspicious of her home life?'

'Nothing major. Her dad has been late a couple of times. I'm just being extra vigilant like my safeguarding course told me to be,' said Alice, sounding haughtier than she'd intended.

'Fine. You wait there.' The woman held up a hand to stop Alice approaching. Which was probably wise given how sticky her fingers were. 'I'll check.' The woman disappeared behind her monitors and began tapping on her keyboard. Her head popped back up again. 'Everything looks in order. Anything else?'

'What do you mean by in order? Are there two parents at home or . . .?' Alice hoped that was a valid question and didn't make it obvious what she was up to. She felt a little flush in her cheeks. She'd make a rubbish spy.

'Like I say, all in order. No issues with either parent. Just the late pick-ups you've already highlighted. Anything else?' The stare that accompanied the question made it clear that there should not be anything else if Alice wanted to get out alive.

'No. You've been . . .' The woman turned back to her

large screens. 'Helpful,' said Alice in a small voice and she slunk away.

She couldn't stop the sigh escaping. That wasn't the information she'd wanted to hear. Dom was in a relationship. At least now she knew and she could erase all fantasy thoughts of him from her mind.

* * *

Nancy was ready and waiting for Freddy the next morning having boiled gently overnight. He needed to take the job seriously or he was going to upset the rest of the team and she couldn't have that. However much she wanted to do a deal with Sir Richard it wasn't worth damaging the team she'd worked so hard to build. And that was the crux of the speech she had prepared. Freddy needed to understand what a privilege it was to be part of their tight, hard-working little team and what an opportunity it was for him to see some of the real world outside of the bubble he'd been living in his whole life. Maybe she wouldn't add the last part. She really hoped he would step up because she also really needed a PA she could rely on.

Nine o'clock came and went and Nancy felt a familiar sense of foreboding that Freddy wasn't going to show up. At 10.40 she was picking and packing with Filip, partly because he had a lot of orders but mainly because she found it quite therapeutic, and she needed to calm herself down – Freddy was driving her potty even when he wasn't there. Nancy popped three balls of Sun at the Summer Fete into the basket when she heard hurried footsteps behind her.

'I am so sorry but you need to know I got here as quickly as I could. I got a lift with Borsch but his flight came into Brize Norton and my car was at—'

'You're late,' said Nancy, trying to hide the fact that she was really quite pleased to see him, having convinced herself that he wasn't going show up. 'Let's continue this in my office.' She led the way and Freddy followed in silence. Nancy took her seat and Freddy slid into the chair opposite.

'Once again I am truly sorry for not being here on time.' Freddy held up his palms in surrender. 'But in my defence, I was in Barcelona last night, which was an absolute blast by the way and I got the red-eye back this morning.'

'By red-eye do you mean a mate's private jet?'

'Yes, but it left Barcelona at silly o'clock and after what I drank last night it was both the red and puffy eye this morning.' Nancy didn't laugh. Freddy lost the grin and continued. 'I misjudged the journey. It's taken three trains, two tubes and a fair bit of walking to get here.'

'Are you expecting me to be grateful?'

Freddy tilted his head and then seemed to think better of it. 'I'm simply trying to explain that I did my best and now I am here and I'm ready to work.' He sat up straight and placed his hands on his thighs. He did look chipper given his arduous trip.

It was very hard to stay cross with him but she was going to try. 'Freddy, you can't walk out early when I've already said you have to work the same hours as everyone else.'

'What, yesterday? I asked and you said it was okay.'

'I thought you needed the loo.'

He laughed. 'You can't blame me for misunderstanding that one.'

'I do because you pointed to the toilets.'

'I definitely pointed at where my car was parked outside . . . oh okay I can see how that might—'

'And it doesn't matter if you're coming from Barcelona or Barking you *have* to be here at nine o'clock. Got it?'

'Barking is a lot nearer . . .' She intensified her stare. 'Yes, got it. Sorry, Boss.'

'If it happens again, it will be a written warning. You'd best get to work.'

'On it.' He got to the door and paused. 'What exactly do you want me to do today?'

Initiative wasn't his strong suit. 'There's a meeting at eleven about a new project which I'd like you to be involved in. You'll need to take notes at the meeting. Okay?'

'Take notes. No problem.'

Nancy really hoped that was the end of Freddy's shenanigans because she needed this to go well.

Everyone gathered for the meeting and Freddy took a seat next to her with his laptop open and fingers poised – it was a hopeful start.

'Most of you know about the new project but for Freddy's benefit I'll go over the key elements. We have had the idea for a book. While there are a number of books on knitting and crochet on the market we feel ours is different enough to get published and sell well. An initial response from a publisher has been promising and I'm visiting their offices tomorrow to pitch the full idea. Claudia has worked incredibly hard on this.' There was an impromptu round of applause and Claudia looked a bit awkward. 'As this is non-fiction we've not had to write the whole thing upfront which is good but it will be a lot of work if we get the contract. And I think it's an area where Freddy would be able to help.'

Freddy looked around, then leaned towards Nancy. 'Sorry I zoned out there, didn't actually get any sleep last night. Did get an hour on the train this morning but then missed my station and had to get the train back to Oxford and . . .' He seemed to sense the irritation radiating from Nancy. 'Should I be typing something?'

'Notes for yourself and then any actions,' said Nancy as calmly as she could manage, she felt the eyes of the team on her.

'Got it. Could you just go over the bit about a book again please?'

Nancy took a deep breath, provided a quick summary and then ploughed on. They had a lot to cover and as with everything she wanted the team to be involved. Claudia ran through the presentation that she and Nancy were delivering to the publishers and Freddy stifled yawns all the way through it, but he did appear to be making notes which Nancy took as progress. At the end of the meeting Freddy shut his laptop and got to his feet.

'Please can I have a quick look at the actions list?' Nancy pointed to his laptop now tucked under his arm.

Freddy narrowed his eyes at her, making him look quite sexy. 'Does someone not trust me?'

'Not really, no,' she said.

'Fair enough,' said Freddy, reopening his laptop and tapping in his password. He turned the screen around for Nancy to view.

There were bullet points in black and red and a list of actions with names allocated as per the discussion. Nancy was disproportionately pleased. She'd make a half-decent personal assistant of Freddy if it killed her. 'What do the red bullets mean?' she asked.

'They're things I'm not sure about so I thought I'd catch up with Claudia so I'm on the ball for tomorrow.'

'Tomorrow?'

'Our little jaunt to the publishers. I thought we could have lunch at Kerridge's at the Corinthia. It's nigh on impossible to get a table but I know someone—'

Nancy held up a hand to stop him. 'Sorry, Freddy, firstly the publisher is in Cambridge not London.'

Freddy looked at her askance. 'Surely all publishers have offices in the city?'

'Not this one. It's more niche and better suited to our industry. Also, I hadn't planned on you coming. It's just me and Claudia.'

He pulled his chin in. 'I thought you said I would be working on this.'

'I meant all the content work but not the pitch meeting.'

'That hardly seems fair,' said Freddy, looking affronted.

'I don't want to go mob-handed and three of us would look like that. Also, you kind of need to earn stuff like that. Prove your worth. But this . . .' she tapped his laptop '. . . is a good start.' Freddy shrugged as if he really didn't care, but Nancy quite liked the fact that he clearly did. He picked up his laptop and left. Nancy stood by her decision. She couldn't risk him being a liability in the meeting. No, Freddy had to earn his stripes.

Chapter Ten

Just before five o'clock Claudia put her head around Nancy's door. 'I'm going to head off,' she said with a deep sigh.

'Everything okay?' asked Nancy.

'Just tired I think. I'll go over tomorrow's presentation one last time tonight and then I'll send you the final version so we've both got a copy on both our laptops as well as the cloud. I don't want anything to go wrong.'

'Okay. Take care of yourself, I need you fighting fit.'

'Yeah. I know. You couldn't do without me blah, blah, blah.'

'It's true,' said Nancy. 'Have you got the samples?'

'Yeah. I'm bringing a wheelie case. Right, I'm off. See you tomorrow.'

'Ooh before you go, did Freddy catch up with you over the meeting points he wanted to clarify?'

'Nope. I've not seen him since lunch.'

Nancy had that now familiar sense of unease. 'Right, well you best get off and I'll make sure Freddy has a long list of things to keep him busy tomorrow. If all else fails I'll ask Filip to get him picking and packing.'

'Okay. Night.' Claudia left and Nancy followed her out of her office. Where the heck had Freddy got to? Downstairs

Filip was talking to the post collection guy so Nancy decided to check the few other places Freddy could be. She very much hoped he'd not gone home early. She really didn't want to have to go through the whole written warning process.

She checked the kitchen – it was empty. She stuck a head around the door of their tiny break room and there was Freddy. He'd pushed two chairs together and he was lying down sound asleep.

Nancy was furious. This guy took two steps forward and then reversed back over them like a getaway driver. She moved nearer to him and clapped her hands by his ear.

'Hell!' shouted Freddy, sitting bolt upright. Nancy folded her arms crossly and stared at him. 'Goodness, Nancy, you gave me a start. Everything all right?' he asked, swinging his legs around and rubbing a hand over his face.

'Freddy, it's five o'clock.'

'Ooh thanks I need to go because—'

'I'm not waking you up so you can go home. You've slept all afternoon. That's not working and it's certainly not what I pay you for.'

'I have said before that while it's a lovely idea, you don't need to pay me.'

'Not the point!' Her frustration and voice were rising rapidly. 'You can't literally fall asleep on the job.'

Freddy smirked. 'Funny story, my old friend—'

'No.' Nancy waved her hands in front of his face. 'No more funny stories. You're a liability and I don't think I can trust you.'

Freddy's expression changed from his usual relaxed state. 'Don't question my integrity, Nancy. I might not be employee of the month but I am making a serious effort here.'

Nancy couldn't help the splutter of laughter that escaped. 'People with integrity don't rock up late and then sleep all afternoon.'

Freddy stood up, making him very close to Nancy but she didn't budge. 'I won't have my integrity called into question.' He'd gone all brooding and looked super sexy.

Nancy tried to concentrate. 'Well I am questioning it so you'd better—'

'I resign,' said Freddy, handing her his laptop.

'You what?'

'I resign. And if you want to contact my parents, go ahead. They will back me to the hilt if someone is questioning my integrity. No job is worth that.'

For a moment Nancy was dumbstruck. Freddy reached for the door.

'Well, you can't resign without giving notice. But you're fired anyway.'

'Fine.'

He walked out of the room leaving Nancy standing there with his laptop and a belly full of rage. How come she was suddenly the bad guy when Freddy had been a nightmare all the way through? She marched out after him, but he was already going out the door. 'Don't expect a reference and don't come back!' The door swung closed which was annoying because she really would have liked to have given him a piece of her mind if that was to be the last time she saw him.

Nancy was still bubbling with frustration when she let herself in her own front door. 'You will not believe what Freddy has done now,' she called up the hall.

A forlorn-looking Alice appeared. 'Dom's not single.' She tried to give a nonplussed face but she was fooling no one. Nancy knew how much of an impact her first encounter with Dom had had on Alice and finding out he was the father of one of her pupils had seemed like fate.

It stopped Nancy's rant that had been brewing. 'The shit.'

Alice gave a one-shouldered shrug. 'Doesn't matter. It's not like we hooked up or anything. It was just a kiss.' The deep sigh that followed contradicted her words.

'Here's what we're going to do. We are going to go *out* out but before that I need some new clothes because while yours are lovely, they're definitely not my thing. First let's head into town, do some shopping and then get a take-away.'

'That might cheer me up, thanks,' said Alice.

'I definitely need cheering up because Freddy turned up late, fell asleep for a few hours and got the hump because I questioned his integrity. He resigned, so I fired him.' Alice looked puzzled. 'I'm getting grumpy again so let's forget men and go shopping.' Nancy picked up her bag and opened the door.

It had been a while since Nancy had been shopping for anything other than work attire. Her one remaining pair of jeans had holes in them and not the fashionable kind. Other than that her wardrobe consisted of leggings, T-shirts and gym kit. Alice seemed to have perked up and already had an armful of stuff for the fitting rooms.

'You need to pick a few things and see how they look on,' suggested Alice. 'They'll look different off the hanger.'

'Nothing's really speaking to me,' said Nancy, turning her nose up at a row of crop tops.

'How about this?' said Alice, pulling out a sequin dress in rainbow colours.

'If I was six maybe,' said Nancy.

Alice frowned. 'I meant for me.'

'In that case. I love it.' Nancy gave a cheesy grin.

Alice added the dress to the pile in her arms. They walked around a bit more and Nancy found some black trousers that she liked the look of. 'I wonder if they have a jacket to go with this?' she said, looking around.

'That would be a suit. You're looking for clubbing clothes. Here hold these.' Alice thrust the pile of outfits she was carrying and Nancy caught them just in time. 'Wait there.'

'I'll have to, I can barely see over the top,' said Nancy but Alice had already marched off. Worryingly Nancy felt Alice was on a bit of a mission. But then if it took her mind off Dom, she was prepared to suffer being a human Barbie. 'Oof,' said Nancy when the weight of another pile of clothes landed in her arms. 'Is that you, Alice, or have I been mistaken for a mobile jumble sale.'

'Come on, time to try some things on,' said Alice, guiding Nancy across the store.

This was the part in films where there would be a lovely montage of them swishing back the fitting room curtains to reveal various different outfits until they both agreed on the best one. The reality was somewhat different. The changing rooms were tiny and the two hooks in each was nowhere near enough for all the clothes they wanted to try on. The attendant had already tutted at the amount they had chosen and had made them leave some with her and only take in ten items each, half of which were on the floor. Nancy had the fitting room by the entrance near the comfy chairs that on a weekend were used as a man crèche for bored husbands, but at least she didn't have far to go to get the next batch of things to try on.

Nancy tried on two outfits. The first one was an over-sized green affair which made her look like the offspring of Kermit and Miss Piggy and the second made Harry

91

Styles's dress sense look conservative – it had so many sequins which scraped her skin as she pulled it off. Nancy was back down to her underwear and trying to pull a very small stretchy dress over her head when the curtain swished open and she froze. 'That you, Alice?' she whispered.

'Of course, it's me. Here, let me give you a hand.' Alice tugged the dress into place. 'I like it,' she said, scanning Nancy.

Nancy looked in the mirror. She could see her underwear through the material. 'Bit tarty.'

'It is,' agreed Alice. 'I like it.'

'Not for me,' said Nancy, trying to roll it up her body.

'Skin a bunny,' said Alice, grabbing the hem.

'You can tell you work with kids,' said Nancy through a mouthful of material as the dress whizzed over her head. 'Do you think I could try jeans and a top. I think that's probably more me,' she added.

'Sure,' said Alice, whipping back the curtain and stepping out leaving Nancy more than a little exposed to the shop, but thankfully there was nobody about, so she quickly pulled the curtain back. No sooner had she done that than it was whipped open again and Alice handed her some black ripped jeans and a trendy top. 'Try these.'

'Thanks,' said Nancy, eyeing the items with deep suspicion.

'This is fun. It's like being a personal shopper,' said Alice. 'Actually, I'm going to get you some more things to try.'

'Hang on . . .' But it was too late, Alice had already exited the fitting rooms.

Nancy looked at the top. It was a bit too sparkly for her taste, so she hung it on top of everything already on her hook and it promptly fell to the floor. She couldn't be bothered to pick it all up again. Nancy unfolded the jeans. Did anyone have thighs that thin who wasn't a greyhound?

She was still shaking her head and muttering to herself as she tried to put them on. With her first attempt she stuck her foot through the torn section and her second saw the stretchy jeans make it as far as her knees. She took them off and decided to try putting them on like tights one leg at a time. Her left leg went in fairly well but now it's unstretched brother was hanging by her groin like an elephant's trunk. She wriggled them down a bit and attempted to shove her foot in the springy material.

Her toe caught on a hole and her weight tipped forward, all she could do to stop herself falling was to hop over the pile of clothes and towards the curtain. She grabbed it for support and only as the rings at the top pinged off in succession did she realise what a bad idea that was. She fell out of the cubicle, clinging to the curtain in a bra, pants and half wearing the pair of jeans. As Nancy fell to the floor pain shot through her wrist and up to her shoulder.

She lay on the floor for a moment. 'What have you done?' said the fitting room attendant, rushing over, but Nancy had a feeling she was referring to the curtain, rather than her arm.

'You okay?' asked Alice, appearing above her.

'Nope. I've done something to my wrist,' said Nancy, feeling that was probably an understatement as she could see the swelling coming up and it hurt like hell. Could today get any worse?

'Nancy is that you?' came a familiar male voice. Chris, her ex, stood up from the comfy waiting area. 'It is you. Mum!' he shouted loudly into the changing rooms. 'Nancy is here. Come and say hello.' *Kill me now*, thought Nancy. *And be quick about it.*

Chapter Eleven

The last people Nancy wanted to see when she was lying prostate on a changing room floor, wrapped in a broken curtain and in a great deal of pain was her ex-boyfriend and his overbearing mother. Especially as they were both standing over her chatting to her as if everything was completely normal.

'We were talking about you only the other day, weren't we, Mum?' said Chris.

'We were. Now where was that?' replied his mother. Nancy tried to turn over but when she put out her right hand she yelped. The way the older woman was standing Nancy could now see up her dress so she averted her eyes.

'We were having coffee,' he said. 'Was it the Marks and Spencer's café?'

The older woman clicked her fingers. 'Garden centre.'

Alice crouched down and leaned into Nancy's ear so only she could hear her. 'Did you really go out with this dullard?'

Nancy tipped her head to one side. This was not the conversation she wanted to have when she was lying on the floor helpless with a direct view of someone's surprisingly lacy underwear. 'Thank you, Alice,' she said in a very deliberate voice. 'I do need some help. I think I may have broken something.'

'You have!' said the assistant. 'The fitting room curtain!'

'Yeah. Sorry about that.' With some help from Alice, Nancy got to her feet. She handed the curtain to the assistant, who did a lot of tutting. Nancy was now very aware that she was only wearing a bra on her top half and a pair of trousers partially covering one leg. 'I'm just going to get some clothes on.' She hung on to Alice and like a lone person in a three-legged race she hobbled into another cubicle and Alice pulled the curtain across.

'Um, Nancy,' came Chris's voice. 'I know you're busy right now, but did you want to catch up sometime. Maybe go for dinner?'

'No thank you. Nice to see you and your mum. Bye,' said Nancy through the curtain. They waited a minute. Nancy pointed at the curtain. 'Have they gone?' she whispered to Alice.

'No,' said Chris from the other side. 'Mum's just trying on a dress. This isn't usually a shop she'd come in, but she saw the one with flowers on in the window and—'

Nancy held up her hands in exasperation. 'Okay then. Bye.' She and Alice had a rushed mimed conversation where neither of them knew what the other was saying. 'Please help me out of these and back into my clothes,' she asked.

'Um, sorry, Nancy, were you talking to me?' asked Chris.

'No!' chorused Nancy and Alice together.

'Right. Got it. Bye then,' he said. 'Call me if you change your mind about dinner.'

Alice helped Nancy change back into her own clothes, taking care with her right arm. Her hand and wrist were now extremely swollen. 'Oh dear,' said Alice as they both inspected the lump.

'It's not good is it?'

'No. Hospital?' asked Alice.

Nancy didn't want to admit it, but she was pretty sure she needed medical attention. 'Yeah, I think so.'

They exited the cubicle and Alice bundled up all the clothes and handed them to the assistant. 'Any good?' she asked.

'Well let's see?' said Nancy. 'This green thing makes me look like a giant Brussels sprout; the sequin-covered top has left me with marks like I've wrestled a tiger; and the super-duper-uber-skinny jeans tried to kill me.'

The assistant blinked a few times. 'Did you want to try another size?'

Nancy was very grateful that Alice went with her to the hospital and tried to keep her spirits up in the waiting area with free-flowing coffee from the overpriced machine and anecdotes from the playground. Triage was quick and painful as the smiling nurse prodded all around Nancy's wrist making a note of each time she flinched. But she did give her a temporary sling to help keep it elevated and something for the pain. About an hour later Nancy was called to X-ray which was a brief intermission. After another hour Nancy's arm was still the same level of swollen but not as painful now the painkillers the triage nurse had given her had kicked in. After all the waiting things seemed to speed up as Nancy was called through by a doctor who declared she had broken her wrist in two places. 'You've done a proper job,' he said cheerfully.

'Great. Do I get a prize?' The doctor frowned at her. 'What happens next?' she asked, although she was pretty sure she could work it out.

'Temporary plaster tonight and then back here to fracture clinic tomorrow where they—'

'No, no, no. I'm really sorry but I can't come back tomorrow I've this big work thing and before you say they'll cope without me it's my business, so I have to be there and—'

'Okay, let me just check who's in the plaster room.'

'Thank you,' said Nancy, attempting to put her hands together as if praying but a sharp pain stopped her.

'No promises,' he said. 'This way.' She followed him through the hospital and he left her on a plastic chair in a corridor next to a young man who had both feet in surgical boots and his arm in full plaster set at an angle.

'You all right?' he asked when her staring had become too much.

'I'm sorry. It's just you look like you've been in the wars.'

'Stubbed my toe,' he said.

'What?'

'I'm joking,' he said with a smile. 'Got knocked off my bike. Cast is smelling so they think I've got an infection in there.' Nancy couldn't help her instinct to recoil. 'How about you?' He nodded at her sling.

Nancy wished she'd spent her two hours in A and E coming up with a better response to this question than 'I got stuck in a pair of jeans and fell over in front of my ex-boyfriend'. She gave a little shudder at the thought. 'I fell. Silly really, just fell over.'

He nodded. 'A fall can cause more damage than you'd think.'

Nancy wrinkled her nose at his turn of phrase. Old people had falls not someone of her age. 'It wasn't a *fall*. I just fell.'

He gave her the sort of look you give the person who is talking to themselves on the tube. 'O-kay.'

She was about to argue her case further when he was called into the plaster room and hobbled off. Shortly afterwards her doctor popped his head around the door. 'You're in luck – my colleague is going to manipulate it for you tonight.' He beamed a smile and she returned it.

'Thank you.'

A lovely nurse showed her to a cubicle and pulled the curtain around. Nancy had a flashback and winced. The nurse chatted to her. 'Doctor will be here in a minute. Then I'll put on the plaster – it's not actually plaster anymore, it's made of fiberglass so it's much lighter. While it's still soft he'll manipulate it so it's in the best position to heal. I've got the gas and air ready.'

Nancy chuckled, the nurse wasn't smiling. 'That was a joke, right?'

'Just take really deep breaths,' said the nurse. 'We've only got orange is that okay?'

Nancy had had enough coffee so orange squash would be just the ticket. 'Sure. Thank you.' The nurse disappeared and Nancy eyed the large black gas canister next to her. Didn't they use gas and air when you were in labour?

'Nancy Barraclough?' asked a jolly-looking doctor who then checked her date of birth and which hand was being put in plaster. She was tempted to say "the one the size of a marrow" but she thought better of it.

The nurse returned and put some stretchy stocking material on Nancy's puffy wrist and all the way up to her elbow and then wrapped it in cotton wool. 'Start taking some deep breaths,' she said, handing Nancy the gas and air tube with a mouthpiece on the end. Nancy did as she was told. Nothing happened to start with and then it felt like her head turned to marshmallow. The nurse had something in her hand that looked like a wet orange bandage which she speedily wrapped up and down Nancy's arm while Nancy breathed through the tube and became even more spaced out. The nurse stepped aside and the jolly doctor took hold of her arm and with a lot of force he bent her wrist over. The pain was so intense she wanted to batter him with the gas cylinder.

'Breathe deeper,' instructed the nurse as Nancy sucked as hard as she could, sounding like Darth Vader having an asthma attack. Was this meant to stop it hurting? Because it didn't bloody work. Nancy closed her eyes as the doctor squeezed the plaster and pain radiated up her arm. Her head was swimming and her wrist was throbbing.

'All done,' he said in a sing-song voice. Nancy wanted to lamp him one. She was still sucking hard on the gas and air and, while it didn't stop the pain, it did make her care less about it. The curtains started to sway and so did the nurse and doctor and Nancy started to giggle. Eventually the nurse was able to prise the tube away from Nancy and after a few fresh breaths her head was back to normal. There was another X-ray after which the jolly doctor declared he was very happy and she'd get an appointment through the post for four weeks' time.

'Four weeks? I've got to wear this traffic cone for four weeks?' Nancy held up her bright orange arm, finally realising that the nurse hadn't been offering her an orange squash.

'Minimum. They'll take that one off at four weeks but depending on how it's going you might need another one. Here's a leaflet about cast care. Take painkillers if it hurts and come straight back if it feels tight or you lose feeling in your fingers.'

It was hard not to be alarmed by that statement. 'It's tight now,' she said.

'That's fine,' he said. 'It's because it's still swollen, as long as it doesn't get any tighter,' he added with a grin broader than the Joker's. She liked to see people enjoying their work but couldn't help feeling he was relishing the pain of others a little too much. Nancy looked at her poor arm – encased in bright orange and bent over like a hook, it didn't look fine at all.

Chapter Twelve

Alice made coffee and toast for a sullen-looking Nancy. They had been at the hospital for hours the previous night and while Nancy had tried to put a brave face on, Alice could tell she was gutted about injuring herself. Nancy had two goes at trying to cover her mouth as she yawned. 'Did you get any sleep last night?' asked Alice.

'I think I dozed off a couple of times but as soon as I moved this woke me up.' Nancy stabbed a finger at her plastered arm.

'I know you're going to say you're busy but should you be going into work today?' asked Alice.

'I'll be fine. Claudia is all over this pitch, she was going to drive us there anyway and she's bringing the samples. I just need to manage my laptop bag and talk. I can do that.' She glanced down at her pyjamas. 'Once I've had a shower and got dressed.'

'I'm going to shower now. Before I do is there anything you need?' asked Alice.

'I'm fine,' said Nancy, waving her good arm.

Forty minutes later the two of them were puzzling over how Nancy was meant to have a shower when her leaflet said in capital letters that her cast MUST NOT get wet.

'Google says you need a special cover off the internet,' said Alice.

'Unless they do delivery in the next five minutes that's not going to work,' said Nancy.

Alice held up a finger to indicate she had found more information. 'Or wrap a towel around it and keep it away from the water flow.'

'Right. I'll try that,' said Nancy, picking up a towel and trying to wind it around her cast. Every time she tried it slipped off. 'Bloody thing.'

'Here,' said Alice, gently holding one end in place, and wrapping it around Nancy's arm. 'If you can hold it with the other hand that might work.'

Nancy did as she suggested. They both looked at the shower and back at Nancy holding the towel-covered cast. 'How exactly am I meant to wash myself with no hands?'

'I don't know.'

'I don't have time for this. Any of this,' said Nancy, irritation tinging her words. 'I just need to get undressed and have a rinse. I'll tie my hair up instead of washing it. It'll be fine.'

'Okay, shout if you need me,' said Alice, exiting the bathroom.

Nancy's phone started to ring. 'Can you answer that please,' called Nancy.

'Hello, Claudia, Nancy is in the shower,' said Alice, picking up on the caller ID.

'Hi, Alice. Please can you tell Nancy that I'm really sorry but I'm not going to make it to the publishers for the presentation today. I've been up all night alternating between throwing up and the world falling out of my bum so I can't be more than three feet from a toilet. Nancy can pick the samples up from my place anytime assuming

I'm not in the loo and . . . Sorry, Alice, I need to go again.'
The line went dead.

Alice got ready for work and came back to stand outside the bathroom door. The shower was off. Alice tapped on the door. 'You okay?' she asked.

There was a loud huff from inside. 'I didn't get the cast wet but I couldn't wash properly or shave and trying to dry yourself with one arm is bloody impossible. Otherwise yes, all okay. Who was on the phone?'

'It was Claudia – she's really sorry but she's sick.'

'Oh come on!' said Nancy, with feeling. 'Sorry, Alice, that was aimed at the universe, not you.' Nancy opened the door a fraction. 'Can I have my phone? I'll call Shona.' Alice went to hand it over, but Nancy was holding a towel in front of her with her only working hand. 'FFS,' she said.

'How about I call her on speakerphone and hold it for you?' suggested Alice.

'Brilliant. Yes please.'

Alice dialled the number and Shona's phone was answered. 'Hi, Shona, it's Nancy.'

'Sorry, Nancy. It's Shona's mum. How spooky. I was just about to give you a call. Shona's having a bad fibromyalgia day, so she won't be in.' Nancy looked at Alice and she pulled what she hoped was a sympathetic face. This was not going well.

'Not to worry. I hope she's over this bout soon. Thanks then, bye,' said Nancy and Alice ended the call.

'Who should I try now?' asked Alice, checking the time. She needed to leave in a few minutes.

'There's only Filip and I need him to keep everything else at Having A Ball running. That's no mean feat on his own.'

'Claudia said you need to get the samples from her house.'

'How,' said Nancy, starting to look flustered. 'I can't drive. Or can I?' Nancy tried to check the leaflet but the thing kept folding itself back up. If she couldn't control a leaflet Alice dreaded to think what would happen if she was trying to control a car.

Alice quietly took the leaflet from her and scanned the information. 'No driving until you are out of plaster and able to perform all required manoeuvres safely.' Nancy muttered something incoherent that ended in 'bugger it'. Alice was starting to think that maybe she should learn to drive, she would certainly have been a bit more help to Nancy right now if she could. Unfortunately, every time she'd booked herself in for lessons she'd had to cancel them. 'Is there anything else I can do?'

Nancy chewed the inside of her mouth. 'You've been brilliant. Thank you, Alice. You might have to cook dinner tonight or we could have that takeaway.'

'Sorry, Nancy, I'm going straight from work on the train to my parents'. It's the start of half-term and I promised them I'd go home for all the school holidays and this time there's the thing I need to do so—'

Nancy waved away her explanation. 'Of course. My mistake, I'd forgotten it was school holidays. You have a fabulous time.' Alice pulled a face. 'Well as good as you can.'

'How are you going to cope?' asked Alice, who was feeling guilty about leaving her already.

'Me? Don't you worry. I'll be completely fine,' said Nancy confidently, lifting up her plastered arm and knocking everything off the bathroom shelf in one go.

* * *

Nancy heard the front door close as Alice left for work. She sat down on the edge of the bath, wobbled and clutched the edge of the bath with her good hand. This

104

was an unmitigated disaster. The one side of her hair that she'd not managed to keep out of the shower dripped into her face. *Start small*, she thought. She'd read a management book that advocated tackling the little things and building up to the bigger ones. She'd tie her hair up and then get dressed. She let go of the bath and picked up her hair bobble. But it was no good, her right hand was no use at all. She couldn't even tie up her own hair. She scrolled through her mobile contacts list. Her mum and dad were away on holiday for another week. Any local friends would already be on their way to work. It wasn't ideal but there really was only one person she could call.

Nancy sighed deeply as she called Freddy's number. As she had expected it went to voicemail. 'Hi you've reached Freddy. Please leave a message. Ciao.' Chow? Nancy curled her lip at the phone until it went beep and she remembered she needed to leave a message.

'Hi, Freddy, it's Nancy . . .' *Where to start*, she thought. 'I had an accident, Claudia and Shona are off sick and it's the pitch to the publishers today. If there was any way you could see past the um . . .' She was desperately trying to think of another way to phrase, 'You being an arse' as she felt that probably wasn't going to help her cause. 'Past our disagreement I would be grateful. If you can help, please call me back. And by that I mean urgently, like now. Please.' She ended the call. She wondered how long she should wait before calling the publisher to rearrange. Nancy wanted to avoid that if she could. She lived in fear of someone beating her to the prize, and of her being the one who missed out. But this time she felt she had little choice.

Nancy wrestled herself into her pants, but her bra was a whole other level of challenge. She decided if she went with a dark blouse and kept her jacket on nobody would know she wasn't wearing one. Nancy decided to send a text to Freddy as well in case he didn't bother listening to his messages. She crafted something oh so slowly stabbing the keys with one finger which made her feel like her Nanna. After she finished, she reread it. She wasn't going to beg. After she'd edited it a few times it sounded just the right side of pleading.

The meeting wasn't until half twelve in Cambridge so she still had time. Perhaps she could go it alone and get a taxi to Claudia's to collect the samples and then onto the nearest train station. She'd give Freddy half an hour before she moved to plan B.

Nancy was exhausted by the time she'd tugged her clothes on. Her blouse cuffs were unbuttoned as they were impossible to do up with one hand and were now scrunched up her arms in her suit jacket making it look like she had muscles The Rock would be envious of.

She'd lost forty minutes to getting dressed and there was no response from Freddy, so she decided the taxi was her best option. As she picked up her phone it started to ring – it was Freddy.

She took a moment to quell her excitement before answering – she didn't want him knowing how desperate she was for his help. 'Hi, Freddy, thanks for calling me back.'

'You said you had an accident. How bad is it?' She was heartened by the concern in his voice.

'My wrist is broken in two places.'

'Anything else?'

'No but it's a pain.'

'Literally and figuratively.'

'Yeah. Anyway, the thing is I need to get to Cambridge via Claudia's in the next four hours. Can you help me?' She waved her arm in frustration and then wished she hadn't. His long pause was infuriating but she pushed her lips together, so she didn't say anything to piss him off and make her lose her best option of getting to the publisher today.

'As I'm a man of integrity, of course I can help. Ping me your address and . . . oh heavens I bet you live near the warehouse in deepest darkest Essex don't you?'

'The warehouse and offices are in Dagenham, which is London. But, yeah, I live in Basildon.'

'Then I'll be a couple of hours.' She could tell he was yawning as he spoke.

'Two hours? Are you coming by roller-skates or donkey?'

'It's going to easily take me an hour and half to get to yours plus I need to—'

'Fine. As quick as you can. Thank you,' she said.

'It's my pleasure, now should we—'

'Can we chat on the way to Cambridge?'

Freddy snorted a laugh. 'Message received. I'll be as quick as humanly possible.'

'Thank you.' Freddy ended the call and Nancy felt she'd swapped one pile of stress for another. A day with Freddy Astley-Davenport was always going to be a challenge.

Chapter Thirteen

The last day of school before half-term holidays always had a heady, slightly wild air of abandon to it where everyone was over-excited and acting up and that was just the teaching staff. Alice had spent a lot of her own time researching the class surnames but had hit a brick wall with two of the names.

'We can't do it as a class exercise if you've not researched two of them.' Mrs Robinson looked personally affronted.

'I did look them up it's just that there isn't any information anywhere about what they mean. But I thought perhaps those children could make up what they thought their name meant.' Alice's shoulders were so high they were nearly touching her ears.

Mrs Robinson became distracted by the headteacher looming around the corner. 'Fine,' she said, taking the folder from Alice and walking in step with the head. 'Can I just update you on something new I'm doing with my class . . .' Mrs Robinson and the head disappeared into the staff room and Alice finally relaxed her shoulders.

Alice got the classroom set up for the session and drew a big colourful shield on the whiteboard for her own name as an example. Underneath her coat of arms, which featured birds, flowers and a suit of armour helmet with an elephant climbing out of the top, she put the origins of the name.

The children all came into class in the usual cacophony as bags, lunches and layers were abandoned in the corner within reaching distance of the neatly labelled pegs. Mrs Robinson came in which caused a flurry of children to race to their allotted seats. 'Today we are going to talk about our last names and where they come from, over to you, Miss Pelling.' And with that Alice was in charge of the class and the lesson. Alice gave a quick overview because with small children it was always best to keep it brief as they had the attention span of an easily distracted fly. 'And this is my name, my shield and where it came from. A long time ago my last name came from a place called Peelings or the people of Pydel . . .' There were a few giggles, Mrs Robinson's eyes had made it to the board. 'Miss Pelling, can I have a word outside?'

Alice hated that, it always felt like she was in trouble, and, to be fair, it generally did mean there was something Mrs Robinson was unhappy about. Once outside the classroom Alice shut the door behind her. 'Everything okay?'

'You can't say piddle in front of a Year One class.'

'I wasn't sure if it was pronounced piddle, pie-dell or pee-dell if I'm honest.'

'Let's go with pie, shall we?' Mrs Robinson didn't wait for a response before marching back into the class. Hush descended.

Alice continued as she handed out the slips of research to each pupil, which had lots of pictures and just a few words that she and Mrs Robinson would help them with. 'I've got information for everyone about their last name apart from two of you, but I thought it might be fun for those two to make up what their names meant.'

'Which students are impacted?' asked Mrs Robinson.

Impacted? Crumbs, it wasn't like she was banishing them to another kingdom. 'Delilah Villin and Kayden Wynker.'

'Miss, Miss,' said William with his hand stretched into the air. 'I know what Wynker means.' Mrs Robinson's eyebrows lifted and stayed there.

Eventually the class settled into their task and soon shields were being liberally doused in paint, and shapes cut out from the scraps box. Two boys had overdone the black paint, which was a regular thing, so Alice cut them out some new shields with the teacher scissors. Bonnie and Delilah had a tussle nearby over some red card, but Alice was able to calm the situation by giving them both a small amount of glitter. Glitter was usually a last resort but seeing as it was the last day Alice used it as an easy fix.

Mrs Robinson was busy in the cupboard, which Alice now realised was code for taking a break to look at her phone and most likely stuff her face with the treacle tart she'd deposited there earlier. Alice was momentarily distracted by Kayden making fart noises on his arm but a shriek from Bonnie had her full attention. Alice raced over to Bonnie, who was at the stage in crying where her face was red and she was sucking in air to her full lung capacity in preparation for a full-on bawl. Alice speedily scanned her for any obvious signs of harm – nothing. Then she spotted the giggling face of Delilah next to her. She was covered in glitter, holding a pair of teacher scissors in one hand and a clump of Bonnie's hair in the other.

* * *

Nancy spent an hour and a half trying to put her hair in a ponytail. The simplest of things had become a Mensa challenge now she only had one fully working arm. The last version of the ponytail wasn't actually the best but she was seriously fed up so it would have to do.

She had given Carrie one-armed cuddles and she was now asleep in her basket where she'd happily stay until Nancy got home. Nancy was waiting by the door with her laptop bag in the crook of her good arm and with her phone in her hand. It was like waiting to go out as a kid, that clamouring need for time to go quicker so she could leave the house. She used the time to call Filip, update him on what had happened to everyone and check he was okay to hold the fort. In true Filip style he was unfazed by being a one-man band for the day and wished her all the best for the presentation. A piece of hair flopped into her face as bits from her ponytail escaped – she'd not tied it tight enough.

At last there was a knock on her door. Nancy was right ready only now she had to put her phone down before she could open the door. There was a second knock. Did people not have any patience anymore? She turned the key which was really tricky because it felt like she was doing everything back to front using her other hand. She opened the door to Freddy's back. He turned around and she was momentarily wowed. His hair was neat, he was wearing designer sunglasses and an expensive suit.

'Uber for Barraclough?'

'Great, a comedian, that's going to make things better.' Nancy tried to blow the strand of escaped hair out of her face.

Freddy lifted up his sunglasses. 'How did the accident happen?'

'Long story that we don't have time for.' She tried to shoo him off her doorstep.

'What are you wearing under that jacket?' He was eyeing her bulging upper arms.

111

'It was very difficult to get dressed and I've rammed the plaster into this jacket so hard I'm not sure if it'll ever come out again and even the simplest task is torture.' She pointed to her head, the effort of which made her wince.

He scanned her up and down. 'Hair by Grayson Perry?'

'Hilarious. If you want your five stars, Mr Uber driver, you'd better take this.' She lifted her good arm where the laptop bag was hanging.

Freddy unhooked it from her arm. 'Seriously, are you okay apart from the wrist?'

'Fine. I'm completely fine. But we need to go.' She waved him down the path.

Freddy's Maserati was parked outside. While he put her bag in the boot she went to get in the passenger side but had to put her phone away first to free up her good hand, by which time Freddy had opened the car door. 'If I'd known you were after the full chauffeur experience I'd have worn my hat.'

'Thank you,' she said, and she got inside.

'M'lady,' said Freddy, closing the door, striding around to the other side and getting in. Nancy felt his eyes on her as she struggled with the seatbelt. 'Here,' he said, leaning across her, taking the belt and swiftly plugging it in.

'Thank y—'

'If you're going to thank me every time I do something for you it's going to be a long day.'

'I think it might be anyway.' Freddy tilted his head in question. 'You know after everything.'

'Lucky for you I don't hold grudges.' He started the engine with a roar and they took off.

First stop was Romford to collect the samples from Claudia, who opened the door, dumped a wheelie case

112

outside, and shut it again. 'Sorry. Gotta go again.' Poor thing was still suffering. Freddy retrieved the case, put it in the boot and after Nancy had had five failed attempts, he helped her put her seatbelt back on. She didn't like it. She felt like a child again where everyone had to do even the simplest task for her. She hated being helpless, it went against everything she was.

She keyed in the sat nav details for the publisher in Cambridge and tried to relax. The seats were very comfortable and Freddy was a confident driver. He was calm and not the boy racer she'd expected him to be. 'ETA one hour twenty-eight minutes, so tell me all about this accident.'

'There's nothing to tell. I tripped and broke my wrist. That's it, end of story.'

'Falls can be tricky if you land badly,' said Freddy.

What was it with everyone calling it a fall? 'It wasn't a bloody fall. I *fell*, that's different.'

'Okay,' said Freddy, not sounding convinced. 'Did people laugh?'

'Goodness no, they didn't laugh.' At least she'd been saved that humiliation.

'If you fall and people laugh, then you're young. If you fall and people look concerned that's when you know you're old.'

'Maybe we should focus on the presentation instead,' suggested Nancy.

'Sure. What would you like me to cover?'

'Nothing. I'd like you to pass round the samples and put them away at the end. That's all.'

'Like a magician's assistant? That's a bit insulting. I was at the meeting, I could go through a couple of slides so it's not just you going on and . . .' He seemed to sense her giving him daggers. 'Different presenters might make it more engaging.'

'We'll see,' said Nancy, turning up the air con. She was starting to overheat.

Freddy talked off and on most of the way there. Various signs they passed triggered amusing anecdotes, but it did make the journey go quite quickly. The publisher's offices were out of town so there was parking right outside and they were immediately sympathetic when Nancy explained both her issues and Claudia's.

The meeting room was all glass and had been heated up by the sun to the perfect temperature for growing tomatoes. Nancy excused herself and Freddy met her in the corridor where she was trying to get her jacket off but all she'd managed was to pull it off both shoulders so now it was restricting movement and more like a straitjacket. 'Let me help,' said Freddy. She didn't have a lot of choice. He took hold of the jacket and Nancy tried to escape. 'Stop moving,' he said. 'Let's slip your good arm out and then . . .' He tried to get the jacket off her cast, but it was stuck fast. They both tugged in all directions but it was no good. 'I'll see if they have any scissors,' said Nancy.

'No need,' said Freddy, producing a penknife from his pocket and deftly slicing the sleeve of her jacket. 'There you go.'

'Bloody hell, Freddy! I was joking! This cost . . .' A glance at his expensive suit told her the price of hers would not support her argument. 'A lot. It cost a lot and more importantly it's my favourite.'

'Ah, apologies but I think having it cut off you was inevitable,' he said, putting the knife away.

'Boy Scout?' she asked with a nod at the knife.

'My cousin's Amsterdam stag night,' he said. He pointed at her crumpled shirt sleeves. 'What happened?'

'I'll just roll them up,' she said, folding her ruined jacket over her arm before they both went back into the meeting room.

After the jacket disaster things improved. A number of the publishing team joined them and they all introduced themselves. The female members of staff were instantly taken with Freddy. 'I'm Nancy Barraclough, owner and CEO of Having A Ball. And this is Freddy—'

'Astley-Davenport,' added Freddy. 'I'm her temporary PA.' Everyone laughed.

'No, he really is my PA.' Disbelieving faces looked at her. How annoying. 'Anyway, shall we go through what we discussed on the phone in a bit more detail?' Nancy knew the presentation inside and out and was passionate about her business. Freddy passed around the right samples at the right time and pitched in with some additional facts he'd picked up on his induction day about their inclusivity and sustainability policies which had heads nodding. At the end Nancy sat down and Freddy gave her a discreet nod that said she'd done well. She didn't need his approval, but it was nice to get some acknowledgement all the same. She'd been the boss for so long she'd forgotten what it was like to get the occasional bit of positive feedback.

The publishing team were enthusiastic. Apparently, they weren't used to being presented to, but they liked that Nancy had thought about the market for the book. They talked about what they could and couldn't do and that they felt it was quite niche but would make a good gifting book either around Christmas or Mother's Day. It was all very positive, and they pledged to be in touch after they had taken the book to their acquisitions meeting, which from what Nancy could make out was where the ultimate decision would be made. It was all good but what she needed now was something concrete. Her little company was a carefully balanced card tower and she wasn't sure how long she could keep going before everything collapsed.

Nancy was packing away while Freddy chatted and laughed with the marketing assistant who kept flicking her hair. Nancy rolled her eyes as she rammed her laptop back in its bag and gathered up the samples. 'Time to go, Freddy,' she called, picking up the laptop bag with her good hand and automatically grabbing the wheelie case with the other. The pain shot up her arm making her let go of the case instantly. No heavy lifting the leaflet had said, and she now realised why. Freddy grabbed the case and steadied Nancy.

'I'll take it from here, Dwayne Johnson. Let's get you home,' he said.

Chapter Fourteen

Alice wasn't looking forward to speaking to Dom but given Bonnie was distraught about Delilah giving her a random haircut she felt she needed to make him aware. It was also her fault because she'd left the teacher scissors unattended, as Mrs Robinson was very quick to point out when she finally emerged from the cupboard brushing pastry crumbs from her lips.

Alice didn't like that she had to make the call from the office with the admin staff listening in, although the nice lady was there and she kept giving her encouraging smiles. The phone was answered just as Alice thought it was going to voicemail.

'Hello?'

'Mr Fisher, it's Miss Pelling from—'

'Alice, hi.' His tone changed instantly. His voice had a deep timbre but all she could think about were his lips and how close they would be to his phone right now. Not helpful. She gave herself a shake.

'I'm calling about Bonnie. There's been an incident and—'

'Is she okay?'

'She's fine. Apart from she's a bit upset because another pupil has cut off a small piece of her hair.' Dom snorted with laughter which Alice felt was both reassuring and a little insensitive. 'We will be making the other pupil's parents aware.' Alice was not looking forward to that call either.

'Okay. What did you want me to do?'

'It was more of an awareness call. You might want to book her in for a hair appointment.' Alice was feeling brave. 'But I think she would really appreciate you being on time to pick her up after school today.'

'Ah, sure. I can do that. Can you give her a hug from me?'

'No, sorry we're not allowed to, but I'll tell her that you sent her a virtual one to keep her going until she sees you.'

'Thanks, Alice. That's kind. And how are you?'

'Busy. If there's nothing else, Mr Fisher.'

'Um no.'

'Thank you, goodbye.' She hastily ended the call.

The call to Delilah's parents was short. They didn't seem bothered about what their child had done or that she had had access to scissors, which was a huge relief to Alice who knew she had a few forms she'd have to fill in. As the teacher scissors had round ends, they weren't exactly a lethal weapon, but they were clearly sharp enough to cut hair so in the wrong hands could have done something worse. It was a big lesson for Alice.

Mrs Robinson was quick to hand a red-faced and sniffly Bonnie over to Alice so she could concentrate on teaching. Alice took Bonnie out of the classroom and managed to console her with a carton of fruit juice and a promise that her daddy had an extra big hug for her at pick-up. 'And it's the holidays. So no school on Monday,' said Alice, trying to distract Bonnie who kept tugging on the short clump of hair at the side of her head.

Bonnie lifted her chin. 'We're going to the seaside.'

'That'll be fun.'

'I've got a new costume with mermaids on it.'

'Lovely. You'll be a super-fast swimmer in that then,' said Alice.

Bonnie shook her head firmly. 'I'm scared of the waves.'

'I like jumping over waves, maybe try that with your dad.' Alice had a brief picture of Dom in swim shorts which she had to shake away.

Bonnie leaned into Alice and whispered. 'I think Daddy is scared of the waves too.'

Alice doubted that but the image of him running up the beach screaming like Hamsi was definitely helping to quell the disappointment of him not being available.

Bonnie leaned against Alice. 'I'd like to jump waves with you,' she said. Alice would have liked that too. She knew she wasn't meant to have favourites, but she had quickly become attached to Bonnie. Moments like this were hard because all Alice wanted to do was give the little girl a hug, but for child protection reasons she wasn't allowed to.

'We'd better get back to class,' said Alice.

Bonnie hopped off the chair and gripped Alice's hand tightly. 'I don't want to be next to Delilah. We're not friends anymore. She's mean.'

'You can sit with me.'

'Good because I like you more.' Bonnie grinned up at her while giving her chopped hair another tug.

Alice managed to persuade Mrs Robinson to let Bonnie take the class toy home for the holidays along with its accompanying diary that had to be filled in. Alice thought it was a lovely idea and really enjoyed looking at the diary when it came back on a Monday. She couldn't understand why all the parents, without exception, groaned when their child came running out clutching it. The toy was a snow leopard which had been a good opportunity to explain to them about endangered animals, making it both educational and fun.

Mrs Robinson was explaining in detail her foolproof approach to matching children to parents at pick-up time and Alice was trying to pay attention as small children bounced around like greyhounds waiting for the trap to open. Mrs Robinson matched a boy with an untucked shirt to a man who was a carbon copy only slightly taller. She was scanning the few remaining adults when Dom jogged up to the door.

'Made it,' he said, looking very pleased with himself and slightly out of breath.

'If you could wait just a second, Mr Fisher,' said Alice, wanting to look professional in front of Mrs Robinson. 'And I'll explain about the incident.'

'Oh yeah, the scalping,' said Dom and a mum next to him gasped.

With a nod from Mrs Robinson, Bonnie ran to her father and he crouched down to intercept her with a bear hug. Alice was pleased he was there for his daughter.

'Mr Fisher,' began Alice, stepping outside.

'Please call me Dom.'

'I think it's best if we keep things professional. Don't you?'

He looked wrong-footed. 'Er, up to you.'

'I'm sorry about the incident earlier today,' began Alice.

'Oh yeah. Let's see?' he asked Bonnie. She stuck out her lip and pointed to the side of her head.

'Woah,' he said but as Bonnie's lip wobbled he carried on. 'That's cool. Nobody else has a haircut like that. I like it.' He grinned at his daughter.

'I don't,' said Bonnie.

'You can have my baseball cap,' he said.

'Cool,' said Bonnie and instantly perked up.

'Problem solved. No need to apologise,' said Dom. 'And thanks for taking care of her. Not just today but all this term.'

'It's my job,' said Alice.

'But you do it very well. So thanks.'

'You're welcome,' said Alice, feeling her resolve start to crumble and she had to concentrate not to stare at those lips. That smile.

'Right, then. We'd best be off,' said Dom.

'Yes,' said Alice, coming out of her brief trance. 'Bye.' Dom turned to go and Bonnie waved at Alice over his shoulder. 'Hang on!' called Alice, remembering something. 'It's Bonnie's turn to have the snow leopard.'

'Bum,' said Dom with a groan.

* * *

Nancy had tried to put a brave face on about her throbbing arm but without her asking, Freddy had found a pharmacy nearby and come back with the strongest pain killers they could sell over the counter.

'Here, take two of these,' said Freddy, handing her the packet.

'Thanks,' she said. She read the back of the packaging. 'To be taken with food. I'll have them as soon as I get in,' said Nancy.

'We can stop for a meal if you want to, there must be some decent country pubs if we take a bit of a detour.'

Usually, Nancy would have been keen to eat out. She was a big fan of pub grub and an even bigger one of not having to cook but it had felt like the longest day and now she was tired and her arm was hurting. 'Actually, if it's okay with you I just want to get home.'

'Of course.'

121

There was a lull in conversation and while Freddy concentrated on the road Nancy watched the world go by out of the window and tried to ignore the throbbing pain in her wrist. She thought about the publishers meeting. Despite her shredded suit jacket things couldn't have gone any better. The hope was that, assuming the book got published, those who bought it would then use Having A Ball for all their yarn and crafting needs as the examples would be using their products. Nancy was already conjuring up a gift box that would include the book, selected yarn and essential tools. It was a good plan, only Nancy hadn't banked on there being hurdles like acquisitions meetings or the long lead time to get published.

'You've gone very quiet,' said Freddy. 'Is it your wrist?'

'It's still giving me gip, but I'll have some food when I get in and take the tablets.' She held up the packet. 'Thanks for getting these.'

'I pride myself on purchasing the perfect gift.' He shot her a cheeky smile and it was hard not to mirror him.

'You know what? It's a shame I fired you because you did okay today,' said Nancy, a little surprised by her own words but they were true. Freddy had been articulate, helpful even, and the fact that he'd charmed some of the publishing staff was a bonus.

'I resigned,' he said.

Nancy wobbled her head. 'The jury's out on that one but take the compliment. You did all right.'

'High praise indeed.'

'As my old nan would say, I speak as I find,' said Nancy.

'I don't suppose you'd consider putting that to paper and—'

'Nope,' said Nancy and she got her phone out to show that the conversation was over.

Nancy was so pleased to see her own front door again. She let herself in and Carrie sauntered over to greet her. Nancy couldn't work out how to pick her up one-handed so crouched down to give her a fuss.

Freddy brought the things from the boot, put them in the hall and stared at Carrie. 'You have a cat.'

'So it would appear. Any comments you'd like to make about me being single with a cat?'

'Not at all.'

'Are you not a cat person?' she asked as Carrie snaked around his legs expertly leaving a trail of white fur on his dark trousers.

'More a dog person really.'

Nancy waited for Freddy to leave but he stood there expectantly. She supposed the least she could do was offer him a cuppa. 'Did you want a coffee or are you after a tip?' she asked.

'I just want to see you take those tablets. If they don't work, I can drop you at the hospital.'

'It's not that bad. I don't think I've damaged it, just aggravated it.'

'Still.'

'Freddy, that's kind of you but I'm just going to peel a few spuds and—'

'How are you going to do that with one hand?'

'Easy . . .' Nancy got out her peeler which made her realise her problem. She couldn't hold either a potato or peeler in her bad hand. 'I'll have a pizza. I've got frozen ones. It's fine.'

'I don't think it is fine. I think you're going to struggle on your own.'

'I don't have a lot of choice about that because Alice is away at her parents for a week and my mum and dad are on the holiday of a lifetime. But I'm a strong independent woman so I can manage on my own thanks.'

Freddy pulled up a chair. 'Actually, I will have that coffee, please.' He was watching her closely like he was waiting to catch her out and she didn't like it. Mainly because she had a sinking feeling that he was right. It was likely that she was going to find things difficult on her own. Despite that she was determined to show Freddy he was wrong. She picked up the kettle and went to fill it. She couldn't hold it and fill it at the same time, so she had to put it in the sink.

'Mind the bottom isn't wet because water and electricity . . .'

Nancy got out a tea towel and put the kettle on it to dry it off before putting it on the stand and switching it on, feeling like she'd cleared the first hurdle.

While it was boiling, she got out the mugs one at a time. She picked up the coffee jar. How was she meant to unscrew a lid? She stuck it under her armpit and gave it a turn with her good hand. Possibly a bit too fierce as the lid came off and the jar spewed coffee all over the worktop, floor and Nancy. 'I'll sort that out in a minute,' she said, spooning some off the worktop and putting it into the mugs. She got a carton of milk from the fridge. A new one posed even more of an issue than the coffee jar. The kettle boiled and she was still trying to undo the carton. 'Did you want milk?'

'Please,' said Freddy. She stared at him, willing him to smirk, but he didn't, he actually looked quite concerned. She didn't need his pity. She could cope.

'I think we'll have it black.'

'Okay. You need to have something to eat so you can take your painkillers.'

'Right.' She was tired and grumpy but she tried not to show it as she got a pizza from the freezer. Opening a box one-handed was virtually impossible. She slammed it on the worktop in frustration. She picked it up and slung it back in the freezer.

'I fancy a takeaway.'

Carrie pawed at Nancy's ankles.

'You can't give the cat takeaway,' said Freddy, sipping his coffee.

And the award for stating the bleeding obvious goes to Freddy Astley-Davenport, she thought as she grimaced at him. Nancy got out a small tin tray of cat food. She tried to grip the tab and open the foil top, but it was impossible and made her arm throb a bit more. Nancy could see Freddy was still watching her, which was annoying. Carrie mewed at her to speed up. At this rate she'd be sharing a Dairylea triangle with Carrie for dinner, assuming she could open one. Nancy got out a knife and began stabbing around the edges of the cat food tin.

'Okay, please stop,' said Freddy, standing up and taking the knife. 'Nancy, I hate to be the one to tell you, because I fear for my safety, but you need to be looked after.' She went to protest but he held up his hands. 'It's miserable being in pain but it'll be worse if you do even more damage.' He put the knife down and with ease removed the foil top on the cat food. Carrie switched allegiance quickly and sat adoringly at his feet – *turncoat*. 'There must be someone you could stay with for a few days?'

Nancy shook her head. 'There's not. It's just bad timing, everyone is away.' Claudia may have been a long shot but even she was out of action. 'I'll just have to manage.' She hated the crack in her voice. She was feeling a bit emotional. She swallowed hard and straightened her shoulders – she didn't want Freddy to see her upset.

'I don't think you should stay here on your own.'

'I've no choice.'

Freddy drew in a long breath. 'I know we're not the best of friends, but you could come home with me . . .' Nancy started shaking her head. 'Hear me out. At least then someone can cook you proper meals, and make sure you don't do yourself any further injury. There's plenty of space so as an added bonus you won't see much of me.' He smiled at her. 'What do you say?'

She was tired, in pain and at the end of her tether. Would a few nights in Belgravia be so bad? 'I don't know.'

'I'll make you a sandwich now, you can have your tablets and then you can decide. No pressure but I'd be a lot happier if you'd come back to mine. Purely on a platonic basis obviously.' He put the food down for the cat and Carrie turned her back on him and got stuck in.

'Obviously,' said Nancy, warming to Freddy. This was really kind of him. Then she remembered something. 'I can't leave because of Carrie.' She felt quite disappointed at the thought. Perhaps she had been coming around to the idea of someone looking after her, even if it was Freddy Astley-Davenport.

'I guess there's room for a fluffy moggy,' he said, stroking Carrie's back. She scowled at the interruption and possibly also at being called a moggy.

'Really?'

'If it means you'll swallow some pride and come too?'

She was struggling to think of a reason not to. 'Just for a couple of days. Once I'm able to use this arm I'll leave. Agreed?'

'Whatever is going to make you feel better.' He smiled

kindly at her as he got out the things to make a sandwich. She'd had worse offers.

'Okay. I'll get my things together.'

Within half an hour, Freddy had fed her, tidied up, helped her pack a case and stood over her while she took her tablets. He'd bundled a rather cross Carrie into her cat carrier and loaded up the car. Nancy got in the passenger seat and instantly started to relax. Maybe it was the extra strong painkillers or perhaps it was the thought of a few days of being waited on in a posh pad in Belgravia but whatever it was, it was making her sleepy.

Chapter Fifteen

Nancy snorted herself awake and blinked. She was still in Freddy's car but now it was dark. A million thoughts swamped her sleepy brain. How long had they been driving? A quick glance at the digital display told her almost five hours. A second thought struck her – *Shit, I've been kidnapped!*

'Ahh Sleeping Beauty awakens,' said Freddy.

'Where the hell are you taking me?' she asked, quickly checking the side of her mouth for any dribble.

'Home. Like we agreed.'

Nancy peered out of the windscreen into the darkness, all she could make out were fields, hedges and lots of trees. 'This is not London.'

'Gold star. That A level in Geography has done you proud.'

Nancy twisted in her seat. She was not feeling good about this. How much did she really know about Freddy Astley-Davenport? She suddenly realised her vulnerability and she didn't like it. 'Freddy, I'm serious. Where are we? Why didn't you take me to yours like you promised?'

'We are about ten miles from Langham Hall, which is my home. And is exactly what I promised. I thought you'd realised it wasn't on Hampstead Heath.'

Nancy felt a little foolish. 'Of course, but I assumed you were taking me back to your place in Belgravia.'

Freddy laughed long and far too hard. Eventually he got it down to a snigger. 'You're hilarious.' He glanced across at her. 'Oh my word. You're actually serious. You thought *I* was going to look after you?'

'Yes, because that's what you said.' She was quite confused.

'No. I suggested that you come home with me because you needed *someone* to cook you proper meals and look after you so you didn't do yourself any further injury. Which is why I am bringing you to Langham because we have an excellent cook and a variety of other staff.'

'Oh.' She couldn't think of anything else to say.

They went the last few miles in silence until Freddy slowed the car by a high wall, turned into a driveway and stopped in front of tall black gates. He buzzed down his window and spoke to an intercom box. 'Hi, it's me.' There was no reply other than the gates slowly opening.

They continued down a long treelined drive and over a cattle grid before they drew up to the house. As they came to a standstill, floodlights switched on, illuminating the front of the large building. It was stunning. A beautiful light grey stone structure with a portico which Freddy crawled the car forward into. A man in a suit strode out and opened Nancy's door for her.

'Good evening, miss, I'm Simpkins, welcome to Langham Hall.' He offered Nancy a hand and helped her from the car.

'Good evening, my lord,' he said, nodding formally as Freddy emerged from the driver's side.

'You can dispense with the usual welcome, Paul, she's . . .' Freddy squinted at Nancy over the bonnet as if trying to work something out. 'Nancy. Nancy Barraclough.'

'I run Having A Ball,' said Nancy, offering Paul a hand which he shook. 'Pleased to meet you,' she added, wanting to get things right. Her dad always said it showed manners to shake hands.

'Likewise,' said Paul.

'Is Percy about?' asked Freddy, scanning the area furtively.

'No, he's turned in for the night.'

'Great. We'll take drinks in the snug, please, Paul,' said Freddy. 'This way,' he added to Nancy, shutting the car door and turning to go inside.

'But my bags are in the boot. And there's Carrie.' The cat was glaring at her from the cat carrier on the back seat.

'I'll bring through any luggage, Miss Barraclough.'

'Please could you pass me my cat? And it's Nancy.'

'Of course. My apologies, Nancy,' said Paul, swiftly removing the carrier from the back of the car. Carrie glared out in protest at being shut in the carrier for the long journey.

'I'm sorry,' whispered Nancy to the cat. 'I didn't know we were going to . . .' She turned to Paul who was opening the boot. 'Excuse me, what county are we in?'

'Devon,' said Paul.

'Devon?!' Nancy couldn't hide her surprise.

'Are you coming?' called Freddy, who was holding open one half of the oversized front door.

Despite her long nap in the car Nancy was tired and wanted to go to bed. She followed Freddy inside. It was like stepping into one of the stately homes she'd been to on school trips many moons ago. She had to concentrate to stop her jaw dropping and her mouth falling open. She was standing in a vast open hallway, surrounded by giant portraits, a large round table big enough for Arthur and plenty of his knights. There was even a suit of armour standing guard at the bottom of a sweeping staircase. This was beyond impressive.

'It's really lovely, Freddy,' said Nancy. 'I mean it's obscenely frigging huge and everything, but it's lovely.'

Freddy smiled. 'I'll do a formal tour tomorrow. For now, let's get you settled in.'

'Frederick?' came a high-class female voice from above. Nancy craned her neck to see a woman in a long shiny dressing gown peering over the galleried landing.

'Good evening, Mother,' called Freddy as he carried on walking away.

Nancy was rooted to the spot as the two women surveyed each other. *Remember your manners*, came her dad's voice in her head. 'Pleased to meet you,' called up Nancy. 'I'm Nancy Barraclough—'

'Goodness me! Nancy, how lovely to meet you. Give me two minutes to get dressed.' Lady Astley-Davenport's aristocratic voice was what Nancy's mum would have called cut-glass and fancy.

'No, don't do that,' said Nancy. 'I can see you're all ready for bed.'

'Nancy!' called Freddy, impatience loaded into her name.

'Keep your hair on, I'll be there in a minute,' Nancy hollered down the hallway. Then immediately cringed at the echoey sound of her London accent as it was repelled by the posh walls.

Freddy's mother chuckled as she came down the stairs. When she reached the bottom, she caught Nancy off-guard with her hearty embrace. 'Oh, um, hello, Lady Astley-Davenport. Pleased to meet you,' Nancy repeated for good measure.

'Please call me Louisa. The pleasure is entirely ours. We can't thank you enough for taking on Frederick. I'm afraid my husband is already asleep. He's on a lot of medication. But he'll be overjoyed to meet you tomorrow. I assume you're not dashing off somewhere?'

Nancy was processing all the information in between what was being said. Clearly they didn't know Freddy was no longer working for her and they weren't expecting her to be staying any longer than overnight. This was awkward. Nancy was forming her words as Paul came in carrying her bag and pulling her wheelie case. Louisa's eyes widened at the sight.

Nancy felt she needed to explain. 'Ah, you see, there may have been a misunderstanding—'

'Nothing of the sort,' said Freddy, striding back into the entrance hall. 'Nancy is my guest, she'll be staying here until her arm has fully recovered. I trust that's acceptable under your new regime of rules, Mother.'

Nancy felt awkward. 'Just for the weekend and only if it's not too much trouble. I've been struggling a bit with this.' She pulled back the sleeve of her coat to reveal the bright orange plaster.

'Oh my dear, you poor thing. Of course, we'd love to have you stay,' said Louisa.

'Shall I take Miss Barraclough's bags to your room?' Paul asked Freddy.

'No!' chorused everyone together. Paul pulled his chin into his chest at the force of the response.

'Queen Sophia's room, please, Paul, and then cocoa in the snug if you'd be so kind,' said Louisa, guiding Nancy down the hallway.

'Of course,' he said, adjusting his grip on the bags and heading for the stairs like he was about to tackle the Eiger.

The snug was not as its name would suggest. It was a large room, roughly the size of Nancy's whole house, where dying embers of an earlier fire glowed in a cavernous fireplace. Louisa ushered Nancy over to one of three elegant dark red velvet settees. 'You sit yourself next to the fire. Have you eaten? Would you like me to see if cook has put any leftovers in the fridge? She did a marvellous venison bourguignon for supper—'

'Mother, please stop fussing,' said Freddy, who was pacing up and down.

'Just a hot drink will be lovely and then I'm going to crash . . . I mean retire to bed, if that's okay?' Why did everything she said sound so common? She knew she had a bit of an accent but for some reason in this setting she sounded pure *EastEnders*.

Louisa sat down opposite, adjusted her dressing gown and clasped her hands together in her lap. 'Now tell me all about what it is that you do.' She fixed Nancy with interested eyes.

* * *

It was late when Alice got out of the taxi at her parents' bungalow. The seaside village was 90 per cent bungalows and 10 per cent retirement flats. Or at least that was how Alice saw it. She felt so much bigger than this small place. She was making her own way in the world. She lived and worked in London, that was her home now, although there was a sense of cosy familiarity about being back. The bungalow looked exactly the same. Nothing here had changed. Before she'd even stepped out of the taxi both her parents were out of the front door followed by their elderly Jack Russell terrier, Cindy. They met her on the pavement and her mum wrapped her in a hug so tight there wasn't room to breathe in comfortably. Cindy made a wheezy sort of noise which in her youth would have been a welcome bark.

'Darling, let me look at you,' said her mum, tears welling in her eyes. 'Are you well? You're thin. Are you eating?'

Usually these sort of comments jarred with Alice. She felt they were a veiled criticism that she couldn't look after herself. But there had been a shift. She was living proof that she could manage on her own.

'Hi, Mum, yes I'm eating and I'm fine.'

'Hello, Alice, love,' said her dad, giving her a squeeze. 'How many bags?'

'Just the case in the boot, I've got the rest.' She held up a holdall and her handbag.

'I'll take that,' said her mum, grabbing the larger bag. 'I'll get the kettle on and then I need to hear all about it.'

'I speak to you virtually every night, Mum. There's nothing else to tell,' said Alice with a snort.

'It's not the same on the phone.' Her mum linked her spare arm through Alice's. 'It's so nice to have you back home.'

'It's only for a week.'

'I know. Now I wasn't sure if you would have eaten so I've done your favourite.'

'Shepherd's pie?' Alice's stomach rumbled at the thought of it. Despite what the week had in store maybe there were some benefits to coming home.

Chapter Sixteen

Nancy didn't have the best night's sleep. She'd been hoping for a Saturday morning lie-in, but her wrist had other ideas. The bed was comfortable, but she couldn't seem to find the right spot for her arm. She tried it in pretty much every conceivable position but it either overheated and became itchy inside the cast or it ached. Carrie was restless too and had walked over Nancy's head a number of times in the night. Nancy did manage to drop off to sleep for a short while with the cast resting on her other shoulder but awoke with a start when the rough surface of the cast felt like it was removing a layer of skin.

She got dressed and went in search of coffee. She walked around for a bit but didn't like to open any doors in case someone saw her and thought she was nosing around the place. As she neared the end of a dark corridor, she heard the low rumble of a growl, making her turn around. She was heading back to her room when she heard footsteps and Paul appeared. He was dressed in a suit and tie. 'Hiya, Paul, I was looking for a kettle to make a coffee.'

'Good morning, Nancy. I must apologise. Freddy said not to disturb you. If I'd known you needed—'

'It's fine. This woke me up.' She held up her arm as evidence.

'Ahh, I see. Would you like to go back to bed and I'll bring you up your coffee. How do you take it?'

'I'm up now. Maybe I could sit in the kitchen?'

Paul looked momentarily startled. 'How about the East Terrace? It's a delightful sun trap at this time of day.'

'Okay. That sounds nice.'

'How do you take your coffee?'

'Instant's fine.'

Paul seemed mildly horrified at the thought of instant coffee. 'I think we can stretch to an americano.'

'If you're going out for posh coffee, I'll have a skinny mocha, ta.'

'Of course. Let me show you to the terrace.'

She followed Paul through the maze of corridors until they walked into a huge, virtually empty room. The ceiling was more decorated than the walls. Nancy stopped walking and gazed around her. 'Wowsers,' she said, taking in the intricate cornicing and scenes of angels and cherubs.

'Forgive me I should have offered you the tour,' said Paul. 'This is the ballroom, reconfigured and decorated in a Regency style by the 7th Earl in 1819. He was an acquaintance of the then Prince George, later King George the Fourth, who stayed at the house for a—'

Nancy tried to stifle the yawn, but it was impossible. She'd had so little sleep. 'Sorry,' she said through the end of the yawn. 'I *was* listening. Honest.'

Paul smiled. 'I'd best hurry up with that coffee. The terrace is through there.' He pointed towards the tall French windows.

'Thanks.' Paul nodded and left the room. Nancy opened the doors and stepped outside. She wasn't sure what she'd been expecting when Paul had said terrace, maybe a bit of patio or decking – this looked like an outdoor restaurant. Five large round tables with umbrellas were spaced across the raised stone platform the end of which looked out over stunning gardens. Nancy walked to the stone balustrade and took in the view: manicured lawn, flowerbeds teeming with colour, avenues of trees and a folly in the distance. She let out a sigh. This place was amazing. There was a rustle below her and she peered over to see someone who looked like they were the gardener.

'Hiya,' she said to the man stooping over a giant ceramic pot.

He straightened himself, pulled off his gardening gloves and eyed her suspiciously. 'Good morning,' he said, his voice far posher than she'd been expecting. 'Can I help you?'

'I'm just admiring the view. I'm not really into gardens and that but this is truly beautiful.'

His features softened at her words. 'Thank you. That's kind of you. Is someone taking care of you?' He pronounced his words very carefully.

'Paul's gone to get me a coffee, thanks.'

'Excellent. I must get on, lovely to meet you,' he said, returning to the pot.

Realisation dawned on Nancy. She'd seen this in books and films. Gardeners didn't have posh voices like that. This was obviously Freddy's dad, Lord whatsit, doing a spot of gardening. She was thrilled not to have walked into the trap.

'Lovely to meet you too, *Lord* Astley-Davenport.' She arched an eyebrow and the man frowned back at her. 'Or should I call you Percy?'

His frown deepened. 'I'm sorry, miss. I think there's some confusion.'

'Shall I leave your coffee here?' asked Paul, appearing with a laden tray.

Clearly Lord Astley-Davenport didn't like being

rumbled. 'Yeah, okay. Nice to meet you anyway.' She gave him a wave and went to get her coffee. 'Thanks, Paul, this looks fab.'

Paul unloaded a large mug, pastries, fresh fruit salad and yogurt. 'I hope it wasn't presumptuous of me to go for a mug over a cup and saucer.'

'Mug works for me, Paul. You've got me nailed.'

'Thank you. What would you like for breakfast?' he asked.

'Just a croissant, ta.' She pointed to the plate of pastries.

'This was just to go with your coffee, I'm making breakfast now.'

'I'm not big on breakfast so this is ace.'

'If you need anything else, ring this.' He placed a hand bell on the table.

Nancy giggled. 'You're not serious?'

'Absolutely. The kitchen is quite a way away but I'm like Pavlov's dog and can hear a bell from the other side of the house.'

'Hang on, there is something. What's the deal with Percy doing the gardening?'

Paul's eyebrows puckered. 'I'm not sure I follow.'

'Goodness me, you're up early,' said Freddy, marching through the double doors in vest top and joggers. She pulled her eyes away from his muscly arms to focus on his bed-ruffled hair. Instinctively she tried to calm down her own bushy mane but for some reason it had gone extra frizzy.

'Didn't sleep well.' She waved the cast. 'It's like sleeping with a cheese grater.'

He laughed. 'Paul's taking care of you, exactly as I said he would.' He patted Paul on the shoulder as he passed. 'I'll be about an hour.'

'Hang on, what am I meant to do?'

Freddy shrugged. 'Go for a swim?' She waved her cast at him. 'Ah, a walk then. Take care on the cliffs. And watch out for Percy!' he called as he ran down the steps and jogged away. He was already too far away for her to shout a reply. This was weird. What exactly was up with Percy? She was starting to think there was something very wrong with his father. Freddy had said he was going to inherit early due to his father's health issues, and she was wondering exactly what they were. She tucked into her croissant and admired the view. She wasn't a gardener, but she did love the intricacy of the vast gardens in front of her. The symmetry was almost as impressive as the colours. Paul returned to check she was okay.

'Paul, what's wrong with Percy?' she asked.

Paul frowned and took a moment. 'I think his issues are age related. He's quite old but still has certain urges. Things have got worse of late.'

'But what is actually wrong with him?'

Paul seemed to ponder the question. 'He's prone to unprovoked aggressive outbursts.'

Nancy knew her eyes were widening. He'd seemed quite sweet when he'd been pottering about the big flowerpot and chatting to her earlier. 'I'm not being rude, but should he be here? You know, for his sake if nobody else's. Maybe he needs specialist care?' She tried to phrase it as kindly as she could, but she was definitely going to lock her bedroom door tonight.

Paul bobbed his head. 'Probably, but Lady Louisa is rather sentimental and while Percy does fly into a rage at the slightest thing and crap on the garden furniture, this is still his home.' He saw Nancy's shocked expression. 'Please don't worry. He's harmless really. Most of the time he just potters about the gardens eating ants. I'd best get on.' He pointed inside. Nancy didn't know what to say so she just nodded. These people were seriously weird.

After breakfast Paul showed her how the shower in the bathroom nearest to her room worked. Paul did a wonderful job of taping a plastic bag over her arm and pledged to have her a proper shower cover by the next morning. She couldn't open the shampoo bottle, so rinsed her hair as best she could with one arm. It was a nice day so she decided she would let it dry naturally, mainly because towel-drying was impossible and a hairdryer would make her look like a mad scientist.

There was a tap on her bedroom door. 'Nancy, it's Paul. I have a suggestion about your cat.' Nancy picked up Carrie and opened the door. 'I wondered if she might like the orangery.'

'She doesn't eat fruit,' said Nancy.

'They don't grow pineapples in it anymore. It's more of a conservatory now but it gets the sun and she'd be fine there if you wanted to explore the gardens.'

Nancy wasn't sure what he was offering but he seemed keen and so far, he'd been very helpful. 'Okay,' she said.

Nancy picked up Carrie's harness and lead and followed Paul downstairs, where people were cleaning. They walked through the house and then into a room full of coats, boots and gun cabinets. Nancy tried to put on Carrie's harness but it was tricky. She looked at Paul. 'Could you give me a hand?'

'Of course.' Paul helped clip on the harness while Carrie swished her tail impatiently. As soon as it was on, she began walking. 'It's unusual for a cat to be comfortable on a lead,' said Paul.

'She's had it from a kitten. Carrie's a ragdoll so she's worth a bit. She's also got no common sense when it comes to roads, so I can't risk her roaming in London.

But she's happy to wear this for a walk around my back garden.' They set off again with Carrie in the lead, out into a courtyard. Nancy was lost already. On the other side of the courtyard were stables where a young woman called 'Good morning' to them both. 'Do you ride, miss?' she asked.

'Sorry. Broken arm,' said Nancy. It felt easier than sharing that she fell off a donkey on Great Yarmouth beach aged five and hadn't been on anything with four legs since. The woman gave her a commiserative grimace which Nancy copied. 'Such a shame.'

On the other side of the stables were paddocks and more green space than Hyde Park. Carrie got distracted by a butterfly and then had an urgent need to wash her bum which delayed the trip a little. Nancy wondered how far away the conservatory was. Weren't they usually attached to a house? 'Sorry, Paul, I expect you need to get to work.' He seemed to be a jack of all trades.

'It's fine,' he said.

'So, Paul, I hope this isn't a rude question but what's your job title?'

'I'm the butler,' said Paul.

'Of course you are,' said Nancy. Butler. Who on earth had a butler in the twenty-first century? The Astley-Davenports, that was who. Her anti rich people prejudice was awakened and then she remembered how kind they were being and shoved it back in its virtual box.

'Being a butler isn't as formal as it was years ago. It's more about making sure the family's needs are met.'

'Sort of like running the house?'

'No, the housekeeper does that.'

'Blimey, how the other half live,' said Nancy. 'Sorry, I don't mean to sound ungrateful. It's just a world away from what I'm used to.'

'They're really nice people,' said Paul. 'If you can see past the money and the title.' She wasn't sure if Paul was scolding her but before she could respond he was pointing. 'The orangery is behind those trees.'

Nancy had seen conservatories before, but this was not the same thing. It was a long, symmetrical, single-storey building in the same grey stone as the house with vast windows along one side. Paul let them in through a door at the side. It was warm and scattered with pots and troughs overflowing with plants of varying sizes. There were sun loungers and rattan sofas and over in the corner were water and food bowls. 'I took the liberty of cooking her some chicken,' he said. Carrie made straight for the dishes.

'She'll love you forever,' said Nancy. 'This is vast.' She walked up to the windows and looked out. The view was over a lake with the house beyond. 'I see why it's all the way over here.'

'It catches the sun for the greatest part of the day. The 4th Earl of Langham, who built it, didn't get on with his wife so he used to come here to paint the plants.'

'An early example of a man cave,' she said.

'Indeed,' said Paul with a smile. 'Do you think Carrie will be happy here?'

Nancy was about to answer but Carrie was already digging a hole in one of the troughs and standing to attention ready to make a deposit.

Paul directed Nancy to a footpath which he said saw a nice circular walk of the prettiest corner of the estate. Corner? She wondered how many acres it was. She followed a high wall from the orangery until she came to a door. Like in all the best horror movies, she opened it. She was astonished to find she was looking out to sea.

She'd not seen that coming at all. She looked around her for more clues that she was at the seaside. In her defence she only knew she was in Devon because she'd asked Paul, otherwise she could have been anywhere. And Devon was a pretty big county, so Nancy felt it was fair enough that she'd not noticed the sea had been on her doorstep. At least that explained what had happened to her hair. She followed the path and was rewarded by a stunning view over a small cove. The wind was whipping across the top of the cliffs. She could see why Freddy had warned her as there was quite a drop. Nancy kept away from the edge and followed the path in the hope of finding a way down to the water.

The path narrowed and wound its way in a zigzag fashion down to a rickety-looking set of wooden steps. The last thing she needed was to fall through some rotten timber – perhaps she'd watched too many Indiana Jones films? She took hold of the rail and placed a foot on the first step, it seemed quite solid. She gave a stomp and it held. Nancy put her weight on the step and it seemed fine so she slowly made her way a bit further down. Only having one arm in use did make her feel more vulnerable which she didn't like but it wasn't going to stop her exploring this delightful place.

Nancy made it to the sand and stood for a moment breathing in the salty air. She felt like she was the first person to discover the place, which she obviously wasn't, but she did wonder how long it had been since anyone had ventured down there. To her left were virtually sheer cliffs with a jumble of jagged rocks to her right and in front of her a couple of large boulders worked smooth by the sea. All around her feet were tiny seashells. Behind her on a natural ledge was a small tumbledown shack that looked like it was leaning against the cliff face and had definitely seen better days. Underneath the steps there was also what looked like the entrance to a cave. The kid inside her felt like she'd stepped into an adventure novel and Nancy went off to explore. There was a rock pool at the entrance to the cavern and the water rippled as its occupants darted for shelter. Nancy shone her phone into the dark. It didn't go back very far at all, but her imagination could still conjure up smugglers and pirates who may have used it as a store.

She put her phone away, took off her shoes and left them on the rock ledge before making her way across the damp sand to the sea. It was warm in the shallows as the sea gently lapped over her toes. It transported Nancy back to her holidays by the seaside as a child. There hadn't been that many so each one was a treasured memory. It had been a big event for them to take a trip to a caravan for a few days and the highlight of that had been the beach and the penny arcades – she still couldn't resist a go on a 2p coin pusher. She couldn't help but think how different Freddy's childhood must have been to her own. Not that she'd not had a good one, it had been the best. She'd had two parents who were happily married, doting on her throughout her formative years, who had saved hard to give her the things they had missed out on like holidays to the seaside.

Time seemed to evaporate in the tiny bay as Nancy paddled, collected seashells, leaned against the big boulder and watched the sea ebb and flow. It was like the breath of the world inhaling and exhaling and she found it incredibly calming. When her stomach rumbled, she decided to face the climb back up the steps. She went to retrieve her shoes and couldn't resist a bit of a nose at the old shack. There were no windows only large shutters that appeared to be made out of driftwood as they were different shades and mismatched. It was an odd little place and Nancy wondered why it was there. Maybe it had been used for storing deckchairs? She certainly wouldn't have wanted to lug one down with her. She'd ask Paul about it later but as there was nobody about, she figured it wouldn't hurt to have a little peep inside. She gently tried the door – it opened. Her heart thumped a little harder. She opened it a crack and then a little wider so she could let in some light. Nancy was surprised by what she saw. There were rugs on the floor, a rustic table and wooden seat against a stone wall to her right and on the other side a bench covered in blankets. She inched inside.

The blankets moved and a grey-haired old man reared up. 'Argh!' screamed Nancy and she slammed the door.

Chapter Seventeen

Alice had surprised herself by how much she enjoyed Friday night with her parents. It was the first Friday she'd not been out clubbing for weeks. They had chatted over a home-cooked shepherd's pie followed by her mother's famous trifle, then they'd all curled up on the sofa to watch some series her parents had been watching. She had no clue what was going on, but it didn't matter. It had been just like old times, the good ones and she'd liked the comfort and familiarity. Unfortunately, Saturday was somewhat different.

Alice had been woken by her mother hoovering outside her bedroom door far earlier than was necessary. During the weekends at Nancy's Alice lay in until lunchtime but that wasn't possible here. Her parents were in their own routine. Alice spent a moment taking in her old room. It was still painted lemon yellow, a colour she had chosen some ten years ago when it had last been decorated. The pink and yellow striped curtains had been made by her mum and she still loathed them but had never had the nerve to say so. The small table in the corner had been her desk where she'd done her homework every night and studied for her exams. Thankfully there were no posters on the walls but the attendance and merit certificates her parents had framed were still embarrassingly on display. It was like a museum of her early life.

Alice dragged herself out of bed and opened the door. 'Did I wake you, love?' asked her mum, switching off the hoover.

Alice rubbed her eyes. 'Yeah, but it's okay.'

'I bet you slept well being back in your bed. You can't beat your own bed for a proper night's sleep.'

'It was okay. But I also sleep fine at Na—'

'What are your plans for today?' asked her mum, cutting her off. While they had been keen to hear about how she was getting on in her job they had not been that interested in anything else about her life in London. But it was probably best they didn't know about some of it, especially not Whizzer or Dom. The thought of the latter made her sigh.

'Err, no plans at all for this week. Apart from Friday.' But Alice was trying not to think about Friday.

Her mother looked astonished. 'Will you not be catching up with some friends? Sammy and Oscar are both home from university.' Her parents had hopes of her settling down with a nice young man, ideally someone they already knew who lived locally.

'Nope. I've not heard from either of them since they went off on their gap year tour of Asia together.'

'I understand Florence is working at Tesco while she waits to hear about jobs. She's on the milking round,' said her mother with a significant nod of her head.

'Milk round,' corrected Alice with a yawn. 'It's nothing special, Mum. It just means she's applying for jobs at the end of her degree course. Lots of businesses focus on recruiting this time of year that's all.'

'She's considering consultancy, and her mother told me there's lots of high-profile companies interested in her.'

'Yeah, well Florence's mum would say that wouldn't she? She's always bigged her up,' said Alice.

'That's not a nice thing to say about your friend, Alice.' Her mum looked shocked.

Alice puffed out a breath. 'I've not been friends with Florence since she stole my penguin bar at Year Six camp.'

Alice's mother laughed. 'Oh you kids. Well, give her my love when you see her.' And she switched the vacuum cleaner back on. Alice marvelled at her mother's ability to engage in a conversation yet not really listen to what the other person was saying.

Downstairs was no different. Her father was muttering into the newspaper until she entered the kitchen. 'Good afternoon, Alice,' he quipped. It was hard to raise a smile to the same old joke.

'Morning,' she said, giving the dog a head rub. Cindy briefly lifted her white-whiskered chin.

'Your mum got your favourite cereal in,' said her dad, pointing into the cupboard as she opened it.

'Coco Pops?' They really did think she was still seven. While she was mildly affronted by the cereal, she had to admit chocolate for breakfast was never a bad thing, so she filled up a bowl and joined her father at the table. He updated her on the woeful efforts of the local football team that she'd never been interested in, and she had a scroll through her phone. There was nothing much of interest until she did a little mild stalking of Dom on Instagram – he'd been fairly easy to find, she only had to search through a few pages of Dominic Fishers until she found him.

What was she hoping to see? She scrolled through all his pictures a number of times and there were only ever shots of him, Bonnie or both of them plus a few of Bonnie's artwork. There were no women in the pictures but then he'd only been posting for a couple of months.

Alice clicked on his latest picture, being careful not to double click and inadvertently like the post. The last thing she wanted was for him to know she was secretly keeping an eye on his movements. Dom had added a selfie of him and Bonnie eating ice creams for breakfast. She instantly felt better about her Coco Pops. Bonnie was grinning and had ice cream on her nose and Dom was laughing. The picture made her smile. Something in the background caught her eye and she zoomed in. She recognised the sign behind them, she'd been to Butterfly Café a million times because it was the next seaside town to where her parents lived. Which meant Dom was less than two miles away right now.

* * *

Nancy was properly startled by the old man and fled from the old shack. She was halfway up the rickety steps before she realised she'd left her shoes behind but there was no way she was going back for them. He'd really given her a fright. What on earth was he doing in there? When she reached the cliff top she was out of breath and her heart was racing. She still wanted to run but there was a twinge of fear in the back of her mind just in case she fell and did more damage to her arm, so she speed-walked as best she could on bare feet. She ended up taking to the grass which was a bad idea – there must have been quite a lot of rabbits about somewhere because their droppings were sticking to her feet – *yuck!*

Langham Hall came into sight and Nancy started to feel calmer. She kept checking behind her, but it was very unlikely the old man was following her. She suddenly felt bad. She'd probably given him just as big a shock and the poor man was probably desperate and homeless. She was still walking at a pace when she let herself through the door in the wall, closing it behind her. When she turned around, she realised it was clearly her day for surprises. She was momentarily startled by a peacock which was right in front of her with his stunningly beautiful tail on full fanned-out display. The rich blues and greens of the feathers iridescent and glinting in the sunshine.

'Aren't you a beauty,' she said to him, trying to pull her phone from her back pocket with her good hand.

The peacock tilted his head to the sky in response and made a noise like a cross between a scream and a fire alarm that felt like it was piercing her eardrums. Nancy shoved one finger in her ear but her bad arm wouldn't bend so she couldn't do the other. She skirted around the deafening bird. This seemed to upset him further and in between screams he lunged at Nancy.

'Whoa!' she said, leaping out of the way.

She daren't take her eyes off him for fear of him pecking her – he had a very pointy beak which was bound to hurt if he hit his target. Each time she leapt backwards he screeched and sprang another attack, beak first, after her.

'Hey!' she shouted, quickly glancing around for some help.

As if on cue Freddy came striding over clapping his hands. He was wearing smart trousers and a plain T-shirt – not your typical knight in shining armour but at least he was coming to her rescue. The feeling was short-lived as the peacock turned on him. 'Run!' shouted Freddy, dancing around. 'I'll hold him off as long as I can.' The bird pecked his ankle. 'Ow! Quick, go!'

Nancy didn't need telling twice. She turned and ran as fast as she dared to. The nearest place was the orangery. She darted around the side and while she was struggling with the door someone jostled her to one side. 'Argh!' she yelled.

'Sorry,' said Freddy, quickly opening the door and

almost shoving her inside. He pulled it closed just in time to stop the peacock following them in. The bird tilted his head up and screeched his annoyance.

It took a moment for Nancy and Freddy to compose themselves. The interruption had got Carrie's attention and she trotted over to see what the fuss was about. The peacock was now strutting up and down outside the large glass windows shimmering his tail and shrieking. Carrie mirrored the peacock and paced along the safe side of the glass.

'What the hell is wrong with him?' asked Nancy when she'd got her breath back.

'I thought you'd been warned about Percy?'

Nancy's head spun around to have another look at the peacock. 'That's Percy? I thought . . .' Freddy was looking at her quizzically. 'Doesn't matter. So *that's* Percy.' She pointed at the shaking tail feathers as they stalked past the window. Things started to make a lot more sense. 'He's the one who craps on the garden furniture and not your . . . um not anyone else.'

'I hope no one else is doing it,' said Freddy with a smile. 'Sorry he attacked you. I'd like to say he's harmless but he's really not. Percy's a nasty little sod.' He rubbed his ankle as he spoke. 'He didn't used to be like this. At one time we had six of them including some hens, but they all got old and died. Percy is still hanging on and he's so ancient we think he's got dementia. The vet thinks he has unsatisfied sexual urges. You could say he's a lover and a fighter. It's that or he's uber stressed by feeling he has to protect this big place all on his own. Which is something I can relate to.'

'Poor thing,' said Nancy. 'Percy. Not you. But thanks for coming to my rescue,' she added, feeling a bit lame.

'You're welcome.' They smiled at the same time but

neither seemed to know what to say next and it became a little uncomfortable.

'I collected some shells.' She pulled them from her pocket.

'You found Seashell Bay then.'

'Good name. Does what it says on the tin?' said Nancy, jiggling her pretty shell collection.

The sound of angry beak on glass grabbed their attention. They turned away from each other to watch Percy and Carrie march in unison on their respective sides of the window. 'Um, what do we do now?' asked Nancy.

'Send for back-up,' said Freddy, getting out his phone.

Paul soon arrived with some grapes and a pineapple which managed to lure Percy a safe distance away. 'We're safe to go,' said Freddy.

'Please can you give me a hand with this?' asked Nancy as she tried unsuccessfully to put on Carrie's harness.

Freddy chuckled. 'Could you not just carry . . . um Carrie?'

'If she freaks out she will reduce my arms to shreds and escape to goodness knows where. And anyway, it's extendable,' said Nancy, holding up the handle end.

Freddy said no more as he fastened up Carrie while she kept her eyes firmly fixed on the peacock. 'You might want to carry her past Percy.'

'Oh Carrie won't go for him.'

'I was thinking more about him being the aggressor.'

'Good call,' said Nancy, lifting Carrie awkwardly with one arm.

Paul gave them a thumbs up and they slunk out of the orangery and back towards the house giving Percy a wide berth. Once they were nearing the formal gardens Nancy put Carrie on the ground and she trotted along happily.

She stopped a few times to sniff places before bounding on ahead.

'She's better behaved on a lead than our dog,' said Freddy. The words were barely out of his mouth before a large black Labrador bounded across the gardens towards them.

Carrie's lead was fully extended. Nancy tried to reel her in like a fish. 'Carrie!' she yelled, sensing imminent danger. But it was too late.

Chapter Eighteen

Nancy wanted to close her eyes for fear of what she was about to witness. She couldn't run fast enough to stop the dog getting to Carrie. She let out a feeble squeak as the animals met.

'Otto. Sit!' commanded Freddy.

The dog's bum hit the grass immediately, making Carrie jump. 'Blimey, that's a good party trick,' said Nancy, hurrying over. The dog's tail was swishing so hard it was spraying gravel across the path. A little belatedly Carrie puffed herself up and hissed at Otto. She'd only ever seen dogs at the vet's before where she was always safely in her carrier. Nancy picked up her wide-eyed kitty. 'That was a close one.'

'Sorry,' said Freddy, petting Otto. 'Home,' he instructed with a wave of his arms and the dog ran off as fast as he had approached. Nancy was staring gobsmacked at his obedience. 'Gun dog,' he explained.

Carrie appeared unfazed by her encounter with a dog about five times the size of her, so Nancy put her down and after having a good sniff at where the Labrador had been, she trotted on happily, but this time Nancy had her on a much shorter lead. They strolled through the beautifully manicured gardens where the floral scents filled Nancy with the smell of summer.

'I was coming to find you when everything kicked off with Percy,' said Freddy.

Nancy felt a squiggle of something in her middle. What was that all about? 'Why's that?' She tried to sound uninterested, but she'd not nailed it.

'My parents are having a welcome dinner tonight, it's a thing they like to do for guests.'

'For me?' She couldn't help but feel flattered. 'Hang on, you've not told them that I've sacked you?'

He held up his hands in defence. 'I am going to tell them that I resigned but now is not the right time.'

'When will be the right time, Freddy?'

'As soon as I've sorted an alternative.'

Nancy faltered. She'd not really considered that he would be looking for an alternative for his fake work experience. 'It's a lovely invitation, so please thank your parents, but I can't go to dinner with a lord and lady when I've not washed my hair for days.'

'I did think of that,' he said, looking pleased with himself.

'Thanks, so you've noticed the state of it too. That doesn't really help, Freddy.' She tried to smooth it down, but she was holding the lead in one hand and the other one was tricky to operate.

'I've booked Mother's hairdresser to come over and sort it out. If I've done the wrong thing, it's easily cancelled.' He checked his watch. 'Although she's probably on her way.'

'That's actually really thoughtful of you.' She gave him a nudge with her good elbow.

He nudged her back. 'You're welcome.'

Having her hair done would definitely make her feel less grotty but there was another issue about being invited to a spur-of-the-moment dinner with the aristocracy.

'Trouble is I've got nothing suitable to wear for a meal with nobility.'

Freddy grinned. 'It's informal. They might have titles but they're probably no different to your parents.'

'Oh yeah, you can't move in my parents' gaff for suits of armour and polo ponies.' Nancy thought about her mum breaking into song while she was pushing the trolley around Aldi. And her dad saying pull my finger just before he'd let a trump go.

'Please try to see past the house,' said Freddy. 'You've met Mother. She's very taken with you.'

Nancy had to admit from the brief encounter with Lady Louisa the previous evening she had seemed genuinely nice. Obviously posh but she'd been interested in Nancy and sympathetic about her injured arm. And they had been really relaxed about her staying in their fabulous home and being waited on by their staff so maybe she didn't need to worry. 'Okay, I'll come. Please tell them that I'd be honoured to accept their kind invitation.'

'Great. They'll be thrilled. I promise you'll have a fun time.' Images of a *Bridgerton*-style ball flashed through her mind.

Lady Louisa's hairdresser was absolutely lovely and came fully equipped. She had set up in a bathroom and it was like a mini salon with a mobile hair washing basin attached to the sink taps and a tilting chair. It was so nice to have her hair washed properly. After a professional blow dry Nancy felt ready for almost anything. She spent a while getting ready. She was changing her top for the umpteenth time when there was a tap on her door.

'Hang on. I'm not decent.'

'It's okay, I'm not coming in,' said Freddy. 'Just to say

I'm going to give them a hand so come down whenever you're ready. You can give Carrie the run of the house because Otto will be with us all evening.'

'Where will we be then?'

'Seashell Bay. See you down there,' he said.

Nancy frowned at the closed door while she processed what he'd said. She had a flashback of the angry old man and she gasped. 'Wait! There's something you need to know there's this . . . Freddy, are you still there?' But there was no reply. Perhaps it was best she didn't tell him. She couldn't be sure they wouldn't turf the poor old bloke out of the little shack and she didn't want that on her conscience.

Nancy covered her boobs with her plaster cast, dashed to the door and checked the corridor – no sign of him. 'Freddy!' she called. Nothing. She was about to dash after him but had second thoughts. She tugged on the top she felt made it least obvious that she wasn't wearing a bra – because putting on a bra with one hand was impossible. She went to leave but realised she had no shoes on. As she'd left them in Seashell Bay and she'd not packed for a stay in a stately home she only had one other option.

Nancy tried Freddy's mobile but it went straight to voicemail. She called out as she made her way through the house. The place was empty. Was she meant to lock up when she left? If she was, she had no idea where the keys were. She shut the doors behind her with a satisfying thud but it still didn't seem right to leave the place unlocked. She wouldn't even leave her little Ikea-filled terrace without locking it up first let alone this one that was full of priceless treasures.

Nancy hurriedly made her way across the lawns, through the door in the wall and out to the cliff path.

It didn't seem as far this time. The sight of the sea would always feel special to Nancy, she wondered if you ever tired of it. As she neared the steps down to Seashell Bay, she could see there were a number of people on the tiny beach. *Safety in numbers*, she thought. If the old man kicked off there were enough people to restrain him. Everything seemed calm so perhaps he'd gone back to sleep. A horrid thought popped into her head. Perhaps the shock of her creeping up on him had killed him? She hastened towards the steps. From the top she could see they were having a barbecue. At the sight of the large black barbecue Nancy instantly relaxed. Not quite the grand ball and dinner she'd imagined – in fact much better.

She made her way down the steps and Freddy came to greet her at the bottom. He held out a hand to help her down onto the sand. 'Hairdresser did okay then?'

'Thanks for arranging that, I feel so much better.'

'You look stunning.' His eyes slid down to her feet. A grin spread across his face at the sight of her footwear. 'I like your slippers,' he said.

'They're furry sliders.' She tried to sound convincing. She'd been distracted from her mission to warn him about the crazy homeless guy living in the shack. 'Anyway, I need to warn you ab—'

'Nancy, good evening,' said Lady Louisa, greeting her with a hug. 'I love your giraffe slippers. How fun! Come and meet everyone.'

Nancy could see Freddy's shoulders were vibrating with laughter, so she gave him a shove as they passed, partly because he was laughing at her favourite slippers but also to get his attention. 'I need to tell you something,' she said, but Lady Louisa was already leading her to the barbecue and introducing her to people.

'Oscar, I would like you to meet Nancy.' The man was expertly turning sausages, but then if he was the chef that wasn't difficult.

'Hiya, Oscar,' said Nancy with a smile. The man was giving her an odd look.

Lady Louisa continued. 'Nancy, this is my husband, Oscar.'

'Crap, you're Lord Langham. I'm so sorry. Pleased to meet you, sir, your lordship.' She did a half curtsey and belatedly offered her left hand for him to shake. She didn't know if that was the done thing, but she was sure as hell that saying crap to a lord wasn't.

'It's either Earl Langham or Lord Astley-Davenport,' he said.

Nancy wanted a very large wave to wash her away. 'I'm really sorry I'm not used to—'

A grin spread across Oscar's face. 'I'm joking. Don't be sorry, it's a bloody mouthful whichever one you pick. Call me Oscar.' He shook her hand that she was still holding out. 'Now are you a sausage or burger kind of gal?' He opened the barbecue with a flourish.

'Definitely sausage.'

'Wonderful.' He clapped his hands together and proceeded to go through the various varieties he had cooking. Nancy glanced at Freddy and he gave her a reassuring thumbs up. Maybe these people were okay after all.

'You already know Paul,' said Louisa as Paul offered her a glass of champagne.

'Hi, Paul, thanks.' She wasn't sure how wise it was to have these very expensive-looking champagne flutes on the beach, so she gripped it tightly. Louisa rattled off a number of names and job titles, most of which Nancy wasn't going to remember.

'This is Allsop our head gardener.'

'Hello again,' said Nancy, feeling her cheeks flush. 'Sorry about this morning. I got a bit confused about who Percy was.'

'Oh dear, have you met our avian terrorist?' asked Allsop, his voice even more upper crust that Lady Louisa's.

'Got herself cornered by the herb garden wall,' butted in Freddy. 'We had to dive in the orangery to escape.' Everyone laughed including Nancy although it hadn't been funny at the time. One of the younger gardeners tapped Freddy on the shoulder and he jogged off to join in a game of frisbee.

Louisa touched Nancy's arm which was when she realised she was staring after Freddy. 'You must think we're crackers making Frederick work for you. I do hope he's explained everything.' Louisa searched Nancy's features.

'He said that his inheritance depended on it.'

'I feared he'd make us sound like awful controlling parents—'

'Which we are,' butted in Oscar. 'But for good bally reason.'

'Please don't get worked up, Oscar.' Louisa rubbed his arm. 'Frederick's not really embraced his duty as we'd hoped he might.'

'Don't get me wrong, we love the boy immensely but managing something like this . . .' Oscar swept a hand up towards the house. 'Is no mean feat and our Freddy likes wine, women and partying far too much.'

'Oscar.' Louisa scowled at her husband. 'He just needs a little steering back onto the right course and that's what we hoped a proper job would do for him. So, thank you.' She took Nancy's good hand in both of hers and gave it a squeeze.

Nancy was uncomfortable, Freddy obviously hadn't

had a chance to update them about losing the job. But then again, how awkward would it be to stay in their home and accept their hospitality if they knew she had fired their son? She wasn't a snake, but she also didn't lie to people. 'Actually, I should explain that Freddy—'

'I thought my ears were burning,' said Freddy, appearing at Nancy's side. 'Watch out or Mother will have the family photo album out.'

'I'm not that bad,' said Louisa with a chuckle. She leaned into Nancy. 'Maybe tomorrow evening. There's the cutest pictures of him sitting by the pool wearing just his armbands.'

'And that's why I have to rescue people.' Freddy guided Nancy away.

When they were out of earshot, she turned to face him. 'You need to tell them that I sacked you.'

'I will but—'

'Freddy, it's lying. You have to come clean.'

'In my defence they also haven't asked.' Nancy gave him a look. 'Okay possibly you're right.' She raised her eyebrows. He held his hands up. 'Stop the interrogation. Yes, you're right. But I wanted to talk to you about everything first.'

'Fire away.' Nancy went to fold her arms and was frustrated that she couldn't. She hadn't realised how much she gestured with her hands until she broke her wrist and no longer could manage simple manoeuvres.

Freddy twisted his lips. 'Not here. Tonight is not about work, it's for relaxing and hoping we don't get food poisoning from Father's cooking. Let's discuss it tomorrow. Is that all right with you?' He put his hands together as if in prayer.

'Tomorrow but then you have to tell them or I will. Got it?'

'Absolutely, Boss.' She arched an eyebrow. 'Sorry, Nancy. Now if Father offers to put his homemade sauce on your food you need to know that it's eighty per cent malt whisky.'

'What's the other twenty per cent?'

'Secret ingredients,' said Freddy. 'Which means it's different every time, but it doesn't matter because you can only ever taste the Scotch.'

While Nancy tucked into her fancy hot dog she tried to see if her shoes were still where she'd left them. She could do with swapping out her giraffes. She caught sight of a movement by the shack and the events of earlier flooded back.

'Freddy, I tried to tell you earlier. There's a tramp living in that shed.' She pointed up the beach. On cue the old man shuffled out and stared across the sand. Oscar started to laugh and everyone joined in. Louisa's lips were pulled together. 'What?' said Nancy to Freddy. Why was it funny? Did rich people find poor people entertaining?

Freddy jogged over to the old man and helped him down on to the sand. 'Grandpa, I'd like you to meet Nancy,' said Freddy with a huge grin.

Grandpa? Nancy was confused. If the old lord was still alive didn't that mean he owned the manor, not Oscar. Or was that why they were keeping him shut in a shed? 'Hello,' she said.

The old man squinted at her. 'You came poking around here earlier. Gave me a fright you did.'

'Yeah. Sorry about that.'

Louisa appeared. 'Dad, this is Nancy, the young woman who has employed Frederick.'

Ahh, thought Nancy, *that makes more sense if he's Louisa's dad.* 'Hiya,' said Nancy.

'Hello, Nancy. Nice to meet you properly.'

'Yeah, you too. What should I call you?'

'Everyone calls me Grandpa,' he said with a warm smile.

'Come and sit down and I'll get you something to eat,' said Freddy, guiding his grandfather to a seat.

Nancy intercepted Freddy. 'Why does he live in there?' she asked.

Freddy snorted but quickly composed himself. 'He doesn't live in the beach hut. He just likes Seashell Bay. He and Granny spent many happy hours in the bay when they visited. I think he feels closer to her when he's here. We've tried stopping him coming down because he's a bit unsteady, but it doesn't work so the compromise is that someone brings him down for a few hours most days. Did you really think he was a tramp?' Freddy's expression said he was judging her.

'No, of course not,' said Nancy, unsure what else to say.

* * *

Alice tried to chill out, but it was almost impossible. If it wasn't her parents fussing over her it was thoughts of Dom being on holiday a couple of miles up the road. She tried to block him from her mind, she really did, but it wasn't that simple. She found she was thinking about his Instagram photos which was definitely unhealthy. What had she been hoping for? An Insta-worthy photo of him and his partner as the perfect little family? She wondered if that would help. If it would stop her fantasising about him. Maybe what she needed was to see them all together. To see him with his wife or girlfriend or whatever relationship he was in with Bonnie's mum. Perhaps that would help her to close the door on that little episode.

Alice wasn't the sort of woman who would pursue someone who was already in a relationship. She had good morals and believed strongly in the girl code. Although right now it was being tested. There was something about Dom. Their kiss had been an accident, but it had had such an impact on her. She'd always thought friends were exaggerating when they said they felt a connection – she'd assumed it was them feeling horny. She knew what that felt like. But however strongly Alice felt, nothing could come of it because Dom was in a relationship.

'Alice, love,' called her mother. Alice had managed to grab ten minutes to herself in her bedroom before her mum had tracked her down. She loved them dearly and it was kind of sweet that they wanted to spend time with her, but it was also quite intense. 'Your dad has got out the Monopoly and we know how you love a game. Shall we set it up?'

'Okay. I'll be down in five minutes.'

Alice sighed heavily and flopped back on her bed. At least Monopoly would take her mind off Dom. She'd never felt like this about a man before, not even when she'd split up with boyfriends. She'd found it easy to move on. This thing with Dom was different but she knew she needed to put a stop to it for her own sake. Maybe what she needed was a glimpse at Dom playing happy families to help reset her moral compass. She checked his Instagram again – no new posts. If Dom wasn't going to provide the pictures maybe she needed to go and seek them out in real life for herself?

Chapter Nineteen

Nancy was surprised at how much she enjoyed the evening. It had been nothing like she'd imagined. She'd made some assumptions, some of those she was prepared to admit were based on the few episodes of *Downton Abbey* that her mum had made her sit through. None of the people she'd met at Langham Hall were anything like the characters on the telly. She watched Oscar trying to force the last of his chilli jam sausages onto Freddy while Allsop refereed a game of football between the younger staff. Freddy's grandpa was asleep in a chair with Otto dozing across his feet. It all felt quite normal really, until Nancy took in the location. A private bay on the south coast. This was a different life to hers and they were different people. She leaned back against the largest boulder on the beach and watched the sun melt into the sea. There was a small boat bobbing in the water that hadn't been there on her earlier visit. She watched as the tide turned it gently one way and then the other.

'You okay?' asked Freddy, joining her.

'I'm good thanks.'

He leaned back against the rock, his warm skin brushing hers, making her shiver. 'Are you cold?' Nancy tried to cross her arms over her protruding nipples – the perils of not wearing a bra. 'Let me get you a blanket,' said Freddy and before she could reply he was wrapping a soft blanket around her shoulders.

'Do you usually leave the hall unlocked?' she asked and Freddy raised an eyebrow. 'I'm not going to be tipping off any crooks if that's what you're worried about.'

'Do you know any crooks?' he asked.

'I might do. Actually a few of the kids I went to school with ended up inside.' Why was she telling him that? 'Not that I'm in touch with them. My mum updates me.' She decided to shut up and stop reinforcing her kid-from-the-dodgy-council-estate stereotype.

Nancy stared at the changing shades of the sky as the sunset bloomed before darkness rubbed out its colour. It was such a peaceful place. She scanned over her shoulder at Oscar and Louisa now holding hands and sipping champagne. She stole a glance at Freddy, the fading light enhancing his features. She'd only been there a day and she'd seen a completely different side to him. 'It's been lovely.'

'How's the arm?' asked Freddy.

'A bit achy but otherwise okay.'

'Should it not be in a sling?' he asked.

'Yeah, it should. I didn't want to spoil my outfit.' Nancy lifted up a giraffe slipper and wriggled her toes.

'Completely understandable. I'm going to be taking Grandpa back shortly. You're very welcome to stay or you can come back with us.'

Something made Nancy yawn. 'I think I might come back with you if that's okay. The combination of champagne and sea air has tired me out.' It was also the fact she'd not slept well thanks to her cast.

'I'll round up Grandpa and we'll make a move.'

Nancy thanked Louisa and Oscar who both kissed her

on the cheek and made her promise that she'd join them the next day for breakfast. Nancy said goodnight to the others and then looked about for Freddy and Grandpa, but there was no sign of them. Grandpa was no longer in his chair and they weren't on the steps as she'd expected. Surely they'd not dashed up them that quickly.

'Hey, Nancy! Are you ready?' called Freddy.

She spun around to see Freddy and Grandpa sitting in the little boat. Freddy beckoned her over. She had to hold her slippers and the blanket in the air as she waded out to the boat where Freddy helped her in.

'Hold on,' said Freddy, carefully wrapping the blanket around her shoulders. He started up an engine and the boat pootled out of the bay before suddenly picking up speed and tearing across the water. Grandpa grinned as they sped along. Nancy tightened her grip. Within minutes the engine slowed and Freddy brought them back into shore, on a much longer stretch of beach. He jumped out into the shallows, pulled the boat in and tied it to a post sticking out of the water.

Freddy helped them both onto the sand and they followed Grandpa up a small ramp to where an old Land Rover was waiting. 'He can't cope with the steps but this is manageable.'

They were soon inside Langham Hall and from a quick inspection it didn't seem that they'd been burgled while they were out which was a relief to Nancy. 'Did you fancy a brandy or a hot drink to warm you up?' asked Freddy.

'But Paul's still at the beach.'

'Hey, I am capable of getting drinks. I'm fully certified as kettle safe, you know.'

'Are you? Because that's a certificate I'd like to see.'

'Okay. There might not be an actual certificate but . . . do you want a drink or not?'

'I'd love a hot chocolate. You know how to make that, right?'

'Actually, I think we've got a machine for that.'

Nancy shook her head at him. 'Show me where the kitchen is in this place and I'll supervise.' He tilted his head. 'Okay, I'm really only coming to point and laugh at you.'

'Your honesty is admirable.' He led the way.

As she'd expected, the kitchen was vast with a huge marble island in the centre. To her left were a row of cookers and stainless-steel work areas, to her right was a pale green country kitchen with a cream Aga – it was like the room had two identities.

Freddy was busy opening and closing cupboards but he noticed her turning her head from side to side. 'Mother wouldn't hand it all over as she likes to cook so this is her half and the stainless steel is better for events so our cook, Mrs Mason, rules that side. It stops any bloodshed,' he said with a smile.

'It's so big.'

Freddy looked around. 'I suppose it is.' He opened another cupboard. 'Found it.' He pulled out what looked like a jug and base.

'I've seen those on the telly,' said Nancy. She'd also looked them up and scoffed at paying over a hundred quid for something that basically warmed up milk. Nancy pulled out a barstool and sat down to watch.

'Standard chocolate or dark mint?' asked Freddy, holding up sachets.

'Standard please.'

Freddy put milk and the sachet contents into the jug and hit the start button. 'Back in a mo.' He dashed off, leaving Nancy swinging her legs. He gave her a cheeky little look as he darted past. She'd never imagined he could be this sweet and attentive. Perhaps she had been very wrong about him. Or was all of this just a ploy to butter her up so that she'd lie about him working for her for six months? Either way Freddy was definitely growing on her.

Carrie announced her entrance with a loud meow. 'Hello there,' said Nancy, realising she couldn't reach the cat without getting off the barstool and she really couldn't be arsed. 'Have you enjoyed having the run of the house?' Carrie sat and stared up at Nancy with her unblinking eyes, which basically meant, 'Cut the small talk and feed me.'

Carrie's ears pricked up, but before either she or Nancy had worked out what was happening, the kitchen was invaded by one very excitable and sandy Labrador. There was no way Nancy could get to Carrie in time. 'Jump!' she yelled at the cat and she held out her arms. Unfortunately, Carrie wasn't as well trained as Otto, so she hot-footed it around the other side of the island. Otto gave chase.

'Shit!' said Nancy, clambering down from her barstool as the animals did their third high-speed lap around the island. Nancy splayed out her arms and legs in the hope of stopping them, but Carrie dashed past her on one side and the Labrador, close behind, on the other. On their next lap Carrie fled out the door with Otto in hot pursuit. 'Freddy!' yelled Nancy as she joined the chase. She quickly lost sight of them but claws on tiles and wooden floor meant she could still hear them. Nancy skidded into the hallway where halfway up the stairs there was a stand-off. Carrie had turned around and was staring down Otto who was standing three steps below with his tail wagging off the scale.

Nancy crept up the stairs. Perhaps she could sneak by the dog and grab Carrie. But suddenly the cat bobbed down and lunged forward, making Otto hop back a step. Otto lost his footing and went further down and before Nancy could grab her, Carrie had run at him. The startled dog tumbled down a couple more stairs, found his feet and darted past Nancy, with Carrie in hot pursuit. They charged through the entrance hall and off down a corridor.

Freddy appeared from the other wing waving a bottle. 'Did you call?'

'Yes, Otto is chasing Carrie. No, other way around. You know what? I'm no longer sure who's chasing who but they went that way.' Nancy pointed.

A shout from Grandpa had them both charging in that direction. Nancy followed Freddy and they both did an emergency stop in Grandpa's bedroom doorway. Grandpa was sitting up in bed with the bedcovers pulled up to his chin while Otto and Carrie bounced around him like they were at a soft play centre.

'Otto get down,' instructed Freddy. Nancy noted that he was rather masterful with the dog. Otto instantly jumped to the floor and stood looking at Freddy as if awaiting the next command. Carrie trotted to the edge of the bed and watched them then bobbed down before leaping from the bed and skidding out of the room. Otto twitched. 'Stay,' said Freddy firmly. He turned to Nancy. 'Otto's only playing.'

'Running for your life isn't the same as . . .' but Nancy didn't finish the sentence because Carrie strolled back in, walked over to Otto, sat down between his front feet and both animals looked up at Freddy. 'Unbelievable,' she said as she started to laugh.

'I'm trying to get some sleep,' said Grandpa, who was narrowing his eyes at Nancy as if she were to blame.

'Sorry, Grandpa, we'll leave you in peace,' said Freddy, holding up the bottle.

'Actually, I will have a little one if you're offering,' said Grandpa. He downed the water in the glass on his bedside table and held it out to Freddy who obliged. They wished Grandpa goodnight and left the room with the animals trotting at Freddy's heels.

'Are you some sort of animal whisperer?' she asked.

'One of my many gifts,' said Freddy, opening a random door as they passed and flicking on a light. The dog and cat filed in, but Freddy carried on along the corridor.

'Hang on,' said Nancy, doubling back. She was still undecided on whether or not Otto was intent on eating Carrie. She popped her head around the door and looked into a vast room. A huge fireplace was halfway down one side, with three large navy sofas pointing at it. Oversized paintings adorned the walls on the same side and opposite were three lots of vast navy curtains between which was a large brown beanbag where Carrie was curled up with Otto sitting on the wooden floor watching her.

'See, they're fine,' said Freddy. Nancy had to agree.

* * *

Alice woke up with a plan and that made waking up in her old childhood bedroom a lot more palatable. She showered and after taking a while to decide she put on a daisy-print T-shirt and pale yellow shorts – she was feeling sunny and her outfit matched. She bounded into the kitchen where her mum was buttering toast. 'You're up early. Did you sleep okay? Is everything all right?' Her mum's brow was furrowed.

'I'm fine, Mum.'

Her dad checked his watch. 'Good morning, Alice, to what do we owe this pleasure?'

Alice got out a bowl and the Coco Pops. 'I thought I'd check out the beach.'

'That's a lovely idea,' said her mum, clapping her hands together. 'We could take a picnic and I could make—'

'Actually, I was just going to walk down there with Cindy.' The dog twitched an ear at the sound of her name. Her mum looked bereft.

'Cindy doesn't go very far these days,' said her dad. 'Any further than round the block and she lays down in protest.'

'I'm sure Cindy'll be fine. I'll take it slowly. And maybe we could have a picnic tomorrow?' Alice felt she needed to offer a compromise to counter the look of disappointment on her mother's face.

'That's even better because then I've got time to bake a cake and think of sandwich fillings. We'd best go shopping.'

'Now look what you've done,' said her dad good-naturedly as he batted her with his newspaper.

Alice was starting to think that perhaps she'd not fully thought through her idea when just ten minutes into their two-mile jaunt Cindy was already lying flat on the pavement and refusing to budge. 'Please walk,' she said, crouching down to the dog who simply huffed. 'I'll take that as a no then.' She looked around. She could carry her home. That was probably the smart thing to do but without the dog her plan didn't really work. Without the dog she was just a sad person stalking Dom and his family. With the dog she was just out on a casual walk and bumping into him by accident. Alice gave another gentle tug on Cindy's lead, but nothing happened. Across the road was a bus stop. Alice had another idea. She lifted Cindy into her arms and carried her over where she scanned the timetable. 'Blimey you've put on some weight.'

'Excuse me?' came a disgruntled voice behind her.

Alice spun around. 'Oh, Mrs Quinn, sorry. I didn't see

you there. I was talking to Cindy.' Mrs Quinn didn't look convinced. 'Do I know you?'

'I'm Alice, Mr and Mrs Pelling's daughter.'

Mrs Quinn's expression immediately softened. Alice was used to this, but it had been a while since she'd used it to her advantage. 'Goodness, Alice. I didn't recognise you. How are you, dear?'

'Fine thanks. Do you know what bus I need for Walton?'

'The ninety-seven which should be along in a few minutes. What are your plans in Walton?'

'I'm taking Cindy to the beach,' she said, turning the dog's bored face in Mrs Quinn's direction.

She recoiled slightly. 'How lovely.'

Thankfully the bus journey was uneventful. Cindy behaved herself and actually seemed to enjoy sitting on Alice's lap and looking out of the grubby bus window as the world whizzed by in dirt-smudged focus. When they got off Alice carried Cindy down to the prom and a little way along until Butterfly Café was visible. This was the location of the last Instagram post from Dom, so it made a logical starting point. All Alice and Cindy had to do was wander around the vicinity until they spotted them – simple.

However, Cindy had other ideas. She wanted to get on the beach, so they went down the concrete steps. Over the years the sand had been eroded and now Alice couldn't see up onto the promenade. Cindy barked at a seagull. Perhaps the beach was a more likely location for a family, anyway. Alice conceded to the dog and they strolled along the sand. Cindy spotted a flock of gulls ahead and with a burst of energy worthy of a much younger dog she gave chase, pulling the lead from Alice's hand. 'Cindy, wait!' called Alice as she sprinted after her. It took a good five minutes to get Cindy back, by which time they were both out of breath. At least Cindy was walking which was a definite improvement. But it wasn't long before Cindy was lying down on the sand and giving Alice her best puppy-dog eyes. 'You're old, I get it,' said Alice. She scanned the shoreline. There were a few families gathered around picnic rugs and behind windbreaks but no sign of Dom. 'Let's walk along the beach until we're level with the café and then we'll go home. Deal?' Alice asked Cindy. The dog huffed out a breath. 'Fine, I'll carry you, but I swear if I see him you're back on four legs.' Alice lifted Cindy into her arms and marched off across the sand and that was when it happened.

Chapter Twenty

Nancy slept better, she wasn't sure whether that was down to her previous lack of sleep, sea air or the brandy Freddy added to her chocolate. The brandy was definitely something she was going to have in her hot chocolate again as it was a very moreish combination. Breakfast was in the dining room which was another new room to Nancy and housed an enormous table and umpteen chairs and very little else.

Oscar pulled out seats for her and Louisa before quickly sitting down himself. Nancy didn't want to make any assumptions, but Oscar did seem fit and healthy which made her wonder about the reasons behind him wanting to hand over the estate early to Freddy. The whole thing made her curious. This was certainly a lot to be handing over – the house was vast, the gardens covered a large chunk of Devon and it had its own beach. As her parents rented a council flat on an iffy London estate *her* inheritance wouldn't amount to much. But she was okay with that. Her parents hadn't had an easy life so she was pleased when they treated themselves, although they weren't able to do that often. One day she hoped she'd be able to help them a bit so they didn't struggle. Her mum and dad had been saving for such a long time to take the holiday they were currently enjoying and she didn't know anyone who deserved it more.

Nancy scanned the table. Despite its size it was set for four with shiny cutlery and what she guessed were antique plates. Oscar poured them all coffee and the three of them sat in silence for a bit.

'I absolutely adore a fry-up on a Sunday,' said Oscar, rubbing his hands together.

'Don't worry, Nancy. You don't have to clog *your* arteries though,' said Louisa.

'I love a bacon buttie,' said Nancy.

'That's my kind of woman,' said Oscar. 'None of this vegan substitute nonsense. If you like bacon eat bacon. If you like vegetables eat those but don't process a bean into something that looks like rashers but tastes like seasoned cardboard.'

Nancy wasn't sure what to say so was thankful for the interruption of the door opening.

'Morning,' said Freddy, coming in with Otto and Carrie trotting behind him like Dr Dolittle.

Nancy immediately got to her feet. 'I'm sorry. Come on, Carrie, you can't be in here.'

'She's fine,' said Louisa. 'We're terribly lax and have very few boundaries with the dog. Bring her over and introduce me.'

'Okay.' Nancy felt like she was presenting a gift to the queen as she picked up the cat and took her over.

'What an absolute beauty.' Louisa scratched Carrie's head as she lay in Nancy's arms – the very epitome of a teddy bear. 'And what's their name?'

'Carrie,' said Nancy, feeling quite proud.

'That's unusual, where's it from?' asked Louisa.

'I'm guessing *Sex and the City*,' said Freddy, taking a seat and pouring himself a coffee.

'Actually,' said Nancy, instantly disgruntled by his assumption, 'she's named after Carrie Chapman Catt.'

'Don't tell me, I know this.' Louisa started clicking her fingers, her eyes tight shut. 'Carrie Catt was a suffragette,' said Louisa, her eyes popping wide open. 'Am I right?'

'Yes. She was an American women's suffrage leader who campaigned for the right of American women to vote. Most people don't get the reference,' said Nancy. She'd spent a number of hours googling until she'd found something she felt was fitting her ballsy little kitten.

'How clever.' Louisa tickled Carrie's tummy. 'Your mummy is very smart, isn't she?'

Nancy gave her best smug look at Freddy, who pushed out his lip and conceded a nod of approval.

While Louisa and Oscar cooed over Carrie, Nancy mouthed at Freddy, 'Have you told them you're fired?'

Freddy's eyes widened. 'Not yet. And I resigned,' he mouthed back.

Nancy didn't like the deception and much preferred to face things head on. 'Freddy, have you had a chance to speak to your p—'

'Good morning,' said Paul, striding into the room. 'What would everyone like for breakfast?'

Nancy put the cat down and Carrie trotted over to the window. Everyone gave Paul their orders and he disappeared, returning them to silence. Nancy went to open her mouth, but Freddy looked pleadingly at her. 'Please don't,' he mouthed. Maybe she could give him a bit longer.

'What happens here on a Sunday?' asked Nancy. She'd assumed her usual routine of big shop, long bath and preparing for work on Monday in her pyjamas wasn't happening. She felt like she'd been away from work for ages.

'We go to the church in the village,' said Louisa. 'You're very welcome to join us.'

Nancy hadn't been to church since her mum's old neighbour died a couple of years ago.

'It's okay,' said Freddy. 'You don't have to come.'

That was all the incentive she needed. 'I'd love to come, thank you.'

Paul arrived with the breakfasts and Nancy concentrated on eating hers with one hand and not dribbling ketchup down her chin.

Oscar shared out a sausage under the table between the cat and dog and Louisa pretended she hadn't noticed until Carrie started mewing and clawing at Louisa's legs.

'Ouch,' said Louisa as Carrie dug her claws in. Nancy went to stand up but Louisa held up a hand to stop her.

'Oscar! That's your fault,' said Louisa, carefully picking up Carrie and putting her on her lap. Carrie's head popped up above the table.

'I'm in trouble again,' said Oscar with a wink. He finished his breakfast. 'Right, I'll drive. See you all out the front in say twenty minutes?' He left the room.

'Mother, you need to do something,' said Freddy, putting down his cutlery.

'Believe me I've tried,' said Louisa, standing up and putting Carrie on her chair.

As they filed out of the room Freddy's phone lit up. 'Hello, Uncle Dickie,' he said.

'Ask him about the contract,' whispered Nancy as Freddy stepped back to let them past. Louisa carried on but Nancy hovered the other side of the door and listened in on Freddy's conversation.

'Something came up . . .' said Freddy. 'I know Arabella was expecting me but . . . Sure . . . I will be there. Okay . . . Yes . . . Bye.'

Freddy walked through the door and was a little startled

to see Nancy waiting for him. 'You didn't ask him?' Nancy was puzzled. 'Why didn't you ask him?'

Freddy scrunched his shoulders up. 'Don't get angry, there's a reason.'

'Which is what exactly?' Nancy waved her arm in a circle in the hope of speeding him up.

'Because I know the answer already.' Freddy's head dropped to his chest before he raised it again and eyeballed her. 'There's not going to be a contract with All Things Crafty.'

'What? Why? What?'

'I spoke to Uncle Dickie a couple of days ago and he said he never offered you a contract. He said you must have got confused.'

'Confused! *I* got confused? He's the one who offered me a contract in exchange for employing you and then has been dodging the deal ever since.'

Freddy waved for her to keep her voice down. 'Did he though?'

'Yes,' said Nancy firmly, although seeds of doubt were rapidly growing into weeds of realisation. 'I was heading down to the tube and I didn't catch all the conversation but I'd pitched to him a few days before and our products are great but he'd turned me down so when he called I . . .'

'Assumed it was about a contract,' said Freddy, filling in the rest.

Nancy's shoulders slumped. 'So there never was a contract?' She looked up at Freddy for confirmation.

'No. I'm afraid not.'

Nancy took a breath. 'Hang on. And you knew this when?'

'Ah.' Freddy seemed to realise his mistake. 'I probably should have mentioned it.'

'You think?' Nancy was so cross she feared she may

spontaneously combust. 'Bloody hell, Freddy. You should have told me. There was a lot riding on that contract.' More than he could ever understand.

*   *   *

Alice hadn't felt that sensation for such a long time. A discomfort in her chest that contained the threat of pain. Her heart was thumping rapidly. She needed to rest. There was a spot of shade by a gnarled and seaweed-covered breakwater where she flopped down, making Cindy land unceremoniously on the sand. As if sensing there was something wrong the dog pawed at Alice's shorts. 'It's okay,' she said in a small voice. Alice closed her eyes and concentrated on her ragged breathing. If she could get that back under control perhaps her heart would join in. She took deep breaths in through her nose and out through her mouth. Her heart was still pounding like she was running a marathon. Alice had a decision to make. If she called her parents, it would worry the life out of them, but then again if she called an ambulance and they called her parents that wasn't much better. The only other option was to sit still and hope her heart calmed down on its own.

As if making the decision for her, Cindy got on her lap, curled up and settled down for a nap. *Animals were meant to be calming, weren't they?* thought Alice as she gently stroked her fur. Alice opened her eyes to see if anyone had noticed but everyone else on the beach was carrying on regardless. A small child was singing to herself as she skipped by with a bucket, a mum and dad were having a crafty cuddle behind a windbreak while a small boy was having a wee on the other side. And another family were arguing over who had eaten the last of the cheese and pickle sandwiches. Nobody had noticed the young woman slumped against the breakwater.

After a few minutes the uncomfortable sensation in her chest eased although she was still short of breath and her heart still thought she was being chased by an axe murderer. The barnacles on the wood were digging into Alice's back and doing goodness only knew what to her favourite T-shirt. She took a few steadying breaths. The simple fact was that she couldn't spend the rest of the day where she was. For one thing the tide was on the way in and drowning was not how she wanted to die. Not bringing a drink wasn't a smart move either as the sun was beating down. She looked over her shoulder at the café. It was really close. If she could make it up the steps there was a little oasis of shade, seating and somewhere she could buy a bottle of water.

Alice took her time to sit up straight and very gradually move from sitting to kneeling. The whole time she was paying close attention to her pulse and her breathing to ensure it didn't worsen. Cindy was not happy at being turfed off Alice's lap. Alice got to her feet as slowly as she could but still she had that horrid faint feeling come over her. She held onto the breakwater for a moment until it eased. Alice locked her sights on the café and slowly made her way up the beach. The sand that had seemed soft and undulating before was now the hardest thing to walk on as it shifted with every footstep. She made it to the steps and held onto the handrail while she dragged in air like an old lady. This wasn't fun and she was starting to panic. Usually episodes didn't last as long as this but then in the past she'd not been out alone in the midday sun when they'd happened.

A gull squawked above them which got Cindy's attention. She barked and then made a dash up the steps dragging Alice with her. She daren't let her run off again because she knew she'd never be able to catch her in her current condition. Apart from the pain returning to her chest Alice was almost grateful for the impetus the dog had given her to get up onto the promenade. She made the few strides across and sat down hard on a plastic chair. She wrapped Cindy's lead around the arm in a rough knot as she gasped for breath. She dug her hand in her shorts pocket and pulled out her phone. She had run out of options.

'Miss Pelling! It is you! It is!' shouted Bonnie as she ran to greet her.

Alice looked up to see a delighted-looking Dom approaching her. *Yep, that is literally the last person I wanted to see*, she thought as everything around her turned to black.

Chapter Twenty-One

Nancy had left breakfast hopping mad that she'd lost the All Things Crafty contract. Although Freddy said that according to his Uncle Dickie there never had been an offer of a contract, she still felt swindled and right now Freddy was in the firing line. Her anger and upset was also driven by the reality that she was fast running out of ways to save her company. It was like she moved from one lifeboat to another and each one had a leak.

Knowing looks were exchanged between Freddy and his mother making her wonder what else was going on that she knew nothing about. Freddy crossed his fingers as they got in the Land Rover and Oscar revved up the engine. Freddy quickly plugged in Nancy's seatbelt before jumping in the passenger seat and grabbing hold of a handle near his head.

'Hold on tight,' said Oscar, looking at Nancy via the rear-view mirror. 'Tally ho!'

The Land Rover skidded away from the house and across the gravel driveway but instead of heading down the tree-lined drive, Oscar veered off. The vehicle bounced over a grass verge down a small slope and started off across the fields scattering confused-looking sheep in all directions.

Oscar picked up speed as he headed for a mound. 'Shitting hell!' said Nancy.

'My thoughts exactly,' said Lady Louisa, as the vehicle was launched into the air and landed with a bounce. Nancy was sure her teeth were rattled loose.

Oscar drove along the edge of a field with two wheels up on a ridge, so the car was tilted at a precarious angle and Nancy hoped her seatbelt was in properly because it was the only thing stopping her sliding along the seat and crushing Louisa who was pushed up against the window.

Oscar suddenly turned the car to point it across an empty field. For a moment Nancy was pleased to be returned to a normal level but as she looked ahead, she could see that although the field was just grass pasture it had likely once been ploughed because there were a series of undulations going from left to right. Oscar put his foot down and the car took off. It went over the bumpy surface with ease, but it was a lot like being on a rollercoaster without the security of a full harness or safety bar.

After a few more minutes of extreme off-roading they joined a rough path, went over a cattle grid and reached a high gate between two imposing pillars. The gates opened and Oscar waved a hand at the camera mounted above as they drove through sedately. Oscar was humming away happily. All his passengers were shocked into silence. They trundled down the side of the church and into the car park.

'How much fun was that?' asked Oscar, twisting in his seat to eyeball Nancy.

Fun wasn't how she would have described the trip, but it had taken her mind off the non-existent contract. 'I think I might walk back,' said Nancy, and everyone fell about laughing.

Church wasn't what she'd been expecting – it wasn't the sombre, dusty affair she remembered. For a start there were quite a few people in the pretty little church. The vicar was funny and everyone joined in with singing the hymns, two of which Nancy knew. Oscar was belting them out. Freddy rolled his eyes at him, but it was lovely to see the obvious affection they had for each other. Oscar had got chatting to someone after the service, so Freddy seized the chance to drive them back and thankfully he took the route via the village on actual roads. It was proper picture postcard with higgledy-piggledy cottages and a thatched pub.

Back at the hall Freddy made himself scarce and Louisa went off to discuss dinner with Mrs Mason, leaving Nancy wondering what to do with herself for the rest of the day. She liked Langham Hall but she had an ailing business back in London that she didn't like being away from. Still, she'd be back there tomorrow so she decided she may as well make the most of the break, because she wouldn't be having another one anytime soon. Nancy perused the bookshelves in the library. There were some beautifully bound books but nothing that was really up her street. She only read on holiday and then it was whatever was on offer at the airport.

Carrie was curled up asleep in the snug with her faithful hound next to her. Nancy sat down in a big old leather chair and when Carrie came to join her Otto followed. The cat curled up on Nancy's lap, Otto sat gazing at Carrie with his chin on the arm of the chair.

Nancy was pondering her limited options of what to do to occupy herself when Freddy marched past the doorway, stopped and reversed to put his head around the door. 'Ah, Blofeld, I've been expecting you,' he said, pointing at Nancy with the fluffy cat on her lap. 'Everything all right?' he asked.

Nancy pouted as she tried to banish the image of Freddy

dressed as James Bond. 'I'm thinking about firing the laptop up.'

'You promised you'd rest.' Freddy wagged a finger.

'But I'm bored.' *And I need to work out a new rescue mission for Having A Ball*, she added in her head.

Freddy rolled his lips together as if considering something. 'I'll be back in two minutes.'

As he turned around Nancy noticed he was carrying a suit carrier. 'You off somewhere?' she asked.

'No. Change of plan.' He gave her a coy smile and disappeared.

* * *

Alice was having a lovely dream. Dom was lying next to her in bed whispering her name. Then he started to shout and that wasn't nearly as nice. Then Bonnie joined in which was downright weird.

'Miss Pelling don't die!' sobbed Bonnie. Alice's eyes snapped open, but it was a few moments before things came into focus.

'Alice, it's Dom, can you hear me?' Dom's worried face loomed into view.

'You're lovely,' said Alice, her voice sounding distant.

'What did she say?' asked a grey-haired woman.

'You're not dead,' said Bonnie, giving her a big hug and blocking out everything.

'Bonnie, give Al . . . Miss Pelling some space.'

'Ambulance is ten minutes away,' said the woman. All the voices were jumbling together and making Alice's head pound.

'Ambulance?' Alice started to come round. 'No, I'm fine.' The pain in her chest had eased and her breathing wasn't as bad. It was funny how fainting made her whole body relax and sometimes improved the situation.

'Can she sit up?' asked the woman.

'I don't think she should,' said Dom.

What had happened began coming back to Alice like pieces of a puzzle. She'd been stalking Dom, but she'd not been able to find him. She'd been on the beach with Cindy.

'Where's Cindy?' asked Alice, trying to sit up.

'Who's Cindy?' asked Dom.

But a gruff bark near her head answered her question. She looked over her shoulder to see Bonnie holding onto Cindy's lead and it made her smile.

'Hello, Bonnie,' said Alice.

Poor Bonnie's face was puffy and tear-stained. Alice put on her best smile. 'I'm okay now, honest.'

'Do you want this ambulance or not? The NHS is stretched as it is without people like you messing them about,' said the grey-haired woman.

'Hey,' said Dom. 'She's got severe heat stroke and if she needs an ambulance then—'

'No ambulance, please,' said Alice, reaching for him and clutching his hand.

'Are you sure? I mean, no offence or anything, but you don't look great.'

Not exactly how she'd hoped their meeting would go. Alice remembered the whole reason she'd been stalking him. 'I'm fine. You need to get back to your wife.'

Dom's eyebrows pulled tighter. 'I think you're still confused.'

'What about this ambulance?' barked the woman.

'No!' chorused Alice and Dom together, making Bonnie giggle.

'Thank you,' added Alice. Manners didn't cost anything.

'I don't know these people,' said the woman, followed by a series of tuts before she explained into her mobile that the ambulance was no longer required.

'What I need is a nice cup of tea,' said Alice.

'Are you staying near here?' he asked.

The worried faces of her parents swam into her mind. 'It's a couple of miles away.'

'Then you'd best come back to our caravan,' said Dom.

'Oh no. I don't want to interrupt your holiday.'

'We were heading back for lunch anyway so it's not interrupting. And I can't leave you like this.' Alice's wasted heart swelled at the care he was showing her. 'I'm not taking no for an answer.'

'Okay then. Thank you, that's really kind,' she said.

'Yes,' squealed Bonnie excitedly. 'We can play frisbee!'

'No, sweetheart,' said Dom. 'Miss Pelling needs to rest up for a bit, but you can show her your new treasures.'

'I love treasure,' said Alice.

Dom leaned into her ear. 'It's rubbish she won at the arcade yesterday so don't get your hopes up.' He leaned back and scanned her over in a way that made her feel exposed. 'Do you think you can stand up if I give you a hand?'

'I think so.'

Dom put his arms around her waist and carefully lifted her to her feet. She felt safe in his arms but her legs appeared to have turned to rubber, so it was a good thing that he deposited her on a plastic chair. 'Take your time and then we'll head off. My car is on the seafront so it's a short stroll up that path. We'll have you back to the caravan in no time, you can lie down there.'

Alice started to see her stalking was a bad idea. She'd selfishly been thinking about what she needed, which was to draw a line under the whole silly Dom crush thing without considering the problems it could cause for Dom. She could not disrupt this family's holiday. The last thing

Alice wanted to do was to cause any issues for him. 'Dom, but won't your partner mind?'

Dom did a slow blink. 'As I've not heard from her for over a year, I think she'll be fine about it.'

Chapter Twenty-Two

Nancy hadn't expected to spend her Sunday afternoon playing board games with Freddy and Grandpa. And what was an even bigger surprise was that she'd enjoyed it. Freddy had returned to the snug with an armful of battered boxes and his grandfather. Some of the games she hadn't even heard of, but Freddy was good at explaining the rules. Grandpa seemed to have forgiven Nancy for the incident at the beach hut and was soon dealing cards with his arthritic hands. He was surprisingly competitive. It was lovely to see the old man come to life and relish the triumph of beating his younger opponents. Nancy suspected there were few things these days that Grandpa was able to beat his grandson at.

'Now I've thoroughly thrashed you whipper snappers I'm off for my nap,' said Grandpa.

'One more game?' Freddy looked at his opponents who both shook their heads.

Grandpa leaned towards Nancy. 'Don't feel pressured to play with him. He's been playing with himself since he was a small boy.'

'I bet he has,' said Nancy with a smirk.

Freddy shook his head at Nancy but he was smiling. 'Come on, Grandpa,' he said, helping him to his feet. The old man's knees creaked in protest but he waved away further help, squeezed Freddy's shoulder affectionately and left the room.

'Sorry,' said Freddy. 'I should have warned you he's a demon at Scrabble.'

'It's nice that his mind is that sharp at his age. I lost my nan to Alzheimer's years before she died.'

'I'm sorry, that's a cruel disease.'

'I guess I thought she was indestructible, so it was tough to watch her fade away.'

'Life doesn't always pan out how we expect,' said Freddy. 'My life was mapped out from day one.' Freddy had a hard done by look about him that instantly irked Nancy. 'As the sole heir to Langham Hall, I inherit, now earlier than planned, and I'm expected to run this place—'

'Bloody hell! I've lost the contract but as usual this is all about me signing off your six months work experience and you getting your own way.'

'I don't always get—'

'Yes you do!' snapped Nancy, her temper getting the better of her and her voice rising. 'You've had things your own way your whole life.'

'Is that what you think?' Freddy clenched his jaw.

'It's pretty obvious, Freddy. Look at this place. The family is obviously loaded. Your parents dote on you. You do what the hell you like when you like.'

'Do you see this?' He ran a finger over the scar through his eyebrow.

'Yes, was it your Jason Momoa phase? Or a battle with Voldemort?' She wouldn't have put it past Freddy to have had it done as some weird on-trend look.

'It's a real scar.' She could tell from his tone he was losing his patience. 'An incident with a horse.'

'Your pet pony was it?' Nancy couldn't hide her sarcasm.

'No, it was Mother's. He was a rescue stallion and she was trying to break him in but he bolted and threw her off. She broke her pelvis but all she was worried about was the horse. So I promised her I'd find him and bring him home. Only he had other ideas. I foolishly cornered him by an old barn on the far side of the estate and he reared up and well . . .'

'I'm sorry you got a hoof in the face but getting hurt doesn't mean you've not sailed through life.'

'If you let me finish,' said Freddy. 'He reared up and knocked me to the ground which was how I cracked my head on the concrete.' He pointed to his eyebrow. 'The horse then came down on my leg.' Freddy rolled up his trouser leg to reveal a large scar up the side of his calf. Nancy winced. 'But he was so freaked out he reared a few more times, each time landing on my legs, shattering my kneecap on this leg and my ankle on the other.'

'Shit,' said Nancy, not sure what else to say and unable to take her eyes off the maze of scarring across his legs.

'Until then I'd had a promising rugby career. I was captain of my university team and signed to the Saracens Academy. I had hopes of playing for England. But that all changed in the space of a few minutes.' Freddy rolled his trousers back down and Nancy pulled her eyes up to his face.

'I'm really sorry, Freddy. That must have been awful.'

'At the time not playing rugby was the least of my problems. I lay there for three hours before anyone found me. Then there were multiple operations. I was in a wheelchair for seven months which was a lot less than the medics predicted. But I waved goodbye to a rugby career and found myself with little else I was any good at.' For a moment he looked sorry for himself but he quickly lifted his chin. 'But I'm still here and we all have something in our past. Am I right?'

'I guess.' Nancy felt scolded. 'I'm sorry about what I said.'

Freddy shook his head. 'Actually, what you said is partially correct. I do come from a privileged background. I have been spoiled by a loving family. But my life hasn't been perfect.'

'I can see how being used as a trampoline by Black Beauty could mess it up a bit.'

'Thank you,' he said, displaying an air of vulnerability she'd not seen before.

'You're welcome. Truce?' Nancy offered her hand to shake.

'What do we do about the job?' he asked.

'We could tell your parents that you're useless and I've sacked you.'

'Ah the truth,' said Freddy with a wry nod.

'Or you could actually do the job.'

'Me work for you on a daily basis?' Nancy nodded. 'What's in it for you?' he asked.

'I desperately need a PA.'

'There's desperate and then there's foolhardy. There are much better personal assistants out there than me.'

'Oh definitely. Carrie would probably do a better job than you. She certainly types faster. But now I've met your mum and dad I get what they are trying to do. They want you to be ready to run this place. It's about you acquiring skills.'

'Is it?' Freddy looked doubtful and a little amused. 'I'm pretty sure it's about trying to curb my lifestyle.'

'That too. To be fair, Freddy, you have been taking the piss.'

He laughed. 'I can rely on you to say it how it is.'

'Always,' said Nancy. 'So do you want your job back or what?'

He took his time before answering. 'Can I have a week off for a polo tournament?'

'Absolutely not.'

'Great, I'll take it.'

*　*　*

Alice felt much better once she was sitting in Dom's car with the air conditioning on full pelt. By the time they had driven to the camping and caravan site Alice's breathing had steadied and her pulse was almost back to normal which was a huge relief. But possibly not as much of a relief as it was to discover that Dom didn't have a partner. He'd not elaborated on his statement that she'd been gone over a year but the fact he was currently unattached had made Alice feel a million times better. Clearly the school hadn't been informed that he was now a single parent.

'We're here!' announced Bonnie as Dom pulled up next to the caravan. 'Are you sure we shouldn't be at Accident and Emergency?' asked Dom, scanning Alice.

'I feel a lot better, honest.'

'Come inside,' said Bonnie, undoing her seatbelt and sticking her head between the seat rests. 'It's really cool, like a little house and we get to stay for a whole week,' she said.

'I'd love to come inside,' said Alice.

'Yay! Let me out, Daddy,' said Bonnie, already trying the door handle which Alice noted didn't budge thanks to child locks. He was a responsible dad, despite the late pick-ups.

When they entered the caravan Cindy made straight for the fire and curled up in front of it even though it wasn't on. 'Is it okay to bring a dog in?' she asked belatedly.

'Yeah. I've seen a few of them on site.'

'There's a place for them to do poos,' said Bonnie, screwing up her nose with disgust.

Alice was quite impressed with the caravan Dom was renting. Not just that it was modern with two bedrooms and two bathrooms but that it was tidy. Her experience of men, with the exception of her dad, was that they were innately messy creatures incapable of folding clothes or returning things to their place. Everything here was neat and tidy, hence he was happy to give her the tour which lasted all of two minutes. Bonnie was very excited to show Alice her bedroom and insisted on introducing her to all of her cuddly toys and there were a lot.

'This is Ellis,' said Bonnie, holding up a green teddy. 'He's best friends with Peanut.' Peanut was a toy sausage dog. 'I always cuddle Rabbit at night unless it's Bumble's turn then . . .'

'That's barely a quarter of them,' whispered Dom, his breath warm against her neck, making her shiver. 'She's got mountains of the things at home. Every one has its own name.' He rubbed his chin. 'Now I think about it I might have gone a bit overboard. Maybe spoiled her because of her mum . . .'

'Trust me, Bonnie is not a spoiled child. I'm a teaching assistant so I know.'

'And these are Pip, Archie, Cookie, John and Bacon,' machine-gunned Bonnie as she reached the end of the row and stood proudly next to her collection with her shoulders back.

'Wow. They are all fantastic. Who is your favourite?' asked Alice.

Bonnie wagged a finger. 'It's not fair to have favourites.'

'You're right. They're all lovely.'

'But I love Rabbit the most,' she said, before leading the

way out of the room. 'Can I have a biscuit, Daddy? Pleeeeeeease!'

'In a minute,' said Dom. He turned back to Alice. 'I think you should have a lie-down. You still don't—'

'Look great?' said Alice with a smile.

Dom seemed awkward. 'I was going to say you don't look back to your usual self.'

'Nice bullet dodging.'

'I thought so.' He shrugged his shoulders bashfully. 'Have a lie-down in my room and I'll bring you a cuppa.'

'And a biscuit,' yelled Bonnie.

'That'd be great. Thanks.' Alice was definitely feeling better.

Chapter Twenty-Three

Alice opened her eyes. She yawned, stretched and looked around the small, unfamiliar room. It took her a moment to remember exactly where she was. She was having a lie-down in Dom's caravan and must have gone straight to sleep. She glanced at the bedside cabinet where a biscuit sat next to a cup of tea with a film on the top. Alice reached out and touched the side of the mug, it was cold. How long had that been there? She checked her watch and then did a double take. It was just after three o'clock – her parents were going to be worried sick. She'd taken the dog out for a short stroll almost four hours ago.

'Dom!' she called and he appeared within a couple of seconds looking concerned.

'What's wrong?'

'The time. I need to get back to my parents.' Alice jumped off the bed but a head rush made her sit back down quickly.

'Whoa, you're going nowhere. Call them and explain that you got sunstroke, they'll understand.'

But it wasn't that simple. A quick glance at her phone told Alice she had a lot of messages and missed calls and there was no prize for guessing who they were from. 'I should probably just get home . . . I mean back to my parents' place.'

'Awwww,' said Bonnie, standing in the doorway. 'Daddy said you'd stay for tea and watch *Moana* with us.'

Alice raised an eyebrow for Dom's benefit, he'd put her in an awkward position. 'No. I said you could ask her, Bonnie, and it was up to her if she could stay.'

Bonnie scrunched up her shoulders. 'Oh yeah. But you do want to, don't you, miss?'

The truth was that she did. She did want to stay with them. 'Let me call my folks and then we'll see, okay?'

'Sure,' said Dom.

'Yay!' said Bonnie, clearly taking that as confirmation that Alice was staying.

Alice picked up her phone and was aware that they were still watching her. 'I'm just going to call them . . .'

There was a delayed reaction from Dom. 'Of course. Come on, Bonnie, let's check we picked up all the Play-Doh you dropped.'

'We did that already,' she said through a sigh.

Dom gave Alice a thumbs up as he reversed out of the door and shut it behind him. She could hear them chatting at normal volume on the other side, which meant they would be able to hear her clearly too, so she'd need to choose her words carefully with her parents. She dialled their number and her mother answered as soon as it was connected. 'Thank the Lord you're alive.'

'Mum, I'm fine. I just lost track of time.'

'But we've been calling and messaging. Your father was about to call the hospital. Why didn't you pick up?'

'I had it on silent, sorry,' said Alice.

'I thought your generation were on their mobiles all the time? It's been hours.'

'Sorry, I met up with a friend and we've been chatting.'

Her mother's tone instantly changed. 'Ooh which friend?'

'It's nobody you know. I'm going to get a bite to eat, watch a film and then I'll head back.'

'What about Cindy?'

'She's fine, she's been asleep most of the afternoon.' *Just like me*, thought Alice.

'Cindy won't like waiting for her tea.'

'I'll grab her some dog food from the shop,' said Alice.

'But she's on a special diet for her kidneys. And she always has her tea at four o'clock.'

Alice felt like she couldn't catch a break. 'Can't she wait until later for once?'

'But she's in a routine. I know, why don't you bring your friend here for dinner. I was going to do sausage and mash but there's not enough sausages to stretch to four because your dad insisted on having a sausage sandwich for lunch but I could make something else from the freezer. And we've got Netflix so you'll be spoiled for choice for films, it's amazing – they have literally any film or TV programme you can think of.'

Alice was silently screaming 'No!' at her phone. There was absolutely no way she was bringing Dom home to be interrogated by her parents and in turn have them parade her life story out. In fairness it was their story too as they had been with her every step of the way but now she was venturing through life on her own and while it was scary, it felt right. Part of this new chapter meant she could be a new Alice, not the girl her mum and dad constantly worried about. So no, she wouldn't be taking Dom home today. Although a little thought popped into her head that perhaps one day in the future she might be looking to introduce him to her parents but that was pure fantasy. Right now she needed to put a stop to her mother's plans. 'Netflix don't have Disney films,' said Alice.

'Disney? Aren't you a bit past that?'

Alice's shoulders tensed, she'd walked into that one. 'We just wanted something easy on the brain and you can't beat Disney for that.'

'Netflix has some great rom coms. There was this one I watched the other night with that chap out of the police thing with the—'

'Mum, I'll see if I can catch up with my friend another night this week and I'll bring Cindy home within the next hour for her tea. Okay?'

'But I can soon whip up a chilli con carne or bolognaise – everyone likes spag bol.'

'Really, it's fine, Mum. Stick with the sausage and mash.'

'Okay, love. If you're sure.'

Alice had never been more certain.

Alice had felt bad letting Bonnie down but a promise from both her and Dom that she would come to the caravan for dinner and *Moana* on Tuesday night had mollified her slightly and had given Alice something to look forward to. It was possibly even better because not only had she seen Dom today now she got to see him again in just forty-eight hours' time, not that she was counting.

Alice pointed out a few local sights on the way to her parents' home and offered some suggestions for places he and Bonnie might want to visit while they were staying in the area. When the sat nav announced they'd reached their destination Alice took over the directions.

'By that second lamppost on the left, number nineteen.'

Dom pulled up opposite. Bonnie was craning her neck from her booster cushion on the back seat to get a look at the property. 'Thanks for everything today,' said Alice.

'I'm sorry you were ill, but it's been really—'

A sharp rap on the driver's window made them all jump. Her dad made the motion of turning a handle in mid-air to indicate that Dom should put the window down. Alice couldn't remember a car without electric windows, but her dad still used this action.

'I need to go. Bye, Dom, bye, Bonnie. See you Tuesday.' Alice snatched up her phone and got out of the car, but she was too late to stop the inevitable as Dom was already buzzing down the window.

'Hi, Mr Pelling, I'm Dom.' He held a hand out of the car window and they shook.

'When Alice said a friend, I assumed it would be someone local,' said her father. Dom's accent had given him away.

'We're on holiday in Walton,' said Dom.

'Dad, can you give me a hand with Cindy.' She didn't need a hand, but she did need her dad to not interrogate Dom.

'Of course.' He moved to the car's back door and immediately clocked Bonnie.

'Hiya,' said Bonnie, bumping her legs against the car seat.

Alice's dad's expression went through a series of emotions including shock and unease. 'Hello,' he said and he offered the little girl a hand to shake. He wasn't really used to children.

'Dad, she's five, she doesn't shake hands. Come on. Bye, Bonnie.'

'Bye, Miss Pelling,' said Bonnie in a sing-song voice which made her dad do another double take. It didn't take a genius to work out how she knew Dom and his daughter.

* * *

Nancy packed the last of her things away, decided it was best not to carry them all herself and went in search of Freddy. She followed the sound of laughter out on to the terrace where the Astley-Davenports were all drinking red wine and chatting.

'Nancy! Marvellous. Pull up a chair. I bet you can answer this conundrum—'

'Actually, I was wondering what time we were leaving.' Nancy was looking at Freddy sipping his wine. She hoped he'd not had much if he was planning on driving all the way back to London.

'What *time*?' repeated Freddy. 'We haven't agreed on a day yet.'

'Err yes we did. We agreed today.' Nancy was aware that her tone was getting on the crabby side, so she took a breath. 'I need to be back in London for work tomorrow.'

Freddy looked confused. 'Really sorry, I somehow missed that brief. I thought we were staying here until your arm got better.'

'No way!' Everyone jolted at the force of Nancy's words. 'Sorry, I mean I simply cannot be away from the office for four weeks. And that would most definitely be over-staying my welcome.'

'Nonsense,' said Oscar. 'It's our pleasure. Stay as long as you like.'

Nancy forced a smile. 'Thank you.' She turned back to Freddy. 'As my personal assistant, you are very aware that we have a lot on right now. I'm afraid staying is out of the question.' Nancy tried to chivvy Freddy with her wide eyes.

Freddy winced and held up his almost empty glass. 'Whoops. This is my second, I won't be driving tonight.'

Nancy's jaw tightened. 'Then I'd best investigate the

trains.' She pulled out her phone. 'Where's the nearest station?'

'Oh, Nancy, please stay,' said Louisa. 'With all the changes it takes hours and hours by train and you don't want to struggle on public transport with your injured arm. I'm sure P—'

Freddy interrupted his mother. 'You know what? There's no reason why we can't work from here. There's plenty of space, we have a printer and you brought your laptop. How about we set up a satellite office from Langham Hall for the next week?'

Nancy was frowning at him. 'There you go, your PA has solved your problem,' said Oscar, looking quite proud. 'That means you can relax.' Oscar picked up a spare glass and poured her some wine.

Nancy was torn. She'd already had a whole weekend off, she wasn't used to this much free time. Her life revolved around her business. This was all quite unsettling. Oscar proffered the glass. Freddy pulled out a chair. Nancy desperately tried to think of another solution.

'I promise we'll be up bright and early tomorrow and whatever is on your to-do list, we'll get it done. Okay?' Freddy was giving her earnest eyes.

At last Nancy took the glass. 'Thank you.' She sat on the edge of the seat and sipped her wine.

Louisa and Oscar resumed their conversation. Freddy leaned forward, placing a hand on her arm, the contact making the hairs on her arm stand to attention. 'This is the part where you relax.'

Nancy awkwardly shuffled back in her seat and tried to move her shoulders down from their 'to attention' position. It wasn't easy.

Two glasses of wine later and Nancy found she was quite enjoying herself. They were exchanging funny stories and Nancy was finally starting to relax. 'I learned my lesson the time I chopped chillies and then blew my nose without washing my hands.'

'Ouch, that must have stung,' said Louisa.

'It did. But as my dad pointed out it was a good job I hadn't needed to wipe my bum.' Thankfully everyone laughed.

Thanks to the top quality wine she woke up with no signs of a hangover and felt as fresh as a Greggs sausage roll. It felt weird to Nancy that it was Monday morning and she wasn't going into the warehouse. But as she struggled to get her top on she was grateful that someone else was making her breakfast and that she didn't have her usual commute. And while she hadn't liked the idea of not working over the weekend she did feel rejuvenated. She wouldn't go as far as to say that Freddy had been right, but perhaps she had been overdoing things for a while.

She'd been mulling over what Freddy had told her about his accident and how his dreams of being a rugby player had been shattered. She'd often thought that money solved most problems, but this was one situation where throwing cash at it didn't change anything. She knew what it was like to be focused on something and then have a nasty reality check. Nancy had dreamed of being the first person in her family to go to university and despite putting in the effort she'd not got the A level results she needed. She'd been devastated at the time, but she'd had to get over her disappointment and come up with a new plan. And that was how she'd come up with her business venture. Nancy had had little choice but to get a job at the local corner shop and work her way out of the council estate. She'd worked a number of jobs while she'd been researching the market and building the knowledge she needed to run her own business. She'd had no Uncle Dickie to tap up for favours. It had been a long journey but she'd turned things around after her setback.

Freddy's response to his life-changing moment appeared to be to have no focus in life other than partying, because unlike normal people who have their dreams shattered, he didn't have to get on with it anyway. He could fill his life with fun and frivolity. However much she was warming to Freddy, there was no getting away from the fact that they were from vastly different backgrounds and because of that they were very different people. And Nancy wasn't a believer in opposites attract. In her experience opposites just pissed each other off.

Carrie had deigned to sleep on Nancy's bed rather than with her new best mate Otto. Carrie rolled onto her back and presented Nancy with her fluffy tummy. The cat seemed to be enjoying her holiday too.

Nancy picked up her laptop bag and went down to find some breakfast with Carrie following her. She was beginning to get to know her way around some of the manor house and could at least find her way to the kitchen unaided. She picked Carrie up so that she didn't dash in and contaminate anything.

'Morning, Paul,' she said, sticking a head around the door along with Carrie.

'Nancy, good morning. Would you like breakfast on the terrace?'

'That would be lovely, thanks. Just coffee and a croissant please.'

'I've got chicken cooling for Carrie,' he said. 'And Mrs Mason was wondering about poaching her a trout.'

Carrie was already sniffing the air. She meowed her response and wriggled. 'I think that's a yes please.'

'I'll take her down to the orangery for the morning and feed her there if that's okay with you?'

'You run a wonderful kitty crèche, Paul, and I'm very grateful.'

'My pleasure,' he said.

Nancy left Carrie pawing at the kitchen door and went through the ballroom and out onto the terrace. The sky was a rich azure blue with barely a cloud. Nancy got out her laptop and switched it on. She could smell the delicate scent of the flowers in the air and the warmth of the early sun on her skin. It was a lovely way to start the day. It was hard to see the screen outside so she was squinting at it when the doors opened and Freddy appeared in joggers.

'Are you working already?' he asked.

'Yep. And you start at nine remember. Even you can't be late when the commute is a few steps.'

'You'd be surprised,' said Freddy. 'But I won't be late. Quick run, shower and I'm all yours.' He gave her a cheeky grin and started down the steps.

'Where shall we set up office?'

Freddy was jogging away. 'I'd assumed the study,' he called back.

'Okay,' she shouted and then realised she had no idea where the study was.

Chapter Twenty-Four

After breakfast Nancy got directions from Paul and set off in search of the study. She must have miscounted the doors in the East Wing because she was pretty sure the first one she opened wasn't the study – or at least she very much hoped it wasn't. The room was in complete darkness, so Nancy felt around for a light switch.

'Argh!' she yelled as the light revealed a giant grizzly bear poised to attack her. It only took a moment to realise it was obviously stuffed but the message took a while to reach her heart which was thudding away. As Nancy looked around she saw that the bear was just the start of the horrors: the room was filled with taxidermy animals or parts thereof. Nancy gave a shudder, switched off the light and hoped the images wouldn't come back to freak her out in the early hours. She reversed out of the room as Carrie shot past her. 'Oh no, no, no!' But it was too late, the cat was in.

Nancy put the light back on, this time ready for the sight of the bear. Although it was still intimidating – the thing must have been over seven feet tall with open jaws and raised paws the size of frying pans. She wanted out of there and pronto.

'Carrie,' she called, followed by a series of kissing noises.

She crouched down and caught a glimpse of her disappearing behind a glass cabinet inside which were otters dressed for golf. She tried more calling and kisses but there was no sign of Carrie. Nancy crept further into the room, carefully manoeuvring herself around the mounted head of some deer-like creature with very long pointy horns. The place had an odd whiff about it too. Was it the smell of death? she wondered. She decided it was more likely dust.

She inched past a forlorn hyena and a series of glass cabinets containing all sorts of birds, most of which Nancy couldn't identify apart from the duck. She turned and came face to face with an ostrich. Its eyes seemed to fix on her. 'Carrie,' she whispered. This place was super creepy. She kept her gaze on the ostrich; it looked so real it wouldn't have surprised her if it had blinked. Nancy stepped to one side but her foot landed on something. A quick glance told her it was a tiger's paw, she gasped and pulled her foot up quickly, her knee hit a mounted badger which knocked over a penguin and sent it crashing to the floor.

'Shit!' Nancy automatically bent to pick it up and came face to face with the snarling tiger. Even though it was dead and apart from the head it was flattened like it had been steamrollered, it still gave her the heebie-jeebies. 'Don't be ridiculous,' she said to herself. She took a deep breath and reached for the penguin which Carrie must have been checking out and didn't appreciate it when the thing bopped her on the nose. With that Carrie leapt over the top of the tiger's head, momentarily landed on a crouching Nancy before exiting the room as if being chased by all the deceased creatures. The brief touch down on Nancy was enough to make her topple. 'Noooo!' she hollered as she fell backwards, her bum hitting the floor and her shoulder bumping into something behind her. Whatever it was tipped forward, thumping into her back before resting there. It was quite weighty and Nancy feared if she moved it would fall down completely. While Nancy hated this sort of thing she had no idea if it was worth a lot of money and didn't want to unintentionally trash something expensive.

Nancy took a breath and slowly looked upwards and behind her. All she could see was the inside of a giant mouth. 'Argh!' She needed to calm down. Whatever it was was dead, but the size of those teeth. What on earth had teeth like fence posts?

'What's this, life-size hungry hippos?' quipped Freddy, appearing at the door and making her jump again.

'Maybe you could help rather than take the piss?' suggested Nancy.

A grinning Freddy came in, moved the large front half of a hippopotamus off Nancy and helped her to her feet. Now she could see it from a different position it was obviously a hippo with its mouth open. 'These are all . . .' She wished she'd not started the sentence because she couldn't think how to end it without potentially insulting Freddy.

'Macabre? Sickening? Hideous?' he offered.

'Yes.' It was a relief that he shared her views. 'They're awful.'

'That's why they're all shut in here. They used to be on display in the trophy room. The 9th Earl was a big hunter and travelled far and wide to shoot innocent animals and yet he loved his greyhound so much he had the folly built in her honour. I can't quite equate the two differing attitudes to the same man. There's a certain irony that the Earl himself was shot dead in World War One. Anyway, what were you after in here?'

'My nosy cat.'

'Where is she?'

'She's long gone. She dashed off at high speed after a disagreement with a large penguin. Unfortunately, she pushed me over in the process. I'm really sorry if I've broken anything,' she said as Freddy began righting things.

'When you say broken anything?' Freddy was scanning Nancy from head to toe.

She held up her plaster. 'Not me. The glass cases with the stuffed remains of murdered woodland creatures. Sorry, I don't mean to be rude, this might be your family's special collection. I mean my gran had those porcelain dolls, they were creepy as hell but, you know, *she* liked them.' Nancy decided it was best if she stopped talking.

'It's fine. We're not fans of taxidermy, with the exception of Lionel.'

'Uh huh,' said Nancy, making her way out of the room. There were far too many eyes for her liking. And most of them were watching her.

'This guy used to scare the life out of me as a boy,' said Freddy, patting the giant bear before joining Nancy at the door. 'He's Wilbur, he's a Kodiak bear.'

'Thanks for scaring the crap out of me, Wilbur,' said Nancy.

Freddy laughed. 'The study is next door.' He opened the neighbouring door and stood back for Nancy to go in.

'Thanks, at least there are no stuffed . . . Holy Shit!' said Nancy, almost walking into a lion.

'Nancy meet Lionel.'

It took Nancy's heart rate a while to slow to a normal pace.

'Sorry,' said Freddy for the umpteenth time. 'I guess I'm used to Lionel.'

Nancy wasn't sure how you got used to the dead body of a ferocious creature sitting in your office but then it was just another example of how different they were. 'He is really beautiful.' She had to concede that it was quite something to see an animal like that up close. She'd always loved the big cats at London Zoo but they were usually lounging in the sun many metres from the viewing area. 'I just think they shouldn't be shot for pleasure. Again, not judging.' She held up one palm in defence.

'I agree,' said Freddy. 'Lionel here was twenty-three when he died of natural causes. That's quite an age for a lion. The 10th Earl, George Langham, my great-grandfather, was hunting in Africa with his father—'

'The 9th Earl,' said Nancy to show she'd been paying attention.

'Very good. Anyway, after George shot and killed a lioness he discovered that she had a cub. It affected him so much that lioness was the last thing he ever killed.' Freddy moved over to some black-and-white photographs on the wall and Nancy followed.

'George brought the cub back to England with him, named him Lionel and he lived here at Langham Hall.' Freddy tapped a series of photographs showing the lion sitting next to a man in Seashell Bay, lying on his back by the terrace steps and standing in the fountain.

'Bloody hell.'

'George loved Lionel and from all accounts the feeling was mutual. They used to eat the best steak together every Saturday. The Earl's was a little more well done than Lionel's. This lion had the best of everything.' Freddy smoothed the mane as he spoke. 'I know it wasn't the life he should have had but I like to think George did his best by him and turned over a new leaf in the process.'

'And then he had him stuffed,' said Nancy. 'Blimey, Lionel, what a life.'

'And he's had *pride* of place in here ever since,' said Freddy.

'Ouch.' She patted the lion on the head. 'I'm sure you were the *mane* man.'

'By all accounts a *roaring* success,' said Freddy.

'Right, well we need to get working rather than *lion* down on the job.'

'That was truly awful,' said Freddy.

'Thank you. Personally, I think it was some of my best pun work. Talking of work. You need to learn how to do some.' Nancy pointed at the large desk near the window. They both went to sit in the overly large chair at the same time and almost ended up on the floor. Freddy grabbed Nancy to stop her falling and in that moment she could see why so many women were attracted to him.

* * *

Alice put off going downstairs for as long as possible. But when her stomach began growling its complaints, she decided she needed to face her parents. The previous evening had been like the Spanish inquisition but with slightly more questions – there was nobody better equipped than a concerned parent for interrogation. But she'd managed to dodge the worst of it by yawning, feigning tiredness and dashing up to her room: it had been a lot like her teenage years.

But now she was an adult so things should be different, right? She didn't have to explain herself to her parents or hide in her room. She could do what she liked, go where she wanted and see anyone she chose to. Although it was one thing to think it and another to convince her parents.

Alice took a deep breath, sneaked out of her room and got two-thirds of the way down the stairs before a creaky step gave her away and both her parents appeared at the kitchen doorway. Rumbled.

'Good afternoon,' said her dad with a smile. So far so normal.

'Did you sleep well?' asked her mum. Alice was instantly suspicious.

'Okay, thanks.' She sidled past them and had made it as far as the cereal bowl cupboard before they started.

'The man who brought you home last night, he's a parent from your school is he?' asked her mum.

Here we go, thought Alice. 'His name is Dom. And, yes, he is a parent but I didn't meet him through school. We met at a club.'

'He was out clubbing when he has a young child.' Her mum was radiating judgement.

'Even single parents are allowed a night off on their birthday.' Alice sat down at the table and poured some cereal. 'What are you two doing today?'

'Gardening,' said her dad. 'Is it serious with this fella?' he asked.

'Daaaad!' She shook her head. 'We're just friends. That's all.' Which was probably true and the thought made Alice feel a little sad. Why was life so complicated?

'But you arranged to meet up.' Her dad leaned a little forward which made Alice feel tense.

'Not exactly.' She'd never been any good at lying. Her mum always knew anyway so it was pointless trying. But she'd give it her best effort. 'We just bumped into each other.' She scooped up a large spoonful of Coco Pops. That would at least give her a moment's thinking time.

213

Although staring at the bowl just made her wonder how long her parents had had the same dinner service. At least twenty years she reckoned.

'But he said he was staying in Walton.' Her dad's forehead was more creased than usual.

'Oh my goodness,' said her mother, her hands shooting to her face. 'You didn't walk poor Cindy all the way there did you? That's miles. It could have killed her.'

'No. I took the bus.'

Her dad lifted his head and narrowed his eyes. 'You took the dog on a bus to Walton and you just happened to bump into this Dom.' Alice decided her dad would make a very good TV detective.

Alice shrugged. Her mum's head tilted to one side. 'Alice, you went following the poor man.' She gasped. 'You're a stalker!'

Alice let her spoon clatter into her bowl. 'I'm not a stalker. He posted some photos on Instagram. I thought I recognised where he might be and I hadn't been there for a while so I took Cindy over there. That's all.' Even to her own ears it made uncomfortable listening. Cindy groaned disapprovingly from her dog bed.

'I think going out of your way to track someone down without notifying them first is the very definition of a stalker,' said her dad. 'I knew no good would come from watching *Hollyoaks*,' he muttered as he retreated behind his newspaper.

'I'm shocked,' said her mum, switching on the kettle and reaching for a mug with a shaking hand.

The worst part of it all was that Alice felt the same, apart from the *Hollyoaks* comment – she'd not hear a bad word said about her favourite programme.

Chapter Twenty-Five

Nancy and Freddy were sharing the huge desk in the study – one on either side. Its leather inlay was worn bare in places, she assumed by countless generations of Astley-Davenports, making her marvel at the amount of history surrounding her. She knew nothing about her family tree, only that Great-Uncle Gerry had once stolen an ice cream van but because he couldn't switch off the music he'd been tracked down in record time.

Freddy had found a chair and fired up his own personal laptop and was going to use that for now as his company one was back at Having A Ball. Nancy found it was a little distracting having him sitting opposite her but she'd had worse views – she'd once worked for a bathroom company and her desk had been surrounded by toilets. The study was small compared to the other rooms in Langham Hall but was still about the size of her living room with dark wood panelling to the bottom half of its walls, an ornate ceiling that rose above them and a pretty view of the gardens out of the window.

She watched Freddy hunting in a drawer for a pen and noticed the scar on his eyebrow. Nancy had been pondering Freddy's situation with his accident and not being able to fulfil his dreams of rugby stardom. 'Have you talked to anyone about the impact of your accident?' she asked.

'Do you mean someone professional?'

'Yeah, a shrink.'

He smiled. 'I've not felt the need to see a psychiatrist.'

'What about a life coach?' she asked. 'Someone to talk through your other options.'

'I think I'm past the point of careers advice.'

Nancy saw that as a challenge. 'Really? I disagree. Let's have a look at what you're good at.' Freddy blinked but said nothing. 'This is where you tell me all the things you excel in,' she said, opening a new document on her computer.

'This may be a very short list.'

'This is not the time to be modest.'

He tipped his head. 'Was there a veiled insult in there, Miss Barraclough? Are you saying I lack modesty?'

'I think you know me well enough to know I'm not big on soft-soaping. I think you are used to people being impressed by your family's name, heritage and bank balance. I'm not sure you're used to looking internally for reasons to impress people.'

'Hmm quite insightful.'

'I know, right?' She winked. 'Off the top of your head tell me ten things you're good at.' Freddy smirked. 'That are not of a sexual nature,' she added quickly.

'That does narrow things down somewhat, but I'll try.' He pouted. 'Ten?'

'Yep.' Nancy had a finger poised over her keyboard. This could be useful for showing his parents where he started and hopefully what he had picked up by the end of the six months.

'I'm a good driver, I did carting for a while but was outclassed. And then there's polo.'

'I'm guessing not the little round mints.'

'No but I am very good at eating sweets if that's a skill. I once ate three Creme Eggs in one go.'

'I'm impressed but I'm not adding it to the list. Eight more things. Anything less sporty?'

Freddy closed his eyes. 'Talking – I can generally chat to most people. Umm I can't think of anything else.'

'I don't want this to sound judgemental but what do you do all day?'

'A little judgemental, but anyway. I run, it's important to keep the strength in my legs to support my knee and ankle. I meet up with friends.'

'And drink.'

'Not always. I'm more reserved than you'd think. If it's a party I'll have alcohol but otherwise I don't,' he said.

'Okay. What else do you do?'

'Riding. But that's about it. You can see why I'm unemployable. And please don't tell them but I have to admit, now we've done this quite frankly pitiful list, I can see where my parents are coming from.'

'Don't get hung up on it. It's just a starting point.' Nancy scrolled to a new page. 'What skills do you need to run the estate?'

'I'm not sure it needs skills as such. It's a giant white elephant that has Father stressed out most of the time. There's always something that needs doing. Something or someone to worry about.'

'I take from that you'd need to be able to prioritise and analyse issues, find solutions and manage them through to resolution. To do that you'd need to be organised, analytical and persistent.'

'I'm none of those things,' said Freddy.

'Ahh,' said Nancy, wagging a finger. 'But you can learn all of those skills and this job is a great start.'

'I'm not sure I believe you, but I love your endless optimism.'

'Just one of my many skills,' said Nancy. 'Right, let's get you to work.'

Having given up on voice recognition Nancy was trying to dictate an email to Freddy. When his phone rang for the third time, he switched it off but not before she noted that it was someone named Arabella calling.

'She's persistent,' said Nancy. Freddy started typing. 'No that's not for the email. I meant the caller. She doesn't give up easily.'

'Oh, I see.' He deleted the letters. 'No, she's certainly tenacious.'

Nancy was dying to ask if Arabella was his girlfriend, but it was none of her business. They carried on with the emails but Nancy couldn't shake her curious mind into submission. She tried to focus on their last month's sales figures and produce a chart with one hand while Freddy worked through the list of tasks she'd given him, and as far as she could tell he was getting on with them. An email popped up from Claudia which made her snort a laugh. Freddy looked up. 'Are you all right?'

'The email you sent to Claudia about explaining the invoicing process to you.'

'What about it?' asked Freddy.

'You might want to proofread your emails. Your one to Claudia starts – "I know you're busty but . . ."' Nancy stopped short of giggling.

'Bugger it,' said Freddy. 'Is she offended?'

'Not so much by that as, to be fair, it is factually correct, but I think she's baffled by a couple of other things where you say further down that you've ordered more strong drugs for Filip and if she had anything for you to do that she should piss it over.'

'*Storage drums* for Filip and *pass* it over.'

'Yeah, I guessed.'

Freddy ran his hands through his hair. 'It's a minefield.'

'It can be,' said Nancy, trying hard not to laugh. 'Just have a quick read through before you press send.'

Freddy nodded. 'Thanks. I'll do that. And I'll message Claudia now to apologise.'

They both went back to what they were doing, Nancy with a big grin on her face as she was still thinking about Freddy's typos, when there was a knock on the door. Freddy and Nancy looked at each other as if both unsure as to who should respond.

'Yep, come in,' said Nancy, feeling a bit uncomfortable. She'd never been that sort of boss.

Paul came in holding a phone which he was partially covering with his other hand. 'I'm sorry to interrupt but I have Arabella on the line. She's concerned that you're not picking up or returning her calls.' Nancy marvelled at how professional Paul was as there was no expression on his face or judgement in his voice.

'Thanks, Paul. Please can you tell her that I'm working and that I will call her back this evening.'

'Of course,' said Paul and he left.

'It's not good when she starts calling the house,' said Freddy. His words were directed at his computer screen, so Nancy wasn't sure if she was meant to answer, but seeing as he'd brought the subject up she wasn't going to miss the opportunity.

'I had an ex like that,' said Nancy.

'She's not exactly an ex.' Freddy sat back in his seat and looked as if he was pondering something.

'Who is she then?' asked Nancy.

'Arabella Boyle is Uncle Dickie's daughter.'

'So, she's your cousin then?' She knew the upper classes

were rife with inbreeding, or so she'd read somewhere on Facebook.

'Uncle Dickie isn't an actual uncle. He's my godfather. I've known Arabella my whole life.'

'She's more like a sister then?'

'No.' Freddy looked alarmed by the suggestion.

'Friends with benefits?' asked Nancy, already forming a picture of the woman.

'You may never meet but I still feel it's not really appropriate for me to divulge any specifics. Let's say we're old family friends.'

'Sure,' said Nancy. 'Makes no odds to me. I guess it's more about what Arabella thinks.'

Nancy put her head down, but she could see Freddy was now frowning and that intrigued her even more.

*   *   *

Alice was in an odd place and by that she didn't just mean her parents' nineteen nineties time warp bungalow with its two-tone walls and floral borders. While she'd defended her actions it had made her think and now she despised herself a little bit. She had a shower, got dressed and lay low in her room for as long as she could stand and then decided she needed some fresh air. She looked out of her window where she could see both her parents busy in the garden. Her father was doing something in the borders with a large fork while her mother pointed and presumably directed. Now was the perfect time to sneak out.

Alice came into the kitchen and took the dog's lead off the hook. Cindy lifted her head and for a moment Alice thought she actually rolled her eyes at her. 'Come on, let's go for a walk,' she said, trying to put on the harness. Cindy didn't move. If anything, she pressed her body further into the bed. 'I promise we're not going far.'

Cindy huffed a reply. Alice wriggled the harness underneath the dog who then rolled over in the hope of getting her tummy tickled. Alice's plan had been to get out of the house as quickly as possible but Cindy was not helping. Alice considered leaving the dog and just going for a walk but now Cindy was lying on the harness she couldn't really change her plans. Alice pulled the clasp around with one hand while giving the dog's tummy a rub with the other. She hastily did up the harness and stood up. 'Right, let's go,' she said. Cindy didn't move.

Alice heard the back door open and she had to make a swift decision. Either stay to face another grilling with some more uncomfortable home truths and feel a little worse about herself and her actions or make a bolt for it. Alice picked up Cindy and ran for the front door.

'Alice, are you—' She shut the door and set off down the road at speed, her heart instantly pounding. The speed of her heart wasn't dangerous, but it still gave Alice a start. She slowed her pace and put the dog down. Cindy looked up at her with questioning eyes.

'I know. But I have already apologised to you about yesterday. Let's just have a wander and—'

'Afternoon,' said someone walking the other way with a smirk on their face. Alice had to concede that she probably looked a bit foolish chatting to a dog. She let Cindy set the speed so they dawdled to the end of the road. Alice kept checking over her shoulder in case they were being followed by her overprotective cross-examining parents but thankfully they weren't. The road they needed to cross was busy so Alice picked the dog up, carried her across and put her down on the grass on the other side. Cindy had a good sniff around but after a couple of tugs on the lead she finally followed Alice over to the bench.

Alice liked this bench. It was overlooking the seafront

and it was the spot where her mum and dad had used to bring her as a child so she could see the sea. She'd also been able to see the other children playing on the beach. It had been her go-to place when she'd got in a strop as a teenager and also where she'd had her first kiss. It was somewhere she came to think, ponder and get things straight in her head. Something she needed to do now. The talk of stalking had upset her and for a good reason – because it was true.

Alice took some deep breaths and concentrated on her breathing. Her heart had slowed to almost a normal rhythm, so she was fine. She wasn't going to experience a repeat of yesterday. She looked out at the view: flower-covered bushes in front of her dropped away to the promenade with its walkers and cyclists and then the wide beach with the sea beyond. It was another sunny day and the sunshine made the water sparkle. Did Alice miss the seaside? Perhaps it was another thing she didn't want to admit to herself. London was everything she'd hoped for and more, but it was also hectic, busy and altogether grubbier than she'd imagined. She breathed in the fresh sea air; you certainly didn't get that in the city.

Cindy came to sit by Alice's feet and did an enormous wee.

'Eurgh, we can't sit here now,' said Alice, hopping out of the way as the puddle became a small stream heading for her trainers. 'You've reminded me I need to dump Whizzer.'

Chapter Twenty-Six

Nancy walked out onto the terrace with her coffee and a croissant that she'd intercepted from Paul and much to his discomfort had insisted on carrying out herself. It was tricky but she wasn't going to be defeated by her broken wrist, although she was very glad to put both down on one of the tables. The morning sunshine warmed her bones as she looked out across the gardens. She was slightly startled by a young woman decked out in full riding gear who bounded up the steps and did a double take at Nancy.

'You're new,' she said, swiping the croissant from the plate. The woman recoiled from Nancy's milky coffee. 'I'll have a black americano. Where's Paul?'

Nancy was miffed by her rudeness. 'Hey that's my breakfast.' She went to snatch back the croissant but as the other woman didn't let go it ripped apart scattering pastry over both of them.

'Eurgh! That's gone all over my boots!' snapped the woman.

'Then brush it off, it's just crumbs,' said Nancy. 'And I'd like an apology.'

'What?!' she scoffed, doing an elaborate head flick which sent her masses of golden hair cascading over her shoulder like a shampoo commercial.

'You just *stole* and then *destroyed* my breakfast.' Nancy held up her half of the croissant.

'You people aren't meant to eat out here.' She waved her hand in a shooing motion.

'You people?' Nancy knew she'd mistaken her for staff but her phrase irked her. 'And who would be my people exactly?'

'Don't make this any worse for yourself,' said the woman.

'I think it's fine to ask politely for an apology when the other person is so clearly in the wrong.' Nancy was starting to enjoy herself.

The woman gasped. 'The audacity. I'll have you fired.'

Nancy took a seat, put her feet up on an opposite chair and picked up her coffee. 'I'd like to see you try.'

The woman's mouth fell open before she stormed past Nancy. 'Paul! Paul!' she shouted as she marched into the house.

Nancy did have a moment where she worried that she'd just upset some very important friend of Lord and Lady Langham but it was quickly interrupted by the sound of ruffling feathers. A sound she would never have thought could have been menacing but when the owner of that plumage was Percy it most definitely was. Percy strutted onto the terrace. With a sharp twist of his iridescent neck he fixed Nancy with the beadiest of eyes. Nancy hastily ripped up the remains of her croissant and began chucking it at the bird.

The ballroom door opened and the croissant thief stepped out with a puzzled-looking Paul following behind her. 'Look! Do you see what she's doing with *my* croissant now?'

But before Paul could say anything Percy screeched and lunged at the woman.

Nancy saw her moment to flee and she raced for the steps. Paul quickly shut the ballroom door, leaving the woman to her fate.

The woman screamed. A sound shriller than Percy and it stopped the peacock in his tracks. Maybe the psychotic creature had met his match. Nancy backed further away and scooted behind the oversized plant pot.

Nancy was watching, from what she hoped was a safe distance, when someone tapped her on the shoulder. She yelped and spun around to see Freddy's grinning face. He pulled ear buds out. 'What are you doing?'

'Percy's having a showdown with Penelope Pitstop,' said Nancy but Freddy was already bounding up the steps.

'Freddy!' squealed the woman. 'Help me!'

'You're okay, he's distracted by the food,' said Freddy. Nancy could see Percy was pecking at the croissant and no longer looked like a threat, although she wasn't taking any risks. When Freddy got within two feet of the woman she slumped against him in the most badly acted fake faint Nancy had ever seen and it made her snort out a laugh. Percy turned her way. 'Shit.' Nancy darted back behind the pot. The peacock slowly strutted his way down the steps. Nancy held her breath. Percy twitched his head and began pecking the ground. He walked off and Nancy darted back up to the terrace. Nancy shook her head as Freddy comforted the woman slumped in his arms – what a drama queen. Freddy gave Nancy a look that she couldn't quite interpret.

Nancy sat down and picked up her coffee. The woman pulled away from Freddy as if forgetting her supposedly weakened state. Her lip wobbled and she pointed at Nancy. 'This woman said awful things to me, Freddy.'

'Ah,' said Freddy. 'You've met Nancy. Nancy, this is Arabella.'

'All righ', said Nancy, deliberately trying to sound common in the hope that it offended her.

Freddy seemed to notice as he briefly frowned. 'Nancy has—'

'She said the meanest things,' began Arabella, phoney emotion bubbling in her words.

'I asked her to apologise for trashing my croissant.' Nancy pointed at what remained of her breakfast, the pecked remnants now liberally scattered at Freddy's feet.

'Do you see what I mean? The sheer impertinence. I mean . . . Freddy this isn't a laughing matter. When staff rebel it's the beginning of anarchy.'

Nancy choked on her coffee. Freddy gave her a stern look. 'You didn't tell her, did you?'

Nancy felt a little sheepish. 'She didn't give me a chance.'

Freddy turned back to Arabella. 'Nancy doesn't work here. *I* work for her.'

Arabella started to laugh. At first it was an affected tinkle and then grew to sound like a vintage car trying to start. When she spotted that no one else was laughing she stopped and pulled her chin into her chest. 'Are you teasing me?'

'Nope, he's my personal assistant,' said Nancy, relishing the look of confusion on Arabella's face.

'Now I know you're teasing. I just don't understand why you, Freddy, would be so cruel. I'll not stay here and be made a fool of,' said Arabella, pushing Freddy away as if he had been holding her, which he hadn't. 'When you've stopped your childish pranks with the hired help I'll be at The Acres.' She flounced off the terrace, down the steps and disappeared towards the stables.

Nancy turned to Freddy and with a mock posh voice she said, 'Well, she's an absolute delight.'

Freddy leaned over the balustrade to check Arabella

had gone. 'She's a little . . .' He turned back to Nancy. 'Highly strung.'

'Just a little,' agreed Nancy, trying hard not to laugh. 'Like a tightrope across the Grand Canyon. Where's The Acres?'

'It's her family's estate. Their land borders ours.' Eventually he took a seat at the table with Nancy but was still looking out beyond the gardens and only really relaxed when they watched Arabella and her horse thunder off across the fields. 'She's cross. She only rides like that when she's cross.' He chewed his lip. 'I expect me not turning up to her party hasn't helped.'

'You missed a party?' Nancy was surprised. She leaned forward. 'Who are you and what have you done with the real Freddy?'

'Very funny,' he replied.

'What was better than an Arabella party?' asked Nancy, interested as to what had changed his behaviour.

Freddy looked uncomfortable which only intrigued Nancy more. 'I had a better offer.'

'Come on, out with it. What was the better offer?'

Freddy slowly drew in a breath. 'Board games with you and Grandpa.'

Nancy started to laugh but realised he was serious. 'Well that would definitely piss her off. But I am honoured that you chose tiddlywinks and Scrabble with me instead of a rave-up.' Nancy tipped her head. 'Are you scared of Arabella?'

Freddy uttered a tinkle of a laugh not unlike Arabella's. 'Gosh, no. Definitely not.'

'You sure about that? Because when she was here you looked pretty tense.'

'I mean she's . . . and sometimes there's . . . but I'm definitely not scared of her.'

'That's good because she's coming back,' said Nancy with a nonchalant nod over his shoulder. Freddy spun around so fast he almost fell off his chair. His head twisted in all directions searching for Arabella. 'Oh no. My mistake, it's Allsop,' said Nancy, grinning as she waved at the gardener.

* * *

Alice spent the day dodging her parents and troubling over her behaviour. That was until she got a lovely text from Dom saying how much he and Bonnie were looking forward to seeing her. All her doubts evaporated – it didn't matter that she'd engineered the meeting because the point was, he was looking forward to seeing her again. It made something squirm in her gut but in a good way. She'd never felt like this about someone and that bothered her. Ever since that kiss in the nightclub she'd known there was something very different about her feelings for him. It was quick, irrational and immense. Was that just a girlish crush? Surely she was too old for those. And if it wasn't a crush, what was it?

'Alice!' Her dad's shout right outside her door made her jolt as if she'd been doing something she shouldn't.

She swiftly opened the door making him jump in return which she felt evened things out a little. 'Yes, Dad.'

'Did you say you were going out tonight? Because me and your mum thought it would be nice if we—'

Alice held her hand up. 'I'm sure whatever you're going to suggest is lovely, but you know I am going out. I'm meeting up with Dom and Bonnie.'

Her dad sighed. 'Can I come in?'

'That depends on whether you're going to lecture me or not.'

He made a cross over his heart. 'I promise no lectures.'

She opened the door fully. 'Thanks.' He came inside and shut the door.

Alice sat on the bed and her father looked around as he joined her. 'It feels like five minutes ago we decorated this room for you when you were on that school trip abroad.'

'France,' said Alice.

'Gosh we worried about you that week. We decorated every night after work just to keep our minds off it.'

Alice couldn't help but feel for her parents. 'But I came home safe. Like I always do.'

'I know, I know,' said her dad with exaggerated nods. 'We'll never stop worrying, Alice, it's only because we care. And if it feels like this room was decorated five minutes ago then it was barely ten minutes ago that we brought you home from the maternity unit in a car seat.' He took a deep breath. 'Tiny little scrap you were. Your mum and I sat and watched you sleep. It was as if we feared if we looked away, you'd stop breathing.' He turned to face her, his features stern. 'That's still how it feels and I'm sorry because I know it's not what you want to hear. I know you'd rather we left well alone but . . . love makes you do strange things.' He swallowed hard. 'And that's all it is, Alice, it's only because we love you.'

Alice linked her arm through his. 'I know.'

He sniffed. 'Look at me going soft.'

'Going?' she questioned.

'Hey.' He tickled her ribs. 'You know if you like this chap, we'll like him too.'

Alice smiled as an image of Whizzer popped into her head. 'I'm not sure you'd feel that way about all of my dates.'

'We just want you to be happy so I'm going to chat to your mum and we're going to try to be less . . .' He looked

229

up at her old Laura Ashley lampshade as if trying to find the right word.

'Intense?' suggested Alice.

'Yes, exactly.'

'Thanks, Dad. That would be great.'

He gave her a hug. 'I did only say *try*. This is your mother we're talking about.' They both chuckled.

Chapter Twenty-Seven

The morning sun was filling the study with light – it was a lovely spot to work. And now Nancy had had a second cup of coffee and replacement croissant all was well with her Tuesday. A padding of paws on the door made Nancy get up and open it. Carrie trotted in but as soon as she saw Lionel she froze and instantly fluffed up like a furry puffer fish.

'It's okay,' said Nancy, giving Lionel a pat. Carrie hissed as she eyed them both suspiciously. She inched up to the lion, sniffed it and backed away. 'Watch your manners because this is what the folks here do to their kitties.' As Freddy appeared the cat dashed past him and out of the study.

'Is she okay?' he asked.

'I think she's unhappy about not being top cat.' She pointed at Lionel.

Freddy and Nancy got on with their work but today, Freddy was noticeably less chatty since the visit from Arabella.

They dialled into a team meeting with everyone back at Having A Ball and Nancy felt a pang of something close to homesickness at the sight of them all sitting at the big table with the colourful shelves of yarn in the background.

Nancy found herself waving and stopped, but she was excited to see them. They were her work family and she missed them.

'Good morning,' said Nancy, unable to hide her grin.

'Hey, Nancy,' said Claudia, leaning closer to the camera. 'How's Devon?'

'It's really lovely,' said Nancy, glancing at Freddy and then hastily looking back at the screen. Had it suddenly got a little warm in the study? 'How's everything back at base?'

'All good,' said Claudia. 'But we'll each do an update in a mo. Morning, Freddy, glad you decided to stay.' Claudia's phrasing was positive and Nancy liked that.

'Pleased to be here,' he said, pulling a notepad and pen over so he was ready to make notes – already he was learning.

'Right, first item on the agenda is supply issues from India,' began Nancy. 'Filip, do you want to . . .' Filip had moved around the table and was now looming large and filling the screen. 'Is everything okay?'

'Is that a . . . a lion behind you?'

The rest of the meeting went well, and it was good to hear that everyone was fine, sales were steady and that current projects were all on track. But that was because only Claudia knew the true situation of the Having A Ball finances. Freddy gave an update on the trip to the publishers which felt like weeks ago instead of just a few days. They put some actions in place to both address and provide contingency for the supply issue and Freddy scribbled notes and actions all the way through. A glance at his notepad made her hope he could read it back because she definitely couldn't.

Freddy went back to his side of the table and put his head down. 'Freddy, is everything okay?'

His head shot up like a startled meerkat. 'Why wouldn't it be?'

There was only one answer to that. 'Arabella?'

Freddy's shoulders slumped. 'It's fine.' Although his face said otherwise.

'Maybe I can help.'

'It's complicated,' he said.

'What relationship isn't?'

Freddy propelled himself around the desk. 'You see that's the main issue. There is no relationship. There's just . . . contact.'

Nancy couldn't help her eyebrows jumping. 'And what do you mean by contact? Physical contact?'

Freddy did an odd chair-based shuffle in an attempt to pull his wheelie chair even closer to Nancy. 'Arabella has always been there throughout my life. And I don't mean in a *Stand by Me* film sort of way, I mean she's just always *there*. As children our parents were close so most weekends, school holidays, birthdays – there was Arabella. Our families ski together at new year . . .' *Of course you do*, thought Nancy. 'We both went to university in London. She went to Queen Mary and I was at UCL. We both have a flat around the corner from each other in the city and our friend groups overlap.' He sighed. 'She's everywhere.' He looked quite exhausted by it.

'That's hard to escape.'

'It is. And the worst of it is that . . . I don't want to sound big-headed but she's—'

'Into you?'

'So it would seem.' He pressed his lips together. 'As you might say, big style.'

'And you don't feel the same way?' She found she was holding her breath as she waited for his response.

He shook his head and Nancy breathed out. 'I'm afraid I don't. We've never dated and yet I feel like we have.'

'Have you tried having an open and honest conversation with her and telling her that you don't feel the same way about her.'

'But how would that change anything? She would still be in the same friend group, our parents still holiday together, her father will always be my godfather. If anything, it would make things worse and unbearably awkward.' He scrunched up his shoulders as if imagining it.

'You're probably right but look at it from her point of view not yours.'

'I am.' Freddy looked affronted.

'You're not. You're thinking about how you will feel, not her.' Nancy leaned closer to Freddy, their heads were almost touching, she was really getting into her role of amateur shrink. 'Worst case scenario, she is madly in love with you and always has been.'

'Heavens, don't say that.' Freddy ran his hands through his hair leaving it skewwhiff and Nancy had to fight the urge to push it back into place.

'Look, Freddy. Not wanting to face the facts doesn't mean they don't exist. Let's assume that's the case, that she's in love with you. How do you think she feels every time she sees you and you keep her at a distance? Each time she's got her hopes up in case tonight is the moment that you realise you feel the same way only for you to blow her off, yet again.'

Freddy winced. 'That's heart-breaking.'

'Precisely.'

Freddy grimaced. 'I need to tell her.'

'Yep, you do,' said Nancy, swivelling back to her laptop, pleased that her coaching course was paying off.

Freddy got up and strode to the door. 'I should tell her now.'

Nancy spun around. 'Hang on, let's not be hasty . . .' But Freddy had already left.

* * *

Alice's day had dragged and now she had an outfit crisis. She had expected to spend the week in joggers, a complete misnomer as they wouldn't be seeing any exercise. In fact, she never made it out of the house when she wore them. Other than those she had barely brought anything resembling proper clothes with her. A quick rummage through her old wardrobe only revealed the horror of her hot goth phase as that was all she had left behind, having taken anything decent with her to Nancy's. There was a fleeting Bridget Jones moment where she imagined she would have to see Dom in something of her mother's before she pulled herself together.

She settled on her cropped jeans and a plain T-shirt. It wasn't the most glamorous outfit but she spent some time on doing her hair. She did her make-up, walked through a light spritz of her favourite perfume and picked up her bag – she was ready.

'You look lovely,' said her dad. 'Do you want a lift?'

'I was going to order an Uber.' But as soon as she'd said it the app was showing her there were no cars available.

'Alice, that's the same as getting in a car with a complete stranger. I read it on Aunt Julie's Facebook page. It's dangerous. Let your father take you and pick you up,' suggested her mum.

Her dad cleared his throat. And unsubtly gestured with his eyebrows. 'Or she could get a local taxi if she wants to.'

'Um . . . of course it's up to you.'

Alice smiled at the pair of them. 'A lift there would be great, but I'll get a local taxi home, if that's okay.'

'Of course,' he said, looking chuffed. 'But we're not bothered, it's entirely up to you,' he added. They were definitely trying to give her some space and she appreciated it.

Her dad dropped her at the caravan site entrance, Alice waved him off and made her way to Dom's caravan. She tapped on the door and was almost knocked off the little steps when the door immediately swung open with force.

'You're here!' cried Bonnie. 'Dad, Miss Pelling is here!'

'You can call me Alice, Bonnie. As long as you remember to call me Miss Pelling at school.'

'Okay,' said Bonnie with a giggle.

'Hi,' called Dom. 'Be there in a sec, I don't want this to burn.'

'Hi,' replied Alice, shutting the door behind her as she was met with a glorious aroma. Dom was stirring something on the hob with a tea towel thrown over his shoulder, making him look at ease in his role of chef. 'Something smells good.'

'It's curry,' said Bonnie, and she pushed her tongue out as far as it would go in disgust. 'I've got chicken nuggets. Would you like the same as me? We bought barbecue sauce.'

'Thanks for the Tripadvisor rating, Bonnie,' said Dom. 'It's a Brazilian chicken curry. Here try . . .' He took a clean spoon from the drawer, scooped up a little sauce and held it in front of Alice's mouth. She blew on it a little. He was watching her closely. She tucked a stray piece of hair behind her ear so it didn't go in the sauce and opened her mouth so Dom could feed her. It was an altogether intimate gesture. Dom was looking intense and she realised he was expecting a response. The sauce was spicy but creamy. 'It's good.'

'Yeah?' He seemed uncertain. It was these little moments of vulnerability that she adored about him.

'Really good.'

He looked genuinely relieved. 'There's rice—'

'Or chips,' cut in Bonnie. 'And chocolate trifle for pudding.'

'I didn't make that,' said Dom.

'It all sounds great, thank you.' Alice scanned the already laid table where in the centre were some wildflowers in a jug.

'I picked those for you,' said Bonnie, wriggling onto the bench seat. 'You're sitting next to me.'

Dom leaned into her shoulder and she thought for a moment he was going to kiss her. 'She's been like this all day. I was hoping she'd calm down once you arrived but . . .' He nodded at where Bonnie was jiggling up and down with excitement. The sight of the little girl grinning back at her made her heart swell. 'It's lovely to see you,' he added. 'You look amazing.' They stayed gazing at each other for a moment too close to awkward.

'My daddy has a penis,' announced Bonnie loudly. But at least it broke the tension.

Over dinner Dom explained that they had recently had the conversation about body parts. 'It's fine. We get that a lot in class,' said Alice. 'Kayden's favourite word is bum.'

Bonnie giggled. 'Mine is puppy.' She pouted hard at her dad.

'We've also talked about the responsibility of being a pet owner,' said Dom. 'Which we're not ready for yet.'

'I liked your dog,' said Bonnie.

'Cindy liked you too.'

'See, Daddy, I'd be a good pet owner.'

'Maybe when you're bigger.'

'Could I have a gerbil while I'm waiting for my puppy?' Bonnie scooped up a lot of barbecue sauce on her chicken nugget and popped it in her mouth.

'We'll see,' said Dom, he turned back to Alice. 'What plans do you have for the rest of the week?'

It was a simple question, but it took her a little by surprise. As long as she avoided Friday it would be fine. 'Not much. Mainly fielding my parents' many questions about life in London.'

'It's nice that you're close. I don't see mine much. They moved to Norfolk to run a post office so they're busy and it's not a short trip.'

'I stay with Nanny and Grandad in the holidays,' said Bonnie. 'But not this time.'

'I don't get a lot of holiday so she spends more time there now she's at school but they love having her and she has fun. Don't you, Bonnie?'

'They don't have a puppy,' said Bonnie with sad eyes.

They finished their meals which Alice was more than a little impressed with. 'You're a good cook,' she said as she helped him wash up.

'Bonnie would disagree. It's hard to find healthy things she'll eat.' He leaned in close and it sent a shiver through her body. 'But I blitz all sorts of veg and hide them in a bolognaise sauce because she'll eat pasta all day long.'

'How much longer?' whined Bonnie from the seating area. 'I want to watch *Moana*.'

'We'll be there in a minute,' called Dom. 'Sorry, she's been looking forward to this all day.'

'It's fine. To be honest I want to watch it too.' She smiled. 'But I'm guessing you've not seen it a million times already.'

'Well . . .' Alice pretended to rapidly count across all her fingers and Dom looked alarmed. 'I'm joking. This will be my first time.'

'You had me worried there,' he said, passing her the last plate. 'It's a good film but it's not *Fast and Furious*.'

'I *love* those movies,' said Alice with feeling.

'Maybe another time we could watch the latest one?' he asked, looking at her coyly.

'I'd like that,' said Alice.

They settled down to watch the film and Bonnie gave a running commentary with added actions all through the first half. They had an intermission for toilet breaks and refreshments before settling back on the seating with Bonnie in between them because she said it was best if she had the popcorn in the middle with her. The adults shared a bottle of white wine while Bonnie had some orange squash. 'I don't like orange,' said Bonnie, glugging down her drink. 'But Daddy won't let me have the one I really like.' Alice looked to Dom for an explanation.

'She loved blackcurrant when she was little but when you've been in the middle of Tesco and your toddler is shouting it from the trolley but only saying the first two and last two letters of currant you learn to avoid it.'

As Alice said the abbreviation in her head, she snorted her drink down her nose. 'I can see why that would be traumatic.'

'I didn't think I was going to make it out of the store alive,' said Dom, laughing at the memory.

'Shhh!' said Bonnie. 'This is the best bit.' Suitably admonished Alice and Dom turned their attention back to the television screen, but Alice was still giggling to herself.

When the film was over Alice called a taxi and Dom insisted on walking her to the park entrance because it was dark. Bonnie was tired so he carried the sleepy child on his shoulders.

'I'm sorry about tonight,' he said.

Alice was confused. 'What are you apologising for?'

'Bonnie doesn't mean to, but she kind of takes centre stage.'

'She's five, that's her job,' said Alice. 'She's a great kid and I've had a lovely evening.' Dom looked doubtful. 'Honestly. The best.' And that was the truth.

'I don't want to steal your holiday, and I guess you were after a break without any kids, but if you fancied spending the day with us we'd be—'

'Yes, I'd love to.' Just when she thought it couldn't get any better he slipped his hand around hers.

Chapter Twenty-Eight

Nancy didn't see Freddy for the rest of the day. Given that she had instigated his rapid departure in search of Arabella she wasn't in a position to complain too much. Although that feeling changed late afternoon when he'd still not returned and she'd heard nothing from him. Nancy pulled her chair back from the desk. She couldn't concentrate on her laptop anymore. She was wondering about Freddy. Not just what was happening with Arabella but also why *she* was thinking so much about him.

Freddy was everything she disliked about the British class system: the rich kid who sailed through life. But she'd learned that despite the money and status his life wasn't perfect. She'd also discovered that Freddy wasn't the enemy, there was a lot about him to like; he was kind, thoughtful even, and it was foolish to ignore the fact that he was ridiculously good-looking. Nancy realised that spending so much time around him was having an effect on her, which was daft because, really, what did they have in common? Nothing. They could not be more different. They would be a complete disaster in a relationship. The fact that she'd even considered that pulled her up short. She got to her feet and did a lap of the room, patting Lionel as she passed.

Why was she even thinking about Freddy like that? The

more she tried not to think about him the more images popped into her head, making her walk faster around the room as if trying to escape. She scooted around the desk a bit too fast and bumped into Lionel, making him wobble. The door opened as Nancy grabbed Lionel to stop him falling over. She froze. Oscar was standing in the doorway. 'Are you cuddling Lionel?' he asked.

'Er, well, not exactly. I was um . . .' What was she doing? *Running away from thoughts of your son* – she couldn't say that. Maybe the painkillers were doing strange things to her. Yes, that was it. Nancy let go of the lion.

'It's okay,' said Oscar, coming into the room. He put a finger to his lips. 'Don't tell anyone but I give him a hug sometimes too. He's also a very good listener. I used to make up stories about his adventures when I was a child. Although there are plenty of real stories about him. He was a bit of a celebrity around the village in the 1920s.'

'So Freddy tells me.'

Oscar held a finger in the air as if suddenly remembering something. 'It was Freddy I was after. Have you sent him on an errand?'

'No, he's gone to speak to someone.' She figured Oscar didn't need to know it was Arabella. She didn't like that Oscar seemed to think running errands was the extent of Freddy's job so decided to put him straight. 'While you're here, Oscar, would it be all right if I explained a little about the role Freddy is doing?'

'I know, he's your gopher. And we are very grateful, that you've taken him on at all.'

Nancy felt defensive. 'No, he's not a gopher. For one thing I'd never treat a member of staff like that, and secondly, he's my personal assistant. It's an important role that requires organisation, attention to detail and reliability.' She had to swallow down the last word, she was sure Freddy would get there eventually. 'He manages my diary which is not an easy task, he schedules meetings, tracks actions and he's really making an effort to do a good job.'

Oscar seemed a little taken aback and Nancy wondered if she'd overstepped a line. And then she thought, sod the bloody line. 'I don't think you should take the piss out of Freddy. It's unfair. He's doing this because you asked him to and I think you should support him.' She almost tried to fold her arms, but remembered in time and instead plonked her cast down on Lionel's head.

Oscar rolled his lips together. Then nodded. 'Nancy, you are a breath of fresh air and you are completely right. I shouldn't ridicule Freddy's newfound work ethic. I will remedy that.' He glanced at the lion. 'Would you mind not leaning on Lionel.'

'Of course. Sorry.' She removed her cast from the poor stuffed creature's head and in the process pulled his mane with it, giving him something of a Mohican.

'Right, well, when Freddy returns, I'd like a word with him. When he's free.'

'I'll pass on the message.'

'Thank you.' Oscar checked his watch. 'If you're finished for the day, would you like to join Louisa and me for predinner drinks?'

She'd worked through lunch with Paul bringing her a sandwich. And she could always do more after dinner. Oscar was looking hopefully at her. 'I would, thanks Oscar.'

'Splendid.' He nodded at Lionel and his sticking-up fur. 'Do you think you could?' He pointed.

'On it,' she said, quickly smoothing down the lion's mane with her good hand.

Nancy was no longer worried about whether she was wearing the right outfit or not. She'd learned that, despite the titles, Lord and Lady Langham were nice people. She joined them in the snug where Carrie was sitting on one of the sofas with Otto on the rug below gazing up at her and Oscar and Louisa on the opposite sofa.

'Evening, Nancy,' said Louisa, greeting her with a kiss on her cheek.

'Has our boy returned yet?' asked Oscar.

'I've not seen him,' said Nancy, trying to sound blasé. The truth was she was itching to know what had gone on with Arabella and why it was taking so long. Perhaps Arabella had persuaded Freddy that he did love her after all, an unhelpful picture of the two of them ripping each other's clothes off popped into her head. No, that was daft. Freddy was clear about his feelings or lack of feelings for Arabella, it was far more likely that she had reacted badly. A picture of Arabella trampling him with her horse shot into her mind – also very unhelpful.

'Are you all right?' asked Louisa, looking concerned.

'Yes, I'm fine, thank you. I think it's because I'm being looked after so well.'

The door opened and Paul came in carrying a silver tray. 'Two bottles of the Barolo Riserva Vigna Rionda Massolino 2012.'

'Blimey the wine has an even longer name than Freddy,' said Nancy with a snort. There was a pause before Oscar began belly laughing.

Paul poured them all drinks from a decanter, which made Nancy think that it could be a couple of bottles of Co-op Merlot in there because who would know?

'Cheers,' she said and she clinked her expensive-looking glass against Louisa's and then Oscar's before taking a swig. That was the point where it was obviously not from the Co-op. 'Ooh,' said Nancy. 'That's proper nice.'

'I agree,' said Oscar, taking a sip and savouring it. 'It's one of my favourites. Having a house guest is an excellent excuse to open a bottle.'

'I'm glad Frederick's not here,' said Louisa, picking up a large leather album and putting it on her lap. 'I was having a bit of a reorganisation of my dressing room and I came across some photographs. Would you like to see them?'

'Too right,' said Nancy, getting up and moving next to Louisa, making Oscar shuffle over a fraction.

Louisa turned the page to reveal a series of pictures of a tiny baby. They weren't like the snaps her mum and dad had of her. For a start her baby photos were in an album that had a picture of a golden retriever on the front which was odd because they'd never owned a dog. All the pictures of Nancy as a baby were taken at home. Some of her in the arms of various relatives, some of her asleep, others with a manky-looking teddy and a lot of her covered in food. Some were slightly out of focus and in almost all of them Nancy either had her eyes closed or wasn't looking at the camera. The pictures in Louisa's album all looked professional. The backgrounds were clear colours, there was no Ikea furniture or homemade curtains to be seen. And in every one, Freddy was smiling broadly and looking directly into the lens unless of course it was a shot where he wasn't meant to be because he was reaching for a pristine toy giraffe.

As the pages turned the pictures became less formal and Nancy warmed to the family shots of picnics and parties that she could relate to. She guessed their picnics were in the grounds rather than the local park but the sandwiches and sausage rolls were the same as was the whole point of the picnic – it was family time. Happy scenes of Freddy through the years in various different sports kits, but always proudly holding a rugby ball, pinched at Nancy's heart. She could see the love and dedication he had to the sport with each turn of the page. Countless pictures of a muddy Freddy scoring tries and holding up trophies told the story. And on so many pages were pictures of Freddy and Arabella together. From a very young age they had been photographed all the way up to their teens and with each one Freddy's grin had diminished until in the last one she was looking adoringly at him, but he had his hands in his pockets and was leaning away. Nancy wondered if Arabella had seen that photograph.

The door swung open and everyone except for Carrie turned quickly to see a flustered-looking Freddy stride in. 'Here you all are. I need your help.'

'Whatever's wrong?' asked Louisa.

'It's Arabella, she's gone missing.'

As everyone else jumped to their feet and left the room Nancy felt compelled to join them, only Carrie stayed exactly where she was. She caught up with Louisa who was putting on her coat. Paul joined them in the entrance hall and handed out torches. 'It's still light outside,' said Nancy.

'But we may be some time,' said Paul and she thought she heard the voice of experience in his words.

Freddy and Oscar came striding up the corridor. 'I suggest we split into two groups,' began Freddy.

'Um.' Nancy tentatively held up her hand. Freddy spun in her direction. 'When you say Arabella's gone missing, is that she's copped a strop and swanned off for a bit or abducted by aliens sort of missing?' She couldn't help feeling that they were overreacting. Freddy gave her a look. 'What? I'm just interested as to why we are sending out search parties for an almost thirty-year-old woman who has been missing for what? A few minutes?' The expressions coming back at her were the looks of people who knew something she didn't. 'Look I want to help but I must be missing something.'

'Fine,' said Freddy, looking agitated and keen to get searching. 'Arabella has a history of . . . shall we say, putting herself in danger.' He gave Nancy a look as if she should know what that meant but she didn't.

'Like what?'

Freddy, Oscar and Louisa all exchanged worried glances with each other as if mentally drawing straws. Louisa took a deep breath. 'She's wandered close to the cliffs a number of times,' she said.

'Bit more than that,' said Oscar. 'She's threatened to throw herself off.'

'What, on your estate?' asked Nancy.

'The cliffs further down aren't high enough for you to kill yourself,' said Oscar and Louisa shot him a look. 'I was simply trying to explain,' said Oscar with added placating gestures to his wife.

'Right, anything else?' asked Nancy.

'She's threatened other things,' said Freddy. 'But we're wasting time. If you're coming, I'd wear a coat,' he added.

'Oh yeah, I'm coming,' said Nancy.

All the kerfuffle disturbed Grandpa who, even after a fraught update from Freddy, was really only concerned about what time his dinner would be. Paul appeared with an oversized Barbour jacket and helped Nancy into it. Grandpa agreed to update Freddy if Arabella turned up there and Paul reassured him that Mrs Mason would serve his dinner on time and reserve meals for everyone else. Paul, Oscar and Louisa headed out the front with the intention of sweeping the driveway and grounds – Paul and Louisa on foot and Oscar in the Land Rover. Freddy,

Nancy and Otto made straight for the cliffs. Freddy had a determined stride and Nancy had to jog a little to keep up. She kept an eye out for Percy as they dashed through the gardens. Nancy upped her pace to walk alongside him. 'So how did it go?' she asked, trying to sound as innocent as possible.

'Are you serious? It was obviously a complete disaster.'

'What did you say exactly?'

Freddy stopped abruptly. 'Do you think we could do the detailed analysis at a later date? Right now, Arabella could be in real danger.'

'Sure,' said Nancy and they carried on with Otto bounding on ahead.

As they neared the cliffs Freddy started calling, 'Arabella!' When Nancy didn't join in he scowled at her.

'Oh come on. I'm the last person she's going to respond to.'

He shook his head at her. 'Arabella!' he shouted as he neared the cliff edge.

'Ooh now, not so close,' called Nancy who had no intention of looking over the edge.

Freddy turned back looking relieved. 'She's not . . .'

'Jumped?' offered Nancy.

Freddy and Otto went down the steps to Seashell Bay at speed and Nancy followed more cautiously. 'Check the beach hut!' she called but Freddy was already on it. He came out shaking his head. He flicked on the torch and went under the steps towards the small cave. Nancy waited, she figured there was little point in her joining him as he'd have the whole area checked within minutes. She looked out across the bay to the sea.

'Freddy!' she yelled, and he appeared under the steps looking up at her through the slats.

'Have you spotted her?'

'No but that's not meant to be there, right?' Nancy pointed out to sea with her plastered arm where the small empty boat bobbed worryingly on the gentle waves.

* * *

Alice had been looking forward to her day out with Dom and Bonnie. It was silly but she missed being around them. They spent the morning on the beach and decided on Walton Pier for the afternoon as somewhere that would entertain Bonnie and it was a trip down memory lane for Alice. She'd spent many a happy time on the pier. A few things had changed since she'd last visited but fundamentally it was exactly the same.

'Thanks for coming today,' said Dom as they strolled along the pier and Bonnie dashed ahead before running back to update them on what she could see.

'Thanks for inviting me.'

'It just feels like fate that we bumped into you here. Sorry, that sounds all gushy. But it can't be coincidence. We met in that club and then at the school and now here.'

Alice felt a pang of guilt but not enough to own up to her having engineered the most recent encounter. 'The universe acts in weird and wonderful ways.'

'It really does.' Dom checked where Bonnie was. She was using an old clunky telescope so was quite safe and out of earshot. 'I'm not imagining that we have a connection, am I?' He reached for Alice's hand and her heart leapt.

'No, you're not imagining it.'

'Phew.' Dom looked genuinely relieved. 'Because I could have looked like a real weirdo there.'

'If you're a weirdo then I am too.' She reached up to kiss him but Bonnie barrelled between the two of them.

'Rides!' she yelled and raced off.

Alice had always loved walking along the old wooden

structure and glimpsing the waves below through the gaps in the planks. It was even better to be doing it holding Dom's hand. She liked seeing the fishermen casting their lines into the deep water, but it was the indoor funfair that they'd come for. Bonnie's eyes were wide at the sight of the carousel. Alice wondered if she'd ever seen one before.

'You'll need to go on with someone,' said Dom, watching the large golden horses and roosters going round. 'Me or—'

'Miss P-Alice!' said Bonnie, followed by a giggle.

Alice was thrilled that Bonnie had chosen her, but she didn't want to upset Dom. 'Is that okay?'

'Of course. You'll have to go on a horse with a double seat. I get a slightly creepy giant chicken all to myself.'

The carousel was the gentle fun Alice remembered although she had to keep her wits about her as Bonnie was forever wriggling and leaning in different directions. Why didn't children ever sit still? But Alice loved her energy. She wondered when it was that you lost that as an adult. Maybe it was simply life that drained your battery. Being with Bonnie and Dom was like having a recharge.

They ticked off the swings, teacups and pirate ships and Bonnie had a go on the trampolines while Alice and Dom watched. Dom was taking photographs and shouting encouragement. It was lovely to see. Next, they went on the dodgems and Alice was pleased that Bonnie chose to ride with her dad. She and Bonnie squealed every time they collided.

They bought some chips and sat on a bench to eat them. When Bonnie had had enough, she went to try and make friends with a seagull nearby.

'She's such a great kid,' said Alice.

'I am so lucky,' said Dom, swallowing hard.

250

'You're a great dad.'

Dom tilted his head and sighed. 'I don't know. Some days I wonder if I'm enough.'

Alice gave his hand a squeeze. 'Look at her, she's a happy child. That's down to you.'

'Thanks. You don't get any feedback as a parent. I get it all the time at work so you know where you need to improve but as a dad it's all a case of trial and error. Most often it's the latter.'

'You're being too hard on yourself,' said Alice.

'I feel I've got to protect her. I've not dared to have anyone in my life since her mother left us. Bonnie was beyond heartbroken. It was like she was ill. I was so worried about her. She stopped talking for a while and barely ate. It was such a worrying time.'

'That must have been tough.' Alice could feel his pain.

'I can't ever risk her getting hurt like that again. I don't want to scare you off but it's better you go now rather than later. Goodness, I'm sorry that sounded awful.' He shook his head at his own ineptitude. 'What I'm trying to say, very badly, is that I care about you, Alice. We both do. And I'd love to get to know you better but if you're not looking for something long-term then . . .'

'It's okay,' said Alice. 'I get it. Serious relationship only. I like the sound of that.'

He gave her a lopsided grin. 'You promise you'll stick around?'

Alice couldn't promise any such thing, but she knew more than anything that she wanted to.

Chapter Twenty-Nine

The previous night had been fraught. Despite an inshore lifeboat being scrambled there was no sign of Arabella. The police were involved as there was now a real concern for her safety. Nancy felt bad about doubting Arabella and thinking it was all just a stunt for Freddy's attention. As the hours had rolled on Nancy had grabbed some sleep but as far as she was aware Freddy had stayed up all night. He was beside himself with worry and guilt. Nancy also got the impression that he was blaming her a little for having suggested that he be open and honest with Arabella about his feelings.

The next morning had been more of the same with Freddy out on both The Acres and Langham estates. Nancy had managed to get a bit of work done but her mind was elsewhere. She took a break and went to see if anyone had an update. Nancy found Paul cleaning guns. 'Hiya, any news on Arabella?'

'I'm afraid not.' Paul concentrated on the gun. 'Are you taking a break?'

'Yeah, it's hard to concentrate.'

'At least there's plenty here to keep my mind off it,' said Paul.

'Have you worked here long?'

'Eleven years.'

'And before that?' she asked.

'Monaco, Saudi, London.' Paul rattled off the locations like they were nothing.

'Wow. Did you not like the travelling?'

Paul smiled and leaned forward. 'Travelling was fine.'

'Ah,' said Nancy. 'The families were the problem.'

'I couldn't possibly comment.' Paul smiled.

'You wouldn't have been here when Freddy was a kid.'

Paul paused. 'I think Freddy was eighteen when I took up the position. He left for university a few months after I joined.'

Nancy nodded. 'Was Arabella about much then?'

'She virtually lived here that summer. There were other friends, but Arabella is something of a permanent feature.'

'So I gathered. I suppose there's plenty of room in a place like this. You'd probably not have noticed if he'd brought his whole year group home.'

'Possibly not. But then they did used to spend a lot of time out on the estate riding, cycling, hiding out in the treehouse.'

Nancy was nodding but as soon as he said treehouse they both halted. They'd had the same thought at the same time. 'I'll call Freddy,' said Nancy.

'Call him on the way. Let's go,' said Paul and they rushed from the house.

Freddy picked up immediately. 'What news?' he asked.

'Not news exactly just an idea Paul and I have had. He mentioned a treehouse on the estate where you used to play as kids. Have you checked there?'

'No,' said Freddy.

'Where are you?'

253

'I'm down on the shoreline at The Acres. I'm checking if anything has been washed up.'

'We're heading over to the treehouse now. Not that I know where we're going but Paul is showing me.' Freddy was quiet. 'Are you okay?'

She heard Freddy slowly exhale. 'If I'm honest I'm worried sick. I've got this awful feeling that she was on the boat.'

'The coastguard said it was an exceptionally calm night so it's unlikely she'd have capsized.'

'I know. I just had this awful sensation in my gut when I saw it floating there. Like I knew she'd gone.' His voice cracked and Nancy wished they weren't on the phone so she could comfort him.

'Let's try and stay positive.'

'It's hard. I've caused all this. Uncle Dickie keeps ringing me. It's horrible.'

'Is he still in London?' asked Nancy, trying not to sound too judgemental.

'There are meetings he can't get out of but if there's no news . . .' There was a pause. 'Either way. Then he'll come down tonight. I can't bear the thought of—'

'Don't torture yourself, Freddy. You're doing everything you can. I'll call you when we get to the treehouse and let you know.'

'I'll start heading that way now. But you'll definitely get there first.'

'Okay. See you there,' said Nancy, cringing at her own upbeat voice.

'Thanks, Nancy.'

'My pl—'

But Freddy had ended the call.

Nancy followed Paul, out through the stables and across the grounds. They walked on past an old barn and small courtyard which made Nancy wonder if that was where Freddy's incident with the horse had happened.

'It's years since anyone has used the treehouse. It's partly derelict so it's a bit of a long shot,' said Paul as they neared the edge of a wooded area.

As they walked through the trees with the light scattering on the woodland floor Nancy thought how pretty and tranquil it was. She could also imagine many happy hours of childhood make-believe in a place like this. A small deer darted across their path making Nancy jump.

'Muntjac,' said Paul and he carried on.

A few more paces and Paul was looking around as if he was no longer sure where he was going. 'Everything all right?' asked Nancy.

'It's been years. I thought it was here but . . .' He turned slowly in a circle. 'There's been a lot of growth since I last ventured through the woods. Perhaps we should wait for Freddy.'

'You wait. I'll have a wander and see if I can find it.'

'Don't go too far, please,' said Paul. 'Let's deal with one lost person at a time.'

'I'll be careful. I promise.' Nancy strolled off with her head in the air searching up high for the lost treehouse. She'd gone a little way when she caught her toe and tripped. 'Shitting hell,' she said as she stumbled forward but kept her balance. She breathed a deep sigh of relief. The last thing she wanted to do was break something else. She cradled her broken arm protectively as she leaned back against a tree and took a moment to calm her panicked heart.

Then Nancy heard a sound. It wasn't the many birds that were flitting around but a sort of creaking, almost like a rusty hinge. Her head automatically spun in the direction of the noise. And through the trees there it was

– the treehouse. Somewhat less impressive than Nancy had pictured it. What she could see was an ivy-clad shed on a wooden platform about ten feet up a large tree. Nancy pulled her head back a little in the hope that she wasn't easy to spot and she waited. Predictably the ivy moved and Arabella's face appeared. She looked about before disappearing back inside. From the brief glimpse Nancy caught of her she looked fine, which was a relief.

Nancy crept over to the bottom of the tree and stood underneath the platform. There was a rickety-looking ladder. There was no way she was going up there. She checked her phone was on silent and she texted Freddy. Unfortunately, she didn't have Paul's number. She may have been doing Arabella a disservice, but Nancy didn't want to alert her that she'd been found in case she bolted. After her earlier stumble there was no way Nancy was running through the woods after her. Freddy texted back that he was not far away and she was to take care of Arabella until he got there. Nancy replied with 'OK'. She stood still. Could she hear voices? That was weird. They were faint but definitely sounded like people rather than animals. She looked around – nothing. The sound was coming from above. When the theme tune to *Gilmore Girls* kicked in Nancy almost chuckled. Arabella was hiding out in the woods with bloody Netflix.

Nancy stepped back to lean against the big tree but she'd misjudged it and she toppled backwards and thumped against it. 'Shi—' She just stopped herself before she fell.

'Hello? Who's there?' called Arabella. 'I know there's someone there. I'll call the police.'

She sounded a bit jittery so Nancy stepped out from under the platform. 'Hiya, Arabella, you all right?'

'Oh my life. You!' Arabella did not look pleased to see her rescue party.

Nancy beamed her a smile and waved. 'Yep it's me. I've come to save you.'

Arabella scoffed. 'Heavens, you're the last person I need. Where's Freddy?' Arabella scanned the wood.

'Looking for you.' Nancy didn't like the smug look of triumph on Arabella's face. Anger instantly bubbled in her gut at the stress she'd put poor Freddy through. 'He's worried out of his mind because he thinks you've drowned yourself. Now why would he think that I wonder?'

'I have no idea,' she said with a swish of her hair.

'Because you unanchored the boat or whatever it is you do to set boats free.'

Arabella tinkled her marbles-in-a-jar laugh. 'You really are an actual idiot aren't you?'

That was like a red rag to an easily pissed-off bull. 'No, I'm not. I'm also not the sort of person who hides away, triggers the call out of the bloody inshore lifeboat and lets Freddy . . . and everyone who cares about them worry that she might have topped herself! That's twisted and sick, that's what that is.'

Arabella gave Nancy the most condescending look. 'Oh dear. You haven't fallen for our dear Freddy have you?'

'What like you, you mean?'

Arabella looked wistful but Nancy was still raging on Freddy's behalf. 'Freddy and I go way back. It's our destiny. Our lives are entwined.'

'Like brambles and nettles? You're delusional.'

'At least I'm not the poor little London urchin in the borrowed coat who thinks she's going to be rescued by the knight in shining armour.' Arabella pulled out her phone and aimed it at Nancy as she cackled a laugh worthy of any of Shakespeare's witches. 'Do you know what Freddy called you?' she asked.

'I've a feeling you're going to tell me.' Nancy didn't like

how much she cared about what Freddy thought but she also knew she couldn't trust Arabella as far as she could shove her with her bad hand.

'Stubborn and bossy,' said Arabella.

Nancy was relieved. 'I've been called a lot worse. In fact, I'll take that as a compliment. One man's bossy is another's leadership skills.' She grinned catlike at Arabella.

Arabella made a sort of screeching noise as she stepped out of the treehouse onto the platform. Nancy stepped back, this time being careful where she was putting her feet. 'You are the *worst* sort of girl!' Arabella's voice was rising. 'You think you can impress Freddy, turn his head. But how long do you think that would last? One, maybe two nights before he gets bored with you and your silly Dick Van Dyke accent.'

'Hey! I love *Mary Poppins*,' said Nancy, now actually enjoying the exchange.

'You don't get it do you? You're a joke. People like Freddy and me, we tolerate trash like you because we have to. Because it's not PC to put you in your place where you belong. You're nothing but a novelty and Freddy knows it.'

Nancy had to admit that stung a bit. 'Maybe he fancies a change from over-styled, spoiled little rich girls.'

'Over-styled? You bitch!' yelled Arabella as she started down the ladder.

'Arabella, what the hell?' said Freddy, striding up to the treehouse and giving them both a start.

'Found her!' said Nancy, pointing and trying hard to make light of the situation.

'Freddy, thank goodness you're here. I was out of my mind after our little tiff and I ran and ran until I was exhausted when I remembered—'

'Netflix,' said Nancy, interrupting Arabella's dramatic delivery.

'What?' Freddy looked at Nancy.

'When I got here she was watching *Gilmore Girls* on Netflix. I could hear it when I was standing under the platform.'

'I don't know what she's lying about now, Freddy.' Arabella's lip wobbled. 'But she's said some awful, awful things to me.' Arabella faked a sob and Nancy had to control her impulse to giggle. Her acting was atrocious.

Freddy held up a hand to stop Arabella. 'Are you hurt?'

'Only my heart.'

Nancy snorted a laugh then waved her apology. 'Sorry, I'd better go.'

'I'll come with you,' said Freddy, which took both Nancy and Arabella by surprise.

'But, Freddy!' called Arabella as she went back up the ladder. 'Please come and talk to me. We can sort this all out.'

'You've gone too far this time, Arabella. I need to make some calls and stop wasting everyone's time.' Freddy spun back. 'Your parents are worried sick about you.'

'What the hell did you tell them for?' snapped Arabella, looking cross.

'*He* didn't tell them,' butted in Nancy. 'The police did.'

'Oh for heaven's sake,' muttered Arabella, pulling out her phone, and she disappeared back inside the treehouse.

That evening Freddy walked into the snug looking bleary-eyed.

'Afternoon naps already. Goodness me. Before you know it, you'll be knitting slippers and polishing your bald patch.' Nancy grinned at him.

'I can't believe I slept so long.'

'I can. You were up all night looking for that daft tar— . . . troubled individual. Anyway. Do you feel refreshed?'

'No. I feel a bit spaced out.' He slumped into a chair.

'When did you last eat?'

Freddy pouted. 'Breakfast yesterday. I had some granola and a yogurt.'

'There's your trouble,' said Nancy, getting up and displacing the cat who scowled at her before she and Otto left the room. 'Let me rustle you up something.'

Freddy looked amused. 'You remember why you're here?'

Nancy held up her plaster. 'I know, but earlier today I gave Mrs Mason a discount code off a crochet-your-own-blanket set so now I'm her best friend and she showed me where all the good stuff is.'

Freddy chuckled. 'How about we both go?' He got to his feet.

They walked through to the kitchen and Freddy took a seat at the breakfast bar while Nancy perused the fridges. 'I'm thinking omelette,' she said, with her head still in the fridge.

'Sounds good to me.'

'I mean I can jazz it up a bit. I wouldn't dream of feeding a lord in waiting a plain old omelette. I'll whack in some wild boar and a sprinkle of truffle.'

'Sounds perfect.'

Nancy pulled her head out so fast she bumped it on one of the fridge's shelves. 'Ow. I was joking about the wild boar and truffle.'

'I know,' said Freddy. 'There's some cheddar in there somewhere. I'll grate that if you can do one-armed whisking.'

'I'll give it a go.'

They had a giggle making the omelette. Nancy almost sent the mixing bowl flying twice but both times managed to recover it at the last moment. Eventually Freddy sat down to a cheese omelette and Nancy kept him company with a cup of coffee and a fancy biscuit.

'That was really good, thanks,' said Freddy, putting his cutlery together.

'My pleasure. I'm sorry if it was me that triggered all the Arabella shenanigans.'

Freddy twisted his lips. 'I still think it was the right thing to do. At least now she knows where she stands. And I understand the level of manipulation she's capable of. I mean she's pulled some stunts over the years but this time she went too far. And I, like a mug, fell for it.'

'Hey,' said Nancy, touching his arm. 'Don't be so hard on yourself.' She felt a bit awkward so she pulled back her hand.

'I've wasted a lot of time on trying to keep Arabella happy. I'm not even sure why, now I think about it. Anyway, not anymore, now she's shown her true colours. Also, her shocking secret television tastes. I mean *Gilmore Girls*.'

Nancy held a palm up. 'Stop right there or we're going to fall out big time.'

Freddy held his hands up in surrender. 'I hope that never happens.'

Nancy wasn't sure what to say and the unwavering eye contact from Freddy was making things swirl in her gut. That or it was the effects of the rich biscuit this late in the evening. Nancy broke eye contact.

'Don't get too excited but I'm thinking of rustling you up a yogurt as pudding.'

'Move over Prue Leith, there's a new gastronomic queen in town.'

'You'd better believe it,' said Nancy, with a laugh.

When Freddy said he had something planned to thank Nancy she went through a number of things it might be.

She didn't want to get her hopes up but in the couple of days since the Arabella fiasco they had definitely grown close – or at least she'd hoped she wasn't doing an Arabella and imagining it. But him planning something was a nice gesture, assuming it wasn't a review of Having A Ball's VAT account.

It was early on Friday morning when Nancy popped on her jacket and met Freddy in the entrance hall before breakfast as instructed. He was scowling as he spoke on his mobile. He ended the call and at the sight of Nancy his expression changed. 'You're here. Great, let's go.'

Nancy was expecting to follow him out of the front door but instead he headed through the house. Were they staying on the estate? A walk perhaps? Or running the gauntlet with Percy in the vegetable garden? They walked through the ballroom and Nancy noticed that today the curtains were pulled shut and the two massive chandeliers were lit up and sparkling above them as they crossed to the French doors which Freddy opened before stepping back. Nancy went to walk out but a very loud noise, like a dragon's roar, made her freeze. She stepped out to see something very unexpected. Beyond the terrace she was treated to a riot of colour as a multitude of hot-air balloons were laid out on the paddocks beyond the formal gardens with a couple of the balloons already being inflated.

'Blimey, we're not going in one of those. Are we?' she said through a laugh which died as she saw Freddy's face.

'Absolutely.' Freddy led the way down the steps.

'It's a nice idea. Really lovely,' said Nancy, trying to keep up with him. 'But I'm not cut out for going up in one of those.' A thought struck her. 'My arm! I can't go in one of those because of my arm.' She tried to replace the relief on her face with a disappointed pout.

Freddy spun around. A smile tweaking the edge of his lips. 'Are you scared of heights?'

'Scared? No,' she said with a snort. Terrified and on the verge of hives would have been a more accurate description but Nancy didn't share things like that. Never show weakness. That had always been her mantra. 'I would absolutely bloody love to go in one of those.' She pointed at the nearest candy-striped balloon as it began inflating. 'But I can't with my broken wrist.'

'I've already checked with a doctor friend, and you'll be fine,' said Freddy and he marched off.

Shit, thought Nancy. 'Actually, Freddy, I've just remembered—'

He spun around and she almost bumped into him. He held her at arm's length. 'Nancy, trust me. You're going to love it.' He beamed at her. She winced a smile. This was an actual nightmare. Usually, it also included her being naked and some creepy dolls who were piloting the balloons but apart from that it was exactly the same, only this nightmare was real.

By the time Freddy manfully lifted her into the basket Nancy had run out of ideas for getting out of the experience and was now concentrating on staying calm. Maybe if she focused on her feet for the whole flight, that might work. As long as she didn't look over the edge. The basket jiggled. Nancy yelped and tried to turn it into a cough. They were off the ground now. This was happening. Nancy's pulse was picking up. Face your fears – wasn't that what people told you to do? Maybe this was a good thing. There was a shout from below, another lengthy roar from the heater and the balloon sailed away from the ground. The safe, firm, lovely ground.

'Heavens above,' she said. The irony of heading in exactly that direction was not lost on her. 'I'm sorry,

Freddy, I lied. I am afraid of heights. I can't do this.' She was shaking her head like the time she'd got water in her ears swimming.

Freddy held out his arms as if offering her a cuddle. Nancy snorted. 'Coming on to me at two thousand feet—'

'About five hundred feet at the moment and I'm not coming on to you. I promise. It's simply that you'll feel safer in a hug that's all.'

Nancy was weighing up the situation when the basket rocked and instinctively she dived into Freddy's arms.

Chapter Thirty

Alice had had such a lovely time with Dom and Bonnie at the pier but what Dom had said to her was swirling in her mind. He'd asked her to promise that she'd stick around. How could she promise something that she had no control over? But then she'd never been so sure about wanting to be with another person. And it wasn't just Dom it was Bonnie too. She'd not planned to settle down young, she wasn't someone who ever felt they had the luxury of being able to look that far forward but now it had presented itself it was all she wanted. She knew it was crazy fast but hadn't someone wiser than her said, 'When you know, you know'? That was how she felt. All the cliches now made total sense to her: soulmate, missing piece, other half, kindred spirit – Dom was all of those things.

Breakfast with her parents was a sombre affair. Everyone was trying to be cheery which meant that ultimately nobody was fooled. Alice ate her Coco Pops, her father read his newspaper while her mother mainlined cups of tea. Alice would be glad when today was out of the way and she could return to London and that life. The life she'd made that was separate from this. The life where she was just Alice, not the girl with the heart problem.

Her annual check-up at the hospital was always

stressful. Not the tests themselves, they were straightforward and non-invasive, but Alice never knew when they'd spot a change. Find something that indicated that all was not well. She'd had the condition all her life and been diagnosed as a baby with pulmonary stenosis – a condition characterised by the narrowing of the pulmonary valve which blocks blood flow from the heart to the lungs.

It was a condition that couldn't be cured with drugs. Alice had had operations as a child to repair her faulty valve. Her regular checks meant that they kept an eye on her condition but there was no guarantee that it wouldn't flare up and be fatal. It was something she and her parents had had to live with. The question was, what did this mean for her and Dom? She usually didn't tell people about her condition. At home she didn't need to because where she grew up everyone knew. Many people had been around when she'd had an episode or had heard about it. In London she had been able to reinvent herself, so she hadn't told anyone. Apart from Nancy, Nancy knew. She'd been great. There were moments when Alice knew Nancy was checking she was okay without being too obvious and it was nice that she cared without the full-on enveloping in cotton wool approach her parents favoured. She'd even managed to keep her scars from Whizzer by always wearing a T-shirt to bed, although in all honesty he'd been so stoned most of the time he wouldn't have noticed if she'd had Harry Styles's face tattooed across her chest.

Alice was waiting in a hospital bed for the next set of tests when a text popped up from Dom – *I can't wait for the school run on Monday so I get to see you again! D x*

She couldn't lie to him. She knew that anyone she got close to would eventually end up heartbroken and she also couldn't risk Bonnie being hurt again. How could she plan a future with Dom when she couldn't even guarantee she had a future herself?

* * *

Nancy wasn't sure how she'd been persuaded into a hot-air balloon and even more astonishingly into Freddy's arms, but she had to admit that she did feel marginally less like she was going to plummet to her death now he had her in a reassuringly firm hug. Nancy had her eyes tight shut and was trying to pretend she was on the tube. The burner wasn't helping by making its deafening noise again in frequent long bursts.

'We're at a good height,' said the pilot.

'Lovely,' said Nancy into Freddy's shoulder.

'Are you okay now?' asked Freddy.

'Erm . . .' As well as feeling safer, Nancy was quite enjoying the feeling of being held. It had been a while since she'd been held by a man and she'd forgotten how nice it was. He also smelled really good.

'If I could let go for a moment I'll pour you a glass of champagne,' said Freddy.

Nancy wasn't sure that was enough incentive, but Freddy was already loosening his embrace. 'Okay,' said Nancy, opening her eyes but keeping her gaze down. She grabbed the side of the basket and gripped it tightly.

Freddy deftly popped the cork and poured the drinks. He held out a glass to Nancy. She looked at her plastered arm and then at the white-knuckled hand holding the basket. 'You know I'm not that big a fan of champagne.'

'It's safe to let go, Nancy.' Freddy held the glass out.

Nancy took a deep breath and tried to let go of the basket but her brain wouldn't let her. 'Nope, sorry. You drink it.'

'Here,' said Freddy, moving closer. 'If you take the glass, I'll put my arm around you. Deal?'

'Hmm.' Nancy was thinking it over.

'I don't usually have to beg women to drink champagne or to let me cuddle them for that matter,' he said. The balloon pilot smirked.

'I'm not one of your usual women though, am I?' said Nancy still trying to motivate herself into taking the glass.

'No, you most definitely aren't,' said Freddy, his expression unreadable. Nancy wasn't sure that was a compliment. 'The champagne will steady your nerves,' he added.

Nancy steeled herself, tentatively let go of the balloon and took the glass, which she realised was actually made of plastic but looked like the real deal. Straightaway a comforting arm slid around her waist. Nancy took a large mouthful of champagne and then thought what the heck and knocked back the rest of it. 'What happens if we come down in the sea?' she asked.

'We're going in the other direction,' explained the pilot. 'See.' He pointed to one side and she foolishly looked. Her stomach nose-dived. In the distance was Langham Hall with the sea behind it and a village in the foreground. It looked like the model villages her parents had once taken her to see.

Freddy leaned in closer and she felt the warmth of him against her. 'Over there is the River Yealm and further this way is Plymouth.'

Nancy could see the urban sprawl in the distance. She looked up to see they were quite near to some wispy clouds. Now the burners were off it was completely silent apart from the occasional creak from the basket. It was surprisingly calm even though she wasn't. Although she had to admit she was feeling marginally less terrified.

'What made you pick a hot-air balloon ride? I mean I'm sure there were lots of equally terrifying options: bareback bull riding, bungee over the Grand Canyon, crocodile wrestling.'

'Funnily enough I did consider all of those. But the local hot-air ballooning club take off from Langham Hall once a month. It's a large area of flat land in the right place. I thought it might be fun to take you up as a little thank you for giving me a second chance with the job and helping find Arabella.'

The basket jolted and Nancy yelped. 'Next time a pack of custard creams will be fine.'

'I'll remember that,' said Freddy.

'Where are we heading?'

'Dartmoor,' said Freddy, sipping his fizz. He was very relaxed given there was nothing but a fancy picnic hamper stopping him plummeting to his death.

Nancy joined the dots in her mind of what she knew about Dartmoor. 'We're not horse-riding are we?'

Freddy laughed. 'No, I thought that was a step too far.'

'Thank heavens for that,' she said, and he gave her a little squeeze. She still wasn't convinced about the balloon, the drop to imminent death was only a hole in wicker away but it was exhilarating and there was definitely something she liked about being held by Freddy. Perhaps the champagne had already gone to her head.

Nancy realised the take-off and being up in the air parts of the balloon ride were not the ones she should have been worried about – it was the landing that was the most terrifying. The lower the balloon drifted the more she realised the speed it had been going. When they had been higher it hadn't been so noticeable and had felt like they were drifting effortlessly, but as they neared the ground it was like they were going supersonic. Freddy had her in a tight hug. 'I've got you,' he whispered into her hair as the basket hit the ground with a juddering thud making Nancy squeal. It was dragged along at a terrifying angle followed by a few more bumps and it righted itself before coming to a complete stop.

Nancy got a fit of the giggles once they were stationary. Within moments a Land Rover appeared, two young men jumped out and began securing the balloon. Freddy hurdled the side of the basket and leaned back in. 'Can I lift you out?' he asked.

Given how high the sides were Nancy wasn't confident she'd be able to climb out and retain her dignity. 'Why not?' She held up her arms like a child and Freddy lifted her out and onto the grass. If it wasn't for the thought of the ponies weeing all over it, she would have thankfully dropped to her knees and kissed the ground.

'Overall, how would you rate your first balloon ride?' he asked.

'Slightly less disturbing than the film *Snakes on a Plane* but more petrifying than actual flying.'

'That's probably fair,' said Freddy, leading them over to a second Land Rover that had now pulled up.

'How did they know where we were going to land? The pilot said he had no way of steering the thing.'

'There's a tracker on the balloon which the ground crew are following.'

'That's pretty cool,' she said as he held open the car door for her.

Ten minutes later they pulled into a layby. If she'd been with anyone else, she'd have thought it very dodgy, but Freddy was full of surprises. He hopped out. 'This way.' He took her hand and helped her out of the vehicle and as they started to walk across the uneven ground she noticed he'd not let go of her. She reasoned that it was sensible to keep hold of Freddy's hand as it was bumpy underfoot but that was easier than admitting to herself that she was quite enjoying the contact.

Nancy took in her surroundings – grass and bushes for as far as she could see. 'Freddy, there's nothing here.'

'Just a bit further.'

They walked over the undulating land until she spotted a flash of colour partly obscured by a bush. As they neared it, Paul stood up to greet them. They sat down on the picnic rug and Paul produced a full cream tea from a hamper including Earl Grey tea for Freddy and coffee for Nancy. 'There's more sandwiches and scones in the hamper. Give me a call and I'll come and pack away,' said Paul and he walked off.

'This is fantastic,' said Nancy. 'Thank you.'

'My pleasure,' said Freddy. 'It was important to me that you had a good time.'

'Was it?' she asked, sipping her coffee and eyeing him over the rim of the mug. 'Now why would that be I wonder?'

Freddy leaned closer. 'Because you fascinate me, Nancy Barraclough.'

'You're full of surprises yourself, Freddy something or other Astley-Davenport.'

Her forgetting his middle name made him laugh. 'You're funny.'

'Am I?'

'Definitely. But you're also smart, spirited and stunningly beautiful.'

The last word caught her slightly off guard. 'I thought you said in the balloon that you weren't coming on to me.'

'That was then and this is . . .' Freddy leaned further forwards until his lips brushed hers.

There were so many reasons why kissing Freddy was a bad idea but in that moment it certainly felt right. She kissed him back. Freddy's phone pinged but they both ignored it. Their kiss deepened. When the pinging increased they both opened their eyes at the same time. Freddy smiled at her. 'That was as perfect as I imagined it would be.' His phone pinged again.

'You'd best see what that is,' said Nancy.

Freddy was still smiling as he pulled his phone from his pocket, but his lips quickly drew a flat line. He frowned hard as he scrolled on his phone. 'What the hell?'

'What's up?' asked Nancy, still feeling like she was floating through the air.

A shocked Freddy turned his phone for her to see for herself. The first thing she saw was a picture of Freddy. He was laughing and had a champagne glass in his hand. Her smile slipped when she saw the very unflattering picture of herself – mouth open and wearing an oversized green coat. Then she realised it was the front page of the newspaper and the heading above read – 'FORTNUM'S FREDDY CONS HIS PARENTS'. Nancy swallowed hard as she read the strapline underneath – 'Freddy Astley-Davenport Plans To Oust His Parents From Their Home Thanks To A Plan Cooked Up By Grasping Wool Shop Owner.'

Chapter Thirty-One

Nancy wasn't one for drama but she couldn't help the gasp that escaped as she reread the newspaper headline. She was still trying to work out how on earth they'd got that awful picture of her.

'This is a nightmare,' said Freddy, getting to his feet and pacing around the edge of the picnic blanket.

'But it's lies, Freddy. Surely we can sue?' Nancy tried to skim read the article. 'This is outrageous. A blatant intrusion of privacy.'

'They know all about the deal. My parents are going to go completely off the scale over this.'

'But most of it is pure fantasy. They say here that you were planning on getting your inheritance and then selling the estate.' Nancy scoffed. But a glance at Freddy made her feel decidedly uneasy. 'Freddy, that's all lies surely?'

He puffed out a breath. 'It's for the best.'

Nancy was shocked. 'Seriously, Freddy? You were planning to get your hands on the place and then sell it?'

'This isn't a snap decision. It's something I've thought long and hard about. Agonised over.' Nancy snorted her derision. She didn't imagine Freddy agonised over anything. He continued. 'Me taking it on is by far the worst option. If it goes to a charity, then it would have to include a large cash payment towards ongoing upkeep. But if it's sold, that money could buy somewhere smaller and provide a good cushion for my parents.'

'Conning them with this *look at me I'm holding down a real job act* only to sell it as soon as you get your hands on it though. That's a really shitty thing to do.'

'You don't understand,' started Freddy.

Nancy tried to stand up, but she couldn't push herself up with her bad arm so had to roll onto her knees which was not her most flattering look. 'Try me,' she said once she was upright and blocking his route around the blanket.

'The estate is a millstone around my father's neck, it's been dragging him down for years. It's wrecked his health—'

'I'm sorry but he seemed pretty healthy to me. I mean, I didn't like to pry as to what's wrong with him but I'm not sure it's all as bad as everyone is making out.'

Freddy shook his head. 'I thought you knew about hidden illnesses. I thought you understood.' He didn't give her a chance to respond. 'My father suffers with his mental health. You were lucky to see him on a good week. Those are few and far between. He's on medication to try to keep his moods even. He's been depressed most of his adult life. And that's all thanks to the historic burden he carries. Tradition dictated that running the estate had to be his job, his number one priority in life and he's dedicated himself to it. But there's never enough hours or money to keep on top of everything. He worries constantly about being the weak link in the family tree that messes it all up. The one who loses the family seat and lets every one of his ancestors down.' Freddy ran both his hands through his hair. 'He's looking to me to fix all the things that he couldn't. That's why he wants to hand it over early. He also thinks it will give me a purpose. But the last thing

I want is to do the same thing for the rest of my life knowing that I'll probably fail at it anyway.'

'But, Freddy, selling it without telling them that's . . .'

'Judge all you like. I can't take that on. I know I'd only let everyone down. It's best I do that earlier rather than later while the estate still has value. I've tried talking to Father about selling up, but he won't hear of it, so this was the only way. Please don't try and convince me that I'm wrong because I know it's what's best for everyone.'

'My dad always taught me to not give up. That when it gets tough there's always an answer, you just have to look in the right place and work harder. You need to stop looking at the problems and focus on the solutions. Your home is a potential gold mine. I've read about other estates turning themselves around. It's the perfect place for retreats, weddings, parties and opening up the gardens to the public.' Nancy's phone rang. 'It's Claudia, I'd best take this as she's probably going to have to field a number of calls today.' Nancy walked away and picked up the call.

'Shit, Nancy, I don't know how to tell you this . . .' began Claudia.

'It's okay I've seen the newspaper,' said Nancy.

'Don't you mean *newspapers*? It's headline news bloody everywhere,' said Claudia. 'Did you know what Freddy was doing?'

'Of course I didn't know,' said Nancy, trying to keep calm. 'I thought the deal with Sir Richard was that we got a contract in exchange for Freddy getting some work experience. It turns out there never was a flaming deal with Sir Richard in the first place and nobody said anything about conning his parents.' She shot a look at Freddy who was scrolling agitatedly through his mobile. 'It's no comment to the press. I'll come up with some wording for a statement. We need to be clear that I don't benefit from this in any way so why on earth would I get involved? It's all about damage limitation.'

'I don't know about damage limitation. But the website hit rate has gone through the roof in the last couple of hours. Let's hope some of those buy something while they're there.'

'Blimey.' Nancy hadn't been expecting that. 'But the point is, I didn't engineer this. Maybe I need to consult a lawyer.'

Nancy was distracted by Freddy waving a hand in front of her face, which was very annoying. 'My lawyer is already on it,' he said.

'I might want my own lawyer,' said Nancy.

'You just said that,' said Claudia into her ear.

'I'm sorry, Claudia, I've got two conversations going on here. Please can you reassure the team that I'm not involved in any con. And ensure everyone is focused on keeping the day-to-day running going smoothly. Also, please can you buy everyone doughnuts?'

'On it. And you take care of yourself. Okay?'

'I will. Thanks, Claudia. You're a star.'

'Twinkle, twinkle,' said Claudia and the line went dead.

Nancy walked back to Freddy, who was on his mobile, the unfinished picnic and champagne glasses at his feet. He ended his call. 'Paul is on his way.'

'Maybe we shouldn't overreact. The paper is printed, there's nothing we can do about it now.' Nancy was also feeling a bit peckish now her jitters from the hot-air balloon had subsided. 'Maybe we could have some break-fast and try to forget about it.'

'Forget about it? Did you read what that rag said about you? This could damage your business.'

'I just spoke to Claudia and website hits are up so every

cloud . . .' Nancy shrugged her shoulders and forced a smile.

'So you've come out of this all right then. Hang on.' He pointed at Nancy and frowned. 'It wasn't you who . . . no obviously not.' Freddy stopped pointing and looked sheepish.

'Bloody hell. Did you think I did this? That I went to the press?'

'Obviously not.' Nancy's eyes widened at him. 'I mean you did once threaten it, but it was merely a fleeting thought,' he admitted.

'Fleeting or otherwise you actually thought I'd do something like this?! You can piss right off, Freddy!' Nancy stormed off. The only problem was she was in the middle of Dartmoor and there really wasn't anywhere to storm off to.

'Is everything all right?' asked Paul, coming the other way.

'Fine. Apart from Freddy being headline news and me not getting any breakfast.'

'Breakfast I can solve,' said Paul kindly. 'Here's the keys, if you'd like to wait in the car.'

'Thank you,' said Nancy, feeling rather foolish for her outburst but the truth was Freddy had hurt her. That he'd thought even for a moment that she would sell him down the river pained her more than she liked to admit. She was also still furious about how he'd failed to share his plans for selling the estate. But then if he had she would never have gotten involved. Nancy sat in the car and fumed.

Freddy got in next to her. 'You okay?' he asked. Nancy didn't respond. 'Are we not talking?'

Nancy rounded on him. 'I'm so cross I'm not even talking to myself right now!' She twisted in her seat to stare him down. 'You've taken me for a prize bloody idiot.

I thought you genuinely wanted to learn skills you could use to manage the estate but the whole time you were counting down until you could sell up.' Nancy gasped as she realised something else. 'Your parents will think I was in on it. You need to put them straight!'

'Because making sure you don't fall out with my parents is my number one priority.' Freddy shook his head.

'Don't worry, I know *you* are and always will be your number one pri—'

Paul opened the car door and presented Nancy with a plate containing a scone smothered with jam and cream. 'Breakfast?' he said. But Nancy was too full of bile to eat anything.

* * *

Alice's consultant typed a lot of notes as she explained about her most recent episode of racing pulse, chest pain and fainting. Excessive notes were never good. She'd been hoping that he'd reassure her that everything was fine and perfectly normal, but he didn't. Alice was pleased that her parents hadn't come in with her. She wasn't proud of herself for hiding what had happened at the beach from them, but she knew how they worried. Was it best to know what she was dealing with and hopefully have a solution before she shared any bad news? Or to forewarn them so they were prepared? She didn't know.

Alice had an intrinsic dislike of hospitals. She'd spent so much time in them as a child that they were both reassuringly familiar and abjectly terrifying. Terrifying because every time she came to one, she was scared of what they would tell her. That the ticking bomb inside her chest was about to stop ticking. There was also that smell that overpowered everything – disinfectant and melancholy. That made it sound like one of those fancy candles Nancy bought.

'Your tests today are definitely throwing up some anomalies. I'd like you to wear a monitor for twenty-four hours so we can get a full picture,' explained the consultant. 'And you need to take things easy for a few days. Nothing strenuous.'

'Okay but I can't spend the rest of my life like that,' said Alice, thinking out loud. 'Unless this is a warning sign that I don't have much life left.' She felt her chest tighten at the thought. 'Is that it? Am I . . .'

The consultant held up a hand. 'Please don't panic. I'm asking you to rest as a precaution. I want a twenty-four-hour ECG so we have as much information as possible before we make any decisions about next steps. There's no reason to fear the worst.'

'And what would be the worst?' asked Alice, although the words were hard to get out because her mouth had gone dry.

'It could be a number of things causing this flare-up but it's likely that some repair work is needed to the fixes that were done when you were younger. You've grown and things wear out. It would be a straight-forward procedure and the recovery is generally very good.'

'Generally? Then there's still a risk, right?' Her pulse rate was speeding up at the thought of more surgery.

He smiled at her. A smile she'd seen a million times before. The one that said, 'I'm sorry but I can't guarantee that you won't die.'

'It's not as invasive as open-heart surgery. Ninety-six per cent of patients survive at least five years. But there's always a risk with any operation.'

'There is to those poor four per cent who don't make it. That could be me!'

'Alice, please try to stay calm. Any treatment we do is

all about improving your health. If I thought there was any immediate threat I would admit you.'

Alice let out a deep sigh. Another bullet dodged, well for today anyway. Now all she had to do was break the news to her parents.

Despite Alice playing everything down her parents still reacted badly as she knew they would. They'd been here a number of times before. When she'd been a child she'd never really understood how serious things were. She'd just known she was different, special even. That was what her parents had told her. As she'd got older she'd felt less special and more as if she'd got a raw deal. She couldn't do what the other kids did. She was always the one sitting out and, more accurately, missing out. Her mum and dad had done their absolute best for her. Her mum had given up a promising career as a chemist to be on hand for appointments and the frequent calls from school to come and collect her. But they'd also been overprotective. Their worry overspilling into control, not that they ever meant that to happen, but it did. They stopped Alice putting herself at risk but that also meant she skipped all the good stuff. She feared that was about to happen again.

'I'm at home all the time anyway,' said her mum. 'Your dad will be back to work on Monday but that's fine.'

'What are you on about?' asked Alice, trying to suppress the familiar niggle of annoyance.

A flash of confusion darted across her mother's features. 'You'll be staying here until we know what's happening.' It wasn't even a question.

'Mum, you don't get to decide where I stay. And anyway, I've got work on Monday.'

'But the consultant said you had to rest. Nothing strenuous,' said her mother.

'You did say that,' pointed out her dad.

Alice chuckled. 'He didn't mean stay in bed and don't go to work. He just meant take it easy.'

'Alice, I know you love being in London but this is your heart we're talking about. You have to be careful.' The tears in her mother's eyes made Alice soften.

'And I will be careful, Mum. I promise. But I have a life in London and I can't not live it.' *Especially when I don't know when it could be cut short*, she thought.

Chapter Thirty-Two

Nancy was fizzing with anger and hurt when Paul pulled the car in front of the manor house where Oscar was waiting and radiating hostility. Freddy got out of the car with his palms up as if being faced with a shotgun which Nancy realised could have been an option. 'I've seen it too. The hacks have gone too far this time. I'm as cross as you are,' said Freddy.

'I doubt that very much. Would you both come through to the morning room, your mother and I would like to discuss this with you.'

Nancy felt like she was being called to the headteacher's office, only worse, because she liked Oscar and Louisa. Oscar's pace seemed to be fuelled by his fury. The morning room was on the same side of the house as the study. It had giant windows which let in light and provided magnificent views past the gardens to the undulating countryside and woodland beyond. Louisa was sitting perched on a sumptuous sofa, her eyes red and puffy which instantly affected Nancy. She might be cross but in front of her was a woman who had been betrayed by her own son.

'Take a seat,' said Oscar formally as he sat down next to Louisa and gave a fleeting squeeze of her hand.

Freddy sat down opposite, leaned forward and clasped

his hands together. 'I understand that you're upset and annoyed and you have every right to be but—'

Oscar spoke over him. 'We have not asked you here to explain yourselves. As it is clear that you are in cahoots. We simply wanted to inform you both . . .' he glanced at Nancy but it was as if he could hardly bear to look at her. '. . . That we are in discussions with a number of heritage charities about handing the bulk of the estate over to them.'

'You can't—' began Freddy but Louisa cut him off.

'Frederick, you've left us no choice. At least this way the property remains intact rather than being bulldozed or converted into holiday accommodation.'

Freddy threw up his arms. 'So that's it. I lose my inheritance because of some tabloid lies.'

Nancy flinched at the word and Oscar saw it. 'But are they lies?' asked Oscar. 'Nancy, I take it you've seen the article.' She nodded. 'And is it entirely fabricated?'

'It's not as simple as that. There's a bit of a story and a misunderstanding because I was on the tube and my phone kept cutting out so I didn't know what I was agreeing to. Then Freddy showed up and I thought he'd come for the job. And he did explain that he needed the job to get his inheritance.' Usually, she was far more articulate. 'But the thing is, right now Freddy *is* working as my PA. Aren't you?' She turned to see Freddy with his head in his hands.

Oscar blinked and shook his head. 'I'll take that as a no.'

It took Nancy a moment to realise. 'I'm getting confused. Is the article *entirely* made up? No. But surely what matters is where we are now. Am I right?'

'I'm sorry, Nancy,' said Louisa. 'I suspect Frederick has led you down the garden path. I don't know what he's promised you. He's fickle when it comes to women and I'm afraid he won't be inheriting anything anytime soon.'

'I take offence at that,' said Nancy and both Louisa and Oscar swivelled in her direction which was quite intimidating. 'I knew some of what I was getting into, yes. I'll give you that. But there was nothing going on between us, if that's what you're thinking. Well not until this morning.' Nancy scratched her head, she'd almost forgotten about their kiss. 'But it was me who said he had to actually do the job. Learn some skills for when he took over the estate. Didn't I?' She looked to Freddy to back her up.

'Really not helping,' he said with a sigh.

'I think it's best if you both leave,' said Oscar, standing up abruptly. Louisa blew her nose.

'Surely we can discuss this rationally,' said Freddy, splaying out his hands.

'Perhaps in time. But not at the moment,' said Oscar. 'Paul!' he called and the morning room door opened.

'Hey hang on,' said Nancy. 'This isn't fair. I know Freddy can be a bit of a mare but this time he's—'

'It's not worth it,' said Freddy, touching Nancy's shoulder. 'They're not listening.' Nancy felt like she'd been tried and sentenced without a proper trial and it infuriated her.

They walked through the door and Nancy heard Louisa burst into tears. Her instinct was to turn back but Freddy stopped her and shook his head. 'Leave it, Nancy.' Why did she get the feeling he thought she'd made things worse?

Paul was his usual kind self and he helped Nancy round up Carrie into her carrier. Otto seemed confused as to why his queen was imprisoned and her poking her paws through the bars only added to his fretfulness. It didn't take Nancy long to pack her things into her case. Now her anger was subsiding she felt awful for the part she'd played in the deception, even though that had been unknowingly. Louisa and Oscar had been so kind and she hated that they thought badly of her. Paul came to carry her things downstairs to where Freddy was waiting in the hall. He made a fuss of Otto who was now lying with his nose at the bars with Carrie's sad face on the other side. Freddy turned to leave.

'Hang on,' said Nancy. She was blowed if she was going to leave with her tail between her legs. She may not have explained the situation well but that didn't mean she was guilty. Freddy might not feel the need to clear her name with his parents, but she did.

'Nancy!' There was exasperation in his tone.

'I'll be two minutes.' *Or less if I get manhandled out,* she thought. But then who would do that? Paul was far too nice.

Nancy dashed through the house and came to face the morning room door. She took a deep breath and knocked.

'Come in,' said Oscar.

Nancy walked through the door with her head held high. Louisa was sipping what smelled like a fruit tea and Oscar was standing by the window. Neither of them looked pleased to see her.

'I'd like to avoid any further upset,' said Louisa.

'I've not come here for any trouble,' said Nancy. 'I'll say my piece and then I'll go.' She didn't give them the opportunity to object. 'I know this is a bugger's muddle.' Louisa's eyebrows rose at her phrase. 'Well, a right mess anyway. And I'm sorry for the part I played. I honestly didn't know Freddy was planning to sell the place, I'd never get involved in something like that. I thought it was a good idea that he had a taste of the real world. And I can share with you proof that Freddy is employed by my company. That was always legit and I would never have agreed to it on any other grounds. You're lovely people, you have a frankly

285

awesome home and I'm really grateful for you putting me up these last few days. That was all I wanted to say really.' When there was no response she headed for the door.

'Nancy,' said Louisa. 'Thank you.'

Nancy gave her a wan smile and left. Maybe it hadn't solved anything, but she felt better for it. All she had to do now was work out how to put things right.

Freddy was in the car, tapping his fingers impatiently on the steering wheel. Paul opened the passenger door and Otto almost dived in ahead of Nancy. 'Hey, boy, you have to stay here,' she told him. Carrie let out a plaintive yowl of one clearly being kidnapped, which made Otto bark.

Paul took hold of his collar. 'Goodbye, Nancy. It's been a pleasure to meet you. I hope we see you again soon.'

'Ah, Paul. I doubt that, sunshine. But thanks for saying it. You're a diamond.' To hell with protocol. She gave him a hug. 'Take it easy.'

'I will certainly try,' he replied with a faint smile.

'Thank you, Paul,' said Freddy as Paul closed the passenger door and led a whimpering Otto away.

Freddy drove out of the portico, across the gravel and over the cattle grid. Nancy looked back at the house. It had been a bizarre week having a peep into a world very different to her own. The big house with all its history, the pretty, tranquil gardens, the private bay full of seashells – it was all the stuff of lottery-fuelled dreams and big euro rollover ones at that. But aside from that it had been the people she'd connected with. That had probably surprised her the most. Despite coming from a long line of gentry, Oscar was a nice guy, Louisa was completely lovely, Grandpa was a legend and everyone needed a Paul in their life. The bottom line was, she'd enjoyed it far more than she'd have thought.

The gates were already open as they approached. Freddy turned out onto the country lane. That was it. She'd not be returning to Langham Hall ever again. She wondered when Freddy would be back. Nancy glanced across at him. His features set to a scowl as he glared at the road ahead. 'It's going to be a really long journey if we're not talking,' she said.

Freddy ran his bottom lip through his teeth. 'I was under the impression that it was you who wasn't talking to me.'

'Yeah well. Devon to London is a long way. But it doesn't mean I'm not still mad as hell with you, because I am.'

'That should certainly make for light, easy chatter.'

'Let's agree not to talk about the newspaper. Okay?'

'That's fine with me,' said Freddy, indicating as the car left the pretty little village. 'What shall we talk about?'

Nancy twisted her lips. Coming up with a neutral topic of conversation was tricky. 'I spy?'

'Definitely not,' said Freddy. Perhaps it was going to be a long trip after all.

Nancy killed time by answering a few emails on her phone, as well as having a little snooze. A high-pitched meow from a forlorn Carrie woke her up and she was sad to remember that she was on her way home. That thought brought her up short. 'Alice is still away,' she said.

'I don't know what you want me to do with that information,' said Freddy, still sounding grouchy.

'I'm thinking out loud. If Alice is away, I'll be on my own.' Nancy had that same image of her and Carrie sharing a Dairylea triangle for dinner. 'But my mum and dad were back from their holiday last night.' It probably wasn't the welcome they needed but they would still be pleased to see her and right now she could do with that. 'Can you take me to my parents' place?'

'You'd best put their postcode in the sat nav,' he said. Nancy guessed that was as good a reply as she was going to get.

There was something oddly comforting about the sound of a police siren as they made their way to her parents' London home. She was a little envious of Freddy who had the best of both worlds with a flat in Belgravia and Langham Hall in Devon. Freddy glanced at the sat nav a couple of times.

'Are you going to go all London cabby on me and say I'd 'ave never come this way, love?' She over-egged her accent for comic effect.

'No, just checking,' said Freddy. Was it her imagination or was he looking a bit twitchy as they entered Hackney?

Past the market and the graffiti-clad buildings they turned off. The sat nav announced that they had reached their destination. Freddy slowed and peered out at the hotchpotch of industrial buildings and terraced housing.

'It's just up there. You can park anywhere. Nobody really bothers,' said Nancy.

Freddy didn't answer. He pulled the car up next to an overflowing skip. 'Do they live there?' Freddy pointed at the high-rise flats.

'Yep. Thanks for the lift. I really appreciate it. I'll need to do a couple of trips for all my stuff and Carrie.' The cat gave a pathetic mew at her name.

'I'll give you a hand,' said Freddy, getting out of the car.

'You don't need to. I get that you'd be a bit twitchy leaving your car here.'

'Oh no, it's fine,' he said, darting a glance over his shoulder.

'Okay, if you're sure.' She handed him her laptop bag. 'Thanks.' Nancy loaded herself up as best she could without straining her arm and led the way. Freddy checked his car was locked twice.

Inside the building it didn't smell great, but the lifts were working so that was a bonus. She jabbed the button for floor twelve with her elbow while Freddy read the notices on the wall that asked residents not to spit, urinate or defecate in the public areas. Probably not the best impression but Nancy wasn't trying to impress Freddy.

What had happened was eating away at her and she couldn't ignore it – that simply wasn't in her nature. 'Look. I'm just going to say it and then we can forget about it. It's not right you trying to rip off your folks. I would never have given you a job if I'd had even the slightest inkling that that was what you had planned. They're good people and they don't deserve that.' She lifted a hand as far as it would go while holding the cat. 'There, I've said my piece.'

'Hang on,' said Freddy. 'You can't be judge and jury. You have absolutely no idea the sort of pressure my father has been under for virtually his whole life. I don't want the same thing to happen to me. If anything, I'm doing my parents and future Astley-Davenports a favour. I'm saving them and myself from a life of mental anguish. And you of all people know how useless I am. Me taking over was always going to be a recipe for disaster. I can assure you that would hurt my parents far more.'

The lift pinged like the bell to signal the end of a round of boxing and the doors opened. 'Maybe we should agree to disagree,' said Nancy.

'Fine by me.' Freddy flared his nostrils as he stepped out of the lift.

They went through some graffitied doors and along the corridor. Nancy knocked on her parents' door. Freddy was checking over his shoulder as if he was expecting to be mugged at any moment. 'I know it's not like having my own village in Devon but it's fairly safe around here, you know,' she said, feeling a bit defensive.

Freddy straightened his spine. 'Of course.'

The dark green door opened on the chain. 'Who is it?' asked Nancy's mum.

'It's me,' said Nancy.

'Nancy, love!' The door closed and there was frantic jangling as the chain was removed and the door reopened. Mrs Barraclough was a small woman with a fierce hug, and she wasn't put off by the fact Nancy had her arms full. 'Let me look at you.' She stepped back and gasped. 'What have you done?' She pointed to Nancy's plaster.

'It's nothing really.'

'You can't say . . .' Mrs Barraclough noticed Freddy for the first time. 'And who do we have here?' She made no effort to hide that she was scanning him up and down. 'My word you're a—'

'Mum!' Nancy shook her head.

'Mrs Barraclough, I'm Freddy Astley-Davenport. I work for Nancy. It's a pleasure to meet you. I've heard so much about you.' Nancy twisted her head so far around she felt like an owl. Did Freddy still work for her? Surely there was no point anymore. That was another conundrum she'd have to sort out.

'Come in, both of you,' said her mum. 'You've clearly got lots to tell us, and me and your dad took a million photos on our cruise. Just back yesterday, Freddy. It was a-maze-ing. You ever been on a ship?'

'He probably owns one,' muttered Nancy, shutting the door with her bum.

Her mother led them through to the tiny sitting room where her dad was waiting patiently. He threw his arms out and Nancy almost dropped what she was carrying on the sofa so she could give him a hug. 'My girl, as beautiful as ever,' he said. They finished their embrace and he eyed the stuff on the sofa. 'You brought the cat? This isn't good. What's happened? Have you not paid your rent?'

'Dad! I've broken my arm and it's tricky doing stuff. I'll only be here one night until Alice is back.'

Nancy noted that Freddy looked slightly surprised to see that her dad was a wheelchair user but he quickly recovered and offered him a hand to shake.

'Mr Barraclough, I'm Freddy. How do you do?'

'All right, son, thanks.'

'Freddy, have a seat,' said Mrs Barraclough almost pushing him into a well-worn armchair. 'That's not the first time she's broken something. Five she was when she shut her middle finger in the door. Went around showing every person she met. Gave the bird to everyone from the doctor to a little old lady at the bus stop. I've never been so embarrassed. Tea or coffee, love?'

'Mum!' Nancy had tried to communicate with her eyes, but her mother was oblivious. 'Freddy can't stop. He's a very busy person. Aren't you?'

'I just need to get the rest of your things from the car,' said Freddy. 'I'll be back in a few minutes so a coffee would be lovely, Mrs Barraclough, thank you.'

Freddy got to his feet and everyone waited until the front door clicked shut behind him.

'Bloody hell, Nance. He's sex on a stick!' said her mum. 'And that voice. He reminds me of . . .' She clicked her fingers. 'Who's that posh bloke I fancy off the telly? Was in that thing and Corrie for a bit.'

'Nigel Havers,' said her dad.

'He's nothing like Nigel Havers,' said Nancy, feeling offended on Freddy's behalf.

Her mum laughed. 'He doesn't look like him. He just

sounds a bit like him. Well posh. Lovely manners. Nice bum.'

'Mum!'

'You know I must have had a premonition because I bought some of those chocolate animal biscuits you like. Want some with your coffee?'

'No thanks. I'm going to put my stuff in your bedroom and let Carrie out in here. Okay?'

'Let me have a cuddle with my grand cat,' said Mrs Barraclough, taking Carrie out. 'You don't want to be shut in there do you, gorgeous?' Nancy took a couple of minutes to ferry things into the only bedroom. She'd be sleeping on their sofa for the night, but it was lovely to see her parents.

There was a knock on the door and Nancy went to let Freddy in.

'This is everything,' he said.

'Great. If you can put it in here.' She held open the door to her parents' bedroom. She saw him sweep his eyes around the small space and it made her shoulders tighten. 'You don't have to stay,' she said in hushed tones.

'I don't, but I'd like to,' said Freddy, walking past her. 'Can I give you a hand with anything, Mrs Barraclough?'

'Call me Debs. And this is Wayne.' She pointed at her husband. 'You put your feet up, lad.'

Freddy relaxed in the armchair, but Nancy was on edge. Wayne was nodding and drumming his fingers on the arm of his chair. Nancy couldn't bear it.

'You look well, Dad,' said Nancy. 'How did you manage on the cruise?'

'They couldn't do enough for me,' he said. He looked at Freddy. 'Can be a bit tricky in one of these. But I've always got a seat,' he quipped.

Debs came in with a tray of drinks and a plate of

chocolate animal biscuits. Freddy got to his feet and took the tray from her. 'Thank you, Freddy. What nice manners.' She signalled her approval at Nancy with her eyebrows. 'Tuck in. These are Nancy's favourites. Get yourselves comfy and Wayne will get out his square thing and show you the holiday snaps.'

'It's a tablet, Mum.' Nancy could feel her shoulders getting tenser. 'And I don't think Freddy wants to see them.'

'You don't mind do you, Fred?' asked Wayne.

Freddy grinned and Nancy wanted to slap him. 'Mind?' said Freddy. 'I'd love to see them.'

Chapter Thirty-Three

Alice was going to need to dig her way out of her parents' bungalow as there was no way they were going to let her leave alone. At least that's how it felt. The consultant had unsettled them all and until they had the full set of results from the ECG machine she'd been wearing even she was a bit twitchy, but she wasn't going to let on to her parents.

She was packing her bag when her mum put her head around the bedroom door. 'What are you doing out of bed?' she asked but her eyes had already spotted what Alice was doing. 'Surely you're not going to go against hospital advice?'

'They said not to do anything strenuous. Getting the train is hardly that.' Alice added a little laugh at the end to emphasise how silly her mum was being.

'And what if you can't get a seat and have to stand half the way to London? Or like that time I came to see you and there was nowhere to put my case, so I had to hang onto it all the way there while people tutted and stepped over it. Now that *was* stressful.'

Alice didn't like that her mum was making her rethink her plans. 'It probably won't be that busy.'

'Half-term week when everyone is heading home from the seaside? It'll be rammed.'

She probably had a point. 'I don't have a choice. I have to be at school on Monday morning.'

Her dad appeared in the doorway. Her mum spun in his direction. 'Will you tell her because she won't listen to me?'

He held up his hands. 'I understand what you're both saying and I'm wondering if there might be another option?' The two women waited. 'Instead of travelling back by train how about getting your friend Dom to give you a lift?'

Both Alice and her mum pouted at him. 'I suppose,' began her mum. 'If you absolutely have to go back to London then being in a car with someone else is probably the best option.' She bit her lip. 'He could drive you straight to a hospital if he had to.'

'Mum!'

Her mother held up her hands in surrender. 'I was just thinking out loud. You have to think of the worst that could happen.'

That was exactly what Alice didn't want to do. 'It's not a bad idea, Dad,' she conceded. The only thing was it felt like a big ask. It would have been so much easier if Dom offered but then he wasn't likely to do that because he had no idea that his potential new girlfriend had a life-threatening heart condition. Her parents were watching her. 'I'll call him and ask,' she said with a smile. They were still staring at her. 'But not right this second.' She turned back to her packing and hoped they'd take the hint.

Alice had pitched it to Dom as a money-saving sugges-tion. Why pay for a train ticket back to London when she could split the fuel costs with Dom? The fact that she already had her train ticket, because she'd bought a return, was irrelevant. Dom had jumped at the opportunity to share the journey home with her which had been exactly the reaction she'd hoped for, and it had ignited that little happy spark inside her. That spark had since been well and truly snuffed out by the worry that her parents were going to give Dom a long list of instructions and by doing that would alert him to her wobbly health. She knew if they were to go any further with the relationship then she had to be honest with him and explain about her condition, but now was not a good time and she certainly didn't want her anxious parents doing the job for her.

They were waiting at the window like the three wise monkeys but with slightly different poses. Alice was nearest the door ready to dash as soon as she saw Dom's car. She'd had two false starts already. Her dad was standing nearby with the TV remote in his hand pretending to check what was on that evening despite his eyes being firmly trained on the window. And her mum had hold of the net curtains and hadn't blinked for about ten minutes.

A car pulled up and Alice bolted for the front door, her parents followed. Alice spun around. 'It's best that we say goodbye here.' She spread her arms wide and her mum automatically hugged her.

'Ring as soon as you get there. Don't overdo it. If you have any symptoms go straight to hospit . . .' Her mum's voice broke and the sound stabbed at Alice's heart.

'I'll be fine, Mum. Try not to worry.' She knew she was asking the impossible.

'Let your dad put your case in the boot of this lad's car.'

'It's fine. I can wheel it to the car and Dom will lift it—'

Ding dong. The doorbell halted Alice's sentence. Her plan had been derailed. Dom was on the other side of the door. 'I really need to go. I love you guys.' She kissed them both.

Alice opened the door and tried to dart through it, but it was hard to move fast with a wheelie case.

'Hiya,' said Dom with a jolly wave at her parents.

They waved back but did not share his happy expression. 'Bye,' said Alice, almost running him over in her haste to get him back to his car.

'Is everything okay?' asked Dom, automatically taking her case from her.

'They're just sad to see me go. You know what parents are like.' Alice did an exaggerated eye-roll. While Dom was putting the case in the boot Alice gave a thumbs up to her mum and dad. She hated to see them looking so down. And it hurt to know that it was her that was causing their pain. Not intentionally of course but their fear of losing her was ever present and that was a heavy cross to bear. She swallowed down a lump of emotion and blew them another kiss before getting in the passenger side.

'Hello, Alice!' said Bonnie. 'Daddy says we can have my music on.'

Dom was getting in the driver's side. 'What I actually said was if Alice can bear it, we can have your music on. It's a Disney films soundtrack album,' he said with a wince as he put on his seatbelt.

'I should think we could listen to it for a little while.'

'Yay!' said Bonnie.

A tap on the passenger window made Alice jump. She'd been so close to escaping. Her dad's face loomed on the other side of the glass. The temptation to shout at Dom like he was a getaway driver was overwhelmingly strong. Dom seemed puzzled as to why she hadn't already buzzed the window down, so he did it for her.

Alice's dad leaned in and Alice held her breath. 'Take good care driving. Our Alice here is . . .' Alice gave the slightest of head shakes '. . . very special.'

'I agree,' said Dom. 'I'll make sure we all get home safe. Lovely to have met you.'

'And you,' said her dad. 'Take care.' He patted her arm before retreating. Everyone was waving like they were at a royal event as Dom pulled away and finally Alice was able to breathe properly.

* * *

Freddy stayed for a very uncomfortable thirty minutes before he thanked her parents for their hospitality and left. There had been an awkward moment at the door when he seemed unsure of how to say goodbye. So Nancy had said, 'The least said the better. And you don't need to work your notice. All bets are off. Take care, Freddy.' She'd opened the door for him. He'd leaned forward and kissed her cheek before leaving without a word. And that was it. Freddy Astley-Davenport had walked out of her life. Nancy felt more bereft than she could have imagined or would ever want to admit, not even to herself.

Nancy walked back into the living room to the expectant faces of her parents.

'Don't go buying hats, Mum. It's not like that.'

Her mum put her hand to her chest. 'Did I say anything of the sort?'

'Your face did.' Nancy flopped exhausted onto the sofa, making a curled-up Carrie bounce up and down.

'It's just nice that you're out meeting people again. And by people, I mean men. It doesn't do to work all the hours God sends. There's more to life than work.'

'If this is the "I want to be a nanna chat" now is not the time,' said Nancy, resting her head back against the sofa and closing her eyes. She wanted to erase the last few hours. It had all been going so well until it wasn't. That seemed to be the story of her life.

'I just don't want you to look back and regret anything,' said her mum. 'Anyway, I'm thinking egg and chips for tea?'

'That'd be great, thanks.' Nancy was grateful that there would be an intermission in the badgering while her mother cooked.

Once her mum was safely in the kitchen her dad wheeled over. 'What's up?' he asked.

Nancy opened her eyes. 'Nothing, I'm just a bit tired that's all.'

'Nice try. If you don't want to tell me that's fine but I'm here. That's all I'm saying.' He reached forward and squeezed her hand. The contact brought an unexpected lump to her throat.

'I let my guard down and Freddy sneaked in. Which is ridiculous because we couldn't be more different if we tried. We have like absolutely nothing in common. He has a massive country estate with a blooming peacock for heaven's sake. There was this spark between us but everything crashed and burned this morning.' She sighed deeply. 'You'll see the newspapers at some point. He's this rich socialite and someone sold a story about me being after his money to save my business and now his parents have kicked him out and my name is mud.'

'He's got a peacock?'

'That's what you take from all that?' She tilted her head.

'It's unusual that's all.' He smiled. 'You know, Nancy, it's not our differences that separate us but our bloody mindedness and inability to admire what makes each of us unique.'

'Bloody hell, have you been watching Open University broadcasts again?' asked Nancy, forcing a laugh.

'I'm just saying everyone is different and that's to be celebrated. I think you youngsters are obsessed with analysing every detail and because of that you focus on the negatives rather than simply enjoying connecting with another human being.'

'Maybe.' Nancy shrugged. She was tired and emotionally bruised and not in the right frame of mind to analyse anything.

Her dad kept his voice low as he leaned forward. 'Are the problems with the business temporary?'

'Who knows?' said Nancy, trying and failing to sound nonchalant.

'If you don't have a solid plan to recover them then they're not temporary.' He was studying her. 'Maybe it's time to cut your losses?'

'I've put my heart and soul into my business, Dad. I'm not going to walk away.'

'Even if it's the smart thing to do?' He tilted his head.

'But you always taught me never to give up.'

'Knowing when to quit is very different to giving up.'

Nancy was pondering her father's words when her mum came bounding out of the kitchen. 'Beans or spaghetti hoops?' she asked, proffering two tins.

Maybe some decisions were easier to make than others.

Chapter Thirty-Four

The car journey back with Dom hadn't been the enjoyable experience Alice had been hoping for. It wasn't anything to do with Dom, he'd been his usual lovely self, it had been her parents' worries that had occupied her mind. They had an uncanny knack of bringing the real world to life and while Alice didn't want to face it sometimes there was no escape from her condition. She joined in with a *Moana* sing-song and a few games of I spy but when Dom started talking about fixing a regular date night, reality gave Alice a bit of a shake.

However much she wanted to be in a relationship with Dom was it really fair to him and Bonnie? She couldn't promise them anything long-term – how could she when she herself didn't know what the future had in store for her? She'd found herself getting quieter and quieter the closer they got to London. She passed it off as tiredness, but she was beginning to realise that the longer she was with Dom the harder it would be to call things off. For everyone's sakes it was better if she did it sooner rather than later. Rip off the Band-Aid. But Alice wasn't very good at things like that, she didn't like confrontation, so when Dom dropped her off, she gave him a hug, waved to Bonnie and went inside. Maybe if she just cooled off gradually that would be easier for everyone?

It was Sunday morning and Alice was thinking through her options while luxuriating in a very full bath with more than a few drops of Nancy's fancy bath essence. The scent of a wild mint and eucalyptus candle was also helping her relax. Alice was enjoying having Nancy's house to herself. Nancy wasn't a neat-freak but she wasn't a slob either so she didn't like things being left out. Alice, on the other hand, liked things a bit more relaxed and comfortable and felt she was just on the right side of messy. Alice was topping up the already full bath with some hot water when she thought she heard something. Was there someone at the door? If it was a delivery they'd have to leave it on the doorstep or with next door. She leaned back and let the warm water soothe her troubled mind. She absent-mindedly touched the scar on her chest.

The front door slammed, making Alice jump and splosh water in all directions, instantly putting out the candle. She remembered the state she'd left the living room in after she'd whipped up a meal out of the freezer and topped it up with snacks. There was more noise from the floor below. Was it a burglar or Nancy? She wasn't completely sure which she'd prefer to face.

'Alice?' called up Nancy.

'Damn,' muttered Alice, clambering out of the bath and taking water with her. 'Hiya! You're back early!' she shouted, grabbing two large towels – one for her and one for the puddle on the floor. She opened the bathroom door a crack. 'I'm just out of the bath so give me a mo and I'll be down to sort everything out.' She grimaced and held the towel in place as she waited for Nancy's response.

'Right,' came back the short reply.

Alice pulled the plug on the bath and willed the water to exit quickly and quietly while she threw on some clothes. She raced downstairs, past Nancy's luggage in the hallway and into the living room where Nancy was surveying the mess like it was a modern art installation. 'Sorry,' said Alice, grabbing up the dirty plate. 'From your message I thought you'd be away for a while.' Alice thought she had at least a day on her own.

'I left another voicemail message this morning to say I was coming home,' said Nancy.

'Did you?' Alice looked about for her phone. 'I left my charger at Mum and Dad's so the battery died. Can I borrow your charger?' she asked with a smile.

Nancy gave her an indulgent look. 'My spare one is in my bedroom. You're welcome to use that once we've cleared this up.'

'Oh yeah, of course,' said Alice, ferrying things to the kitchen. Alice didn't have a sister, but she felt Nancy had the big sister authority vibe nailed. She only had to look at her.

Once the little house was tidy again, Carrie had been let out of her carrier so she could inspect everywhere and Alice had taken Nancy's things up to her bedroom, Alice was at last able to plug in her phone. It flashed to say it was charging and then sprang into life as several alerts popped up for texts and voice messages. Alice listened to the messages while watching Nancy unpack. There were three from her parents because she'd not let them know she was home but that was okay because they'd rung the house phone the previous evening in a panic so she'd already straightened that out. The last message was unexpected. She listened to it twice.

Alice stared at her phone.

'Everything okay?' asked Nancy.

Alice tried to swallow but her mouth had gone dry. 'Er not really, no.'

Nancy automatically put an arm around Alice and sat down on the bed next to her. 'What is it?'

'My test results are back. My consultant says it's time.' Alice looked at Nancy and saw a lack of understanding on her face. 'He wants to operate again. They said they may need to when I'd reached adulthood and stopped growing but I'd always hoped that they wouldn't.'

'When will it be?' asked Nancy.

'As soon as they can fit me in. His secretary is going to call me, but it'll definitely be within the next four weeks.' Alice tried to control her breathing, but it was hard not to gulp in air. 'I don't want another operation.'

'But if that fixes your heart once and for all that's a good thing, right?'

'It's a major operation, Nancy. I could die.' The word stuck in her throat.

'Try to stay calm,' said Nancy, rubbing Alice's back. 'These people are professionals and you've been here before and you were absolutely fine. Your aunt told me about all your operations growing up and how brave you were.'

Despite the panic rising in her, Alice spluttered a laugh. 'Brave? I wasn't brave. I had no idea how risky it was. Nobody told me I could die every time they opened me up. They don't tell you that when you're a kid. It's all positive and happy. I had no idea of the danger I was in and having time off school was brilliant. I almost liked it. That sounds weird but my mum and dad always bought me something cool afterwards and made a big fuss to cheer me up so it was like a bonus birthday. So even though I was sore for a bit, going into hospital didn't really bother me. But now I know what's going to happen . . .' She'd run out of words so she shook her head instead.

'It'll be okay,' said Nancy, giving her a squeeze.

'Will it though?' asked Alice. She wished she shared Nancy's positivity.

* * *

Nancy was happy to be in the office on Monday morning. Even though some things were tricky with her broken wrist, it was good to be surrounded by her team in familiar territory. Claudia was thrilled to have her back; she'd done a brilliant job of holding the fort but there was quite a bit of catching up to be done. They sat down together to go through the highest priority items.

'What's top of your list?' asked Nancy.

'What was Freddy's gaff like?'

'Really, that's top of your list?'

'Trust me, the list doesn't make pretty reading so let's have a bit of light relief first. Come on, spill.' She looked eager to hear all about it.

Pictures of Langham Hall played through Nancy's mind like a movie montage. The long drive, the large house and the potty peacock. The rooms, the history and Seashell Bay as well as Paul and all the other staff. There really was too much and no way to share it without it sounding like she was either showing off or overly impressed. 'Nice,' said Nancy.

'*Nice*.' Claudia screwed up her nose. 'It looked like Buck House to me from that last video conference we did. I've not got over them having a whole stuffed lion in the house. Lord and Lady wotsit are proper toffs eh?' Claudia laughed.

Oscar and Louisa flashed into her mind. 'They might be Lord and Lady but they were lovely people. And the house was big, but it was somehow homely too. They're really not that different to you and me.' They had made it feel that way. They'd been so welcoming and she hated to think that they thought the worst of her.

'Yeah, you can't move in my place for stuffed lions and the bloody buffalo in the bathroom although his horns make a great towel rack.' Claudia chortled at her own joke.

Nancy gave her a look. 'Right, let's focus. Payments out, is there anything outstanding?'

'Where do I start?' asked Claudia, who was no longer joking.

Over the course of the meeting her dad's words came back to Nancy more than once. The business was on a precipice. The piece in the paper had generated a lot of interest in the company but that hadn't really converted into sales. The last thing she wanted was to go bankrupt and she knew it really was make or break time for Having A Ball.

They were packing up and discussing lunch options as they'd missed the sandwich van when Claudia started pulling faces. 'You all right?' asked Nancy, becoming a little concerned.

Someone behind her cleared their throat. Nancy stiffened. 'Hello,' said Freddy.

'Hiya, Freddy,' said Claudia. She turned back to Nancy. 'It'll be sandwich roulette for lunch,' she added.

'Great. Just don't get the tuna surprise. My guts couldn't take that again,' said Nancy.

Claudia gathered up her things and disappeared. Nancy turned to properly face Freddy. He was wearing a blue suit, his hair a little dishevelled and his hands in his pockets. Still just as gorgeous as ever. A part of her was pleased to see him but mostly it triggered the irritation that was just below the surface. 'What do you want, Freddy?'

'I need your help.'

'Who are you trying to swindle this time?' She stared him down.

'Ouch. I guess I deserved that. If you've not had lunch, perhaps we could go somewhere . . .'

'Claudia's getting me something.'

'Salmonella by the sound of it.' He smiled, Nancy didn't join in. 'Come on, Nancy. At least listen to what I've got to say. In your words, it's right up your alley.'

'Unless it involves putting things straight with your parents then I'm not interested.' She turned her back and started up the stairs and for the first time ever she was grateful for the loud echoey sound they made.

'Actually, it does!' called Freddy over her footsteps.

Nancy halted. Bugger. Now she'd have to go back downstairs and hear the rest of what he had to say. She looked over her shoulder. 'You had better not be lying to me.'

'I'd never lie to you, Nancy.' He held her gaze, which was uncomfortable so she came back down the steps as quietly as she could which was still pretty noisy.

'One hour,' she said, emphasising her point with a finger.

'That's all I need,' he replied with a big smile. Before she had a chance to argue he was guiding her out of the warehouse and to his car.

He opened the door for her and she paused. 'Where are we going? Because I don't want to fall asleep and wake up in Devon again.'

'Woodford. Turns out there's a Michelin-starred Indian restaurant there. That okay with you?'

'If we split the bill,' she said, getting in the car and

hoping that the Michelin star didn't double the price of her biryani.

They didn't talk on the way apart from a brief discussion about the unpredictability of the weather. Inside the restaurant was busy and the waft of food was divine. They were shown to their table and Freddy began perusing the menu.

Nancy needed to not get distracted. 'Actually, before we get caught up in ordering and eating can we sort a few things out please?' asked Nancy.

Freddy put down his menu. 'Do I need to apologise again?'

'Might be a good start.'

'I really am sorry, Nancy. But in my defence, at the start I did think you knew what you'd signed up for, but I guess I should have realised that Uncle Dickie hadn't been straight with you. Please accept my apologies.'

'Apology accepted.' Freddy picked his menu back up. 'For that at least,' she added.

Freddy eyed her. 'What else do I need to apologise for?'

'Er, the newspaper headlines. You thought I was involved in that and I got splattered across—'

Freddy waved the menu to get her attention. 'Again, really sorry. Do you think we can draw a line and move on?'

Nancy straightened her shoulders. He was right. Going over and over it didn't serve any purpose. 'Fine by me.' She picked up her menu and tried not to show her alarm at the prices. It was twice the price of her local TikkaTastic and she was pretty sure they wouldn't be upgrading her naan for free.

'Nancy.' The way Freddy said her name got her attention. He was giving her one of his intense looks. 'I've been thinking about you.'

Nancy put her menu down. 'Have you?' She'd been thinking about him too. And there had been one particularly x-rated dream but he didn't need to know about that.

'You've been on my mind constantly since we left Devon.'

Nancy couldn't help the smile on her lips. Clearly asking for her help was just a ruse to get her alone. Nancy pushed her hair behind her ears. She studied him closely. He was so handsome and underneath all the bravado, the family estate and the pedigree bloodline she felt she'd found the real Freddy. It was alarming how quickly she'd grown close to him but if he felt the same that didn't matter. This was a moment and she wanted to remember it.

Freddy shrugged. 'I've not stopped thinking about what you said.'

Nancy remembered a lot of shouting and the kiss but she couldn't think of anything profound she'd said. 'What did I say?'

'About the estate and the business possibilities it offered.' Nancy blinked more times than was necessary as she processed the fact that Freddy really *did* want to talk about business and not about them. 'You said it had huge potential to be a gold mine. Retreats, weddings, parties and opening up the gardens to the public.'

'So I did.' She had a vague recollection of the conversation, but it hadn't stuck in her mind as something memorable.

Freddy leaned forward. 'I don't want to muddle along like Father but if you really believe the place has potential perhaps, with your help, I could consider it further.' He looked at her expectantly.

'It's great that you value my opinion, Freddy, but I've got to be honest with you.' She glanced around

309

but literally nobody was taking any notice of them. 'My business is in trouble.' Freddy's expression changed to one of shocked concern. 'The All Things Crafty deal was a lifeline. Or it would have been.' She waved that old story away. 'We've been fending off debts left, right and centre and . . .' In that moment she had to face the truth. 'I need to either find a buyer or call it a day before I end up bankrupt.' The word sent an unpleasant shiver down her spine.

Freddy leaned back. 'Goodness. I wasn't expecting that.'

Was that disappointment she could hear in his words? 'Well, we've not all got an Uncle Dickie who can help us out if things get too hard.' She snatched up her menu.

'Can I take your order?' asked the waiter. Nancy was glad of the intermission. Freddy was a fantasy that was all, because he obviously didn't think of Nancy in any other way than a business associate and after her revelation about Having A Ball he now probably regarded her as not a particularly good one at that. The memory of the kiss popped into her head as if her brain was trying to find a counter-argument. That was just them being caught up in a moment, that was all and nothing more. The thought made her sad but today was the day for facing reality on a number of levels.

They gave the waiter their orders and he took the menus away which meant Nancy now had nothing to do with her hands.

'Where do we start?' asked Freddy.

'With what?' Nancy was confused.

'With transforming the Langham estate or at least working out how we could transform it because I need to be able to persuade Father. The more I thought about it the more I realised that even though running the estate was never my first choice for a job, selling it would be wrong and I definitely can't let it go to some charity. I think that might break my father and despite everything I've said, a charity running Langham Hall is not what I want either. Langham is my heritage and while I worry that I'm not the safest pair of hands I am quite excited about what we could do differently to share it with others, like you suggested.' He nodded at Nancy.

'But I think we've seen that I'm all ideas and not much substance.'

'Rubbish,' said Freddy. 'Your business has hit a blip. Get a loan.'

Nancy was too tired to get cross. 'It's not that easy for people like me. I'm struggling to pay off the loans I already have. Looking back, the move to the warehouse was probably too soon. I need something special to save the company at this stage.' Her mind wandered off to big marketing campaigns and all the things she could do if she had the cash.

'Maybe I could help,' said Freddy.

'Why would you want to invest in a failing crafting business?'

'I don't,' he said, looking puzzled. 'But if we did crafting retreats at Langham you could supply the wool.' He looked mightily pleased with himself.

'Yarn,' corrected Nancy. 'Thanks, but I don't think a dozen balls are going to get me out of this hole. And who is going to teach the people to knit and crochet? You?' She spluttered a laugh but at the same time a seed of an idea was forming.

Chapter Thirty-Five

Nancy only stopped talking to eat her food, which was astonishingly good. Unfortunately, most of the conversation was Nancy trying to persuade Freddy around to her way of thinking.

'I'm sorry, Nancy, but I don't see how me learning to crochet can be some huge breakthrough for your business.'

'Even the recent headlines haven't dented your huge number of followers. I saw all the likes your Instagram apology got. You have a massive media following. Both traditional newspapers and social media. You're an influencer. Think what Tom Daley did for knitting! You could be the next Tom Daley.' Nancy was getting herself overexcited at the thought. An image of Freddy in Speedos popped into her mind. 'I can see it now – billboards, posters on the underground, giant image of you with balls—'

Freddy almost choked on a mouthful of food. 'Let me stop you there!'

'I was going to say, balls of yarn beamed onto the Houses of Parliament,' she said with a grin.

'Sorry, that's not going to happen.' Freddy forked up some rice.

'Okay. Let's put that idea down as a maybe,' she said, scribbling something illegible with her left hand on the envelope she was using as an action list. Freddy shook his head. 'Do you have any celebrity friends we could teach to crochet?' She waited expectantly.

Freddy looked bored. 'It's not that I don't want to help you shore up Having A Ball. Obviously, I do. But I was hoping to go through ideas for the future sustainability of Langham Hall.'

'Yeah, we're coming to that,' said Nancy. She made a mental note to check Freddy's Instagram for potential famous people he could tap up for a favour. They would be good for promoting Langham Hall as well as Having A Ball.

'Could we discuss it now?' he asked.

Nancy put down her tiny pen which was on an extended loan from a certain catalogue company. 'Of course. Let's split things into long-term and quick wins.' She turned over the envelope and realised there wasn't much space to write on the other side.

'Go on, I'll make notes on my phone,' said Freddy, getting out his mobile.

'You'd make someone a good PA,' said Nancy. Freddy stuck his tongue out. 'Right, quick wins,' she said. 'The gardens are always beautifully kept, so they are visitor ready. You'd need to find out what permissions you need for letting the general public onto your land and any additional insurance requirements. Some sort of kiosk or table as somewhere to take money and a robust recording system for accounting. Might be an opportunity to sell some plants, there were lots in the orangery.'

Freddy tapped away. 'Great. Anything else?'

Nancy pondered for a moment and was aware of Freddy's gaze on her. It made her go all weird, so she shut her eyes and concentrated. 'You've got loads of space so I'm thinking you can charge companies and groups to use it for like cinema nights and car rallies – they should be low effort and reasonable income for you. Nature trails in the woodland, den building and beachcombing if the tides are right but all with an educational and environmental spin which schools might be interested in. I don't know about history, but Paul certainly knows his stuff, maybe do tours of the house and grounds and badge them as Tudor themed or whatever.'

Freddy looked impressed. 'The original house was built in Tudor times.'

'Lucky guess,' said Nancy, dipping naan in her curry.

'Nancy you are so good at this.' Freddy paused and from the way he was looking at her she wondered what he was going to say. 'You could do this professionally. Help other businesses to realise their potential and charge them a consultancy fee.'

'Brilliant idea. You're my first client so I'd best remember to send you an invoice.'

Freddy looked astonished. 'Then I definitely want my money's worth. Any long-term ideas?'

'Loads. For a start, music festivals rake it in. All you need is a couple of fields.'

Freddy pulled a face. 'Have you seen the aftermath of Glastonbury? I think we'll give those a miss.'

Nancy wasn't going to be so easily rebuffed. 'Or you could target a more responsible audience like folk or jazz lovers.'

Freddy pouted thoughtfully and began tapping again.

'How about holding a country fair? These things do take a lot of organising but there's a lot of dosh to be made because you charge everyone who wants to enter competitions like the biggest carrot competition, cutest puppy, best Victoria sponge, etc. You also charge anyone wanting to sell anything on a stall or a food van. *And* you charge admission. It's a licence to print money.'

Freddy paused. 'Actually, there used to be a fair in the grounds before the war. We've got photographs with Lionel somewhere.'

'Maybe leave out the lion this time. "Langham Lion has Locals for Lunch" is not a headline you'd want.'

'Definitely no plans for more lions. But I love the country fair idea. We could use some of the old photos for publicity and badge it as bringing back local traditions.'

'You see. Now you're thinking like an entrepreneur. Last one for now. Weddings and parties.'

Freddy pulled a face. 'I'm not keen on having all and sundry traipse around the house.'

Nancy had a thought. 'When Arabella was missing, Paul and I walked past some massive barns where um . . .' Her eyes were drawn to Freddy's scar.

'Where I had my accident?'

'Yeah, I guessed as much. I get why they've been abandoned. Do you find that area triggering, does it hold bad memories?'

'Not in the slightest. They're simply not used anymore. They are from when the estate had cattle which we haven't had for almost a hundred years.'

'Awesome. Then I think with a bit of investment you could have yourself the most amazing party and wedding reception venue. Imagine the photographs of the bride and groom on the beach, in the woods or on the cliffs with the sea behind them. I mean where else do you get that kind of choice? You can convert one of the other buildings into a state-of-the-art kitchen and maybe team up with a local chef or catering company or you can sublet the catering so brides can have whoever they want.' Nancy sat back in her seat feeling that was a bit of a mic drop moment.

Freddy carried on happily tapping. 'There's even another

entrance on that side of the estate so they wouldn't come anywhere near the house.'

'Perfect. Now all we have to do is convince your parents.'

Freddy instantly lost his jubilant air. 'And that's where I'm really going to need your help.'

* * *

Alice's first day back at work was an odd one. Everything was pretty much the same as she'd left it and yet everything felt like it had changed. She'd been happy and care-free before the school holidays or at least that's how she chose to remember it. Of course, her illness was always a little cloud that followed her around but now it felt like the grim reaper himself was wielding a scythe behind her. On top of that Bonnie had called her Alice twice already and Mrs Robinson had noticed. She'd not said anything, but her narrowed eyes were enough to tell Alice she needed to tread carefully. Alice also wasn't entirely sure that either time had been a mistake on Bonnie's part because she'd giggled and put her hand over her mouth in a very staged way before saying, 'Oopsy, sorry, I forgot.'

At break Alice had been tasked with updating the staff notice board which had become a dumping ground for people trying to sell stuff and promote local events, most of which were long out of date. But at least it got her out of playground duty which was always a blessing. The head came in brandishing a poster and stuck it in the middle of the now clear board. 'Summer Fete, Miss Pelling. You'll manage a stall, won't you? Any boyfriends you can rope in to help with the football tournament?' She waited for a response.

She thought of Dom and her heart squeezed. Then she thought of Whizzer on a bouncy castle and it scared her.

'Er, well, there's um . . .' This was awkward. 'There's not really anyone at the moment who would be appropriate to bring along.'

'But you will help out of course.' She tapped the poster which made Alice have another look at it. The date jumped out at her. It was four weeks away. Her operation dominated her thoughts – she might not even be here for the Summer Fete. One twitch of a scalpel and it was all over. Almost immediately it felt like sucking in air to her lungs was a difficult thing to do.

'Are you all right?' asked the head.

'Fine,' she managed. 'Touch of hay fever.'

The head seemed happy with this. 'I'll put you down for the tombola,' she added and exited the room. Alice flopped onto the edge of the teachers' sofa and received a number of glares in response. But her chest was so tight she couldn't even tell them where to go.

She'd managed to calm herself down just in time for the bell and was pleased to see that she didn't have anything specific to do in the next lesson other than helping those students who generally struggled with their writing. She loved this part of her job. Actually, there wasn't much she didn't like when she thought about it. Perhaps the looming hospital visit was making her see things through rose-tinted specs, but she had definitely found her vocation in teaching.

Kayden was sitting staring out of the window, so Alice went over. 'Do you need any help, Kayden?' she asked.

'My mum's having a baby,' he said, looking glum.

Alice was slightly wrong-footed. She crouched down. 'That's exciting. You're going to be a big brother.'

'I'll have to share my stuff.' His lip wobbled.

'But you'll always have someone to play with. I often

wished I had a brother or sister growing up. What are you hoping the baby will be?'

Kayden paused for a moment. 'The Hulk!' he said loudly.

Mrs Robinson glared at Alice. She gave a smile that she hoped said 'I have this under control'. She turned back to Kayden. 'I meant a boy or a girl,' explained Alice.

Kayden looked thoughtful. 'Is there a girl Hulk?'

'Er, I think there might be,' said Alice.

'I think boy Hulk would be best,' he said, picking up his pencil and starting to practise the letter H. Alice hoped she had a few months to work on managing Kayden's expectations in time for the arrival of his non-Marvel-badged sibling.

Alice was on lunchtime playground duty so was trying to referee four simultaneous games of tag while eating her sandwich. 'Alice!' called Bonnie, running up to her.

Alice wasn't great with facing things head on, but she knew she had to this time. 'Hi, Bonnie. Do you remember we talked about you having to call me Miss Pelling at school?'

'Oh yeah, I forgot.' Bonnie giggled.

'Bonnie, I don't think you did forget. And it could get me into trouble if you don't call me Miss Pelling.' Alice kept her serious teacher expression firmly in place.

Bonnie pouted. 'I don't want you to get into trouble.'

'That's good then.' A tennis ball whizzed past Alice's ear. 'No higher than tummies remember, boys!' she called.

'Sorry, miss!'

'But Al—I mean Miss Pelling, you don't call me Miss Fisher, you call me Bonnie.'

Alice realised the discussion with Bonnie wasn't over.

'That's right because I'm the teacher and you're the student.'

'But we're friends,' said Bonnie.

This was getting very tricky and Alice was starting to see why dating parents was frowned upon. This situation was only going to get worse as she tried to distance herself from Dom. 'Not at school, Bonnie. When we are here, I'm at work and you are here to learn so I'd like you to call me Miss Pelling, have I made that clear?'

The little girl looked a little taken aback. 'I don't think we're friends anymore, Miss Pelling,' said Bonnie, turning around and stomping off across the playground, narrowly missing an incoming tennis ball. Alice sighed; no this wasn't going to be easy at all.

Chapter Thirty-Six

Nancy was truly grateful to Alice for stumping up and doing more cooking while her arm was in plaster although it was likely driven by self-preservation when she'd caught Nancy wielding a knife. Partly as a thank you and partly because Alice was looking glum Nancy had bought a bottle of wine.

'It's not bad considering it was on offer,' said Nancy, taking another sip of the cheap Shiraz.

'Sorry?' Alice appeared miles away.

'The wine, it's all right.' Nancy lifted her glass.

'Oh, it's nice.' Alice took a sip and winced which probably meant there was a good reason it was on offer.

'Is everything okay?' asked Nancy.

Alice sighed. 'It's Dom.'

'You've not split up, have you?'

Alice pushed a pasta bow around her plate. 'No, but I think we should. But it's not just Dom I'd be breaking up with, it's Bonnie too. But then if I don't end things now . . .'

Nancy waited for a moment for her to finish the sentence, but she was still doodling with her pasta. 'Then what? I thought you two were the real deal?' Or at least she was certain that that was what Alice had thought a couple of weeks ago.

Alice looked up from her plate. 'If things don't go well with my operation.'

'You can't think like that,' said Nancy.

'But I am thinking like that. I can't stop it. Isn't it best to be pessimistic and then have a nice surprise rather than the other way around?'

'No,' said Nancy with a laugh. 'Life is precarious, I agree. And you have had more than your fair share of . . . precariousness.' She wasn't sure that was a real word but she went with it anyway. 'But you have to try to be positive.' Alice's darting eyes said she disagreed. 'If you don't then the negative stuff wins because you feel bad all the time. Have you told Dom how you feel?'

'No.' Alice slowly shook her head. 'And I've not told him about my condition.'

'Ah, maybe that's step one.'

Alice pushed the pasta to the edge of her plate and put her fork down. 'When I get a date for the operation I'll tell him then,' she said. Nancy wasn't getting the feeling that she would.

Nancy was both delighted and surprised to find Freddy already in the office when she arrived for work the next morning. He did look hot in a crisp white shirt. 'Morning, Boss,' he said, handing her a branded coffee cup. 'Grande, skinny mocha.'

'Perfect, thank you.'

'I've been fleshing out each of the ideas for Langham as per your suggestion,' he said, whizzing around his laptop screen to show her. 'I thought we could build on it this morning.' He gave her a smile worthy of a toothpaste advert.

'Freddy, it's honestly great that you're getting into this. It really is. But I have a day job and one that desperately needs me to be fully focused right now. I figured you were no longer working as my PA but if you are then I've got a list of stuff for you to do.' She didn't want to dampen his enthusiasm, but she also had to be practical and put her own company first.

Freddy's smile wilted but he quickly recovered. 'I suppose it's only fair that I do something to help out. Your business first, saving Langham Hall second.'

'I'll work on it with you at lunchtime and after work.' It was in Nancy's interest to get things moving because she wasn't joking about a consultancy fee and right now every penny in the pot counted.

'Okay. Then I am your PA. Let's have the list.' He held out his hand.

'I've not got an actual list but now I know you're staying I'll send you an email.'

'Great. Until then I'll crack on with the Langham project.' He turned his laptop back around.

Huh, thought Nancy. 'Or you could use your initiative and get on with something useful that's Having A Ball related.' Freddy opened his mouth but before he could ask what, she threw something out there. 'Picking and packing, chasing up any outstanding payments . . .' And in her head she added, *And anything that justifies me having to pay you because right now you're a luxury I can't afford.*

Freddy snapped his laptop shut. 'On it, Boss,' he said, and he picked up his computer and left. Nancy had grown very close to Freddy, and there was an undeniable attraction, but he still annoyed the crap out of her.

Nancy had a busy morning. She held off a few suppliers who were demanding payment with calming phone calls. She'd chased the publishers but they had no news and she'd done some investigation into billboard costs – far too expensive. She looked out through her glass office but there was no sign of life. Both Freddy and Claudia had vacated their usual spaces. Nobody had asked her about lunch, so she figured she'd best go in search of some food. As she came down the stairs she discovered where everyone was. They were all huddled around one end of the big table, apart from Freddy who was enthusiastically doing some order picking.

'Everything okay?' she asked as she reached the bottom of the steps.

Guilty faces spun in her direction. Nobody spoke but the expressions and body language were enough to tell her that everything was definitely not okay. Filip cleared his throat. 'We're wondering if we should be looking for new jobs.' Nancy scratched her head, what was he on about? 'We've heard on the grapevine that the company is in trouble,' he added, lifting his chin as if in challenge.

Nancy hated being caught off guard. She glared at Claudia who was already shaking her head and pointing in Freddy's direction. Nancy's mind rewound to the restaurant – *Heavens*, she thought, *has bloody Freddy shared everything I told him?* 'I don't know what has been said but you definitely don't need to look for new jobs. Right now, we need everyone concentrating on what they're doing.'

'But if the company is going bankrupt . . .' said Shona.

'It's not,' said Nancy. Lots of disbelieving faces stared at her. 'Look I'll be straight with you all. Things are tight but it's not the end of Having A Ball by any means. I've got ideas and projects in the pipeline that could get us out of our current and hopefully temporary cashflow crisis.' It didn't sound that robust even to her own ears.

'But how long until we're back here again?' asked Filip.

'This is still a relatively new company. The first few

years are usually unstable, but we can overcome this. We just have to all believe and keep focused and not get distracted by stuff like this.' She scowled at Freddy who was oblivious as he slam-dunked a large ball of Subtle Sienna yarn into a basket. 'Anyway, we need lunch. Anyone fancy doing a trip to the supermarket?' She received glum looks all round. 'Freddy! Supermarket sandwich run please,' she said, striding over and steering him out of the building.

Once outside she rounded on him. 'What the hell, Freddy?'

'I'm sorry, I don't follow.'

Nancy did a dramatic step back. 'You spilled your guts about the company. All the stuff I told you in confidence at the restaurant. You told everyone.'

'I don't recall you saying it was top secret,' he said.

'Bloody hell, could you not work that out for yourself?' She threw up her arms and almost decked him with her plaster.

'It came up in conversation. Had I known you didn't want your staff to know the situation, of course I wouldn't have said anything.'

'You've stirred up a right shit storm. The last thing I need is my team distracted by bankruptcy worries and looking for new jobs. Argh!'

Freddy recoiled a little as she vented. 'I'm sensing I need to apologise.'

'Yeah, that'll fix everything, Freddy.' She shook her head as she stomped off to his car.

In the car the atmosphere was frosty. 'I am sorry that I spoke out of turn. But in my defence, I believe I was only confirming what they already suspected.'

Maybe Nancy hadn't hidden things as well as she'd hoped. 'Still wasn't your place to say anything.'

'You are absolutely right. I am incredibly sorry. I will buy the doughnuts. That's the answer, right?'

Nancy's shoulders dropped. She had been ridiculous trying to smooth over her problems with doughnuts. She was in a heap of trouble and deep-fried treats weren't going to solve it. 'I need more than doughnuts this time,' she said.

'Then why not let others help?'

'I'm not stopping anyone.' It was hard not to be defensive.

'But you are because you think you have to solve everything on your own and you don't. Your team adore you. Granted they're a bit fed up right now but that will pass. And I suspect it will pass quicker if you ask them to help.'

'Thing is, I don't know if anyone can help.'

'Goodness, that doesn't sound like the Nancy Barraclough I've come to know.'

Nancy sighed. 'Maybe it's time to throw in the towel.'

'Oh come on!' said Freddy with a force that gave Nancy a jolt. 'Nancy Barraclough doesn't give up. You've taught me that there's always an answer, you just have to look in the right place and—'

'Work harder.' Nancy smiled.

'For a start tell me what I can do to help and I'll do it. I'll not have you giving up on Having A Ball or yourself. You didn't give up on me.' He shot her a look that sent all kinds of shivers through her.

* * *

Alice only checked her phone a few times a day and then only when it was appropriate. Each time she did there was another message from Dom. Her coward's approach of cooling off wasn't working at all. She knew it would be even worse to send a text to end their relationship even though it was quite appealing. But Dom deserved better than that. Alice pledged to call him after she'd finished work. Dom sent back a lovely text saying he was looking forward to it. Now she'd made it even more awkward. At least she had an afternoon of rounders and counting to work out what on earth she was going to say to him.

Rounders was a complete and utter fiasco. Despite explaining the game with a big diagram on the whiteboard before they went outside it quickly descended into bedlam. What was it with small children and outside activities? They became instantly overexcited and even the calmer ones acted up.

An over-enthusiastic Delilah spun around in a full circle every time she took a swing at the ball. The other waiting batters were incapable of staying in line as most of them were making nests out of the grass cuttings. Half the fielders had abandoned their bases and were making daisy chains while the others were running around with their PE tops over their faces like celebrating footballers. Bonnie was one of the few still paying attention, but she dived out of the way whenever the ball came near her – ironic really as she never managed to dodge them in the playground. Jaxon was running around in his socks. Kayden was practising catching by throwing Jaxon's trainers in the air and managed to throw them both over the school fence. William skidded unnecessarily into fourth base and took the skin off his knee and when he showed it to Hamsi, she screamed and threw up all over William's new plimsols, so both children burst into tears. When Alice had finally calmed everyone down, Delilah was so surprised at finally hitting the ball, she had a mild asthma attack.

If the idea of rounders had been to tire them out it had had the opposite effect, as afterwards they were bouncing around on a post-rounders high in the changing rooms. Alice, on the other hand, was exhausted and ready to curl

up in the corner. She managed to get the thirty-four children into uniforms and back to their classroom although
as the afternoon went on she realised that quite a few of
them weren't wearing their *own* uniform and if they were
it was inside out.

Counting was thankfully less eventful and Alice was
overjoyed when the end of day came and Mrs Robinson
handed the children back to waiting parents. Alice ducked
out and went in search of Jaxon's trainers which had landed
in a neighbouring garden. She took her time thanking the
resident and didn't rush back. She knew it was cowardly,
but she couldn't face Dom. Since the holidays he'd been
on time at every school pick-up where he'd given her a
smile and a wave. She suspected she wouldn't be getting
any more of those after their phone call tonight.

Chapter Thirty-Seven

Whether it was the little pep talk from Freddy or the sugar rush of three doughnuts, Nancy wasn't sure, but she spent the afternoon generating ideas with her team. By the end of the day they had a list of potential things that could drum up some additional business and a second list of how they could streamline processes and save some money. Nancy didn't know if the two-pronged attack would work but she knew she had to have one last try. As everyone left for the day Claudia put her head around Nancy's door. 'Are you okay?' she asked.

Nancy thought for a second. 'Yeah, I'm fine. It's actually better that everyone knows. I didn't like keeping stuff from them and as it turns out the best people to find ways to improve stuff are the ones doing the job.' Nancy nodded at the lists on the wall.

'Try not to worry. And don't stay here too late,' said Claudia.

'I'll do my best. See you tomorrow.'

'Yeah, I think I'll come back. There's only ironing and daytime telly waiting for me at home,' said Claudia. She left and Nancy was contemplating whether to call it a night or get herself a coffee when Freddy bounded in.

'Is now a good time?' he asked.

'A good time for what?'

'To go through project Langham? All my PA work is up to date apart from two people I'm waiting to call me back.' He looked pleased with himself. 'What do you say? Can I walk you through what I've done?' Nancy couldn't stifle the yawn that escaped. 'I'll take that as a no.'

Nancy sat up straight in an attempt to wake herself up. 'It's not a no. I'm just tired that's all.'

Freddy slid into the seat opposite. 'Is it worrying about this place?'

'A bit but it's mainly this.' She held up her cast. 'You try sleeping with a concrete bollard – it's not comfy.'

'You don't have to tell me, I know exactly what that's like.'

Nancy raised an eyebrow. Freddy held up his palms. 'Oh no! Not a euphemism. Real concrete bollard. Stag do in Benalmadena. Anyway . . .' He waved his hands, looking a bit flustered. 'You get off home and I'll take you through my stunningly brilliant plans some other time.'

Nancy's curiosity was piqued. 'Could you give me a whistle-stop tour of them?'

'I'd love to. Over a takeaway at mine?'

'Okay, but I'm not staying late. Alice isn't herself at the moment.' Nancy couldn't elaborate further.

'Brilliant!' said Freddy, jumping to his feet. 'About coming to mine. Not about Alice.'

'Yeah, I figured,' said Nancy, smiling at his enthusiasm.

Despite being tired Nancy was glad she'd agreed to go to Freddy's. She wasn't sure why but she'd been expecting somewhere that was like a mini version of Langham Hall but Freddy's London apartment couldn't have been more different. It was in a converted stucco-fronted building with a large shiny black entrance door. The flat itself was painted entirely white and accessorised with grey and black and looked a lot like a show home to Nancy. Even the grey cushions on the black sofa had a dent in the top. 'You've got a lovely . . . second home,' she said, following him past the sofa to a round black dining table surrounded by four grey upholstered chairs.

'I like it,' said Freddy, pulling out a chair for Nancy. 'Mum did it all,' he added, following Nancy's gaze.

'I didn't know she dabbled in interior design.'

'She doesn't get to do that sort of thing at Langham. I think that's why she likes the place in St Kitts; she's always changing colour schemes out there.'

'She's got a real eye for it. If we could get her involved in the look and feel of the barn conversion . . .'

'We need to convince her first,' said Freddy, sitting down. 'The tabloids might have forgiven me but my parents have not.'

Nancy tilted her head at him and his puzzled face stared back at her. 'Yes, please, I'll have a coffee,' she said.

There was a small delay before the penny dropped. 'I'm a shocking host. Coffee coming right up.' Freddy got out his phone. 'I can get that on Deliveroo, right?'

Nancy's eyes widened in shock. 'Don't tell me you can't make coffee.'

'I'm kidding. Back in a mo.' He winked as he got to his feet and left the room.

Nancy was impressed with the amount of work Freddy had done. It was good to see him taking it seriously. After they'd ordered their takeaway she listened and drank her coffee while Freddy went through all the research he had done on similar ventures to the ones on their very long list. He had obviously put in a lot of time and effort.

'What about costs and projected income?' she asked.

'You evil genius. You've spotted the flaw in my plan. I ran out of time, but I'll work on those next. Assuming my harridan of a boss doesn't overload me.'

Was he calling her a dragon? Nancy felt burned. 'Harridan?' she questioned as she sipped her drink and tried not to look hurt.

'It means strict.'

'Does it?' She studied him.

He stuck out his chin. 'As well as a belligerent and bossy older female which you obviously aren't.' He seemed to notice that she wasn't amused. 'It was meant as a joke, not an insult.'

'It is insulting though.'

'Nancy, I was being ironic. If you were anything like a harridan do you think I would have said that? You're a brilliant boss. For a start you've even managed to get a no-hoper like me working and please don't tell anyone, as I have a playboy image to uphold, but I am rather enjoying it. And that's entirely down to you.' She looked doubtfully at him. 'And the picking and packing. I bloody love that. If Filip ever leaves, I want that job permanently.' Nancy laughed. 'I mean it. Forget running the estate I want to match yarn to orders. It's oddly therapeutic.'

She had to admit that she knew what he meant. There was something very satisfying about making up orders. Seeing what people had chosen, packaging it up and imagining their delight when they unwrapped it. She thought back to Freddy's reasons for not wanting to run the family estate. 'But I thought you didn't want to do the same thing for the rest of your life?'

Freddy became animated. 'That's the joy of all these ideas. It won't be the same thing. We'll make changes. Good long-term, well-thought-through changes, not sticking plaster solutions that don't hold. And we can keep

331

moving forward. Have a rolling five-year plan so as the world changes, we do too.'

'Blimey. Calm down, Elon Musk. I've created a monster.'

'You said to stop looking at the problems and focus on the solutions. So I did.'

She was clearly far better at solving other people's issues than her own. 'How do you feel about taking on the estate?'

Freddy puffed out a breath. 'Completely terrified. Still worried that I'll stuff it up and disappoint everyone as per my track record. But I'm willing to give it a shot.'

'You have to stick at it though, Freddy. It's all exciting now. What will you do when things get tough?'

'Work harder.' Freddy beamed at her. 'And I'll have you.'

Nancy's stomach did a couple of flips. 'When you say – you'll have me. What exactly do you mean? Is that as a paid consultant or what?'

Freddy leaned forward and Nancy held her breath. 'That's really up to you, Nancy.' Freddy looked deep into her eyes. How could one person both have an instant calming effect one moment and drive you crazy the next? Freddy was a one-off and there were so many reasons why they would never work as a couple and yet Nancy was drawn to him. He ignited something in her – the Nancy who had been fearless and up for any challenge came back to life in Freddy's presence. And the kiss they had shared had told her there was a spark of something else that she very much wanted to explore.

'I think—'

The door entry bell buzzed. 'Dinner's here,' said Freddy, jumping up and dashing off. Nancy let out the breath she'd been holding in. She very much hoped there'd be time for answering that question later.

* * *

332

Alice had been dreading the phone call with Dom. She knew it wouldn't be until after he'd put Bonnie to bed so she thought that would at least give her time to think through what she was going to say. What it actually did was give her far too much time to fret and worry about the conversation. She had hoped to talk it through with Nancy first. Nancy had become like a big sister and was someone she could rely on for sound, impartial advice. Unfortunately, something had come up at work and she wasn't going to be back until late. Nancy had checked a few times that Alice was okay and that she would feed Carrie and Alice had lied and said everything was fine.

Alice gave Carrie her dinner and made herself a pot noodle, but she couldn't eat much of it. She was too full up with guilt at what she was about to do. But despite how she felt and the obvious upset to Dom and Bonnie, she knew it was the right thing.

Dom had sent her a text to say that bath time had gone on a bit too long and he still had to read Bonnie a story so he wouldn't be free for a bit. Alice could picture him as the doting father and that didn't help the situation at all. She went to the freezer and pulled out the ice cream Nancy kept for emergencies – she was pretty sure this qualified.

She was digging her way through the tub of Cornish vanilla when her mobile sprang to life. It was Dom. She wasn't ready for the call. What was she going to say? 'Um, hi,' she said through a spoonful of ice cream.

'Hi, Alice, I missed you at pick up today.' He laughed. 'I'm such a loser, you should dump me right away. No, I'm joking, don't do that.' Alice's heart squeezed. 'I hate going a day without seeing you. It's crazy, isn't it?'

Rip off the Band-Aid, she thought. 'I know how you feel, Dom—'

'Oh, that's good. I'm glad it's not just me. Sorry I was late calling. Little miss had other ideas. We had a long discussion about rounders. She really enjoyed it.'

'That's good. It was a bit of a nightmare if I'm honest.'

'Bonnie is now an expert thanks to your fabulous teaching. She was a bit disappointed that rounders player isn't a recognised career path, but she quite likes the sound of baseball and cricket. My dad will be pleased as punch if she takes up cricket. That reminds me. I did something daft and I need to confess.'

'Okay but then I really need to tell you something.' Alice's heart thudded in her chest. She felt like she was going to put down a puppy.

'Of course. My confession is that I stupidly mentioned you in conversation with my parents and now my mum is choosing hats, you know what they're like. And I said I'd met your mum and dad so then the next question was "when do we get to meet Alice?" I hope you don't feel it's too soon but I thought we could go over one weekend. Is that okay with you?'

This was worse than a nightmare. 'Dom, I'm really sorry but the thing is—'

'It's too soon! You're right. I'm an idiot. I'm really sorry. I shouldn't have put pressure on you like that. I'll call them and put it off for a bit. Does next year sound okay?' He chuckled.

Alice felt sick to her stomach. This was awful. She was tempted to bottle it, but she knew she was only putting off the inevitable.

'Alice, are you still there?'

'Yep.'

'Is everything okay?'

'Er, nope. Dom, I'm really sorry but you have to trust me when I say that it's best for both of us. Actually, Bonnie too.'

'What is? That we postpone you meeting my folks?'

She took a deep breath. 'It's best that we don't see each other anymore. It's nothing you've done. It's entirely my fault and I am so, so sorry.'

There was no answer at first, but she knew he was still there. 'But it was fate,' he said at last. 'You and me meeting. First at the nightclub, then at school and then on holiday. Serendipity.'

'My mum loves that film,' she said and then gave herself a shake.

'Mine too. Alice, I don't understand.' There was emotion in his voice.

'It's too hard to explain but it's for the best. Trust me. Bye, Dom.' She had to end the call before she got emotional herself. She reached for the ice cream but Carrie had already got there and looked up with a guilty face covered in Cornish Vanilla.

'You're in big trouble,' she told Carrie. 'But I can't eat it now so you might as well finish what little there is.' She put the pot back in front of Carrie who looked at it as if she'd been offered poison. Why did cats only want things if they were forbidden? Before Alice could sort out the cat, the doorbell sounded. She opened it to find her parents on the doorstep. This was all she needed.

Chapter Thirty-Eight

Alice took a moment to pull herself together. The last thing she needed was her parents realising she was upset, although it was hard to think of anything worse than them turning up at Nancy's out of the blue. 'This is a surprise. Why are you here?'

'We can pop by, can't we?' said her mum.

'This is where you usually invite us in,' prompted her dad.

'Sorry. Come in,' she said with a forced smile. Her mum walked in and her dad followed, carrying a small case. *Oh, no*, thought Alice.

'Shall I put the kettle on?' asked her mum.

'I can do that,' replied Alice, dashing into the kitchen and throwing the pot noodle in the bin.

Alice was grateful to Carrie who entertained the visitors while she hid in the kitchen making drinks. She took the mugs through to the living room and sat down. She saw her mobile was flashing – Dom was calling again. She picked it up and switched it off.

'Where are you off to then?' asked Alice, with a nod at the case.

'To see you, silly,' said her mum.

'But you said you were popping by. You don't usually pop by with luggage,' said Alice.

'We're staying at the motel place up the road. I got a very good deal. You see if you go direct then you don't pay commission . . .' Her dad was interrupted by her mum putting a hand on his knee.

'What's going on?' Alice was more than suspicious. 'Oh no. It's Cindy, isn't it?'

'Goodness no, she's fine. Bit of wind and arthritis that's all. She's staying with your Aunt Julie for the night,' explained her mum.

'Then what is it?'

'Your mum was worried about you.'

'But I'm fine.' Her mum's eyes rested on the ice cream tub. Carrie was unhelpfully sat under the table staring up at it. 'Really. You have to believe me.' Alice splayed out her hands and tried to look fine when it was the last thing she felt. It was like she'd been hollowed out. Breaking up with Dom was horrible. She wanted to curl up in a ball and cry which she probably would do the moment her parents left.

'We're going to do a spot of sightseeing. It's been years since we looked around London. Your mum wants to go to the Victoria and Albert Museum. Which I found out is completely free. Then we can all go home together.'

Alice narrowed her eyes. Here it was. 'All go home. Who? You and Mum?'

Her mum shuffled along the sofa until she was close enough to reach for Alice's hand. 'We were both worried about you, love. Maybe you'd be best coming home before your operation. I can feed you up a bit so you're fighting fit. And . . .'

Alice shook her head. 'I don't want any fuss.'

337

'There won't be,' said her mum, looking affronted.

'*This*.' Alice animatedly waved her arms about. 'This is fuss.'

'Alice, would you listen to your mum?'

'No,' said Alice, standing up. 'I'm sorry. But I'm an adult and *I* will choose if and when I go to the hospital. Not you.'

'If?' said her dad as they both stared at her.

'I haven't decided if I'm going ahead with the operation.'

'But, Alice, you can't,' said her mum, gripping her husband's arm so tightly her knuckles turned white.

'Actually, I can.' Her parents looked affronted. The doorbell went. 'For crying out loud,' said Alice and she stomped to the front door.

'Alice, we need to talk,' said a dishevelled and wretched-looking Dom.

'Not now, Dom. It's not a good time. My—'

'Hello, Dom,' said her dad, leaning past her to shake Dom's hand. 'Good to see you, lad. Perhaps you can talk some sense into Alice here.'

Oh, no, no, no, thought Alice. 'Dad, can I have a minute with Dom, please.'

Carrie came to greet the visitor, closely followed by Alice's mum so they were now all squashed into the very small space by the door. 'Aren't you going to invite him in?' asked her mum. 'Goodness London has impacted your manners. Come in, Dom. The kettle's just boiled. Tea or coffee?'

Dom looked awkward as he followed Alice's mum up the narrow hallway. 'Tea please, Mrs Pelling.'

Alice was a bit delayed closing the door. She left her dad making a fuss of Carrie and went to undertake damage limitation in the kitchen where she found her mum mid-conversation with Dom. '. . . I said that's stalking but Alice insisted that it wasn't. She was determined to find you. You see she recognised something in one of your photographs on Insta is it?'

'Ahh that's not exactly what happened.' Alice was trying to signal to her mum to shut up, but the message wasn't getting through.

'It was. You remember. You said you were taking the dog for a walk, but you took her on a bus ride and were gone hours and me and your dad—'

'Thanks, Mum!' Alice guided Dom into the hallway.

'I can explain,' she said.

Alice expected Dom to be cross but if anything, he looked even sadder. 'Not fate then,' he said to Alice.

'The nightclub was. And Bonnie being at the same school where I work.' He raised his eyebrows. 'But not finding you on the beach. Although I did walk a long way that day trying to find you.'

'If you went to all that trouble then why dump me now?'

Alice's mum's face appeared at the kitchen door. 'Was it tea or coffee, Dom?'

'He's not stopping, Mum.' Alice was desperate for Dom to go. The last thing she wanted was her parents spilling out her life story and Dom feeling sorry for her.

'I just don't understand.' Dom shook his head. 'Surely we can talk about whatever it is.'

'I'm sorry I can't explain right now. Please leave.'

'If that's what you want.' Dom turned and left.

'Bye.' She managed an embarrassed wave, but Dom was already shutting the door behind him. She tried very hard to hold onto the fact that this was what she wanted but that was impossible to do when her heart was breaking.

* * *

Nancy didn't see Alice as she was home late that evening and out early the next day. She'd stayed far later than she should have done at Freddy's before getting a cab home. Time seemed to slip by when she was with him. They'd chatted and laughed as well as fleshed out the plans for Langham. Seeing Freddy so fired up about what he could do with the estate was infectious, but Nancy knew she had to stay focused on her own business, which was why she was up bright and early and in the office. Now was the time to call in favours. She'd made some good contacts over the last couple of years and been a sounding board for quite a few people so now she was going to ask them for their support. She also had a meeting with an online marketing optimiser although right now she lacked the spare cash to do much, but she was hoping for some insight into where she should focus any money she did have. She still thought a large poster of Freddy crocheting would work wonders, but he wasn't keen.

She'd brought Carrie into the warehouse so that she could take some promotional photographs of her. With any luck she'd get a clip of her playing with some yarn and it would go viral on TikTok – she could but hope. It was nice to have a bit of company although Carrie was far too busy investigating Nancy's office. Claudia arrived with warm croissants. 'Are you some sort of mind reader?' asked Nancy, tucking into the flaky pastry.

'If I'm honest I thought you'd be late in and would have skipped breakfast.' Claudia gave her a wink.

'Why?'

'Because Freddy sent a couple of emails late last night and happened to mention that you'd just gone home so . . . Do I need to update the company policy on relationships at work?'

'Firstly, we don't have a company policy on relationships

at work and secondly the key part of your sentence is *gone home*. There's nothing going on between me and Freddy.' Although as she said it her cheeks heated up – what was that all about?

'Yeah. I don't buy it.' Claudia munched on her breakfast. 'You must have noticed the sexual tension between the two of you?'

Nancy spluttered out a few flakes of croissant. 'Bloody hell, Claude. Have you been on the Mills & Boon again?'

'Don't diss the M & B.' Claudia looked serious and pointed a finger at Nancy.

Nancy held her palms up. 'Sorry.'

'Apology accepted. Anyway, you're too buttoned up to be a Mills & Boon heroine.' Claudia took a swig of coffee.

'I'm not buttoned up.' Nancy self-consciously ran a finger around her shirt collar.

'I know you're not really but that is how you come across to men. Because you're all work, work, work, it makes you seem standoffish and unavailable. There's no way the hero would have a clue that you were into him unless you gave off more . . . allure.'

'Allure?' Nancy and Claudia both started to laugh.

'Good morning,' said Freddy, striding over and swiping the last croissant.

'Hey! Who are you, Arabella? That's my breakfast,' said Nancy. Claudia gave her a look. 'Well, second breakfast.'

'Split it?' said Freddy, offering her the untouched end.

'Ta.' Nancy tore it in half.

'Thanks for last night,' said Freddy. 'You are brilliant.' He carried on into the little kitchen.

Nancy was grinning when she turned back to Claudia who had her chin pulled in and a knowing look on her face. 'Thanks for last night,' Claudia repeated with a posh

Freddy twang which did give her more than an air of *Downton Abbey.* 'Maybe not as buttoned up as I thought.'

'We were working,' said Nancy. 'And that's what you should be doing.'

Claudia got up from the table. 'I know *who* you should be doing,' she muttered as she walked away.

Nancy's morning was busy. Carrie was a total pain in the bum. She kept scratching at everything and when Nancy tried to take her photo with lovely colourful balls of yarn Carrie kept turning around so Nancy had loads of pictures of the cat's bum which was not the sort of promo she was after.

Nancy was also distracted by Freddy and Claudia who kept putting their heads together. She wondered what they were up to and then decided that she was just being paranoid and it was most likely Freddy was asking how to set up a conference call for the umpteenth time. After her conversation with Claudia earlier she really hoped she wasn't trying to match make. That would be too cringey. If Freddy had been at all interested, he wasn't the sort to be coy, he would have made a move since they'd returned from Devon.

Nancy was pleased to meet the rep from the new marketing firm, but her mind kept wandering off.

'So, Nancy, that's the key deliverables of our initial marketing review. Does that sound like it would be beneficial to Having A Ball?' asked the trendy marketeer in front of her.

'Yes, absolutely it does. But I was hoping we could look at where to get the most bang for my buck so to speak.'

'That would all be detailed in our report and proposed marketing plan after we've undertaken a full review.' That was what she was worried about. She'd have to spend a wedge of cash before she even got to the useful part.

They continued discussions but Nancy was aware of both Claudia and Freddy pacing outside her office. Carrie was sitting on the inside watching them like it was cat telly. Nancy started to get an uncomfortable feeling which was nothing to do with two breakfasts and too much coffee.

As soon as she wrapped up the meeting and pledged to let the trendy guy know when he could come back to review the company's online presence she was pounced on by Freddy and Claudia.

'There's a problem,' said Freddy. 'Paul rang to tip me off that Mother and Father are meeting with a big stately home charity today.'

'Okay,' said Nancy. 'But that doesn't mean they're signing Langham over. Does it?'

'It's not the first meeting and Uncle Dickie is going to be there. I think this is something significant. I need to go to Langham urgently and speak to my parents before they sign anything.'

'Right. What do you want me to do?' asked Nancy, keen to help but also a little unsure as to what she could do if his parents were at the point of handing over the estate – horse and bolted sprang to mind.

'Will you come with me?' asked Freddy. 'You're so much better at presenting this sort of thing than I am.'

'Oh, I don't know. I don't think they'd be that chuffed if I rocked up and butted into what is a family affair.'

'I think they're more likely to hear us out if we both go. If it's just me, they'll dismiss it as my latest flighty whim but whatever has happened, I know they see you as a serious businesswoman. Someone level-headed, dependable and restrained.'

Crumbs, maybe Claudia was right about her being buttoned up. 'Freddy, that's all very flattering but I have stuff here. I can't drop everything and clear off for a day or so.'

'Yes, you can,' butted in Claudia. Nancy gave her a look. 'I can manage this place. Filip and Shona are in, we'll be fine.' Claudia leaned in to whisper in Nancy's ear. 'And it might be worth your while. Trust me.' She pulled back and winked at Nancy. What did that mean?

'Please,' said Freddy, going full puppy dog. It was a look they both knew could win her over.

'When would we need to leave?' she asked.

'About half an hour ago.' Freddy winced.

'Then what are we waiting for?' said Nancy, feeling like she was in an action adventure.

'Just you. I've got the presentation on my laptop.' He went to guide her downstairs.

'Actually, I had better put my out of office on and I need to make a quick call to—'

'No, I'll do all that,' said Claudia.

'What about Carrie?'

Claudia picked up Carrie and handed her to Nancy. 'Take her with you. She loved it last time. Text me anything else. Go!' said Claudia with another wink. Nancy stared at her. 'Too much winking?' asked Claudia.

'Far, far too much,' said Nancy.

'Thanks for the feedback.'

'You're welcome,' said Nancy and with the cat in her arms she followed an agitated Freddy out of the building.

Chapter Thirty-Nine

Nancy had to admit it was quite exciting dashing down the motorway on a mission to save the estate even if updating the presentation with one hand while balancing the laptop on her knees was a little tricky. They went over the key points of the pitch and who was going to cover off which slides as well as discussing how excited Otto and Carrie would be to see each other again. Nancy had to admit she was pleased to be going back to Langham Hall. She hadn't stayed there long but in that short time it had made a big impression on her. She was also looking forward to impressing Freddy's parents.

She couldn't say the journey flew by, because it was a really long way to Devon, but she definitely enjoyed the trip. They stopped at a drive-through coffee shop which was like having a mobile picnic.

It was both a relief and a thrill as they pulled up to the giant gates and Freddy buzzed the intercom. This was it. Freddy's future depended on them getting this exactly right. There would be no second chances.

'Freddy, at last,' came Paul's voice and the gates opened.

They went quicker up the drive than they had previously, and Freddy pulled up short of the portico where Paul was already waiting. 'Thanks for the call. I really appreciate this,' said Freddy, shaking Paul's hand and pulling him into a man hug.

'I don't know if it's enough. They're all in the drawing room and have been for a while.'

'Don't worry. Leave it to us,' said Nancy, buoyed with adrenaline.

'Ah, and I should warn you Arabella is with Sir Richard.'

That only strengthened Nancy's resolve. She had a score to settle. Carrie was yowling from the back seat. 'I'll take Carrie,' offered Paul. 'The gentleman from National Heritage is very allergic to pretty much anything with fur. Otto is shut in the boot room so they'll both enjoy a walk.'

'Thank you,' said Nancy and Freddy together. They looked at each other.

'Ready?' asked Freddy.

'Never more so,' said Nancy and they strode inside.

Freddy knocked on the door but didn't wait to be invited in. With chins high they walked in together and the conversation in the room trickled away.

'Frederick!' Louisa was on her feet and wrapping her son in a hug.

That's a good start, thought Nancy. She strode up to Oscar and offered him a hand to shake. There was only a slight hesitation before he did. 'Good to see you again, Oscar.'

She turned to Sir Richard and Arabella who both looked surprised and slightly smug, which was worrying. She bypassed them and went towards the stranger in the room: a robust gentleman who looked discombobulated by the interruption. 'Good afternoon, I'm Nancy Barraclough. I work with Freddy.' As she said it, she saw Freddy look her way and there was a definite connection. They were a good team and they had this covered as long as they weren't already too late.

There were documents laid out on the coffee table. 'Simon Lillicrap from National Heritage. We're in the middle of a meeting with Lord and Lady Langham.'

'That's precisely why we're here,' said Nancy,

Freddy greeted everyone in the room although the reception from Arabella was decidedly frosty. 'If we can have your attention for a few minutes we'd like to share our business plan.'

'It's your plan, Freddy. I just gave you a few pointers,' said Nancy.

Freddy paused and smiled. 'I couldn't have done it without you.' For a moment they could have been anywhere – just her and Freddy. But the moment was fleeting.

'This is all rather irregular,' said Mr Lillicrap.

'Give me ten seconds to set up.' Freddy handed Sir Richard a whisky glass as he grabbed the small table it was on and placed it in the middle of the room. He put the laptop on it and flipped it open with the screen directed at his parents.

'Come on, Freddy,' said Sir Richard. 'I think this is a bit late in the day. The contract with National Heritage is drawn up.'

'Well, actually . . .' started Mr Lillicrap.

Sir Richard continued. 'Everything is being finalised. If this is a last-minute attempt to trick your parents, it's a jolly poor show.'

Nancy was riled. 'If you don't mind me asking,' she began, although she couldn't care less whether he minded or not. 'Why are you here, Sir Richard?'

Freddy's eyebrows twitched in recognition of her questioning, and she felt a bubble of pride. Nancy and Freddy stood side by side and waited for his response. 'I'm here in an advisory capacity.'

Nancy looked from Sir Richard to Oscar who was fiddling with a teacup. 'Oscar, what does that mean exactly?'

'Well, it's partly that Dickie wanted to check everything was all in order with National Heritage, what with him having neighbouring land, and also that he's offered to take on some of the land to make the estate more manageable for National Heritage.' Oscar pointed at Mr Lillicrap.

Freddy turned slowly back to eyeball Sir Richard and Nancy very much liked the look of slightly menacing Freddy. 'And how did you come to agree on a price for that land I wonder?'

Sir Richard beckoned Freddy forward with a finger and absolutely had the menacing thing nailed. 'Let's not go into battle over this or that could end badly for you. Understand?'

'I understand who has the most to lose here.' Freddy stood up straight. 'This coming from a man who offered Nancy a contract in exchange for—'

'I've warned you,' snapped Sir Richard.

'I think everyone knows about that now,' said Nancy. Louisa and Oscar shook their heads. 'Oh, right. Sorry. Sir Richard asked me if I would pretend to employ Freddy in exchange for a contract with his company.'

'No, I didn't,' said Sir Richard.

'You're right,' said Nancy. 'It was my mistake, I thought that was what he had offered but I wouldn't pretend to employ Freddy instead I made him do the job.' Arabella giggled and looked pityingly at Freddy.

Freddy tilted his head. 'Actually, Nancy, that wasn't what I was talking about.' Now Nancy was as confused as Oscar and Louisa looked. 'There was a more recent situation where Uncle Dickie offered to set up a substantial contract with Nancy's company.'

'Was there?' asked Nancy. She would have liked to have heard about this before. Why on earth had she not been involved? But before she could ask more Sir Richard was on his feet and pulling Arabella from the sofa.

'We're not listening to this. You're lying as usual, Freddy. Or probably on drugs. Perhaps the papers would like an update on your latest outrageous behaviour. Trying to stop your parents from their final attempts to save their home.' He looked meaningfully at Oscar and Louisa before marching to the door with Arabella in tow.

'In exchange for the contract all I had to do was marry Arabella,' said Freddy just as Sir Richard opened the door.

'What?!' Arabella spun around looking furious.

At that moment, Carrie charged through the open door followed by a bouncing Otto, the pair were clearly over-joyed to be reunited. Mr Lillicrap leapt to his feet and emitted a high-pitched squeal as he jumped onto the sofa. For a few minutes chaos reigned as Arabella was shouting at her father, Louisa was trying to catch Otto, Oscar was apologising to Mr Lillicrap who was scrambling across the furniture in a futile attempt to get away from the excited animals. Nancy was still processing what Freddy had revealed when a harassed Paul dashed in.

'So sorry. Boot room door was ajar and they both escaped while I was getting the leads.' But it was hard to hear him over the noise.

Oscar clapped his hands. 'Otto, heel,' he said and the Labrador darted to sit at his side. Carrie continued to harass Mr Lillicrap, who was scratching at his already rather red neck. Nancy scooped up her cat. Everyone glared at each other.

Arabella cleared her throat. 'Freddy, is this true?'

Sir Richard butted in. 'Of course it's not. The boy is a habitual liar.'

Arabella held up a hand to her father who looked taken aback. 'Freddy?' she asked.

Freddy got out his phone and it started to play back a conversation. 'Obviously, there would be other benefits to being my son-in-law . . .' came Sir Richard's voice.

'That's illegal!' Sir Richard raised his voice. 'You, Freddy, will be hearing from my lawyers and, Oscar, the deal for your scrap of land is off.' Sir Richard stormed out.

Arabella blinked slowly as if trying to compose herself. 'How humiliating,' she said.

'I'm sorry, Arabella,' said Freddy.

'No need to apologise this time. I should be thanking you for not marrying me, which feels quite bizarre.' The sadness showed in her eyes and Nancy felt for her. She obviously cared for Freddy but even Arabella didn't want to snare him like this. 'I'll make sure Father doesn't take this any further. And it's a good thing the land deal is off as Father wasn't offering you anywhere near what it's worth.' She nodded at Oscar and Louisa and left.

There was a brief silence before Mr Lillicrap spoke in a wheezy voice. 'I think I need my inhaler.'

* * *

Alice's morning had gone very differently to what she'd expected. She'd woken up to a message on her voicemail from her consultant. It said he'd had a cancellation. She knew what that meant. People didn't cancel operations like this – they died before they had the procedure. It pulled her up short.

The consultant was offering her an afternoon slot if she didn't eat anything and could get there for one o'clock. As terrified as she was of having the operation the thought of the poor person who no longer needed theirs was enough to scare Alice into action. She discovered she was far more frightened of dying before having the procedure than of actually going through with it.

Alice had called her mum and dad who she caught just before they were about to leave their motel to go sightseeing. They rushed over and within forty minutes of picking up the call from her consultant she was on the way to the hospital. Alice called the school from the car and they were so supportive and understanding it almost made her cry.

When they arrived at the hospital her dad took ages to choose a car parking space but they were still there on time. After everything had happened in a rush it then all slowed to a snail's pace. Once checked in she had a pre-med and then she had to wait. And wait. And wait.

'Shall I ask where you are on the list for this afternoon?' asked her mum.

'It's okay,' said Alice. 'It won't change anything.'

'If you're not down until later I could go and grab a sandwich,' said her dad, looking up from his newspaper.

'Ooh I could just go for a ham sandwich,' said her mum with feeling.

'You can both still have a sandwich,' said Alice.

'I don't want to miss you um . . .' Her dad didn't say 'going into theatre' he just made twirly signals towards the door. There was a lot about her parents that was really annoying but right at that moment she couldn't have loved them more.

'I don't want you conking out,' said Alice.

'Maybe I'll get a soup from the machine in the corridor,' said her dad, not looking excited at the prospect.

Alice's phone vibrated. She'd put it on silent. It was Dom. She cancelled the call but not before her mum had noticed. 'Did we cause a problem between you and Dom last night?' she asked.

Alice could have said that having them blurting out that she'd been stalking him wasn't exactly helpful, but in the back of her mind was the niggle that she might not come through this operation and that really wasn't the last conversation she wanted to have with her parents. It was much better that it was about sandwiches and vending machine soup. Alice patted her mum's hand. 'Nah, some things just aren't meant to be.' Alice had to swallow hard as the words seemed to stick in her throat. Maybe that was because she'd been so sure that she and Dom were right for each other. The perfect little ready-made family she'd never known she wanted. A weight seemed to descend into her gut. She knew what she had to do. She tapped out a text which broke her damaged heart a fraction more: *I'm so sorry, but we can't be together. Please stop calling. A x*

She stared at it and then deleted it, perhaps there was another way.

The hospital curtain was pulled back by a jolly-looking nurse. 'I've called a porter, so you'll be on your way to have your anaesthetic shortly.' This was it. Alice's heart rate picked up. She needed to stay calm as much for her parents as for her own sake. Her phone vibrated again. Alice's dad reached and picked it up and cancelled the call. 'I'll look after this until you come round. Okay?'

'Er, yeah. Switch it off would you, Dad?' Alice had an image of Whizzer messaging something wholly inappropriate.

'Don't worry, love. All done,' said her dad, popping the phone in his pocket. 'Don't you worry about a thing and we'll see you when you come round.'

Alice hoped with all her broken heart that he was right.

Chapter Forty

Alice was dreaming. She was lying in the bright sunshine with Dom. It was a nice dream. He was reading to her. She tuned into his voice. He was saying something about the price of sandwiches. That was odd. Alice opened her eyes but the light was too much, so she closed them again.

'Hello, Alice,' said her dad. 'Your mum's just gone to get a sandwich. How are you feeling?'

She went to scratch her head, but her arm felt heavy and there was something attached to it. She tried to lift the other arm, but someone was holding her hand. She remembered where she was. She was in hospital. If she was waking up, she'd made it through the operation. A wave of emotion flooded her system and she choked on unexpected tears.

'Alice?' It was Dom's voice again.

Was she in hospital or had she died? She'd not reckoned on there being a lot of sandwich talk in heaven. Alice's eyes snapped open and she squinted to focus.

Two faces loomed in, making her blink – her dad and Dom.

'Dom?' she said through sobs.

'Good you've not forgotten me,' he said, leaning forward to kiss her forehead.

'Mind her chest,' said her dad. 'All went to plan. You've just missed Mr Johnson-Brown.' He turned to Dom. 'Alice's consultant is a lovely fella. He's recommended a little deli around the corner that does good sandwiches and he says they aren't too pricey.'

Alice spluttered a laugh through her tears. 'That's good to know, Dad.'

'I'd best find your mother or there'll be hell to pay that she missed you waking up. Maybe try and look a bit more drowsy when she comes back,' he said, getting to his feet and disappearing from view.

She turned to look at Dom. 'It's lovely to see you but I kind of thought . . .'

Dom was shaking his head. 'You can't shake me off that easily. Unless of course you want me to go.' Worry lines appeared around his eyes.

'No, please stay. I'm sorry about everything and I shouldn't have tracked you down like some deranged stalker.'

'But if you hadn't then maybe I wouldn't have fallen in love with you.'

Alice's tears kept coming but for a different reason. The words she'd so wanted to hear. 'I love you too,' she said in a croaky voice. 'But how come you're here?'

'Mrs Robinson said you were off long-term sick and I was worried. I kept ringing, but you didn't pick up. I sent a message and your dad called me back on your phone. I might have told him I love him too. Before I realised it wasn't you.' Alice laughed. 'Anyway, your dad explained about your operation and that he thought you might be pushing people away so that they didn't get hurt.' Her dad was far more perceptive than she gave him credit for. 'He also told me about a good budget hotel up the road which I couldn't resist,' said Dom with a smile.

'Where's Bonnie?' she asked.

'She's with my mum, she drove over to babysit for a couple of days. Bonnie made you a get well soon card and Mum sent me a photo of it.' Dom held up his phone for Alice to see. There were three smiley faces surrounded by love hearts. It was too much and Alice was back to crying happy tears.

* * *

Once things had calmed down and Mr Lillicrap had had his medication and returned to a more healthy colour, Paul took him off for a calming cup of tea away from the furry creatures. Nancy, Freddy, Oscar and Louisa sat down in the drawing room. Otto and Carrie happily curled up together in Otto's bed.

The silence was a bit much for Nancy, so she waded in. 'It's not what we planned but I'm glad Sir Richard has been outed for his shenanigans. Which means we're in the clear, right?' She looked hopefully at Oscar and Louisa.

'What was it you had planned?' asked Oscar. 'To scupper our chances with National Heritage?' He frowned at his son.

'Not at all,' said Nancy, feeling defensive of Freddy. 'If you would give him a few minutes he can show you.' Nancy elbowed Freddy and he jumped into action.

They went through the presentation in record time. Freddy was very good on his feet. Maybe that was something they taught you at private school. But more than that, his passion for the project came across. Freddy flicked onto a sparse slide.

'This one is really about the impact on the local community. Once we're established, we'd be able to showcase other local businesses at fairs and events and it would be important to me that we had an inclusive recruitment policy for any additional staff we take on. I want Langham to be a disability positive employer, so we'd be actively looking to recruit from the disabled community wherever possible.' Freddy glanced at Nancy and a lump formed in her throat. Towards the end Louisa was nodding, but Oscar remained stony-faced.

Freddy and Nancy sat back down. 'Do you want me to go over any of that again?' asked Freddy, looking between his parents.

'I think there's a lot there to think about,' said Louisa. 'But it was very good. Well done, darling.'

Freddy smiled at his mother before turning to his Father. 'Pa, what do you think?'

Oscar turned to Nancy. 'And you'll be part of this will you, Nancy?'

Given the state of her own business she probably wasn't the asset Oscar thought she was. 'I'll definitely be on hand if he needs me.' She looked to Freddy and he smiled. A smile that seemed to turn her insides to mush. She definitely needed to do something about this silly crush she had.

'Hmm,' said Oscar. 'We need to think about this.' He looked to Louisa and she nodded.

'Of course,' said Freddy, standing up. 'We'll leave you to talk things over.' He reached for Nancy's hand and pulled her to her feet and the contact sent a shockwave through her.

Nancy and Freddy chatted as they wandered away from the house and found themselves in the little cove.

'Not quite how we planned it,' said Nancy, kicking off her shoes. 'But I think it went okay.'

Freddy joined her and rolled up his trousers. 'We'll only know that if Pa opts for me over National Heritage.'

'But you should be proud of what you've done with the whole project even if . . .'

'It goes tits up?' said Freddy.

'Well, I obviously wouldn't use language like that but yeah. You did good, Mr Astley-Davenport.' She nudged him with her shoulder.

'You weren't too shabby yourself, Miss Barraclough.' He nudged her back.

They walked down to the water and Nancy dipped in a toe. 'I can't believe Sir Richard tried to get you to marry Arabella.' She sucked in air through her teeth.

'I think you can,' said Freddy. 'I'm sorry for not telling you before. I gave him a call to see if he would step up to help Having A Ball and that was the offer he put on the table.'

'And you weren't prepared to marry Arabella to save my company.' Nancy tutted. 'What kind of employee commitment is that?' She laughed.

'I couldn't marry Arabella.'

'Of course, you couldn't, not like that.'

'I couldn't ever marry Arabella because . . .'

'She's up her own bottom? Is a bit of a cow?' offered Nancy. 'Looks like she can constantly smell a turd?'

'No.' Freddy paused his paddle and stared at his feet, making Nancy do the same. She wriggled her toes into the wet sand. 'It's because I think I might be in love with someone else.'

'Get out!' said Nancy, kicking out and splashing him with water – a bit more than she intended but the declaration had taken her by surprise. The leaden weight of disappointment that dropped in her stomach told her how much she cared about Freddy. 'Who is she then?' asked Nancy.

Freddy surveyed his wet trousers. 'It was this amazing woman who barrelled into my life with her indominable positivity and sharp cockney tongue. But now I'm not so sure.'

'Why?' questioned Nancy, hoping very much that the description was meant to be her.

'How could I love someone who ruins my designer suits?' He splayed out his arms and studied her with warm eyes and a cheeky grin.

'Because she's adorable?' said Nancy, booting the water and soaking him further.

'She's not that adorable when she attacks me with sea water.' Nancy kicked more at him. He looked shocked. 'Huh! Outrageous behaviour. Human Resources!'

Nancy squealed and tried to run through the shallows but it was harder than it looked. 'You can't get my cast wet!' she shouted.

Freddy scooped her up into his arms and carried her up the beach. They fell laughing onto the sand which was harder than Nancy thought it would be. 'Ouch,' she said.

'You've not broken anything, have you?' He looked concerned.

'No, I'm quite tough really.'

'Oh, I know,' said Freddy, leaning up on one elbow and giving her that look that laser beamed her insides. 'I want your advice,' he said.

'Go on.'

'I'm thinking about entering into a long-term relationship with my boss. What do you think?'

It was hard to concentrate with his body up against hers and his lips so close. 'I think I'd better give HR that call,' she said and she pulled him towards her. As their lips met all sorts of sensations zinged around Nancy's body. But unhelpfully a little doubt poked at her brain. She pulled away. 'Freddy, we're from very different worlds.

You're from a long line of genuine lords and I'm from an disorderly bunch of Londoners. Is this a bad idea?'

'You know what? I don't think I give a shit,' said Freddy, brushing his lips against hers.

'That's good enough for me,' said Nancy, pulling him back towards her.

Their heated kiss was interrupted by someone clearing their throat. 'When you're done, Freddy. I'll have a ride back in the boat,' said Grandpa, making Nancy and Freddy dissolve into hysterics.

They were in the little boat when Freddy's phone pinged and he handed it to Nancy. It was Oscar asking them to join them to celebrate. This was it. The decision had been made. They'd done it, Project Langham was go. Nancy whooped and hollered, Freddy laughed and Grandpa held on tight to the boat.

They went from boat to car and were helping Grandpa walk the last few steps to the house as a car tore up the driveway and skidded to a halt on the gravel. Sir Richard got out, ignored them and began striding towards the house. He'd almost made it to the front door when he was ambushed. Percy darted out from behind a bush and went for him. Sir Richard yelped and danced about waving his arms which didn't distract Percy for a second. Sir Richard was shouting as Grandpa shuffled by. 'Pull yourself together man,' said Grandpa, letting himself in.

Sir Richard seemed stunned and made the mistake of taking his eyes off Percy who lunged at him and pecked him in the trouser zip department. The man dropped to his knees with a pained expression on his face. Percy strutted off the victor.

Louisa and Oscar appeared at the door. 'Whatever's happened?' asked Louisa.

'Sir Richard just got pecked in the—'

'Uncle Dickie,' said Freddy.

'I bloody love karma,' said Nancy as Freddy held her hand and they walked inside Langham Hall together.

Epilogue

Six weeks later

Langham Hall was preparing to be party central. Thanks to a lot of hard work, mainly on Freddy's part, they had a schedule of planned events and tonight was the big launch party. Nancy was already feeling bubbles of excitement as she came down the big staircase with Carrie trotting at her heels. Freddy was waiting at the bottom wearing full dinner suit and carrying a bouquet of yellow roses and a bag of dried fish. He looked so handsome and he was all hers. 'Dried fish, you know how to spoil a girl,' said Nancy.

'I certainly do,' he said as Carrie dashed to greet him. She snatched the treat and sauntered off.

'Will I do?' asked Freddy.

'Wow,' said Nancy, launching herself at him.

Freddy did his best to catch her with one arm as he held the flowers out of crushing distance. 'We said casual so what's with the penguin suit?' she asked and then felt a sense of dread. 'You're not stopping are you? Some fancy thing that's more important has come up?'

'Woah. I dressed up for you. I thought it would be fun. I can go and change into jeans and T-shirt if you think that would be better?'

Nancy scanned him up and down. He looked like he'd stepped off the cover of a magazine. 'Nah, you're all right. I think we'll stick with this. But I can't guarantee you'll make it through the party without me jumping you.' She kissed him.

Her dad cleared his throat behind her. That was the trouble with wheels – you rarely heard them coming. Nancy felt it would be rude not to prise herself off her boyfriend.

She straightened Freddy's bow tie, took the flowers and whispered in his ear. 'Later.'

Nancy and her dad, Wayne, went through to the kitchen which was a hive of activity as Mrs Mason was putting on a magnificent buffet, much to Oscar's disappointment as he was hoping to share his special sauce with everyone at a barbecue, but he had been outvoted.

Wayne put his head in the fridge. 'Have you seen how much champagne there is in here?' he asked, taking out a bottle and sucking his teeth at the name on the label.

'Ooh champagne?' said Alice's mum, coming into the kitchen.

'We've lots to celebrate,' said Nancy. 'Especially Alice's recovery.'

'Her consultant, Mr Johnson-Brown, is a miracle worker. I'd get that man knighted if I could,' said Alice's mum with a chuckle as she picked up a tray of food and left the room.

An icy sensation flooded Nancy's bloodstream and for a second she was frozen to the spot. 'That's a coincidence, right? That's another Johnson-Brown who's a doctor?'

Wayne put down the bottle, wheeled over to Nancy and took her hand. 'Nancy, you have to let it go. I have.'

'I don't get how you can be okay with what that posh

twat did to you. To all of us. I was a kid and I thought my dad was going to die.' Nancy choked on unexpected emotion.

'Nancy, you know it was a combination of factors. He was driving a bit too fast and I stepped out on the crossing without looking. It's time to forgive.'

Nancy's shoulders tensed. 'I don't think I can. He got off with a few points on his licence and a couple of hundred quid fine. All because he was an upper-class wally with letters after his double-barrelled name.'

'But mainly because he was a doctor trying to get to a patient in time.' Wayne gave her a hug. 'Say it is the same bloke. Then look at the good he's done in his life. He's saved countless people including Alice.'

'But he put you in a wheelchair!'

'Not on purpose. It's time to let it go, Nancy. Please.'

'I'll try.'

'Thank you,' said Wayne, looking relieved. 'And anyway, if you marry Freddy you'll be a posh twat with a double-barrelled name too!'

She took a swipe at him with a tea towel and missed.

The evening flew by and thankfully everyone attending seemed impressed with the plans for the future of Langham Hall. Louisa and Oscar had looked on proudly as their son had given an impassioned speech. The formal part of the evening segued into the fun part as the ballroom came to life as it had likely done many times before, but perhaps not previously to the sound of Dua Lipa. Nancy watched as a very healthy-looking Alice danced with Dom and Bonnie while her parents watched from a respectable distance and Grandpa joined in the fun with a tambourine. Freddy took Nancy's arm and guided her outside.

'We can't wander off. You're the host,' said Nancy, relishing the feel of her hand in his.

'They can manage for a while. I want to show you something.'

'Freddy, I said later—'

'Not that,' said Freddy. 'Come on, this way.' He led her across the terrace and down the steps.

'Watch out for Percy,' she said, checking in as many directions as she could swivel her neck.

'He's gone to a local farm.'

'Oh no. The farmyard in the sky. I had a few goldfish go there when I was a kid.'

'No, an actual farm. They've got a variety of birds including some peahens. He's ruling the roost once again but this time the inhabitants are happy about it.'

'Aww that's lovely.' They made their way out of the grounds, along the path and down the steps to Seashell Bay. The tide was going out so the sand was damp underfoot.

'Right, stand over here and close your eyes for a minute,' said Freddy.

'What's going on?'

'Trust me. You'll find out any second.'

'Okay.' Nancy did as she was told. Her stomach had more knots than a macramé pot holder. She listened hard but all she could hear was the sound of the waves gently lapping the shore behind her. There was a click and then a buzz.

'You can look now,' said Freddy, who was now standing right next to her.

'I'm not sure I want to.' Nancy slowly opened her eyes and was blown away by what she saw. Projected onto the beach hut was an advert for Having A Ball and there was Freddy crocheting one of their blankets. 'What the actual—'

'You don't like it?'

'Freddy Astley-Davenport, I love it and I love you too.'

'Claudia lent a hand. I hope it helps to turn things around for your company. I've called in some favours from friends who have lots of social media followers so with any luck it will be going viral any time now.'

'Thank you,' she said, giving him a kiss. 'You know what? You're all right you are.'

'High praise indeed,' said Freddy, as fireworks erupted on the cliff above them.

'And if this ad campaign works, I might be able to afford a qualified personal assistant.'

'Thank goodness for that!' he said, and he picked her up and spun her around as explosions illuminated the night sky.

Acknowledgements

Thank you to the fabulous team at Avon – with special thanks to my editors Cara Chimirri and Rachel Hart. Thanks to Holly MacDonald and Enya Todd for the gorgeous cover.

Huge thanks to my agent Kate Nash for helping to get another book out into the world.

Thanks to my brilliant subject matter experts:

Charlotte Hancock – thanks for the valuable insight into life as a teaching assistant. Also our chat about crochet and yarn which was the inspiration for Having A Ball.

Dr David Boulton – thank you for answering my many questions and for helping to diagnose my character's illness.

Warwick Castle – The Peacock Garden and Conservatory Tea Room helped to inspire Langham Hall and one feathered resident in particular. It was also thanks to a trip around their ice rink that resulted in a broken wrist – so thanks for that too because it's all material!

Thank you to all my wonderful writing friends – I am so lucky that there are now far too many of you to name!

Huge thanks to my family for putting up with me when I broke my wrist, for ignoring the muttering that came from my desk and for still delivering tea. I love you!

Much love to everyone in the book blogging community, booksellers and librarians for their continued support.

And lastly, but by no means least, a whopping big thank you to you my readers who have bought or borrowed my book and taken the time to read it.

**One blind date. One chance encounter.
One life-changing moment.**

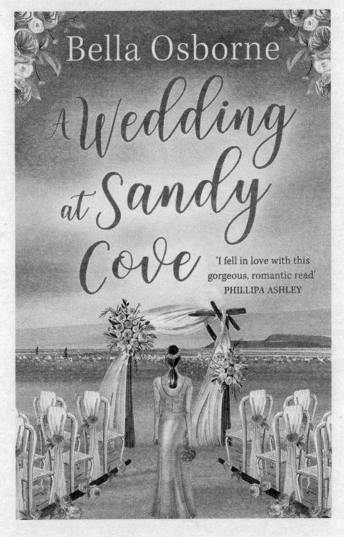

Bella Osborne

A Wedding at Sandy Cove

'I fell in love with this
gorgeous, romantic read'
PHILLIPA ASHLEY

Available in all good bookshops now.

Ruby's life is about to change for ever . . .

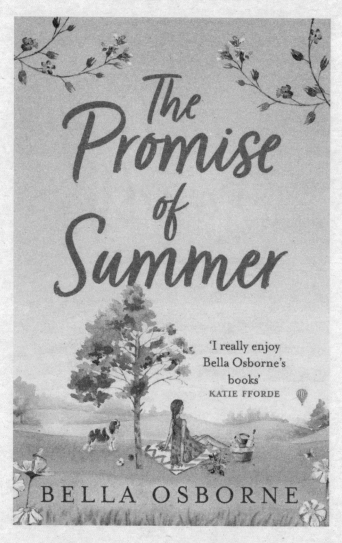

The Promise of Summer

'I really enjoy
Bella Osborne's
books'
KATIE FFORDE

BELLA OSBORNE

Available in all good bookshops now.

A big family. A whole lot of secrets.
A Christmas to remember . . .

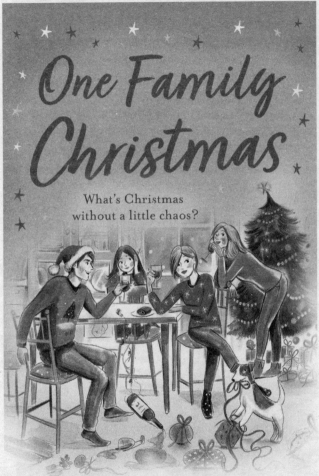

One Family Christmas

What's Christmas
without a little chaos?

BELLA OSBORNE

Available in all good bookshops now.

Regan is holding a winning lottery ticket.
Goodbye to the boyfriend who never had her back,
and so long to the job she can't stand!
Except it's all a bit too good to be true . . .

Available in all good bookshops now.

Life's not always a walk
in the park . . .

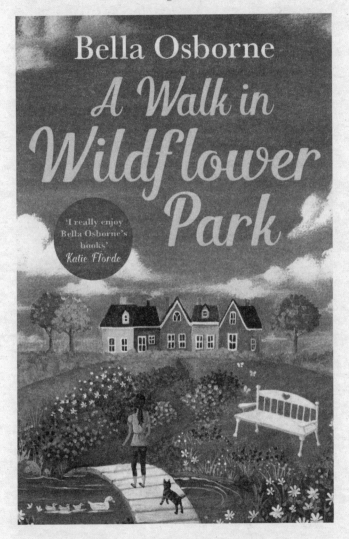

Bella Osborne

A Walk in
Wildflower
Park

'I really enjoy
Bella Osborne's
books'
Katie Fforde

Available in all good bookshops now.

**Join Daisy Wickens as she returns to
Ottercombe Bay . . .**

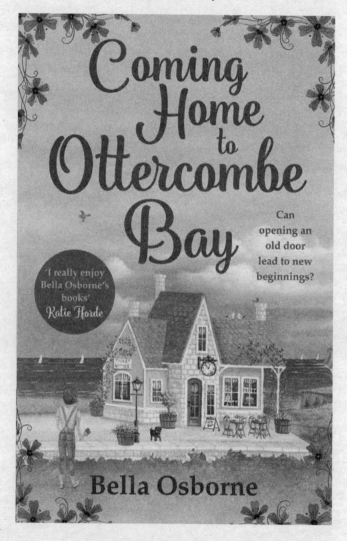

Available in all good bookshops now.

Don't miss these delightful cottage adventures . . .

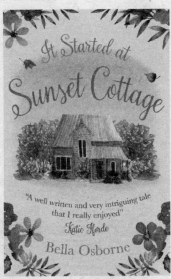

Available in all good bookshops now.

Tempted to read another heart-warming romance by Bella Osborne?

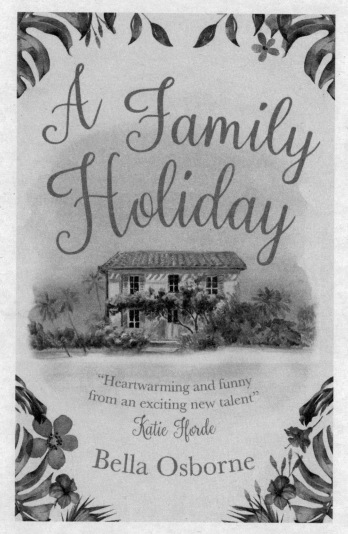

Available in all good bookshops now.